HOSTAGE

PREDATORS
MC

JAMIE BEGLEY

Young Ink Press Publication
YoungInkPress.com

Copyright © 2016 by Jamie Begley

Edited by C&D Editing
Cover Art by Young Ink Press

All rights reserved.

No part of this book may be reproduced in any form or by any
electronic or mechanical means including information storage and
retrieval systems, without permission in writing from the author.
The only exception is by a reviewer, who may quote short excerpts
in a review.

This book is a work of fiction. Names, characters, places, and
incidents either are products of the author's imagination or are
used fictitiously. Any resemblance to actual persons, living or dead,
events, or locales is entirely coincidental.

*This work of fiction is intended for mature audiences only. All sexu-
ally active characters portrayed in this ebook are eighteen years of age or
older. Please do not buy if strong sexual situations, multiple partners,
violence, drugs, child abuse, domestic discipline, and explicit language
offends you.*

ISBN: 0692725946
ISBN-13: 9780692725948

Connect with Jamie,
JamieBegley@ymail.com
www.facebook.com/AuthorJamieBegley
www.JamieBegley.net

PROLOGUE

Friday

"Do you take sugar?" Penni waved a packet of sugar in the air.

"Yes, please." Grace opened a drawer next to her, looking for a spoon. "Why do you only have plastic silverware?"

Penni opened the package of sugar into the coffee cup in front of her then handed it to her friend. "I keep meaning to buy some more silverware. For some reason, they keep disappearing." She poured herself a cup of coffee, leaving it black, as she watched Grace take a sip, wincing at the strong flavor. "Sorry. I like my coffee strong."

"Now I know why you're always so hyper."

"I'm hyper without it. The coffee just makes it worse. I appreciate that you didn't mind working here today instead of the office. I hate the smell of fresh paint. The building owners promised it should be finished by tomorrow, so we can go back to the office on Monday." The owners were in the process of renovating the building, and the smell of the fresh paint had given her a persistent headache. Thankfully, that part of the renovations was almost over.

"No problem. It's a nice change of pace. I brought my laptop to go over the venues for the tour dates."

As tour manager of Mouth2Mouth, it was Penni's job to set the tour schedule. Grace had proven invaluable as Penni's assistant, handling the office when she went on tour with the group.

"Let me grab my laptop, and we can work at the kitchen table. I'll be right back." Penni went into her living room then carried her laptop back into the kitchen seconds later. She came to a stop when she saw Grace about to open the sliding door to her backyard.

"Don't go out there!" Penni rushed forward, shutting the door quickly and locking it.

Grace stared at her, open-mouthed at her reaction. "Sorry. It's really pretty outside, so I thought it would be nice to work in the fresh air."

"I would love to; except, we wouldn't get much work done if we went out there." Penni pointed out the clear door. "Look at the bushes."

She loved working in the backyard on the days when the weather was warm. It was small with a little table and chairs that had comfortable cushions. It had a five-foot stone wall that created privacy from her neighbors with a hedge of bushes in front. The bushes were what she was pointing at now. It didn't take Grace long to see the problem.

"Good grief! How many of them are there?"

"I don't want to know. I'm not going out there to count the mean fuckers." Penni eyed the innocuous bushes that were very pretty...until you noticed the large amount of bees flying in and out of the greenery.

"Kill them," Grace advised.

"I thought of that; believe me. The last time I got stung, I notified the landlord. I should have stayed in my apartment," Penni admitted glumly, eyeing the bees that prevented her from going outside to indulge in her favorite pastimes of sunbathing or reading, which were the reasons she had decided to rent the house.

"So why didn't he take care of it?"

"Did you know bees are becoming extinct?"

Grace shook her head. "No."

"Neither did I. The exterminator my landlord hired notified Fish and Wildlife. Now, not only can I not kill them, but I have to put up with them another couple of weeks until they move the colony. The University is going to take them to a spot where they can be researched."

"That's a bummer."

"No shit," Penni replied caustically. Any sympathy she'd had for the bee population had disappeared after the first couple of stings.

Grace laughed, shaking her head at Penni. "They'll be gone in a few weeks. Then you'll have your backyard back. Look on the bright side; they're a hell of a deterrent for burglars."

Penni shook off her ill humor, mentally throwing her negative thoughts into the air. It was a habit she had developed for when she found herself focusing on only negative thoughts. She hated to be in a bad mood. Her brother Shade had that covered. He was in a perpetual bad mood. Well, he had been before he'd married her bestie, Lily.

"I don't need bees for protection. I can take care of myself," Penni boasted. She was sure she could handle any situation. Besides, her brother was an enforcer for The Last Riders, and he had taught her how to defend herself as soon as her mother had bought her first bra for her.

"Don't jinx yourself," Grace warned.

"I don't believe in luck." Penni felt the chill of foreboding going down her spine. Shrugging it off, she also threw that out into the air. "Let's get to work before that badass husband of yours comes back to pick you up."

Penni settled down to work, forgetting about Grace's warning. It was a warning that would come back to haunt her.

* * *

Monday

"I'll take a Café Mistro," Penni placed her order, reaching into her wallet to pull out her money.

"I have it." A ten-dollar bill passed in front of her toward the waiting cashier.

Penni snatched the money out of the cashier's hand and handed it back to the man she absolutely loathed with every fiber of her being.

"Thanks, but I can pay for myself," Penni snapped at Jackal.

The enforcer for the Predators MC narrowed his eyes at her angrily, but Penni refused to be afraid of his intimidating glare.

Determined to ignore him, she handed the cashier the money to pay for her coffee then moved to the side to wait for her order.

"I was only trying to be nice." Jackal shook his head at the cashier, who took his order, before moving to stand next to Penni.

Penni rolled her eyes. "Your idea of nice and mine differ. You can pretend to be nice all you want, but I know you're an asshole, remember?" She knew the enforcer hated it when she reminded him of the time he had kidnapped her, holding her hostage until The Last Riders had returned one of the Predators who had been taken prisoner. She had been forced to spend several days alone with Jackal on the road from Queen City to Treepoint, Kentucky. The jerk had made the swap for one of the Predators in front of both clubs.

"How long are you going to hold that against me?"

"Um...let me think a minute...until Hell freezes over."

Jackal's lips tightened at her sarcasm. "You're not even giving me a chance."

"No, I'm not. You're a freaking caveman, manhandling me every opportunity you get; you kiss Ice's ass; and every man, woman, and child in Queen City is afraid of you."

"Except you?"

"No, I'm not afraid of you." Penni moved sideways, trying to distance herself from the biker.

His scarred face, which could never be described as handsome even by his mother, became even angrier, only to be smoothed out and replaced by a twisted smile that Penni assumed was his attempt at being charming.

Her name was called, so moving forward, she took her coffee from the busy waitress. When she turned to leave, she found Jackal standing in her way.

"That's good, because I don't want you afraid of me. You should come out with me sometime, give me a chance to show you that we could have some fun together."

Penni almost choked on her sip of coffee. "Some fun together? You mean, riding around town on your motorcycle then going back to your room at the clubhouse for a night filled with sex? That kind of fun?"

He had the audacity to shrug. "Sounds fun to me."

"I would rather become a nun than have sex with you."

Penni stepped around him and was two steps away from him when she heard his snide comment.

"You don't have to be such a fucking bitch."

Fury coursed through her bloodstream. She hated the B-word. Whenever men didn't like something a woman had to say, it always seemed to fly right out of their mouths.

Deliberately pasting a seductive smile on her lips, she turned back toward him. "I'll tell you what, Jackal," she purred, which warned him she was up to something. "I'm busy tonight, but tomorrow night, I'll leave my backdoor unlocked. If you can make it, I'm all yours."

Jackal's eyes narrowed on her, wondering what the catch was. "You serious?"

"Oh, yes, I'm deadly serious." She masked her aversion to him, stepping closer. Then she placed a kiss on the corner of his mouth, letting her tongue flick out briefly before quickly withdrawing.

"Why not the front door?"

"I don't want my neighbors to know I'm dating the most feared man in Queen City." She fed his already overblown ego, knowing he couldn't resist.

"What time?"

Penni almost rolled her eyes again. Men's egos were their weakest spot and a woman's greatest weapon.

"Any time after six."

She was leaving for the next Mouth2Mouth concert at five, so that gave her plenty of time to be far from home before he arrived.

"I'll be there." Jackal gave her another twisted smile, holding the door open for her.

Penni's conscious kicked in as she headed toward her car, which hadn't been parked at the curb when she had entered, nor had the other two bikers who were waiting on Jackal with his bike.

"Dammit," Penni swore. She couldn't do it. She couldn't send a man deliberately to his death, no matter how much she detested him. She needed to learn to control her temper, mentally throwing her antagonism into the wind.

She was about to go back and tell Jackal she had been joking when her cell phone rang. Juggling her coffee and purse, she grabbed her cell phone from the depths of the huge bag, hearing the motorcycles roar to life behind her.

"What's up, Grace?"

"The executive officer of the arena in California called, Erick Dunaway...He said he didn't receive the signed contracts you faxed to him, and if he doesn't have them in ten minutes, he's rebooking."

"Dammit, I know I sent them. I'm on my way." Penni disconnected the call, hurrying to her car.

By the time her key went into the ignition, she had a niggling feeling she had forgotten something important. Had she forgotten to send the contracts?

Oh, well, she would be at her office in five. It wasn't like it was a mistake that couldn't be fixed.

CHAPTER ONE

Penni snatched the coffee from the cup holder.

"Dammit!" She slammed down the empty coffee cup into the hapless cup holder. That wasn't the only thing on empty. The red light was flashing in the dim lighting.

Hearing the phone ring, Penni pressed her hand to the steering wheel, answering the call.

"Hello?"

"How did the concert go?" Grace's voice filled the interior of her car.

"Great. It went off without a hitch."

"Where are you now?" Grace asked.

"About three hours away from home."

"You're making good time. Why didn't you just catch the bus back?"

"Too many roadies." Penni squinted at the gas gauge. Was it her imagination, or was the red light becoming brighter in the dim lighting of the car?

Grace's voice sharpened. "Kaden warned the men no women were allowed on the tour bus. He said the roadies should drive their own cars."

"It's easier said than done," Penni commented wryly.

"Not when Kaden hears about this. He's going to be furious."

"He's not going to know. Sawyer and Kaden wanted a small vacation. They're on their way to Kaden's cabin, which is why I'm driving my own car."

Grace laughed. "When are you going to get tired of keeping the band out of trouble?"

"I don't know. Maybe about the time I can stop renting and buy myself a big home. Even better, when someone buys me an even bigger diamond ring," Penni joked. "Or when Kaden fires me." This time, she was only half-joking. While she was considered friends with him and his wife, he expected the business to stay separate.

"You should tell him before he finds out on his own," Grace warned.

"Nope. I'm not a stool pigeon."

"You're not going to listen to me?" Grace muttered then changed the subject. Penni's friends were all too familiar with the stubborn streak that would make a Rocky Mountain jackass proud. "I need to be off Monday. I'm sorry about the notice—"

"Thank God!"

"Penni?"

"Sorry, I found an exit. I'm almost out of gas." She gripped the steering wheel as she drove the lonely road.

"How many times have I told you to fill up your car before you drive?"

"Hindsight is a pain in the ass!"

"Where are you?"

"Calm down! Jesus, I'm fine." At least, she thought so.

The red sign hanging in front of a bar glinted through her windshield then turned off as she drove closer. Her prayers had been answered. She wasn't stranded on a highway during the middle of the night, but the uneasy feeling brushing at the back of her neck had her vowing to delete the numerous *True Nightmares* shows she loved to watch.

She reluctantly slowed to a stop in front of what seemed to be an old saloon.

"What's going on?"

Grace's demanding voice had her nearly jumping out of her skin.

"Nothing. I need some gas and, if I'm lucky, some coffee. Take whatever time you need. I'll talk to you when I see you Tuesday."

"Wait…Why are you being so nice? You were just bitching at me last night because I came in late yesterday."

"Because you were late since you were boinking Ice." Penni stared around the empty parking lot. Despite what her misgivings were telling her and all the hours of watching *True Nightmares* had shown her, she ignored the folly of what she was about to do. "I need to go. The bar's closing."

"*Bar?*" Grace shrieked. "What bar?"

"Actually, I think it's a saloon."

"Call me back as soon as you get back on the road."

"Don't be such a worrywart. Get to bed. Give Oceane a kiss for me and another one for that handsome father of yours."

"She heard you."

Penni smiled, hearing feminine laughter that relieved the stress of the situation she had found herself in, all because she had been too stubborn to ride the bus with the band.

"She said to be careful," Grace passed on her mother's words.

"Tell her I'll be fine. What could go wrong at a saloon called Hay and Fiddle?"

* * *

Jackal didn't miss the glances that came his way as he entered the clubhouse. Ice's mouth had dropped open at the rough appearance of his clothes. Even Max was stunned by the dirty condition of the clothes Jackal couldn't hide as he limped into the packed clubhouse.

"Give me a whiskey!" Jackal snarled at Rave who wasn't able to hide her reaction to the rank smell that had reached her before he had.

She nearly dropped the whiskey bottle before hurriedly pouring his drink and escaping to the opposite end of the bar.

"What the hell happened to you?" Ice, as club president, didn't make it a habit to stick his nose into the brothers' business, but this was one thing he couldn't ignore.

Jackal finished his whiskey before answering, "I had a date with Penni." Jackal didn't know which one burned worst: his pride or the whiskey. He wasn't going to be able to downplay just how big a fool he had made of himself tonight.

"Grace told me Penni was out of town tonight." Ice shifted away, his nostrils flaring at the rank smell stealing through the clubhouse.

Jackal's mouth tightened as he reached for the whiskey bottle that Rave had set near for him. He hadn't kept his interest in Penni a secret from the club.

"So I take it that you didn't know?" Ice probed.

"That's a fucking understatement." Even when he had been the poorest in his high school class, the rich bitches had lined up to take him to the movies on a Friday night.

Ice poured more whiskey into his glass as the brothers gathered to listen.

"What happened?"

"She stood me up. Penni told me to meet her at the back of her house. Not only was she not there, but her whole yard was covered in bees."

Ice was the only one of his friends who didn't try to hide the fact that he was laughing at him.

Jackal pushed Stump back toward Max when they began waving their hands in the air to dissipate the stink coming from his clothes.

"What did you say to her?"

"She's not answering the phone." Jackal grasped the glass in his hand to keep himself from smashing it against the wall.

"That's some fucked up shit. He could have been hurt." Rita wrapped her arm around his waist. Jackal kind of admired her for not showing an aversion to the odor fouling the surrounding air.

"Are you going to finally listen to me and quit chasing after that fruitcake?"

Jackal was aware Ice already knew the answer to his question because of the mocking sneer on his lips.

He stared down at his whiskey glass as Ice poured him another one. "I'm never afraid of a challenge."

"Brother, she's one bitch that you would be better off stepping back from. You've had a hard-on ever since you met her." Max snorted. "It's not like you have a chance with her, anyway.

You would have to wear a bulletproof vest under your leather to fuck the girl."

"I'm not worried about Shade. He'll eventually get used to Penni being my old lady. Besides, he lives in Kentucky."

"You keep telling yourself that." Max shook his head, but Jackal didn't give a shit.

"Penni and I will be good together. If I had never taken her hostage, we would have already been together. I didn't expect her to hold a grudge against me for so fucking long."

"You doing crack?" This time, Ice couldn't hold back his amusement.

"You watch and see." Jackal began to get angry at the men for laughing at him. "She's attracted to me." Jackal had seen the interest in her eyes during the road trip to Treepoint. Penni hadn't been able to disguise it when they had returned to Queen City, either.

"I believe in you, Jackal." Rita licked her lips, dropping her hand down to cup his ass.

Ice rolled his eyes. "You never did explain why you smell like dog shit."

"Had to jump into the neighbor's yard, and the son of a bitch had two guard dogs."

Now Ice couldn't hold in the laughter. "The only way that fruitcake becomes your old lady is hell freezing over."

Jackal hated to admit it, but he was finally going to have to agree with Ice. He tugged the hair surrounding his face.

Was it his face? Did she find the scar on his cheek repulsive? Were Max and the rest of the brothers right? Was he just wasting his time?

"I need a shower. Want to party, Rave?" Jackal's voice rose so she could hear him from the other end of the bar.

Rave covered the bottom half of her face as she heaved at the thought. "Sorry, Jackal. Another night?"

The club wouldn't let him forget anytime soon that his pride had taken a hit. A big hit.

As an enforcer in a club the size of the Predators', his reputation not only reflected on himself, but on Ice for picking him. An enforcer who wasn't feared became a liability.

"I'll party with you, Jackal," Rita spoke up, ignoring the brothers' laughter.

Jackal's eyebrows rose. He hadn't fucked Rita since she had landed on Ice's shit list.

"I'll even wash your back for you," she offered.

"Why not? Give me enough time to get most of the stench off before coming to my room."

"I've got some shower gel that will get rid the smell right off. I'll run to my room and meet you there."

Any humor on Ice's face evaporated as Rita darted toward her bedroom. "You're better off waiting for Penni to get back and smacking her ass."

Jackal shook his head. "Rita is a raving bitch, but I can handle that. What I'm tired of is Penni chasing after every man in Queen City who wears an expensive suit and turning that snobby nose up at me."

"I don't think that's why she doesn't like you—" Rave started to speak up then hastily snapped her mouth closed at Jackal's glare.

"It doesn't matter." Jackal slammed his fist down on the counter of the bar. "Fuck her. It's not like I was in love with the girl."

Max pounded his hand on his back." Fuck her," he agreed, showing his support then grimacing as he wiped his damp hand off on the sleeve of Ice's T-shirt. "The bitches all look good in the dark. No need to put up with the shit Penni's dishing out."

"You're right! She's not the hottest tail in Queen City."

"There you go!" Max's encouragement had Jackal's sore pride finally kicking in.

"Thanks, brother!" Jackal missed the appalled look behind his back as Max tried to avoid coming into contact with Jackal's soggy clothes.

Ice leaned against the bar, watching as Max and the men snickered as Jackal cockily headed toward his bedroom. "Since when do you give a flying fuck who Jackal does?"

"Can you seriously imagine Penni as Jackal's old lady?"

Ice frowned at the brothers' expectant faces. Obviously, all of them believed he would agree with them.

"You don't think Jackal could handle Penni?"

"Brother, I think she'd shoot off his dick."

CHAPTER TWO

Penni stepped out of her car. She had barely managed to pull into the parking lot before her car had died. It wasn't the only thing not working.

Penni gave a frustrated sigh when she tried to call Grace back. Blanking, she glared at the cell screen, hoping the bars would mysteriously reappear.

"What the hell?" She had just had phone service when she'd talked to Grace. Penni had decided to call Grace back to have her help find a road service.

A car was parked beside the dark bar, the dark windows showing no welcoming gleam from inside. The only thing that resembled a saloon was the crooked sign and the music she could hear escaping from inside.

Penni snagged her purse from inside the car, sliding the strap firmly over her shoulder. The assortment of self-defense weapons she had inside gave her flagging confidence a boost as she walked toward the front door. With her other hand, she kept trying to call Grace back.

Her fingers trembled as she opened the door. Penni's instincts screamed, telling her to run, and Shade had always warned her to follow her instincts. However, before she could take her brother's advice, she felt the door jerked from her grasp.

Panni gasped as a man barreled into her. Horror had her gasp becoming a scream when she realized the man's chest was covered in blood. The lethal weapon poking out of his back seemed incongruous. Her first instinct was to try removing the weapon, but her survival instincts kicked in when she realized there were two occupants involved in the deadly duel.

Unable to stop herself, Penni reached forward to aid the man who seemed to need the most help with the vicious weapon sticking out from his back.

His brown face was filled with agony. He appeared to be Shade's age, in his thirties. While Shade was lean and athletic though, this man had a slim frame, which wasn't a match against the muscular guy intent on finishing the fight that had started before she had come in the door.

The two men directly in front of her were silent, temporarily stunned by her appearance, but the scream that filled the dingy saloon had each scrambling to find an advantage to break away from the deadly struggle.

The poor man with the knife sticking out of his back stared at her as if she could somehow help him.

Penni dropped her phone to the floor as she reached out to catch him. The one standing behind him didn't give her the opportunity, though, pulling the knife out with a sickly squish, only to thrust downward again into his helpless victim.

Penni scrambled back a step, holding the man as he slumped into her.

The other man stood as if frozen to stone. He appeared to have just come out of the bathroom. He was young than the other men, his actions showing he didn't know how to react to the life and death struggle. Penni didn't think he was friends with the other guys; his clean clothes might have come off the rack, but they had high price labels. Penni had the feeling he had been as shocked by the stabbing as she was. He must have come out of the bathroom as she had entered the front, both of them getting a shock they didn't know how to respond to.

Penni didn't have much time to react before she felt the victim grasping her harder. The man's weight buckled his thin frame as she frantically tried to catch him. She was sickened by the fear she saw staring back at her.

"Help us," Penni appealed to the man across the room who was coming out of the bathroom.

He gripped the backpack slung over his shoulder. "What's going on?"

The shaky voice didn't belong to a man with a backbone. Penni considered herself a good judge of character. Shade had often bragged to his friends that she could guess which of them had swiped another beer out of the refrigerator or who had taken the last piece of chicken leftover from dinner. Penni would bet her last dollar the stranger gawking at her was going to run.

She felt her own legs give out under the weight of the man she wanted to save.

"Please…" Penni flinched at the womanish sound that emerged from the man at her plea.

The stranger across the room released a squawk before the coward ran across the room, sliding between her as the stranger hanging on to her released his final breath.

The man who had jerked his knife out of his victim's back tried to stop his escape, slipping in the blood that showed the brutal evidence of his crime.

"Striker, hold on. Be cool."

Another feminine groan brushed past her ear, and the coward disappeared out of the closing door.

"Fuck me!" Penni toppled over when the murderous rage was directed to her as his other victim escaped out the door behind her.

"Bitch, you're going to pay for that!"

Penni found herself trying to struggle free from the limp body pinning her to the ground. She finally gathered her senses and managed to scoot out from under the body to make her own dash for freedom. A hand burying in her short hair brought her to a sudden standstill.

"Who the fuck are you?"

Penni tried unsuccessfully to pull her hair out of his grasp. The more Penni tried to tug away, the harder he held her.

"Let me go!" Penni's demand was ignored as he pushed her farther inside the bar.

Penni blindly stepped over the blood-soaked man she had been unable to save.

She was released, finding herself staring up at an angry male face. It wasn't the first time she had dealt with that reaction, but she wasn't used to having a knife pointed at her. For the first time in her life, Penni found herself speechless.

She felt the sharp point of the knife under her chin.

"Who are you? This is the last time I'm going to ask!"

"Penni!" she barely managed to gasp out.

"Your DJ's girl?"

"No." Penni tried to shake her head yet stopped when she felt the knife nick her skin. "I don't even know who DJ is."

A tug on the back of her hair had her figuring out the man lying near her feet was the unlucky DJ.

"You were with Striker? Did he have you waiting outside?"

Penni didn't flinch as his hand threatened to cut out her throat if he thought she was lying to him.

"I ran out of gas."

Her eyes widened when she heard him begin to laugh.

"You don't know DJ or Striker?"

"I've never seen either one of them in my life," Penni confirmed truthfully, praying he would believe her.

The smug look filling his face did not bode well that she would escape unscathed.

"Then you were in the wrong place at the wrong time."

Nope, it isn't going to go down well for me at all, Penni thought dismally.

"You're not going to let me go, are you?"

"What do you think?" His sarcastic reply had her unobtrusively searching for her purse, which wasn't easy with the knife pointed at her.

"You could just let me leave," Penni mumbled with forlorn hope when she saw the spark of desire in his eyes as he glanced down her body.

Penni's breath caught in her throat. The beating of her heart sped up when she felt the danger race toward her as he moved closer to her.

"That could be hard to do since you're out of gas."

"I can walk."

The man didn't seem to appreciate the humor.

"That doesn't work for me. You might decide to call the cops."

Penni wrinkled her nose as the smell of alcohol on his breath wafted closer.

"I know you don't know me, but I'm really good at minding my own business."

"Shut your trap."

Penni winced as a drop of blood slowly dribbled down her throat. She didn't dare glance toward her purse. Carefully, she used the heel of her tennis shoe to drag her purse closer.

When the stranger cupped her breast in a forceful gesture, Penni didn't scream, trying to keep him distracted.

"Are you just going to leave him there?" She nodded toward the dead body.

"Why not? It's not like he's going to complain."

The man became even bolder when she didn't struggle against his hold. Her top was slipped from under her jeans as he burrowed his hands underneath, wrenching several buttons loose on the front of her blouse. Penni was tempted to use one of the chairs on a table to brain the man intent on raping her.

Biding her time, she used her tennis shoe to reached for her purse. She bit the inside of her jaw, ignoring the sensation of his tongue entering her mouth. She damn near vomited. She wanted to rake her hands down his face. Instead, she pretended to like it as she searched her purse for what she wanted. The disgusting excuse of a man really believed she was responding to him. Thankfully, her fingers curled over what she wanted.

"Woman, we're going to have a lot of fun."

"Yes, we are," Penni promised as he shoved his disgusting tongue down her throat.

Not able to control her gag reflex any longer, she pulled her tongue from harm's way. The teeth that her dentist had charged a small fortune for bit down, nearly ripping the offending invader from her mouth, but he couldn't seek sanctuary.

She ignored the bloodcurdling screams that filled the bar as she pressed against his chest, engaging the trigger on her Taser.

Penni didn't let him go until he was writhing in agony and had pissed himself. Then she stumbled to her feet, grabbing for her purse as she ran toward the door. She almost lost her balance in the flight but managed to right herself as she reached the door.

The humid air filled her lungs as she took a flying leap off the step. Then...

"No!" Penni found herself pinned within a pair of strong arms that refused to relinquish her struggling body.

"I didn't know we're having a party, Hennessey."

Penni found herself surrounded by at least twenty men. She was under no illusions that she had found a savior. The arms that were wrapped around her roughly were covered in tattoos. The one who had two tear drop tattoos at the corners of his eyes had her wishing fervently Shade would miraculously show up.

The dark-skinned man came to stop next to him. "If Ricky and DJ are screwing around when they're supposed to be watching for Striker, I'm going kick their asses. Cruz, you're responsible if they screw up this meeting," Hennessey threatened, coming to a stop, his eyes widening in surprise.

Penni saw the expression mirrored on their faces when the door opened behind her.

"What the fuck happened to you?" The man holding her—named Cruz—was obviously angry.

"The bitch almost bit off my tongue."

"What did he say?" Hennessey questioned the man Penni guessed was his second in command from his appearance.

Penni tightened her lips. Damned if she would help the bastard explain himself.

The man who had tried to rape her jerked her out of Cruz's arms. She wasn't given time to react before she felt her cheek absorb the shock of landing on the ground.

"Fucking bitch! I'm going to kill you." Boots kicked out at her out, one after another, as she tried to catch her breath.

Penni used her nails to crawl away from the attack until a large pair of boots had her looking up.

Hennessey stared down at her furiously. She refused to flinch as he picked her up.

Penni waited for the attack to continue. She was smart enough to realize the man holding her wouldn't be as easy to escape from.

As soon as the dark man had touched her, Ricky had stepped back. The man who had her now was the one calling the shots. Yes, this man was the president. His towering height had her standing up straight, glaring into his eyes. Penni made sure to notice every detail she could use as a weapon, like the diamonds in his ears glinting in the light from the door.

The expensive jewelry could potentially be used as a weapon, but it would be one of the only ones. The president was easily as big as Max with a bald head that made his frown even more menacing. Penni knew he was the more dangerous one.

"Cruz?"

"Got her."

"Sy, let me know when Striker gets here."

"No problem." The biker who answered took a seat on one of the bikes, looking like he was pissed about missing the confrontation brewing between the two bikers.

"He's already shown up." The man who had chased after her from inside of the bar glared at her with retribution in his eyes before his face filled with fear at the dark brown man who was unsettled by his answer.

"He showed early?"

Penni found herself handed back over to the stranger who had stopped her panicked flight. He carried her back inside the empty bar.

"Why'd he show?"

The twenty men who followed them in came to a stop at the sight of the body lying on the floor.

"DJ better be sleeping." Hennessey's growl had her attempted rapist paling.

"It was an accident..." Ricky stammered.

Penni wanted to place herself as far away from the body as she could. Unfortunately, the man in charge and his men blocked her escape route.

She didn't flinch when Hennessey pulled out a gun from under his leather vest.

"Why is the only other black brother dead?"

"I caught DJ calling Striker, telling him to show up early. He was going to take the money and disappear before you and the brothers could get here. If I didn't try to stop him, he would have taken off with our money."

"He's lying," Penni found herself saying then found herself shoved into a chair. Cruz placed a heavy hand on her shoulder.

Ricky had taken a step toward her, but Hennessey blocked him before he could reach her.

"She's lying." Ricky's raised his hand as if he were going to strike her.

"I'm not." Penni glared back, lifting her chin, prepared to tell the truth, even if it meant taking a hit from the man glaring at her, promising retribution.

Hennessey caught Ricky's arm in his grip, and Ricky's expression became a mask of fear.

Penni's bottom lip curled in contempt. The biker was making a fatal mistake by letting the men see his fear.

"He didn't have a cell phone in his hand when he was stabbed in the back as I came in through the door. Ricky would have had time to call you if he wanted to," Penni explained.

"She's lying!" Ricky screamed as Hennessey aimed his gun.

A pool of blood appeared on his thigh.

"Dammit, listen to me."

Another pool of blood appeared on his other leg.

Ricky fell to the floor with Hennessey standing over him.

"Dumbass, DJ would have never betrayed me. He knew the price for betraying me." The gun was pointed at Ricky's temple.

"Please, brother..."

"Don't call me brother when DJ's blood is smeared all over your boots."

Penni covered her mouth with both hands when the shot rang out in the bar. Sadly, she didn't feel any sympathy toward the dead man a few inches from her feet. He would have raped her and probably buried her where she would have never been found. Then the other bikers would have shown up to find their friend dead with no one able to prove the lies Ricky had told.

She stared mutely at the bald-headed president with his diamond earrings glinting at her, which seemed to mock her emotionless response to the killing that had taken place in front of her.

"Get that piece of shit out of here," Hennessey ordered, not taking his eyes off her.

"What do you want me to do with DJ?" Cruz removed his hand from her shoulder.

"Call Stefan; he'll take care of him for me."

Penni pressed her back against the chair as the black president took a step toward her. Penni expected him to strike her; instead, he crouched in front of her.

"You better have been telling me the truth."

"Why would I lie?"

"You tell me. Maybe you were trying to cause trouble between my men."

"Maybe you should have figured this out before you killed him."

"Maybe I should have, but he pissed me off."

"Do your friends usually end up dead when you get pissed off?"

He shrugged. "Only one of them was considered a friend."

Penni lowered her eyes to the pistol resting on his thigh. "I'm feeling like I need a friend myself right now."

"You're shit out of luck. You're not black the way I like my women, and you're definitely not a brother."

"Maybe not, but I can keep my mouth closed, and I don't care what deal you and your men have going down. I just need enough gas to get to the nearest gas station, and you never have to see me again."

"Why would I trust you?" The man's lip was set in a sinister sneer.

"Because I know how you can find Striker."

CHAPTER THREE

Jackal hazily blinked at the light filling his bedroom.

"Turn off the fucking light," he growled, searching for a pillow on his jumbled bed. Muttering to himself, he managed to find one jammed against Rita's side. He drunkenly dragged it upward to relieve the headache hammering a hole through his brain.

"Ice wants you."

Jackal could barely make out Stump's serious features as he jerked away the pillow providing the only buffer from the daylight that was beginning to lighten the darkening sky outside his window.

"Dammit!" He managed to raise himself to sit on the side of the bed, shrugging off Rita's clinging arms that twined around his waist as he tried to get to his feet.

Jackal reached down, tempted to break her fingers to make her release him from her greedy clasp.

"Come on, Jackal...You promised me that—"

Jackal leaned over to grab his jeans from the floor, swaying as he tried to slide his clothes up his legs. Maybe the extra bottle of whiskey he had made Rita get him had been a mistake.

"Hurry, Jackal; Ice is getting pissed." Stump helped him get to his feet, handing him a T-shirt that was sitting on the bed.

Jackal wrenched away from him. "Tell him I'm coming."

Stump nodded, giving him a warning that Ice wouldn't be kept waiting much longer.

Jackal took only the time he needed to take a piss and wash his face before heading into the clubroom.

He came to a stop at the sight of the empty room. "I thought you said that Ice is waiting—"

"He is. He's waiting for us at Penni's house." Stump didn't give him the chance to ask any questions before he left out the door.

Stump had already started his bike and was driving out of the parking lot before Jackal started his. The last person he wanted to see this morning was Penni. It was Grace's day off, so why would Ice or any of the other Predators be at her house?

As he made the turn onto Penni's street, he saw the brothers already parked out front. Jackal brought his bike to a stop. She wasn't going to be happy to see the men gathered around her yard.

As he slid off his bike, he realized Penni's car wasn't parked in her usual space. It was early on a Sunday morning, but Jackal saw the barely perceptible movement from more than one window of Penni's nosy neighbors.

He walked up her path to the door that was already open. Ice had his back turned to him as he spoke into his phone.

"I'll take care of it. I'll call you back as soon as I find out something new. I promise," Ice assured whomever he was speaking to. The Predators' president didn't make promises he didn't intend to keep.

Jackal looked around Penni's apartment as Ice finished his call. It was what he had imagined her home would look like. It was filled with flowers and the frills that always made him feel uncomfortable. Potted plants rested against the windowsill, and family photos had him sauntering closer to pick up one that caught his attention. His hand circled the picture frame containing the image of the woman who haunted his dreams.

"What's up?" Jackal asked as he felt Ice move near him.

"Grace called me to check up on Penni to make sure she's home. She's worried about her. Seems that she ran out of gas last night, and Grace hasn't heard from her since. She keeps trying to call her back, but it goes to voice mail."

Anything that upset Grace made it Ice's problem, not the club's.

"And you woke me up because Grace is worried about Penni?"

"Yeah."

Jackal slammed the photo down. "I'm out of here, brother."

He tried to sidestep Ice, only to find his path blocked.

"You're not worried? I thought you had a hard-on for this bitch?"

Jackal's eyes and hands returned to the photo. Penni's blue gaze stared at him from the picture. His soul tried to shrink from her scrutiny as if she were really there. Her blonde hair and direct gaze were the direct opposite of her brother Shade, who stood next to her. They were at someone's wedding. Everyone in the picture seemed happy, especially Penni who was surrounded by several men.

Jackal knew most of them were The Last Riders. As the Predators' enforcer, he had made sure to know the men Penni had come into contact with when Colton had asked for their help to find a childhood friend of Vida's. Sawyer and Vida had discovered Lily, Shade's wife, was their missing childhood friend whom they had assumed died when they were all little.

The Predators had been willing to help Colton, especially when they had realized King was Lily's father. When one of the brothers had been sent to keep an eye on her and the Last Riders and then subsequently disappeared, Jackal had taken Penni as insurance until they could get him back.

The trip to Treepoint had been more aggravating than he could have dreamed possible. Penni had become a raving bitch, trying to escape despite his assurances that she would be turned over to Shade as soon as Eightball was released. She had nearly crashed his motorcycle twice, bit him hard enough on his back to leave a scar, and it had taken two weeks to heal from the scratches she had made sure hurt like hell. At one point, Jackal had nearly left her stranded at a rest area. Ice's anger when he had called him to give him the location of the meet with The Last Riders had forced him to turn around to get her back.

Jackal had never met a woman who wasn't afraid of him. When he had pulled into the meeting place, he almost hadn't stopped. Only keeping his word to Ice had kept her safe as he'd forced himself to let her climb off his bike. She had spat at him before sedately walking away.

Jackal wasn't sure why he had let Penni go. He was a hard-ass and didn't care what any of the Predators thought of him. Fuck, that was why he was the enforcer. They preyed on the weak. They took what they wanted, when they wanted. The only reason the Predators were involved with Lily in the first play was because King had made it worth their time.

When Penni had walked away from him, his eyes had met with Shade's. Her brother was as ice cold as his half-sister was volatile. Jackal had felt the chill coming from halfway across the parking lot. He was smart enough to recognize Shade for what he was—a killer. Jackal knew because he was one, as well.

The men gathered on the parking lot had vowed their loyalty to their respective clubs. With one glance, Jackal could tell the difference between the men facing off against each other. The Last Riders held a loyalty to the club that the Predators were missing. All The Last Riders had bonded together to protect Lily, while the Predators were monsters no one could control. They were willing to help King for a price, whereas Eightball had been returned at any price because no one took what belonged to the club.

Jackal stared down at the picture, wondering if Penni knew how dangerous Shade was, how dangerous he was.

"Not since she nearly killed me." Jackal didn't try to keep the irritation out of his voice.

Ice stopped him again. "I didn't think there was a woman you couldn't handle."

Jackal studied Penni's living room. Something was missing, but he couldn't place his finger on what.

"Sometimes, the work isn't worth the effort." His hand went to his scarred cheek. "I learned a long time ago from Camy that you're not going to steal a woman's heart when she doesn't have one."

Camy had been his old lady. He had been nineteen and stupid, believing in forever. He had gone for lunch one day and found her fucking his father, who had stopped by to tell him he was out on parole. The two men had fought, and the cops had been called. When the cops had tried to stop the fight, his father had pulled a blade, cutting him from his brow to the corner of his bottom lip. He had been arrested, still trying to get away from the vicious attack.

"All the women like Penni." Ice braced his legs apart as he leaned over to look out the window.

Jackal set the photo back down. Jackal was right; Penni had dozens of friends. Many were captured in the pictures placed around her living room. Her smile displayed evident humor as she grew older in her photos. The only thing missing from family and friends were boyfriends. None of the pictures seemed to show old love interests. Maybe he had been wrong. Maybe women didn't want be reminded of old boyfriends.

When he had pressured Ice to find out whom Penni was dating, Grace would only tell him that she had seen several men, but she didn't believe Penni was in an intimate relationship.

Jackal had been shocked. His jealously had fueled his imagination, picturing her with numerous one-night stands, some of them with the members of the Mouth2Mouth band she managed. According to Grace, though, that couldn't be further from the truth. Penni would get all gung-ho about meeting particular men, looking forward to getting to know them, only to never see them again after the initial date.

"The women at the strip club all like her, too. Even her fucking neighbors like her. They think she's sweet."

Jackal snorted as he leaned next to Ice. "I bet they've already called the cops." Jackal nodded his head toward where the neighbors could be seen as more of the Predators filed into the house.

None of the neighbors would think of confronting them. Hell, they'd probably have nightmares later. When Penni got home, she was going to be furious with Grace for letting the Predators inside her house.

Ice's contemptuous gaze caught his. "I'll get Colton to talk to them. Penni's had him and Vida over to dinner a couple of times."

Jackal made damn sure he stayed as far away as possible from the cops. The only ones he came into contact with were the ones he paid to turn a blind eye to the Predators' activities.

Jackal heard Max and Stump enter the room from the flight of steps.

"She's not upstairs."

"No shit, Sherlock."

Max clenched his jaw at Jackal's sarcastic words. "Her car isn't outside, and I didn't see her car parked in front of her office."

"How do you know she wasn't parked at her office?"

Ice shook his head at Max when he took an angry step toward Jackal at his jeering comment.

Jackal shrugged, and Stump went up the stairs. He knew Stump was going to go through her things. Ice wouldn't stop him. Despite his denials, he didn't want the brothers snooping through Penni's belongings.

He heard the sound of boots upstairs then the sound of opening and closing drawers. Then Max opened the refrigerator, helping himself to a beer and making himself at home.

Jackal couldn't understand why the brothers were getting on his last nerve. He had once imagined he would be the only one to step foot into her house. He'd had it all planned out the night she had stood him up.

Jackal had planned to take her out to dinner and had even paid for a fancy bottle of wine that had been chilling, waiting for them to arrive. He had worn his best jeans, the ones he was now going to throw away, and even splurged on a haircut. The whole night had been one fuck up after another, all because Penni had decided to deceive him on a whim. Because of this, he shouldn't care that the brothers were making themselves at home in her place.

Thank God none of the brothers could hear the thoughts going through his mind. They would laugh their heads off to know he was still pissed off for being stood up.

Jackal moved away from the window, leaned on the back of the couch, and crossed his arms against his chest to keep himself from punching out at his aggravating friends.

"I'm going back to bed. You and Grace can deal with Penni. I don't know why we would even give a rat's ass about wherever she is."

"Grace is out of town, visiting her parents. If she doesn't show up soon, Grace will catch the next flight into Queen City."

"What's wrong with that? I'm surprised you're not booking her flight for her. She's visiting her parents a lot lately."

Ice's eye's shifted away from him.

Jackal had assumed Ice's marriage seemed to be going well; had he been mistaken?

Jackal knew better than to stick his nose into any of Ice's business. After all, when Ice wasn't with Grace, the club President became a man to fear. However, it was becoming more and more obvious something was going on with Grace.

"Grace's mother is sick."

That bombshell had all the brothers staring at Ice in shock.

Jackal straightened from the couch. "How bad is she?"

"Bad."

Jackal didn't know Oceane personally, only from the snide comments Ice said his mother-in-law constantly slipped in during conversations when she visited. To keep them from fighting, Grace would occasionally fly to visit her parents.

Jackal buried his hands in his pockets. He was going to have to help. Jackal considered himself a hard-ass, but he did have a soft spot that had gotten him in trouble a time or two.

"When's the last time Grace heard from Penni? She sure she just didn't forget to call?"

"She's sure. Penni and Grace have grown close since they've been working together."

Stump came down the steps with a mocking smile. Jackal nearly wasn't able to stop himself from planting a fist on his smirking face.

"She sure Penni didn't go see her brother or his friends this weekend?"

"Penni would have mentioned it to her. Why?"

"I found her toy boyfriend in the drawer beside her bed." Stump waved a picture. It took Jackal a second to recognize it.

"Who's that?" Ice turned to Jackal, expecting him to have the answer he wanted.

Jackal wondered if he expected him to know because it was his job as the club enforcer or because Jackal would have made it his business to know everything that concerned Penni.

"Train." Jackal stepped forward, snatching the photo from Stump.

Penni was standing next to Train. The tall man had his arm casually wrapped around her shoulder. Train's expression was carefully remote. Penni's wasn't. Jackal wanted to tear the picture into a million pieces. Instead, he tucked into his back pocket.

"He's one of The Last Riders."

"You think they could be together?" Stump asked as he took the beer Max handed him. The two men dropped onto the couch, hiking their boots onto the coffee table, carelessly dropping magazines to the floor.

"How have you kept Casey from throwing your ass out the door?" Jackal bent down to pick up the magazines, hitting the tips of Max and Stump's boots to make the brothers lower them to the floor.

"She'd miss my dick too bad to throw me out!" Max jammed his elbow into Stump's side.

"Maybe Penni got tired of needing batteries and decided to drive to Treepoint." Stump jammed his elbow back into Max's side as the two dumbass each laughed at their lame jokes.

Jackal couldn't handle the two stupid men any longer.

Using the magazines, he began battering them as they tried to avoid the vicious blows.

Ice held Jackal back. "I don't think so. Penni wouldn't have left Grace so worried for her."

"Me, either." Jackal hated to admit it to Ice.

The last thing he wanted was to be dragged into Penni's disappearance personally. He thought she was safer away from Queen City until his temper cooled.

A sudden thought had him coming to the perfect solution for both his and Ice's problems.

"Call Shade. Let him find out what happened to her."

"I thought that, too, right up until Grace told me the name of the place where she stopped for gas."

Jackal could tell from Ice's expression that he wasn't happy with his answer.

"Grace said Penni was at a place called the Hay and Fiddle."

Jackal and the brothers all stared at Ice in disbelief. Only Penni would find the one place in a million she should have never gone into. Hell, there wasn't a Predator who would willingly walk into the den of the most bloodthirsty road bandits known to ride a bike.

Max and Stump stared at Ice then Jackal. "You're fucked."

Jackal stiffened. "Why am *I* fucked? It's Ice problem, not mine." He stubbornly crossed his arms.

"If the Road Kingz have Penni, they won't give her back." Max leaned toward Jackal as he watched his reaction. Max always came across as a cuddly teddy bear to the opposite sex, but he was the club's pain in the ass. He loved to aggravate the brothers in every way he could. The only one worse than Max was Stump, and the evil smile curling his bottom lip had Jackal's asshole clenching tight.

"I think we should let them have her." Jackal shrugged. "They'll give her back in a couple of days."

The men both knew he was bluffing.

"Are you telling me that Hennessy can't deal with Penni?"

Jackal still felt the bee stings on his back. "I'm telling you those motherfuckers will throw her back on our doorstep."

CHAPTER FOUR

"You hungry?"

"No." Penni rested her bruised cheek on her knee. Curling into a ball, she tried to ignore the man standing in the doorway of the room she had been dragged into.

After the intimidating biker president had forced her into the back seat of her car, she had watched as they had used fuel from their own bikes to start the sluggish motor.

She had made sure to look out the window so she could remember the way she had been taken. *That's what kidnapping victims do,* Penni had told herself despite the darkness out her window making it difficult to spot any signs she could use to find help.

"Hennessy's not going to give a fuck if you're hungry or not." Cruz placed the take-out bag on the bottom of the bed she was sitting on.

Penni lifted her head to glare at the biker who had uncaringly forced her into the messy bedroom that made her skin crawl at the thought of the germs she guessed were on the filthy mattress.

She was tempted to reach out with her foot and kick the food into his face.

"I wouldn't if I were you."

Penni arrogantly sniffed the air as he bent over to grab the bag. Reaching inside, he pulled out a hamburger and took a large bite of the cholesterol ridden burger that had her wishing Shade and The Last Riders were there to rip out his clogged arteries before letting her dance on what was left of his heart.

"I'm not frightened of you or your men." Penni stubbornly stuck out her chin. "A smart man would let me go."

Cruz wiped his greasy hand on his jeans. "I've never been accused of being smart."

"That's a shocker."

Penni included the dark man entering the bedroom into her fierce glare.

"You threatening my men again?"

She clenched her fingers on her thigh. "If you know what's good for you—"

Hennessy's laughter had Penni ready to jump off the bed to claw out his eyes.

"My brother and his friends are going to make you wish you had never been born."

"Let me guess; he will come for you, and he will kill me? Does he have a particular skill that I need to be worried about?"

If the man standing at the bottom of the bed hadn't been holding her captive, Penni would have found him very attractive. Even Lily and Grace, whom she considered her BFFs, would find him attractive, and they each had handsome men keeping them warm.

"Actually, he does," Penni taunted. "He damn sure has more men at his back than I saw riding with you."

Hennessy's smile disappeared. In a split second, he was bent over the bed and over her.

Penni winced as his hand clenched her jaw. Bravely, she stared up into his eyes.

"Your brother belongs to a motorcycle club?"

"Maybe," she spat out.

"Is that why you were at the Hay and Fiddle?"

"No. My brother wouldn't be interested in a club like yours," she retorted.

"What's the name of your brother's club?"

Penni snapped her mouth closed as Hennessy intentionally lowered his body over hers. She didn't give in to the body braced over hers. Men pissed her off when they used that dominating bullshit.

Their eyes refused to back down from each other's.

"She's lying."

Penni didn't look his way when Cruz spoke from her side. She had no expectations of him interfering with whatever Hennessy planned to do with her.

"She's not lying," Hennessy stated, staring down at her. "It's only a matter of time before I find out, anyway. I gave Apoc your driver's license."

Penni had seen him searching through her purse when she had been shoved into the backseat of her car. She had no intention of giving him any information on The Last Riders; she wasn't an idiot. Thank God Shade and she didn't share the same last name. She was sure Hennessy would eventually find out, though. Hopefully before then, she would be back home, or Shade would find out she was missing.

"Good luck," Penni snarled. "You need to let me go before my brother finds out I'm missing, or you and your men will get seriously hurt."

She shivered at the menacing twist of his lips.

"I can take anything your brother wants to dish out."

"Really? He wouldn't be your only problem." Her cheek was beginning to sting from the pressure he was exerting on her face. She forced herself to hold still as he settled even more weight on top of her.

"You're just filled with surprises. You want to tell me who else will be looking for me?"

"What? And spoil the surprises?" She let her mocking smile slip to a serious expression. "Listen, I really don't give a damn what was going down with your men. Just let me go. I'll go home, and you'll never hear from me again."

"And I'm supposed to believe you?"

"Yeah, I haven't been hurt. Why would I care about a dead biker?"

"Sorry, but that's not going to work for me." Hennessy eased his grip on her cheek. His touch became a caress as he trailed a calloused palm over her throat before covering the beating pulse at the base of her throat.

"Why not?" Penni had a sinking feeling she wasn't going to like his answer.

He released her abruptly and stood next to Cruz. "Did you forget about Striker?"

Penni lowered her eyes. "What about him?"

"Don't play games with me." He angrily moved toward her again, but Cruz gripped his arm. Hennessy shook him off, taking several minutes to straighten his jacket.

Cruz gave her a warning nod of his to tread carefully with the man who seemed to have reached the end of his temper with her.

Penni turned to sit on the side of the bed. "I'm not playing. I told you I could recognize him."

"See? You can help." He brushed his leg up against hers, not letting her move away from him. "You help me, and then I can help you. If I don't find Striker, the cartel I bought the drugs from will wipe out my club. So you can see the pussies from your brother's pretend motorcycle club are the least of my problems."

"What do you need me to do?" Penni asked, knowing she only needed to keep herself safe until Shade found her.

"I told you she was a smart girl, Cruz." He kept his gaze directed on her. "All I need from you is to go for a ride."

Seeing the surprise she made no effort to hide, Hennessy stepped back, giving her a reprieve from the forcefulness of his presence.

"It won't be so bad. You might even have some fun."

"You'll let me go home when I show you Striker?"

She didn't miss the sarcastic exchange between them that Hennessy and Cruz thought she was too stupid to recognize.

"It seems I don't have a choice, do I?" She sighed.

"No, you don't."

Penni firmed her chin. She was determined to show him that he needed her until he could find Striker. "It seems we're stuck with each other, then. I'm hungry."

Both men were surprised at her sudden change of conversation.

"I thought you fed her."

Cruz gave her an angry glare at Hennessy's question. "She refused to eat, so I ate it for her."

"I'm a vegetarian."

"Go get her something else to eat," Hennessy ordered then gave her a hard stare. "I have better things to do than send out my men on your errands. Next time, tell him what you want, or you'll go hungry."

Penni nodded, and then the men left the room without saying anything else to her.

Left alone, she was tempted to pick the lock, but she had already seen the man standing on the other side of the door when they had entered her room.

The room only held the bed and an adjoining bathroom. She had searched furtively through the drawers in the bathroom without success. There was no escape from the prison that she had been locked into. All odds of coming out unscathed were against her.

Penni did what she always did when she felt overwhelmed. Taking a deep breath, she gathered her worries into her hands then threw them out into the vastness of the cosmic wilderness. The situation she was facing seemed bleak, but Penni's brother had faced insurmountable odds when he had been in the service. He had remained alive, not letting them steal his soul when so many men had returned without theirs. She couldn't do any less. She was a survivor; it ran in their blood.

Penni remembered the name of the club printed on their vests. The Road Kingz didn't know what was in store for them.

CHAPTER FIVE

Jackal parked his motorcycle a few inches from the door of the Road Kingz' clubhouse. One of the soldiers standing guard outside snapped to attention, his hand going behind his back. Not taking his eyes from Jackal, he opened the door and yelled out to someone inside the club.

Jackal tuned off his motor and waited expectantly for the shit to hit the fan. It didn't take long before the front door was thrust open.

He lifted his hands in the air as the Road Kingz gathered in a show of force. Then Jackal carefully slid off his bike, making sure to keep his hands visible as he lowered them to his sides.

He searched the faces of the men threatening to attack any second.

"Hennessy? Since when do have to hide behind your men?" It might not have been a smart move to call him out, but Jackal didn't have time to play the bullshit game with the rival club.

The tall, dark man easily stepped around the men standing in front of him. Hennessy's gleaming white teeth were bared in an unwelcoming snarl.

"What the fuck are you doing here, Jackal?"

"I thought I'd come for a visit."

The Road Kingz' president looked at the white do-rag on his head. A mirthless smile was Hennessy's only response. The man had always been an asshole.

"We need to talk."

"We don't have shit to talk about. Get your ass off my club's property before one of my men takes that white rag and shoves it up your ass."

"I'm doing you a solid by coming here."

"Really?" Contemptuously, Hennessy walked around him.

Jackal didn't move as Hennessy lifted his black leather jacket, searching for weapons. Then Jackal received no warning before there was a hard shove to his back. Managing to catch himself, he moved toward the doorway that the men had moved away from so he could enter.

Jackal scrutinized the place as he crossed the threshold of the clubhouse. Damn, his brothers didn't know how good they had it. The Predators' clubhouse was like the Marriot compared to the Road Kingz'.

The large room was filled with broken pieces of furniture, empty beer and liquor bottles littering every available space. The lone trashcan was filled to capacity with empty bottles scattered on the floor. Jackal pictured the lazy bottom dwellers pitching the empties, too busy playing video games and smoking joints to take out the trash.

Hennessy didn't give a fuck about Jackal's opinion.

"You're not going to offer me a beer? It's been a long drive."

The Glock Hennessy pulled out from his back showed the large man was fed up with Jackal's attempt at small talk.

"I'd tell you that you have five seconds to tell me what you want, but you've already used three of them." Hennessy pressed the Glock to his temple. "And don't think I don't know why you're here. That bitch yours?"

"Hell no." Jackal stared him in the eyes so that Hennessy could see he was telling the truth.

"You didn't tell me you had a sister when we were in juvie."

"She's not my sister."

"So if she's not your sister or your bitch, why are you standing in my club?"

"She a friend of the Predators'."

"Shit." Hennessy snorted sarcastically. "You're lying. The Predators don't have any friends. I can vouch for that." He lowered his weapon, replacing it behind his back.

"Technically, she is. Ice's old lady is Penni's employee. Ice is worried that his woman won't get paid since she's not there to sign the check."

"Don't make me pull out my gun again. This time, I'll shoot your lying ass."

Jackal sighed. "Ice has gotten soft in his old age. His woman and Penni are friends. Ice doesn't want her upset since they found out her mother's dying."

No hint of compassion touched Hennessy's chiseled features. "She's not here anymore."

Jackal arched his brow humorlessly. "Now who's lying? I told you I was doing a solid. I didn't take part when the Predators tossed you and DJ out of the club—"

"You didn't step in, either, did you, brother?" Hennessy snarled.

"No, I didn't. I would've if you would have been willing to cut DJ loose."

"He's dead." Hennessy didn't show any of the pain Jackal was sure he was feeling.

"Sorry."

Hennessy shrugged. "It's been coming for months."

Jackal agreed. Some souls were doomed from birth. DJ had been one of them.

DJ, Hennessy, and Jackal had joined the Predators around the same time, each coming from a screwed up childhood, searching for some place to call home. Jackal had found it with the Predators. Hennessy could have, too, but he hadn't wanted to leave DJ. DJ had nearly gotten them all killed during a buy. He had been weak, and the Predators had cut him loose. Hennessy had known DJ wouldn't have survived without him taking his back. It seemed even that hadn't been enough to keep him alive.

"I don't want to butt into your club's business, but Ice is willing to pay for her and make sure there won't be any blow-back to the Road Kingz." Jackal didn't know how Ice was going to keep that promise. Penni would drive to the police station as soon as she was released. The only reason Jackal hadn't been arrested when he had kidnapped her was Shade had explained how the Predators had helped reunite Lily and her childhood friends.

"She's not here." Hennessy repeated. He had been the best poker player in the club when he had been a Predator.

"Penni was on the phone with Grace when her car ran out of gas."

His face didn't twitch at Jackal's words.

Sighing, he nodded his head at the cell phone sitting on top of the trash can.

Hennessy furiously smashed his elbow into the face of the soldier standing next to him. "I told you to get rid of it."

"I can see how you managed to take control of the Road Kingz," Jackal remarked.

At one time, the Road Kingz had made bikers quiver in fear. It had been a long time since then, and most of the members had aged or ended up in prison. Before Hennessy had taken over, the Predators would have struck the Road Kingz' clubhouse and stolen her back before they would have been able to retaliate. However, Hennessy being there made it more difficult.

Without him, the Road Kingz were like a snake with its head cut off—useless.

To give Hennessy credit, he had begun restoring the club's reputation with fights that had made the news. Jackal had actually been surprised when he had checked out the Road Kingz that Hennessy wasn't still in prison.

"Like I said, Ice is willing to make it worthwhile to the club. The Predators would even be willing to get Rita to clean the clubhouse." Getting rid of Rita would be a bonus for both Ice and him. He had made the mistake of using her to take his anger out on Penni. Now the bitch thought she was his lady, despite his angry protests.

Jackal could see the Road Kingz were tempted by the offer. Colt, Arkansas was a rural county. It couldn't be easy to find women to become club whores.

"You're sure there won't be any blow back?"

Jackal nodded. "Ice said he would give his word."

"Fine. You can have her back next Sunday."

Jackal felt his victory slipping out of his grasp. "That's not going to work for Ice."

"That's the deal, the only one you're going to get," Hennessey stated. "Count yourself lucky. That bitch is a pain in the ass."

Jackal took a step forward, his eyes narrowing malevolently at the men surrounded him. "Then we're going to have a problem."

"The only one with a problem is the Predators. Get his ass out of here," Hennessy ordered the soldier he had punched.

The soldier didn't hesitate. Reaching out, he took Jackal's shoulder, shoving him in the back. Jackal spun, breaking the restraining hold before the others could interfere. Placing his arm around his neck, Jackal put him in a choke-hold, holding his head to the side.

"I'll snap his fucking neck if they don't back off."

Hennessy didn't move. "Hell, you'll be doing me a favor."

He might not care, but his men did. Jackal saw the discord brewing among the others in the club.

"I told you I was doing you a solid." Jackal made sure Hennessy knew the repercussions if he didn't listen to reason. "Brother, you've stepped into a pile of dog shit, and I'm trying to help you scrape it off before you get buried in it."

"Let Apoc go. I'm not talking until you do."

"I thought you didn't care."

"I don't, but Cruz is getting ready to put a bullet in that big head of yours. If you want me to listen, I suggest you let him go."

Jackal tossed Apoc toward the Road Kingz, and two men moved toward him, but Hennessy motioned them back.

"You remember King?"

This time, Jackal got the reaction he wanted. Fear entered Hennessy's eyes.

"What about him?"

"Penni is under King's protection." She would be if Ice called him.

"Then why didn't he call me?" Hennessy was no fool.

"I knew, if I called King to ask you to release Penni, you would be a dead man."

Hennessy stared at him doubtfully. King didn't bother himself in other people's business unless there was a profit to be made. Jackal would have to give him the partial truth while protecting King's secret.

"King is friends with Penni's brother."

"Does this bitch know everybody?" Finally, Hennessy's frustration was beginning to show. Penni did have that effect on men, which was why Jackal had taken his time to try to charm Penni into his bed.

Jackal had used his contacts to find out any information on her. With the exception of her parents, she only had one brother. Her parents were an open book, working nine-to-five jobs, while her brother was a different story.

Shade was shrouded in mystery with little or no information available. Fortunately for King, who had wanted to know everything about his son-in-law, Jackal knew how to pay for the information he needed. Shade had entered the Navy at eighteen and stayed there until he had finished his tour. That was his official record. His unofficial record was buried and attainable only to those who had the clearance to see the carnage he was capable off.

Shade was an assassin who took out his targets without leaving a trace. He demanded a high fee for his expertise, but

Jackal didn't think many of the recent deaths were contracted. Those had been done for free, enemies of The Last Riders.

The part that had made the hair on the back of his neck stand up was his psychological report, performed when he had applied to the Navy SEALs. Jackal considered himself fucked up, but Shade was *seriously* fucked. At least he knew he had issues. Shade, on the other hand, didn't care. Shade was an unemotional bastard with only one weakness—Lily.

The first time he had met Shade, Jackal had looked into his eyes and seen death. The man was a natural born killer. Even knowing what he had found out hadn't prepared him for the soulless eyes staring back at him, though. They had stared at each other, recognizing each other's capacity to deal death without remorse. Kind recognized kind. One predator recognized another.

The difference between the two men was that Jackal was willing to bet most of Shade's kills had been sanctioned, while his own had been a matter of survival.

The corner of Jackal's mouth curled into the only semblance of a smile his scarred flesh allowed. "She tell you about her brother?"

"Jesus, now I'm supposed to be afraid of her brother?" Hennessy kicked out at a chair, forcing the laughing, gathered men to step back. "Shut up! You pussies are afraid of King, but I'll be damned if I'm going to be afraid of someone before—"

"You ever hear about The Last Riders?"

"No." Hennessey picked up the chair. Sitting down, he leaned forward, placing his hand on his thigh. "I don't give a fuck who her brother is. I don't care who The Last Riders are. Tell King I'll give my word to give her back, but she has a job to do for me first."

44

Jackal stiffened. "Doing your men?"

"My men haven't touched her."

"Then why keep her prisoner?"

"I need to ride with her to the Spring Rally."

Hennessy wasn't stupid. He wouldn't jeopardize his men's lives unless he had no choice.

"Talk."

Jackal could see Hennessy was weighing his options.

"Core?"

A man walked from behind his back when Hennessy called his name. "I've heard of The Last Riders. The Road Kingz won't win against them."

"I'd take your enforcer's advice. I wouldn't have warned you had it been anyone else. When you saved my life and took me to Gert to patch me up, I told you then I pay my debts. But, brother, you're making it hard for me.

"I found out about The Last Riders because of King. Before then, I thought he was the meanest son of a bitch I had ever met. He wasn't. The Last Riders are filled with them. They'll kill for each other, and what makes them even more dangerous is they'll fucking die for each other.

"Shade is their enforcer. He is the one you will not escape from. He is the reason the Road Kingz or even the Predators can't defeat them. I thought of taking on Shade, and King laughed at me. Fucking laughed at me!"

"And King would drag The Last Riders into a war with us?"

Jackal shook his head. "King wouldn't, but Shade would. Shade is Penni's brother."

CHAPTER SIX

Penni walked back and forth across the small room. When she heard the door open, it took everything she had not to attack.

She stumbled over her own feet when she recognized Jackal.

When he closed the door behind him, fury and fear had her throwing her body against his.

"You bastard!" She tore a chunk of his hair out as she used his hair to slam his head against the wall.

"Are you fucking nuts!" Jackal twisted her hands behind her back.

Undeterred, Penni kicked then bit him on the shoulder. Struggling against him, she found herself thrown backward onto the bed. Then she found herself pinned underneath Jackal's weight as she tried to rise from the bed.

"I hate you! When I get away, I'm going to kill you!" Penni glared up into his imperturbable expression.

"I'm here to try to save your ass." He turned his face to the side when she attempted to rake her nails down his cheek.

"I don't believe in turning the other cheek."

Penni found herself lifted up like a rag doll, tossed head first over Jackal's lap. Then a series of harsh spanks pounded down on her unprotected bottom.

"You big ape!" Penni bit down on Jackal's thigh as she tried to throw herself down to the floor.

"I wouldn't put up with that spoiled bitch behavior from any other woman. Quit biting me, or I'll pull your jeans down and carry you down to the front room and let them take turns turning that ass you're so proud of red."

Penni stopped biting. The thought of the bikers witnessing the aftereffects of the spanking was incentive enough, but she still struggled. And the more she struggled, the harder his hand struck her bottom.

"Did you think it was funny leaving me waiting? I was nearly stung to death. I had to jump over your wall into your neighbor's yard, and they had fucking German Shepherds. You think this hurts? One of those sons of a bitches nearly bit off my balls."

Penni raised her head as Jackal furiously ranted and spanked her again. What was he talking about…?

She pressed her hand to her mouth as he described having to jump into her neighbor's pool then maneuvering through piles of dog shit as he ran from the dogs.

"I bet you laughed your ass off!"

"I forgot, Jackal! I swear!" Penni wiped away the tears that fell from her eyes. It took all her will not to laugh out loud at Jackal's injured pride.

She looked up at him to see him frowning down at her. Jackal jerked her up to sit on his lap. Wincing, Penni shifted so the globes of her butt bore her weight. The bastard knew how to give a spanking, placing most of his smacks on the tender flesh between the top of her thighs and the bottom curve of her ass.

"I waited for you for over an hour."

Penni bit her bottom lip. "I'm sorry. I forgot. I swear, Jackal, I was going to tell you I couldn't make it, but Grace called me, and I forgot." She saw no need to confess that she had originally planned to leave him to face the bee's alone.

Jackal wasn't buying her bull and dropped her unceremoniously on the bed.

Penni watched as he straightened his T-shirt making the tan skin of his waist was visible. An irritating quiver of excitement held her still as Jackal regained his temper. Without realizing it, she had raised her hand, letting another thing go.

"What are you doing?" he asked her.

Penni lowered her hand back to her side. "Nothing."

"Were you going to hit me again?"

"No." She shook her head. "It's just a habit I have."

Suspiciously, Jackal stared back at her.

Penni tried to divert his attention from the silly habit she'd had since she was a young girl. "Are you going to get me out of here?"

"Any sane woman would have asked me that question when I came inside the room!"

Penni flushed. He was right.

"I've been cooped up here for two days. When you walked in the door, I took my frustration out on you. Shade keeps warning me my temper will get me in trouble."

"Don't mention Shade to me. I blame him for turning you into a spoiled brat—"

"Don't you dare bad mouth Shade!" She yelled as she rose to
her knees in the middle of the bed. "It's not his fault I'm here.
It's my own fault for running out of gas."

Penni's head reared back when Jackal grasped her shoulders, forcing her gaze to his.

"Any other woman would have called a tow truck. I told
you when we went to Treepoint that you were writing checks
with your attitude that couldn't be cashed."

"Like I would take any advice from you." She jerked back
from his hold. Rising, she moved to the opposite side of the bed.
More than getting fed up with him manhandling her, Penni
didn't want to deal with her unwanted reactions to Jackal. It
was a losing battle she had been dealing with since she had first
seen him sitting on his motorcycle in front of a hotel years ago
when she'd had the interview with Kaden Cross.

Penni had prayed for the job as tour manager for
Mouth2Mouth. It gave her the perfect excuse to move from her
overprotective parents and brother. It also gave her breathing
room from the man she had fallen in love with when she was
just thirteen years old.

"Then you better start. The Road Kingz aren't like the
Predators; they don't give a damn that King ordered Henry and
the Predators to watch out for you."

"I don't—"

"Shut up!"

The sound of Jackal's boots striding across the floor had her
backing up to the wall.

Jackal braced his hand on the wall near her head. "The only
reason those men haven't already gang raped you is because of
Hennessy."

Shocked speechless, Penni reached for her own throat.

"Instead of using your head and bargaining with them, what did you do? You fucking told them you could identify who took off with their shit!"

"How was I supposed to know?" Penni interrupted another long-winded rant then quickly changed her mind at the contemptuous sneer that reminded her of Shade when he was angry.

"That know-it-all brother of yours should have warned you!"

She trembled as Jackal ran his hand down the curve of her cheek, coming to a rest on the curve of her breast.

He lowered his head, placing it next to hers. "I swore I would let you get out of this mess yourself."

"Why didn't you?" she whispered.

"Grace has enough to worry about."

"Her mother is worse?"

"Yes."

Penni held back the tears at his stark answer.

"I've really screwed up."

"Yes."

Penni felt the tip of his tongue explore the corner of her lips.

"Are you trying to pay me back for tricking you into showing up at my house?"

"Maybe…" Jackal murmured.

Penni clutched his shoulders, fighting the urge to respond to the enticement of him nibbling on her bottom lip. She firmed her mouth. She had made a promise to herself years ago that the only man who would share her bed, despite her yo-yo dating, was her childhood crush, whom she told herself she would get over when she met the right man.

Penni had lost count of how many times she had made a fool of herself to keep him off her mind. She forced herself to concentrate now.

"Did you work out a deal with Hennessy to let me go home?"

"Kind of. First, we have to go to the Spring Rally—"

Penni brought her knee up in a sharp movement. She tried to squeeze between him and the wall, but Jackal closed the space between them.

"We don't have a choice."

"I'm the only one here who doesn't have a choice. I want to go home. If you're not here to help me, then why are you here? Did Hennessy call you to get me to cooperate?"

"No. If you want to go home, then you're going have to do what Hennessy wants. This isn't a conspiracy between the Road Kingz and the Predators. Ice wants to help get you back for Grace. Grace could have found another job months ago. The only reason she hasn't is because of her relationship with you. It might not mean much to you, but she loves you, and the last thing she needs right now is to be worried about you, too."

Penni was filled with turmoil. Seeing Jackal watching her, she kept her hands from reaching upward toward the universe. Penni could imagine the man judging her. Shade was aware of her strange habit, and he would roll his eyes when he saw her praying to the universe.

"So, the only reason you're here is to help me?"

"Yes. I'm the best chance you have to get out of here alive. If you don't help the Road Kingz find Striker, Hennessy said none of us are going to live. The cartel the Road Kingz bought the drugs from want their money."

"Shade will save me—"

"You believe that Shade can walk on water, but he's still in Kentucky, and he doesn't know you're missing."

"But—"

"Can you listen to me just this once? Did I let anything happen to you when I took you to Treepoint?"

"You mean when you kidnapped me?"

"I didn't kidnap you. The Last Riders, King, and the Predators all explained we needed to keep Lily safe."

Penni nodded her head. That was what they had all explained to her, but they had all lied to her, too. She had been kidnapped and used as a pawn. The only one who had told her the truth had been Lily. No one would ever be able to break the bond that existed between them.

Lily knew how important the truth was to her. Not many other people could understand, but Lily was one, and Grace was another.

"I'll trust you, Jackal, but you better not be lying to me." Penni held out her hand. "Let me have your cell phone. I'll call Grace and Shade—"

"Hennessy doesn't want you making any calls."

"What about Grace? I don't want her worried."

"Ice will take care of Grace."

Her hand dropped. He was lying to her. She could spot one a mile away.

"Let's get some sleep. We leave at first light."

Penni felt the shot of adrenaline she had experienced when Jackal had entered the room wear off. Sitting on the side of the bed, she stood back up when she saw Jackal lie down, making himself comfortable.

"You're not sleeping here!" Penni insisted, reaching down to shove his shoulder and make him move.

"There isn't an empty bed in the clubhouse, and I'm not fucking sleeping on the floor."

"I don't care where you sleep as long as it's not with me."

Jackal stretched out his arms, tugging her down to the bed. A long leg wrapped over her, holding her in place. Penni began to struggle against him but stopped when a seductive whisper had her freezing.

"Go to sleep," Jackal ordered. "It's not like it's the first time we've slept together."

Penni moved to the side, burying her face in the crook of her arm. Just like anytime she began to feel nervous, she moved her hands upward toward the stars she wasn't able to see.

The stars were filled with good energy, guiding her to a calm when she needed to release her inner turmoil. It was a lot easier than going to a psychiatrist or prison when she wanted to knock sense into someone.

Jackal wove his fingers between hers, pressing them to her belly. "Go to sleep, Penni."

Wearily, she decided she was on her own tonight. The universe had other souls to be concerned with.

Her mind went back to Grace and Oceane. It always took Penni a long time to settle down into sleep. Shade had told her that normal people lived their life on cruise control, while she pushed the speed limits.

She concentrated on their linked hands, unconsciously gripping his hands more tightly, sinking into the warmth at her back as her lids lowered. Some things in the universe were inevitable.

Why was Jackal the only one who seemed able to shift her mind to neutral and calm the constant turmoil in her soul? Penni should have been grateful to have someone to lean on while playing the Road Kingz' hostage. However, she couldn't shake the feeling that her savior may be the devil in disguise.

CHAPTER SEVEN

"Get dressed." Jackal dropped his saddlebag onto the bed then watched as Penni opened the bag. It didn't take long before he got the reaction he was waiting for.

"These are my clothes?" She picked up her clothes, giving him an accusing glare.

"Ice used the key you left for Grace to water your plants and feed the ducks."

Jackal could tell she was torn between having her privacy invaded or leaving her precious plants and ducks without proper care.

"Is Ice taking care of my things?"

Jackal's amusement had Penni throwing the empty saddlebag at him.

Dodging the missile, he sat down on the foot of the bed. "Calm down. Grace would kick Ice's ass if anything happened to your precious plants and ducks. How did you get railroaded into taking care of a pond of ducks, anyway?"

"They're not ducks. They're swans. I was elected into the position during the yearly HOA."

"You were elected? You mean more than one person volunteered to feed them?"

Penni nodded eagerly. "Yes, well, I mean...One other person volunteered to feed them, but nobody liked her."

"But they liked you?"

"Yes. I offered to pay for their food. The feed had gone up in price, and I offered to pay."

"Why? You haven't lived there long."

"Because they're beautiful."

Jackal stared at Penni. Her expression went soft, and her blue eyes looked luminescent. He shifted on the bed.

He had been attracted to her since he had seen her walking out of the hotel lobby in Queen City. In his experience, when women saw the Predators, they either ran the other way or turned into provocative whores. Penni had flipped him off because he was parked in the wrong space. Then, when he had kidnapped her then released her, she had shown her disgust in him by spitting on him.

After Ice had married Grace, he had seen Penni at a couple of the parties that Grace had invited her to. It had only fueled his attraction.

Jackal had discovered she made friends easily, but only kept a few. It was the same with him. And she had dated most of the men in Queen City. They didn't last long, and if they did, they joined the ranks of her friends.

He'd had no intention of being a friend. Playing the waiting game, he had patiently used any excuse to come into contact with her, only to become the brunt of her insults. Why Jackal had put up with it was uncertain. It was as if a part of her were calling out to him.

It was why he had been so pissed off when she had stood him up. When Penni had said sorry last night, Jackal had believed her, but he had also noticed that her contrition had been brief.

Jackal tilted his head as he studied Penni. King had warned him long ago that there was more to her than showed. Jackal agreed. He didn't think he would live long enough to figure her out.

His stiff dick was tired of waiting, and he had missed having her in his bed like when they had gone to Treepoint. The Spring Rally was a four-day ride. That gave him four nights to build a fire that Penni would beg for him to put out.

Penni stared at him suspiciously as she headed into the bathroom. "What? Why are you staring at me like that?"

Jackal smoothed out his features as he picked up his saddlebag. "Nothing. Get changed. Hennessy is getting the bikes gassed up."

"Why can't we just take off while they're gone?"

"A guard is outside."

Disappointed, Penni went inside the bathroom.

Jackal had already considered making a run for it with her. However, they wouldn't make it out of the clubhouse. The Road Kingz' fate was in Penni's hands. If they didn't find Striker, none of them would come out alive.

When Ice had told him that the Road Kingz had Penni, he had been ready to call Shade and hand the mess over to him. However, it would have been a death warrant for Hennessy, and Jackal hadn't been able to forget the fact that he had saved his life. Then Ice had further convinced him it was a bad idea.

Ice saw the benefit of having the Road Kingz if they ever needed to join forces. It was a risky move, but Ice had given his approval, letting Jackal face the Road Kingz alone.

Jackal stood when Penni came out of the bathroom. Her jeans looked like an old pair, hugging her slender legs snuggly. The blue, long-sleeved T-shirt was tight with a bright rainbow plastered across the front of her taut breasts. It was going to be a long ride to Riverside, California.

"Ready?" He dug his fingers into his back pockets to keep himself from touching the firm thrust of her breasts.

"Do I have a choice?"

"No." Jackal knocked on the bedroom door. Hennessy had assigned Core to stay with them until they were ready.

Jackal took Penni's arm, leading her to the clubroom where Hennessy waited.

As they approached, Hennessy nodded toward Core. "Go on outside. We'll be there in a minute."

What he wanted to say, he didn't want his man to hear. Jackal had a feeling he knew what had his former friend incensed.

"Call them off." Hennessy's order wasn't one that Jackal could follow. Trying to play peacekeeper between the two clubs was going take every skill he had.

Out of the corner of his eye, Jackal saw Penni's attention go back and forth between him and Hennessy.

"They'll stay back, but Ice wants to make sure Penni doesn't end up as a casualty between you and all the shit you've got going down."

A split second was all Jackal had to prepare before Hennessy launched his giant body at him. Planting his feet, he braced for the pain coming his way.

Hennessy barreled into him, and Jackal released Penni's arm then wrapped his arms around Hennessy's waist, putting him in a bear hug, trying to stop his momentum and keep himself from crashing to the floor.

He didn't stand a chance of breaking Hennessy's hold. Jackal couldn't match his weight, but he clamped his arms tightly around him, giving himself time to reason with the raging giant.

"Ice will stay back," Jackal grunted. How much did the fucker weigh? "If anything happens to Penni, King will kill all of us. Think about it! If you can't find Striker, you're going to need the Predators."

Hennessy threw him off, breathing hard. "I don't need the Predators."

"Are you sure about that?" Jackal took the time to catch his breath, expecting Hennessy to attack again.

Hennessy rubbed angrily over his bald head.

"There's going to be over eighteen motorcycle clubs at the rally. You think you're going to deal with all off them and a cartel that wants their money back?"

"I have it under control!"

"Brother, you lost control when you snatched Penni. I'm trying to keep you and her alive. If she gets hurt, you won't live to see another day." He sighed out in frustration. "Let me help you. Ice won't interfere unless you need back up. When you get your money back, I'll take Penni, and we'll disappear. We'll all get what we want."

"I don't know what trouble you're in, but I would listen to Jackal if I were you."

Jackal shook his head at Penni. Hennessy would drop down dead before he took any advice a bitch gave him. Surprisingly, however, he stared across the room at him as if he was considering her opinion.

"You'll keep Jackal's word and not run to the cops when I let you go?"

Penni narrowed her eyes at him. Jackal expected her to spit at Hennessy for his question.

He tried to silently warn her of the repercussions if she lost her temper. Penni had been too sheltered by Shade. Bikers were notoriously controlling. They expected their bitches to do what they were told and not argue. Penni was the exact opposite.

"Yes." Penni looked like she was about to choke on her answer.

Hennessy wasn't convinced.

Jackal moved closer to Penni, laying an arm across her shoulders.

"She'll do what I tell her." His arm tightened around her, giving her the only warning he could. He could only do so much.

"That right?" Hennessy didn't look like he believed him.

She leaned into his side. "Jackal's the boss." The nails digging into his back would leave marks, but at least Hennessy's doubts had been taken away.

"Go make us some sandwiches. If we don't get on the road, the rally will be over before we even get there."

"I'll help," Jackal spoke up. "It'll be faster." Not to mention, he didn't want to eat anything Penni made while in the mood that was brewing in her eyes.

"Don't take long." Hennessy left them, slamming the door to show he wasn't happy that Ice was nearby.

"When this is all over—"

"You want us to make a sandwich for you?" Jackal addressed the man Penni had forgotten was lying on the couch behind her.

Her eyes widened at Jackal's reminder that Hennessy wouldn't be stupid enough to leave them alone.

"No, thanks. I'll make my own." Cruz laughed. "If I want to eat food that will kill me, I'll eat at Chip-n-otle."

"Be my guest—"

Jackal covered her mouth with his then hastily jerked it back. "What she means is I'll pay for lunch. It'll save some time." He tossed some money at him. "Grab some burgers."

"What do you want me to grab for you?"

Jackal stared at Penni in confusion as Cruz waited for her answer.

"Get her a burger, too—"

"She doesn't eat hamburger; she's a vegetarian."

He almost burst out laughing at Cruz's comment. Jackal had seen Penni eating too many chicken wings and hot dogs. He wasn't going to bail her out of this one. It was going to be a long road trip without the foods she loved.

"Get her a veggie burger," Jackal said mockingly. "Grab me two burgers. I'm all of a sudden hungry."

CHAPTER EIGHT

"I'm getting cold!" Penni yelled into Jackal's ear above the roaring motor.

She held him more tightly as he accelerated. Why was he speeding up instead of slowing down? Had he not heard her from behind the visor of the helmet?

Penni saw Jackal give Hennessy a hand signal. Then the bikers Jackal had passed gradually pulled off to the side of the road. When he came to a stop, Jackal slid his leg off his motorcycle to stand stiffly. The cars whizzing past them made her nervous.

"I'm freezing. When are we going to stop?" Penni complained through chattering teeth.

"Not for another hour."

She gaped as he tugged off his leather jacket, holding it out for her to slip on.

Penni tried to move away, shaking her head. "You'll get cold."

He ignored her, zipping up the jacket then getting back on his motorcycle. "I'll be fine."

Jackal carefully watched the speeding traffic then skillfully maneuvered back onto the road.

Penni felt as if her ass was numb, and her head would fall off. She pressed into his back, hoping to share her warmth. She didn't know why it bothered her that he might get cold.

Resting her head on his shoulder, she felt strangely secure despite the traffic. She had ridden with Shade a few times, and Jackal was almost as good. She would grudgingly admit he might even be better, but Shade was her big brother, and Penni had hero-worshipped him since she had been old enough to walk.

She was relieved to see Hennessy taking an exit with several hotel and food signs an hour later.

Jackal had ridden in the middle of the pack, surrounded front and back by the Road Kingz. The large group of bikers riding down the road were an impressive sight. Penni would have appreciated it much more if she been there willingly.

Penni attempted to get off the motorcycle when they pulled in front of the hotel.

"Wait."

"My butt is killing me," Penni protested yet remained seated at Jackal's order.

"It won't take long."

Thankfully, Cruz came out of the office not long after, handing out room keys.

Penni wanted to cry in relief when Jackal parked his bike in front of a room. Every muscle in her body ached as she slid off the motorcycle. She didn't know how she was going to make it three more days.

When she had ridden to Treepoint with Jackal, she hadn't appreciated how easy he had taken it on her, giving her time to rest and more breaks. Hennessy didn't give her the same consideration. He was pushing her on his timetable, not caring how uncomfortable he was making her.

Jackal took her arm to steady her. Penni was self-conscious as he led her to the hotel room.

She looked around the room when Jackal flipped on the light switch. It was much cleaner than she had expected.

"I need to use the bathroom."

Penni tightened her lips as Jackal strode across the room. His lean body moved with ease despite riding on the motorcycle as long as her. He went through another doorway, and a light came on.

"It's through there." He raised a brow at her resentful expression.

Penni waited for him to step to the side before going inside and closing the door behind her.

Mumbling to herself, she relieved her aching bladder then washed up with the clean washcloth. When she finished, she sat down on the side of the tub.

The tiny room didn't even have a window. How could she escape if they didn't give her the freaking chance? Her normally cheerful attitude was cracking under the strain.

She heard male voices outside the door then the front door closing.

"Cruz is getting us some food."

Yippee!

Penni didn't respond.

Reaching into her back pocket, she pulled out her useless cell phone. As they had left the Road Kingz' clubhouse, she had seen it sitting on top of a trash can. She had refused to get on the back of Jackal's bike until he had gone back inside and retrieved it for her.

"Hennessy took the SIM card, so it won't work."

She had snatched it from his hand with a genuine smile.

She was more upset about the loss of her contact list and pictures that she'd never had the time to get printed. Penni was hoping that, when Hennessy released her, he would give the SIM card back.

She rolled her eyes toward the ceiling. The universe had gifted the huge man with an arrogant nature. It was no wonder he was the president; his size alone made it difficult to stand up to him.

Penni ran her thumb over the black screen, tempted to throw it against the wall. As an alternative, she tucked it back inside her pocket.

"You're not the only one who needs to take a piss." The sound of Jackal's voice on the other side of the door had her rising up to open the door.

"Sorry."

Jackal tilted his head. "I get an apology two days in a row? I'm amazed."

She removed his jacket, handing it back to him. "Thank you for letting me borrow it."

"You sick?"

Penni frowned in confusion. "No, why?"

He shrugged. "I thought you would have to be stinking drunk to say anything nice to me."

Before she could reply, he went inside the bathroom.

Ashamed, she sat down on the bed, folding her legs crisscrossed. It took her several minutes before she realized she might have a chance to escape. She was about to jump from the bed when Jackal came back into the room. Folding her legs again, she resumed her meditation position.

When a knock sounded on the door, Penni didn't show any interest, not even when she smelled the aromas coming from the bag that Jackal placed on the nightstand.

She ignored the sandwich he held out to her.

"I'm not hungry."

"It's a hamburger."

Before he could snatch it back, Penni took it from his hand. Unwrapping the burger, she didn't even care that it had a sauce she hated.

Jackal sat down on the bed, pulling out his sandwich and taking a bite. After she saw what he was eating, she winced.

"You're eating the one Cruz got for me?"

"Yes."

"Why didn't you just tell him I was lying about being a vegetarian?"

"I figured, if you wanted him to know the truth, you would tell him." Jackal's mouth twisted. "Besides, I knew you were doing it to bug Cruz."

"I was being a bitch," she admitted, taking another bite of her own sandwich. "I'd share with you, but it's not that good. The veggie burger is probably better. The special sauce sucks."

Jackal handed her a bag of chips. "Special sauce?"

Penni licked her bottom lip after she finished the last bite. "Every restaurant makes their own sauce. Usually, it's ketchup and Thousand Island. One time, I ate it, and I swear they used tartar sauce. It was disgusting."

"Why didn't you just tell them to leave it off?"

"You're kidding, right? I know how to order the way I want it, but somehow, in every drive thru, they screw my order up. Don't they mess yours up?"

"No."

I bet they don't, Penni thought to herself. The sensual man sitting across from her probably had dozens of women jumping to make a burger for him.

"Well, they do mine." Dropping a chip back into the bag, she uncurled her legs. "How did you and Hennessy become friends?"

Jackal neatly placed their trash in the take-out bag then put it in the trash can beside the bed. "Hennessy would tell you we were never friends, especially in juvie." Jackal sprawled out on the foot of the bed. "It was a couple of weeks doing guard duty for the Predators before he would even say hi when we went on duty. It was another month before he stopped walking away when I tried shooting the shit with him. Guard duty is boring as fuck. He finally started talking to me, and we would have beers every now and then, but we were never best buds."

"But you did." Penni remembered the flash of emotion on Jackal's face when he had convinced Hennessy to let Ice back him up. "Will he let me go?"

"I'm not going to give him a choice."

She believed him.

"You're lucky that you were on the phone with Grace when you ran out of gas."

"Yes, I am. I'll have to invite Grace and Ice to dinner when this all over," she joked.

"What about me?"

Penni didn't know how to respond. The thought of Jackal in her house was nerve racking. "You convince Hennessy to give my purse back, and I'll fix you a four-course dinner."

Her gaze dropped to his bottom lip. The jagged edge of the scar ended at the corner of his mouth. When he was angry, it had the effect of appearing harsh, but when Jackal was in a good mood, the effect was a sensual feast that, combined with his muscled body, had her stomach doing somersaults.

"There's not a chance in hell of that. You keep a fucking arsenal in your purse."

"That's an exaggeration." Penni pouted, throwing a pillow at his grinning face.

Jackal turned serious. "Kiss me, and I'll get him to give it back."

Penni shook her head. "I don't want it back that badly." As soon the words came out of her mouth, she realized she had screwed up.

Jackal's expression became shuttered, and it didn't take much to figure out how angry he was at her abrupt rebuff.

"Go to sleep. Hennessy wants to be on the road as soon as the sun comes up."

"Jackal..." Penni moved to grab his arm. "I didn't mean it the way it sounded—"

"What did you mean, then?" Jackal pulled his arm back.

She twisted a lock of her hair. "Why do you always make me the mean person? Everyone likes me." Penni stopped then clarified, "Maybe Killyama doesn't like me, but everyone else does." She waved her hands emphatically. "You kidnapped me! I was minding my own business, and the next think I know, I'm driving around the freaking country with my hands cuffed around your waist. How was I supposed to know that you and the Predators were trying to protect Lily?

"I'm really a nice person! Did I call the cops when you let me go? No!" Penni took a deep breath then resumed her tirade. "Did I jump on the chance to go out with you when you asked me? No, I don't like the way you manhandle me. For your information, throwing a woman over your shoulder stopped with the cavemen!" She took another breath. "The women you go out with might appreciate it, but I do not! I think they need their heads examined to put up with the games you play with them."

Penni pointed a finger in his direction when he attempted to stop her tirade. "Most of the women who work at Purple Pussycat all know you fuck them individually depending on the day of the week. The only one who thinks it's a secret is you. You're a manwhore. I was smart not to fall for that bullshit in high school, and I'm damn sure not going to fall for it now." Before she finished, Penni wanted to get something that bugged her the most about Jackal off her chest. "And don't ever call me a bitch again!"

When Jackal didn't say anything, she couldn't stand the silence. "I'm a really nice person."

"You said that three times; I believe you. If I promise not to call you a bitch, do you think we can start over?"

How could she say no without coming off as the bitch he believed her to be?

"Okay." Penni tried not to look like she was about to eat a burger with secret sauce.

"You don't look like you mean it."

"I do." Penni pictured a baby duck in her mind, trying to appear more convincing.

Jackal brought his hand to the back of her neck. "Prove it." He brushed his lips against hers.

She placed her hands on his chest, expecting him to take advantage of the opportunity. Before she could pull away, Jackal was already backing up.

"Friends?"

Penni stared back, struck dumb. She cleared her throat.

"Friends," she agreed softly.

"I'm going to take a shower. If you need anything, yell out."

Nodding, she watched as he closed the bathroom door. A second later, she heard the shower.

"Damn."

The tender kiss Jackal had pressed against her lips had been exactly like she had always imagined the man she had loved since being a teenager would kiss her.

Immediately, she pressed her hands upward, throwing her worry to the universe. Usually, the simple gesture provided a calming effect, but not this time. Neither the universe nor Shade were going to help her out of this mess. She was on her own.

CHAPTER NINE

"We're five minutes away." Jackal raised his voice so Penni could hear him above the wind. He felt her perk up at his back.

He was as relieved as she was. If her ass was as numb as his was, she was going to be in bad shape. Should he offer to massage it for her? He laughed, knowing she couldn't hear him. Since the first night they had stopped, he had made sure to treat her the same way he had seen her girlfriends behave when they were together.

Suspicious at first, she had gradually become more comfortable around him. *Riding a motorcycle practically nonstop would do that for you*, Jackal thought sardonically. He didn't know why he hadn't tried the friend trap before.

Parking his bike next to Cruz, Jackal helped Penni off. When she would have fallen, Jackal caught her by the waist.

"Thank you."

Jackal kept her at arm's length, solicitously releasing her as soon as she caught her balance.

"You're welcome."

He was wound so tightly from being near Penni it was everything he could do not to throw her down on the nearest bed. Jesus, he was being a fucking saint. The Road Kingz and the Predators would laugh their asses off at the dick-less way he was treating her. He was doing everything but painting her fingernails. He had never put so much work into getting a bitch in his bed, and he couldn't explain to himself why he was now.

He had learned at an early age not to become a dependent on a particular woman. Jackal's father had beaten that into him when his mother had left.

His mother had disappeared one day when he had gone to school. At eight years old, he had waited for her to come back. His father had told him that she wasn't going to, that she had taken off with another man. Jackal hadn't believed him at first. Then, as the days and months had passed, he had finally accepted that she wasn't returning.

His father hadn't seemed to miss her. Women would show up and stay a day or two then leave after an argument. Jackal was ten when he had begun calling him the nickname his drinking buddies called him. Bulldog had been waiting for him one day after school. From his furious expression, Jackal had known he was going to get a beating.

He had received a letter from school that he had been late three times. It hadn't been surprising since Jackal had been the only one responsible for getting himself dressed and walking to school since he had usually missed the school bus. It had been a blessing in disguise when Bulldog had broken his arm. An ER physician had reported his father to the cops, and Jackal had been placed in foster care. It had taken Bulldog three months to get custody back. What had followed were years of being in and out of foster care. Then, when the beatings had become severe enough to send him back to the ER, Jackal had asked his father why he had even bothered to get him back from foster care. His answer had run chills down his back.

"I made sure that bitch you called a mother didn't take you when she tried to leave me, and I'm fucking sure as shit not letting you leave me unless you're in a casket."

Bulldog had done his damnedest to keep his word. The scar that marked his face was the reason his father had received a prison sentence that was almost over.

"We're not going to a hotel?"

"No, Hennessy wants to take a break."

"Don't make me regret my decision to let you take her in with us," Hennessy warned.

Jackal wrapped his arm around Penni's waist as they walked toward the restaurant to keep her from replying to Hennessy's warning.

The town was filled with motorcycle clubs showing off during the Spring Rally. Several bikers eyed them as they neared the doorway of the restaurant, but none of them spoke. Jackal wondered which of their group they were most cautious of starting a fight with: his scarred face was a hostile mask; Hennessy's height easily towered over the rest of them; and Cruz at the rear was no slouch, his muscular build drawing their attention.

Inside, Jackal led Penni to a booth near the front door. She slid in, and then he slid in after her. Hennessy and Cruz sat down across from them while the rest of the Road Kingz took two other booths beside them.

Jackal ignored Penni's attempt to put more space between them, sliding another inch to pin her closer against the wall. If shit went down inside the restaurant, he would be able to block her from getting hurt.

"Do you mind?" Penni tried to push him back.

"No. I have plenty of room."

"Good for you," she snapped. "But you're squishing me."

"You could come over here and sit next to me," Hennessey offered. "Cruz can sit at another table."

"Never mind." Penni quickly looked down at the menu she took from the waitress.

Jackal and Hennessy shared a grin across the table. It reminded him of the old times from before Hennessy had become consumed with watching out for DJ.

"What can I get you?" the waitress asked.

"I'll take a steak and baked potato," Jackal ordered.

"I'll take the same," Hennessy ordered, leaning back against the booth. "You're buying."

"Me, too," Cruz repeated.

"I hope I have enough in my account to pay," Jackal complained.

When Penni didn't order, he looked at her then almost laughed out loud. She had kept up her pretense of being a vegetarian. He had taken several of her meals that they had ordered for them, but he had eaten his last veggie burger or bean burrito. She was on her own.

She pushed her short, blonde hair back from her cheek as she studied her menu, frowning. When she bit her lip, Jackal broke. Damn, he was a sucker when she did that. It sent a lightning bolt to his dick.

"Give her the same as me. You can blame me later. You're going to need the protein for what I'm going to do to you tonight."

Her mouth dropped open as the waitress snickered while she walked away. Penni's face turned a bright red.

Leaning down, he brushed her hair back. "You want me to order you something else?" he teased then jerked back when she dug her nails into his thigh under the table.

"I can order for myself."

He stared back at her, finally understanding why Penni had claimed to be a vegetarian. She had resented them making the choice for her instead of being asked what she wanted to eat. Penni was a control freak. Jackal wasn't surprised. Penni and Shade didn't share the same father, but they did have the same mother. The apple must not have fallen far from that particular tree.

"Aw, don't feel bad about last night. I'm sure it happens to all men," Penni cooed with a malicious glint in her eye.

Hennessy and Cruz shook their heads. "Not me," they spoke at the same time.

When the Road Kingz looked with sympathy at him while they shook their heads, Jackal was tempted to spank her ass in front of the whole restaurant.

If he hadn't been pretending as if he were her BFF, he would show her exactly...

The door opening distracted him from planning his revenge. The Predators filed inside as if they owned the restaurant.

"What the fuck!" Hennessy growled as he and the Road Kingz moved to stand up.

"Back down," Jackal hissed. "The Road Kingz aren't the only club here for the rally. The Predators are as tired as we are."

Jackal laid his hand over Penni's on his thigh. She was looking at Ice, Max, and Colton as if they could save her. It was the way he had wanted her to look at him. Jackal's hurt pride had him pulling away from her.

"Ice doesn't want any trouble. He just wants to feed his men and give them a chance to rest."

"If he gets near Penni..." Hennessy sat back down.

"You keep your word to give her back, and Ice will keep his. Besides, if anyone starts some shit, Ice can help out."

"I don't need the Predators' help."

Jackal believed him. The Road Kingz weren't cowards, and they all appeared ready to fight. Hennessy seemed to be returning the Road Kingz to their former glory.

The waitress arrived with their plates, and Jackal didn't miss the beseeching look Penni shot her. When she lowered hurt-filled eyes as the waitress walked away, Jackal swallowed his hurt pride.

"You're going to be okay."

She nodded but didn't look up, beginning to eat her food. He was a freaking sucker where she was concerned. He didn't want her sitting there, disappointed that the Predators weren't making a stand to force her release.

He wanted Penni as his woman. He wanted her to learn that, if anything happened to him, the Predators would take care of her.

"As soon you show me Striker, you can go. I don't get my kicks from threatening women."

"That's not how it seemed when you took me hostage."

"Don't get me wrong; I'll do what I have to in order to keep my men safe. To do that, I have to find Striker. Finish eating and let's get out of here. The Predators are ruining my appetite."

His word had the desired effect, and she began eating. Jackal spared Hennessy a grateful look for reassuring Penni.

Penni was one of the most confident women he had ever met, but even she had to be worried about her safety surrounded by so many outlaw motorcycle clubs. Hell, he was worried. The restaurant was filled with at least four different outlaw clubs that he recognized from their colors and patches.

When the waitress returned, Penni turned her head away. Jackal took the check when Hennessy mockingly handed it to him.

"If Jackal keeps feeding us like this, we might need decide to keep him," he joked.

"If you would give me my purse back, I'd pay."

"That's not going to happen. I almost lost my hand when I searched it, and I should have sent Cruz to the ER for the cut on his finger."

"I told you not to open it."

"Yes, you did."

Hennessy and Cruz stood up as Jackal reached out his hand to help Penni slip out of the booth. The Predators stared at them coldly as they filed out the door. Hennessy acknowledged Ice's cold stare, saluting him mockingly.

Penni sat down on his bike. As he was about to get on, though, she stopped him.

"Ice did that for me, didn't he?"

"Yes, he did." he answered, knowing she had referred to Ice's menacing attitude.

Sitting down, Penni perched her chin on his shoulder. "I'll have to make him a cake when I get home. Grace said he loves cake."

"You're not making Ice a fucking cake." Jackal started his bike, revving the motor then backing out of the parking spot.

"Why not?"

He wanted to snarl jealously at her, but he reminded himself to play it cool. "He's on a diet."

"Really? He doesn't look like he needs to be on a diet. He looks really good to me."

Jackal, backing up, planted his leather boots on the pavement. *Did she just say that to me?*

He'd had more of the BFF bullshit than he could stand. The thought of her staring at Ice's body had him wanting to hit the nearest wall.

"Yeah, Grace is complaining he's getting a big gut," Jackal lied without remorse.

"I don't want to break his diet."

He nodded, relieved he wouldn't have to kill his president because of Penni making him a fucking cake. He lifted his boot to the foot peg, accelerating toward the busy street.

"I'll have to give him a big hug."

His bike jerked when she yelled in his ear.

When he came to a stop at a red light, he turned back to her.

"I know something you can give him."

"What?"

"Buy him his favorite liquor."

"That's a good idea. What is it?"

"Hennessy." Jackal revved his engine. "And put a big ol' bow on it."

CHAPTER TEN

"We're not staying. Hennessy's only giving us time to shower. He wants to find Striker."

Penni paused as she was about to lie down on the hotel bed. "I'm not going to argue with that. The sooner, the better." She brushed her fingers through her tousled hair. "I want a shower, but I don't have any clean clothes to put on. The clothes I washed last night are still damp, and the ones I'm wearing are the only other pair I have."

"I can go and buy you some clothes while you shower..."

A sharp knock on the door had Jackal opening the door, only to see no one there. Penni watched as he leaned down to pick something up. She almost jumped up and down in excitement when she watched Jackal lay her overnight bag and purse on the bed.

"Hennessy must like you."

"What?" Penni unzipped her suitcase, pulling clean clothes and underwear into her arms.

"He gave your things back. He would have tossed them in a dumpster if he didn't like you."

"He must not like me too much; my purse is practically empty." Penni searched the purse which now had a busted zipper. "He didn't even give my wallet back."

"At least you have your clothes back."

She was too thrilled to have clothes again to get upset. If anyone tried to use her credit cards, they would be disappointed. Her new home had put a big dent in her checking account and credit limit. She had sacrificed everything but the bare necessities since she had moved in, and then she had found she couldn't really enjoy the backyard she had been looking forward to because of the damn bees.

"I'm going to take a shower."

Jackal lay down on the bed, turning on the television. His T-shirt rode up his waist, exposing his tan skin. How could he be that dark when it was still early spring? Penni felt her mouth go dry and unconsciously wet her bottom lip.

When she didn't move, Jackal turned from the television. "You need something else?"

Penni shook her head, escaping into the bathroom before she did something she would regret.

Leaning back against the closed door, she took several deep breaths, calming her rioting nerves.

It was easy to see why the women who worked at King's former bar were all at his beck and call. Jackal had a lazy sensuality that drew women in. He wasn't a man whom women would run over. With Jackal, you knew exactly what you were getting—a male chauvinist who called all the shots in the short-term relationships he had.

Could they even be called relationships? According to her friends, they were nights of sexual excesses that had them begging for repeat performances.

Penni began to question the futility of her virginity. The man she had been saving herself for treated her like a little sister. Shade had told her over and over again she was wasting her time, and Penni had huffily told him that he had waited for Lily and hadn't given up hope. Her brother was now happily married with a baby boy. Giving up hope wasn't in their DNA.

She removed her clothes then stepped into the shower. The warm spray didn't cool the heat that Jackal had built.

"Jesus," Penni mumbled, shoving positive thoughts through her mind instead of focusing on the picture of Jackal sprawled out body on the bed on the other side of the door.

She hurried through her shower. She needed to find Striker and get the hell out of Dodge before she attacked Jackal and was arrested. He had astonished her by being well-behaved, showing a sense of humor she hadn't known he possessed. Penni had begun to like his friendly overtures when he would ask about her work with Mouth2Mouth. At first, she had believed he was trying to find out if she had any relationships with the band. The more they had talked, the more he had seemed interested in whether she enjoyed the work she did. Even Lily and Grace became bored when she discussed her work. She found out that he grasped the concept of the huge amount of work and attention to detail it took to pull off a concert with thousands of screaming fans.

Penni dried off then got dressed. Then, using whatever makeup Hennessy had left inside her purse, she made herself feel almost normal again. If she ever got home, she promised herself to pack a larger suitcase and to keep it in her car. Changing her mind, she promised herself to ride the bus from now on. She believed in learning from her mistakes, and not following Kaden's orders had been a doozy.

It didn't take long for Jackal to shower. Penni waited patiently, trying not to imagine his naked body on the other side the door. She was all about being friends with the opposite sex, but Jackal was a temptation who was becoming a fascination she was having difficulty resisting, and the man didn't even realize she was becoming attracted to him. It was like watching a car wreck in slow motion and knowing it would end in disaster, but you still couldn't look away.

She thought they would drive, but when she moved toward Jackal's bike, he took her hand and pulled her through the crowd, walking through the parking lot. Hennessy and Cruz walked next to them.

"Thank you for letting me have my things back," she muttered to Hennessy, unsure how to talk to the imposing man, but she couldn't resist criticism on the way her things were returned. "It would have been nice if I had my wallet in case I wanted to buy something."

"If you want something, Jackal can buy it. He has all kinds of money."

Penni couldn't understand his mysterious comment, though she didn't miss the sharp look Jackal gave Hennessy. It would have been nice to have her wallet if she managed to slip away from the Road Kingz. Obviously, Hennessy had thought of that, which was why he hadn't given it back.

Like escaping is going to happen, anyway! Penni snorted to herself. She was surrounded by Hennessy and his men.

"Where are we going?" Penni asked Jackal, curious about how Hennessy planned to find Striker.

Hennessy was the one who answered. "To the Night Owl. It's a bar where most of the clubs hang out. Cruz and I will be next to you the entire time, so don't think you can sneak away. The men there won't give a shit that you don't want to be there." He turned toward her, giving her a calculated glance. "Hell, it'll make their fucking night, and you'll find yourself in more trouble than you bargained for. The clubs there are one percenters, and they aren't squeamish about slitting our throats and raping you before they buy everyone at the bar a round of beers."

In other words, they weren't The Last Riders. Penni wondered how the Predators behaved when they were away from Grace, Vida, and Casey. Their husbands seemed happily married, but did they act like the men who were lining the streets?

Flushing, Penni saw women within the groups wearing shorts and tops. She was wearing jeans and a sweatshirt, and she was freaking cold. These women didn't even look chilled.

Penni was relieved and terrified when she saw the huge sign for the Night Owl on top of a building that had a massive crowd out front.

"I can't believe there aren't any signs of the police."

"Believe it," Jackal replied sardonically. "It would take the National Guard to get a squad car through this part of town."

Both Jackal and Hennessy shifted closer to her side as they entered bar with the Road Kingz at their heels. Penni felt the room sizing them up as Jackal found an empty spot at the corner of the bar.

She shook her head when the bartender asked if she wanted a drink, too disgusted at the behavior taking place in the bar. If the women had been scantily clad in the street outside, the women inside were wearing next to nothing. There were even three dancing on a stage in the front of the packed bar.

Jackal took his beer, not paying attention to the women nearby who were doing their best to get his attention.

"Do you see him?" Hennessy spoke softly into her ear.

Penni pried her eyes away from one pretty blonde woman who was speaking to Jackal out of her earshot. She forced herself to concentrate on the males in the bar. Once or twice, she caught her breath, thinking she saw him, only to realize it wasn't Striker.

Her shoulders drooped. "I don't see him."

Hennessy's mouth quirked in a smile. "It's early. Don't worry; he'll show tonight or tomorrow."

"Are you sure he'll show?"

He ignored her question. "I'll take a Hennessy," he told the bartender before turning back to answer her question. "He has nowhere else to go." Hennessy waved his hand around the bar. "Everyone he does business with is here."

"You could stop all of this and let me go. Is the reason you're trying to find Striker worth dying for?"

Hennessy stared at her, his eyes going hard. "I am trying to stay alive. If I don't find Striker, my men and I will be eating dirt."

Penni turned away and toward the bartender. "I'll take what he's having."

Jackal and Hennessy watched as the bartender poured her the drink she had requested. Penni took a sip of the amber liquor, enjoying the taste. It wasn't as strong as she had expected, but it wasn't bad.

"I'll have to buy a bottle of this for Shade when I buy one for Ice."

Hennessy choked on his drink. "Ice hates Hennessy. It's an acquired taste."

"Really? Then why did Jackal tell me he likes it?"

Suspiciously, Penni glared at Jackal's innocent expression.

"He's acquired the taste for it since you left the Predators."

Hennessy didn't seem to believe him anymore than she did. She took another sip of her own drink then motioned for the bartender to give her another one.

"Take it easy on those. I want you to be sober enough to recognize Striker when you see him," Jackal warned, reaching out to take her drink away.

"I don't get drunk," Penni bragged, moving out of the way.

Jackal helped the man seated next to her, who looked like he'd had too much drink, slip off the bar stool.

"What? I was tired of standing." Jackal leaned back against the counter, his thigh brushing against hers.

Penni finished her drink in one swallow. How could his leg against hers feel so good? She tapped her glass with a fingernail.

"I don't have time to keep filling her glass." The bartender set the bottle down in front of her. "Who's paying?"

Jackal reached into his back pocket, pulling out his wallet. Penni laughed at his disgruntled expression when Hennessy poured himself another drink.

"Will you two remember why we're here? I'm going to be broke before I get back to Queen City."

"Was Jackal always such a sour puss when you were in the Predators?"

"Depends."

"On what?"

"On which bitch he had in his bed or who he was fighting."

Penni wished she had keep her mouth shut. She really didn't want to hear about even more of Jackal's women or his criminal activities. The more she spent time with him, the more she wanted to know him better, especially when he was sweet, like sleeping on the floor or waking up early to get her a cup of coffee. The man she was beginning to care about didn't match the image she had been given from others who knew him better.

Suddenly, her stool was spun around.

"Is that him?" Hennessy hissed.

Penni narrowed her eyes. It was difficult to see through the smoke-filled room. She had thought smoking in bars was a thing of the past. Then she recognized the smell assailing her nostrils, and it had her giving an appreciative sniff.

"Greer should come here. He would love to know what green they're smoking."

"Your bitch has the attention of a gnat."

"Did you just insult me?"

"Yes. Is. That. Striker?"

Did he seriously just talk to me like I'm a child? Penni fumed, refusing to answer.

When he clenched his hands into fists, Jackal stepped from his stool, blocking Hennessy.

"Penni, in case you didn't notice, Hennessy isn't playing."

"I'm not, either. It wasn't Striker."

"She couldn't have answered that when I asked her?" Hennessy snarled at Jackal as if she weren't there.

"Next time, don't make me mad. Don't call me a bitch, and especially don't refer to me as Jackal's woman."

"Bitch, I'll call you what—"

"She'll be gone as soon we find Striker. Get Cruz to buy you a bud." Jackal wound his arm around her waist.

"I need more than one to deal with her."

Penni was so aggravated with Hennessy she almost didn't tell him the man he was searching for had come into the bar. Jackal, providing a barrier from the Road Kingz, reminded her of the Predators who were waiting to go home, too. They were here because of Grace. As much as she hated the Road Kingz and didn't want to help them, she despised Striker. He had left her without a second glance when she had begged for help. If the Road Kingz hadn't shown up, Ricky would have raped and killed her, leaving her family and friends wondering for the rest of their lives what had happened to her.

"Let someone else have the table. Striker just came through the door."

"Where?"

Penni was lifted off her feet before Jackal could block him again. The Road Kingz surrounded them.

"Don't draw attention to yourself. I don't want him taking off."

Penni nodded at Hennessy. "He's wearing a black jacket..." She kept trying to spot Striker again and couldn't see him. "I can't find him." Frustrated, she tried to peer over Cruz and Jackal's shoulders.

"What color was his shirt?"

"I didn't notice," Penni admitted.

"Fuck." He glared warningly at her. "Here's what we're going to do. We'll walk around the bar, and as soon as you see Striker, show me, and then Jackal will get you out of here. Understand?"

"I do understand English."

Penni became afraid. Hennessy looked like Killyama when Penni had visited her in the hospital after the incident.

"Cool down, Hennessy." Jackal gripped Hennessy's hand. His knuckles were white as he tried to exert pressure to get her

87

released from his hold. The men were fighting over her like two dogs fighting over a bone.

"We can stand here all night to see who wins this argument, or we can go find Striker. I'm going to get another drink. Let me know when you two goons make up your minds."

Hennessy dropped his hand from her arm. "Let's go. I'll take the lead. When she sees Striker, tap me on my back."

"Will do." Jackal pulled her closer to his side.

As they began skirting the outer edge of the bar, Penni inspected each face for the one she was looking for. They were all either young or old, and some were downright scary. Penni pushed closer to Jackal until she wound her arm through his.

"Scared?"

"What do you think? Some of these men would terrify their own mothers." She shuddered when a biker with a Mohawk caught her eye. Not wanting him to think she was staring at him because he was ugly, Penni forced a trembling smile to her lips.

"What's your name, sweetheart?"

"Uh...uh..." She didn't know if she should answer, but politeness won out. "Penni."

"Wanna dance?" The biker drew closer.

"Keep going," Jackal cautioned her.

Penni swallowed hard as the friendly biker tried to keep up with their trek through the crowd.

"There isn't any music."

"I don't need music to dance with you."

This man might have been the first charming biker she had ever met.

"Quit talking to him." Jackal used his shoulder to force the smooth-talking biker back.

"Cunt, you talking to me?"

Penni's mouth dropped open when her charming biker became a raving maniac. The biker took the bottle he was holding and crashed it on top of Jackal's skull.

She reacted without thinking, wanting Hennessy and his men to help Jackal, but they were so busy trying to find Striker that they hadn't noticed the attack taking place on the side of the bar. Trying to find their attention, Penni reached out to tap Hennessy on his back.

Hennessy turned around. "Where is he…?"

Penni screamed as another biker who had been standing close when the lothario decided to butt in crashed a stool into Hennessy's chest before he could finish turning around.

Penni began to fall back, pushed by the building momentum of the fighting between the Road Kingz, who were trying to protect their stunned president, and the other men in the bar.

Penni saw the floor rushing toward her, and then her vision unexpectedly cleared to see Ice's cold face as he hauled her to her feet.

"You have her?" Jackal asked, hurrying to their side.

"I have her."

Jackal's forehead had blood running from his scalp. Penni reached out to wipe it away yet received a glare for her effort. After securing her to him again, she found herself pinned against a wall with Jackal blocking her from the massive fight that had spread from where they were to encompass the whole bar.

Jackal hit anyone who came near her. Hennessy was taking on two men who nearly equaled him in size. Penni saw Max tear one away, punching him in the nose. She felt bile rising in her throat as blood sprayed from those unfortunate enough to be fighting close to him.

Penni couldn't help herself; she moved to help the man.

"Don't you fucking move."

She froze when Jackal spoke, not taking his eyes off the fight.

"Ice, the one on your left!" Jackal yelled out as a biker fighting Cruz began flashing a knife.

Ice moved in behind the man who was about to gut Cruz. As he held the man from behind, Ice snapped his hand down on the man's wrist, breaking his hold on the knife.

"The bartender has a gun," Ice grunted out as he kicked away the knife that had fallen to the floor.

Shots were fired toward the ceiling.

"Son of a bitch! He'll cause a shootout!" Jackal reacted before the second shot hit the ceiling.

Penni found herself thrown over Jackal's shoulder as he and the Road Kingz ran out a door with an exit sign. She pounded on his back as she tried to throw herself from his shoulder.

"Why are you running? The cops are here." Penni saw her escape slipping away as they continued to run, not stopping until they barreled into their hotel room.

She sat up on the bed where Jackal had dumped her as the Predators and Road Kingz crowded into their room.

Jackal opened the connecting door, giving them breathing room. They needed it. Hennessy and Max were bent over, gasping for breath. Evidently, the two men's exercising routine didn't include running.

"What in the fuck happened?" Hennessy was finally able to gasp out.

Jackal frowned at Penni. She sensed his hesitation to admit her involvement.

"It was my fault," she confessed. "A biker asked me to dance, but to be fair, it wasn't all my fault."

Jackal stared at her as if she had lost her mind. "Yes, it was. If you had just kept walking—"

"Was I just supposed to let him beat you up? If I hadn't tapped on Hennessy's back, he would have—" A startled scream escaped Penni as Hennessy lunged at her.

"So help me God, I'm going to strangle her with her own tongue."

"Jackal, lock her in the bathroom until Hennessy and I talk. It'll give him time to cool down."

Before she could object, she found herself pushed into the bathroom. Penni considered banging on the door then changed her mind. She didn't want to talk to them, either. The assholes were blaming her! They were the ones who had kidnaped her!

She slid down the closed door, sitting on the bathroom floor. Her hands mimicked a series of snapping motions that she had seen Jackal use on anyone who had come too close during the fight.

Bravely, she yelled out, "My brother would have whipped all their asses!"

A fist pounded on the door at her outburst.

Tilting her head to the side, she tried to listen to what was going on in the other room. The sound of shuffling had her rising to lock the door. Then Penni lifted her chin to rest on her bent knees.

"Big brother, where are you when I need you?"

CHAPTER ELEVEN

Jackal pushed his plate away. "So now I'm getting the silent treatment?"

Hennessy had found a hole-in-the-wall café to feed them lunch.

Penni's silence was unexpectedly pissing him off. Other than her lips tightening, she didn't respond.

Hennessy mocked him from the next table, lifting his coffee cup to salute him.

He should fucking get on his bike and leave Ice to deal with the mess Penni had created. After all, Hennessy had boasted last night that he didn't need his or the Predators' help. So fuck it!

The waitress laid the check in front of him. Snatching it up, he was about to slide out of the booth when Penni looked up from her untouched plate.

"I'm sorry I screwed up." Her subdued apology was a fireball to his nuts.

"It's okay. We'll find Striker."

What the hell? What crap had just come out of his mouth? It would be a fucking miracle if Striker were still in town.

"I'll do whatever you tell me to do from now on. No more screw-ups, I promise."

"It wasn't your fault." Even he had trouble swallowing that load of bullshit, but if it took that miserable expression off her face, then it would be worth the muted "pussy-whipped" that Hennessy mumbled as he stood.

"We're going to walk around town. You're going to keep your eyes open and your mouth closed. There's going to be a poker run then a wet short contest. If that doesn't make you horny, they're having a tattoo contest. The groupies get to count them. They collected money from them to buy a limited edition Gold Desert Eagle. Any man who has a dick will be there tonight, and so will we."

"Free pussy and guns. That's asking for trouble." Penni's anxious features had the men coming to a stop outside the café.

"You worried we can't protect you?"

Her expression cleared at Hennessy's wounded pride. "No."

"I didn't doubt you could. You all proved that last night."

Jackal smiled, taking the compliment the way it was intended. The massive fight in the bar hadn't left him with a hair out of place. That was more than one of Hennessy's men couldn't say the same.

They walked back to the hotel to their bikes. Penni's searching the crowd as they began walking down the street had Jackal thinking she was finally taking the predicament she was in seriously. She at last had realized that finding Striker was a matter of life and death.

Hennessy chose two men to ride on the poker run as they remained in the hotel parking lot. Jackal knew he was hoping they would hear of someone who had a large supply of coke for sale. It wasn't likely they would catch a break, but the longer Striker held on to the cache of drugs, the greater his chances of having them stolen or a cheese sniffer ratting him out.

Jackal was proud of Penni for sitting on the seat of his bike as the men stood there, talking with other clubs staying in the hotel. He could see the influence he'd had on her when she didn't interrupt the conversations, despite the crude language they were using as women began mingling with the bikers.

It wasn't the first rally he had gone to. With as experienced as he was, he was able to recognize which women were there for a good time or to fish for a new back to hang on to. The bikers at this rally were mostly there for fun and games, but if trouble showed up, they were ready for that, too.

"She yours?" One biker talking to Cruz nodded to Penni sitting sedately behind him.

"Yeah," Jackal answered, waiting for a smart-ass comment from Penni. He wanted to kiss her when she remained silent. He didn't count the snort he heard at his back. No one but him heard it.

"Lucky man."

"I tell her that all the time." Jackal knew he was egging her on, but he couldn't help himself. Part of Penni's attraction to him was her unwillingness to take any shit from him, unlike the whores who were beginning to outnumber the bikers.

"I lost my woman on the way here. She wouldn't stop whining about missing the kids, so I dropped her off at a truck stop."

"Mine knows better." Jackal turned to see her about to break her vow of behaving.

Taking her hand so she could stand, Jackal sat down on the motorcycle seat. Breaking the taboo in his own code, he sat her down in front of him, his arm snaking around her waist, flattening his palms across her tummy.

"A smart man would patch her."

"Jackal likes to keep his options open." Penni circled her hands around his wrists yet didn't twist away from his touch.

"Options are good." A woman wearing a dress that was meant to be a beach cover-up smiled at him seductively. She wasn't wearing anything underneath. Jackal could easily see her breasts and the naked pussy that was within easy reach.

Jackal felt Penni tense, and he lowered his chin to her shoulder.

"A man doesn't need options when he has Penni. She's a handful." He tightened his arms around her. "She doesn't need a patch; Penni knows who she belongs to."

"What about them?" The biker nodded to the large group of bikers gathered around the parking lot.

"I can protect what's mine." Jackal stared at the biker who was measuring him up before his greedy gaze traveled down Penni's body to where Jackal's hands possessively rested on her belly. "We gonna have a problem?"

The biker got his message, shaking his head. "No problem. Like I said, you're a lucky man." He stepped away, unfortunately not taking the whore with him.

"My name's Misty."

"Jackal."

"My name is Penni."

Misty ignored her, her fingers tracing down the sleeve of his leather jacket. "I've heard of the Predators." She dropped her hand down to his thigh. "Let's go for a ride."

Jackal pushed her hand away. "No."

She pouted. "We could have a good time."

"Fuck off."

Her face fell. "Could have been fun."

Jackal didn't watch as she disappeared.

"Don't let me stop you from having *fun*."

"I am having fun; can't you tell?"

Her infectious giggle had him smiling down at her.

"Smiling isn't your best feature," she commented.

"Max says that all time, but I tell him he's just jealous."

"I don't think Casey would agree."

Seeing Penni loosen up had him wanting to carry her into the hotel and lock the door. Jackal would rather be fucking her than forced to sit next to her while Hennessy and the Road Kingz tried to find out if anyone was hustling in large amounts of coke. Jackal thought they stood a better chance of getting arrested from an undercover cop.

The bikers became more boisterous as the day dragged on. When it began to get dark, Jackal walked with Penni into the park where a stage had been set up. There were at least thirty women waiting for the wet short contest.

"Want to join in?" He joked at her wide-eyed stare. Jackal knew it wasn't the mostly shirtless male bikers crowding around the stage that had her attention. The women even made him look.

He ran a hand across the back of his neck. Jesus, it looked like a tit-fest.

"I thought it was a wet 'short' contest."

"It is. That's why they can't wear anything else."

"I didn't know a thong is considered a pair of shorts." Penni stared at him accusingly.

Jackal held his hands up. "Hey, it wasn't my idea."

"Most of those women look drunk. You're gonna watch, though, aren't you?"

He turned his head to where the women were waiting for their turn. "Damn straight."

Laughing, he dodged the fist that was aimed at his shoulder.

"Don't worry; none of them can hold a candle to you."

She quit hitting him. "Like you're ever going to see my boobs."

Jackal watched her cross her arms in front of her chest.

"Afraid you can't measure up to the competition?"

"Good things come in tiny packages," she said stiffly.

"Yes, they do. Don't worry; I saw the picture Casey sent Max. Believe me; you have more than enough for me. If you were up there, you would win my vote." Jackal's attempt to placate Penni backfired when Hennessy looked her over critically.

"He's right; you should do it."

"Not in a million years." Penni glared at Hennessy with a mask of resolution.

"You would be able to see up there. You could spot Striker and tell Jackal where he is."

"No!"

"We're never going to be able to spot him in this crowd."

Jackal had to admit Hennessy was right.

"Penni...?" He stared back at her, letting her have the chance to let the truth sink in. She was going to have to do it.

"I'm not going to take off my top and show my breasts to hundreds of people! I don't even have on shorts."

"You're wearing a thong," Jackal reminded her.

"I'm not going out there in a damn thong!" She began walking away from them. The Road Kingz closed their ranks around her, not letting her go anywhere.

With remorse, he saw her angry eyes flick toward his. She expected him to put a stop to Hennessy's order.

"Most of the men here are so drunk they won't remember…" Jackal realized he wasn't helping. "I'll make sure no one touches you."

"Don't do me any favors." She turned to face Hennessy. "Any of you assholes have a knife?"

Did she seriously expect him to give her a weapon she could use against them?

"As much as I want to use it on you, I want to cut off my jeans," she explained.

Hennessy didn't trust her, but he took out his knife.

Jackal took out his own knife. "I'll do it."

Bending down, he began cutting away the legs of her jeans. When he would have stopped at the middle of her thigh, she demanded, "Higher." When Jackal would have stopped at the middle of her thigh, Penni pointed the top of her leg.

"No."

"Either you do, or I get Hennessy to do it."

Jackal tightened his jaw. The son of a bitch would do it, and if Hennessy touched where she was indicating, they would have to call the cops.

After cutting her jeans to the tops of her thighs, he stepped back. Swallowing, he watched her fold the top of her jeans down then tuck the frayed ends of her makeshift shorts.

Everyone in the audience would be able to see the intimate flesh she was exposing. There wasn't a hair on her pussy visible. *Fuck me.*

As if reading his thoughts, Penni turned her back on him. He followed stiffly as she got in the long line of women waiting their turn.

"You didn't have to cut them that short," he said hoarsely.

"I always say go big or go home." She turned her cold eyes on him. "I'm going home."

CHAPTER TWELVE

"Back up, sister; I need more room."

Yes, she did.

Penni took a step back as the woman danced to "Bad to the Bone" that was spilling out of the speakers,

Penni found herself eye level with a large pair of breasts that were so perky she was amazed they weren't slapping her in the face.

"You think she'll be offended if I ask her the name of who did her breasts?" She elbowed Jackal in his gut when he didn't answer.

"Huh?"

"Never mind." If she ever got home again, she would never have to see him again.

The line was creeping closer with five women in front of her.

"Sweetie, you're going to have to take that shirt off." The woman in front of her stared back at her as if she wouldn't be caught dead in the purple sweatshirt she was wearing.

"I'm cold."

The women standing nearby were nodding their heads with big smiles.

"That's kinda the point." She snickered. "The cold makes your nipples bigger. Wait until they pour the cold water on them."

"Obviously, the organizers haven't heard of hypothermia," Penni said snidely.

"You're kidding, right? Most of the men here can't even spell hypothermia."

Penni smiled. She liked a woman who could be as salty as her. "My name is Penni."

"I'm Mandy."

She winced at the response that came out as a breathy voice, a cross between a sex kitten and a sixteen-year-old.

The line was down to four. The water from the stage sprayed on her trembling legs.

"Sweetie, if you move, it'll warm you up."

"Hell, it'd warm me up, too."

If the man didn't shut up and put his eyes back in his head, she was going to plant her elbow in his crotch instead of his stomach.

The line was down to three. The music switched over to "What Do You Want from Me." The woman at the front of the stage was dancing, her nude body swaying to the music, her voluptuous form hiding the thong within her folds of flesh.

Why the hell am I doing this? Penni jammed her hands into her sweatshirt pockets. There were enough people around her that someone should come to her aid if she screamed for help. Dammit, she was agile enough that she could take a leap off the stage and disappear into the crowd.

"Don't do it." Jackal's low warning had Penni hesitating. "Hennessy would have you out of here in a second."

There were at least two dozen people standing on the stage and at least three hundred in the audience. Penni debated yelling out for help.

The line was down to two. It was now or never.

She took a step to the side, preparing herself to start screaming bloody murder. She was prepared to take her chances with Hennessy's fury rather than flaunt her pint-sized boobs.

"Trust me." He knew she wasn't going to do it. "You'll let loose a powder keg. How do you think this will go if a fight breaks out with so many people around? Remember what it was like last night? Most of the clubs are packing and drunk. By the time the cops broke up the fight, almost all of them would leave in body bags, including us."

Dammit, he was right. She was going to have to do it.

Penni didn't care if the Road Kingz were hurt; they had put themselves in this position. The Predators, on the other hand, were there to try to help her. Penni wouldn't be able to look Grace in the face if anything happened to Ice. She had enough on her plate dealing with her mother's sickness. Grace didn't need her husband getting killed.

The line was down to one. The DJ started "Motorcycle Mama," nodding to Misty that it was her turn.

"Good luck, sweetie."

Penni forced herself not stare at Misty's breasts as she wished her good luck.

"You're next." Jackal's quiet reminder was unnecessary.

"No shit, Sherlock." Penni clenched her hands into fists as she watched Misty strut to the front of the stage.

"You need to take off your top."

"If you say one more word, I'll take your knife away and stab you."

Jackal shut up.

The DJ started "Highway to Hell" as Misty began to walk to the rear of the stage where all the women were dancing in a line, giving the men in the audience a chance to choose who was going to be the winner.

Penni turned to see if she could let any other woman go, but the line was empty. She was the last one.

I'm going to have to do it, Penni kept telling herself as she lifted the bottom of the sweatshirt over her head. Goose bumps broke out over her body as she shivered. Maybe it was getting dark enough that the men wouldn't be able to see her that well.

Someone at the edge of the stage flicked on a switch, surrounding the stage in blazing lights.

"That's about right."

"What did you say?" Jackal stepped back when she took a step toward him.

Penni looked down at her pretty dusty rose bra and unclipped it, tugging off the fragile material and handing it to Jackal.

"I want that back. It cost me a freaking fortune."

She looked at the biker waiting with the water hose then at the women on stage, shorts plastered to their body. Reaching into her jean pocket, she pulled out her cell phone, handing it to Jackal.

He was smart enough not to open his mouth, simply shoving it into his jacket pocket with her bra.

Penni bravely walked toward the stage. When she got back to Queen City, she was going to make Henry give the women strippers a raise. It was worse than she thought, but it was easier than she imagined.

The man at the front of the stage who was pouring the water over the women's bodies wasn't given the chance to douse her. Jackal's cruel visage had him handing the water hose over. She was so preoccupied with the freezing water hitting her body she didn't have time to be embarrassed. The other women had been hit with the water on their breasts or pussy. Jackal aimed at the top of her shorts. Her breasts were still wet, but she wasn't hit full force the way the other women had been.

Jackal jerked his head toward the crowd, reminding her of the reason for making a fool of herself.

She swayed toward the front of the stage, carefully scanning the audience for Striker.

Please be here, Penni pleaded to whatever powers in the universe that were listening as she tried to take her mind off the cold water. Of course, she didn't hold out much hope anyone was listening with the loud music playing.

Her eyes were shifting from the middle of the crowd when she saw him. Excited, she turned toward Jackal.

"He's over there, standing with the bikers with the orange happy faces on their jackets."

Jackal immediately handed the water hose back to the biker he had taken from then took out his cell phone from his jacket. "You sure?"

"Yes." Penni could barely answer him through her chattering teeth. She moved toward the steps off the stage as he talked to whomever was on the other end.

"Not yet." Jackal blocked her before she could reach them. "What is he wearing?"

She had been so busy looking for his hair she hadn't noticed his clothes. Penni turned to look again, but could not find him. She wanted to scream and cry at the same time. Where had he—

Then she saw him again when one of the men he was standing next to moved.

"He's wearing an orange T-shirt—" Before she could say anything else, Jackal was leading her down the steps.

Cruz appeared.

"Take her to the hotel room," Jackal ordered, wrapping a large towel around her shoulder that he had taken from a stack by the steps.

"Did you see him?"

Penni grabbed a handful of his leather jacket before he could leave, excited that her ordeal was almost over.

"I saw him, baby. Get changed. When I get back, I'll take you home."

Penni lowered her lashes so he couldn't see the happy tears in her eyes.

"No way. I used to envy anyone who rode a motorcycle. From now on, my ass is only sitting in a car."

CHAPTER THIRTEEN

Where is he? Penni had expected Jackal back an hour ago.

She sat there, staring blankly at the television screen, not watching the movie she had turned on to fill the silence in the room.

She turned and jumped up when heard the door open, her expectant smile dying as she saw Cruz in the doorway instead of Jackal.

"Hennessy wants you."

Confused, she slid her bare feet into her tennis shoes. "Where's Jackal?"

"He's waiting, too."

She wouldn't find anything out being stuck in the hotel room. It wasn't like she had a choice, anyway. Therefore, Penni went with Cruz, climbing onto his bike sitting outside the door.

The streets were strangely quiet as they passed the businesses that had been busy just an hour ago. Where were all the bikers in the bars? Her silent questions went unanswered as Cruz's bike rode outside the city.

Penni began to feel afraid. Had Hennessy decided to kill her after all and bury her body in the desert?

As they rode, Penni saw the orange glow of a huge fire in the sky. Cruz slowed his speed, and Penni was able to see motorcycles parked in front of a huge bonfire.

Cruz maneuvered his bike through the swarming crowd. Relieved, she saw Jackal sitting on his bike with Hennessy and the Road Kingz. After they were parked next to Jackal, she leaped off Cruz's bike, anxious to go home. At this point, she was even willing to ride Jackal's bike to Queen City.

"Are you ready to leave?"

Penni didn't like the grim expression on Jackal's face as she eagerly came to a stop next to his motorcycle. Hennessy didn't appear to be in a better mood than Jackal.

"There's been a snag," Jackal confirmed the dread she had been feeling when she had seen the Road Kingz stop talking when they had spotted her.

"I don't care. You told me that, if I found Striker, you would let me leave. I'm holding you to your word. I want to leave now!" Penni demanded, facing Hennessy, her hands clenched on her hips, trying not to strike him. His men would probably kill her for disrespect, but Penni was at the point of not caring.

Jackal reached out, lifting her off her feet to sit sideways across the front of his bike. "Penni, I know you're upset. Calm down and take a deep breath. It's almost over. We only have one thing left to do, and Hennessy said we can ride out of here tonight."

Penni clenched her jaw shut, unconsciously leaning back against Jackal's chest.

"We talked to Striker. Unfortunately, he found another buyer." Hennessy's face looked so angry it was frightening.

"Since he already took our money and doesn't want to give me the product he has for sale, we're at a stalemate."

"What does this have to do with me? I can't make him—"

"Yes, you can. I mentioned your connection to The Last Riders. Evidently, Striker has heard of them."

Penni felt the angry flush heat her cheeks. She tried to pull away from Jackal. "Who told you about The Last Riders?"

"I did," Jackal admitted. "I had to give him a reason to keep you alive. You might not have figured it out yet, but Hennessy doesn't really like you."

"Really? Let me tell you how I feel about him." Penni shot her tennis shoes out, trying to kick him.

Jackal slid his hand intimately down her thigh, forcing her to stop kicking out. Cruz, who had made the mistake of stepping in between Hennessy and her when she had lashed out, found himself doubled over in pain.

"I'm killing the fucking bitch..."

Penni found that funny since he was still unable to move.

"Touch me, motherfucker, and—"

"You two shut the hell up." Hennessy helped his enforcer stand up. "Take a walk," he continued when Cruz managed to move. "Your brother teach you that language?"

"No, his friend Knox did. Want to meet him?"

While Knox and Hennessy were the same size and both shared the same lack of hair, Penni bet on Knox beating the shit out of him. Knox would jerk one of those diamond earrings out of Hennessy's ear and use it as a tongue ring. The thought had her twitching in humor, making the men believe she had lost her mind.

"I'll pass. The Last Riders might have everyone afraid of them in Kentucky, but I'll put my money on any of these clubs from California."

"You'd lose," Penni confidently contradicted him. "You may not have heard of The Last Riders, but Striker's heard enough that he's going to hand over what you're wanting."

"That doesn't mean shit—"

"You two stop arguing. I'd like to enjoy the music before Striker gets here. Cruz, go find us some beers. Hennessy, those bitches over there have been trying to get your attention for the past ten minutes."

Penni refused to look up at Jackal as the men stepped away.

"You cold?"

She remained silent, and Penni heard his sigh above her.

"The silent treatment again?"

She bit down on her lip to keep from replying.

"Your blaming me for Hennessy making you stay?"

This time, she couldn't hold her tongue. "I blame you for telling him about The Last Riders and for not keeping your promise to get me out of here tonight."

"Baby, I'm good, but I can't perform miracles. You might think that Hennessy listens to me and we're friends, but we're not. He's keeping you close because he thinks you're too much trouble."

"If he thinks I'm a pain in the butt now, wait until he meets Shade."

Penni heard the amusement in his voice when he said, "I don't think he's wanting an introduction."

"He may not have a choice," she muttered.

His voice became hard as he lifted her chin up so she could see his serious eyes. "Have you managed to contact Shade?"

"Why do you care? I thought you said you're not his friend."

"You're the one I care about," he said impatiently. "If Shade and The Last Riders show up, I don't want you hurt if—"

"Shade would make sure I wasn't hurt. You don't care about me," Penni denied his assertion.

"Then why in the fuck am I sitting with you?"

She frowned. "Because of Ice. You'd do anything he told you to do."

Jackal's hold loosened, his touch becoming a gentle caress. "Baby, I'm the enforcer, but not even for Ice would I let one of the other men play babysitter."

"Hennessy has Cruz watching me, and he's an enforcer."

Jackal laughed. "Because you're a lot of trouble, and the Road Kingz don't know how to handle you. The Predators wouldn't have the same trouble. Either Stump or Fade would have been able to watch over you."

Her thoughts became a whirlwind as she tried to think of how she felt about Jackal's admission.

"So, you like me?" Penni probed.

"Yeah."

"You like all women."

"No, I don't. I have sex with a lot of women; that doesn't mean I like them all."

Penni turned her face. She had known that becoming involved with Jackal would be like watching a car wreck in slow motion. Now the asshole wanted to give her fair warning that it was going to hurt. No thanks.

When she fell in love, Penni was going to have a love like Shade and Lily shared. It was going to be all or nothing. Whatever Jackal was offering by laying his cards on the table, she was going to walk away with it.

Shade had taught her long ago how to spot a card shark, and Jackal had dealt her a losing hand.

CHAPTER FOURTEEN

"Where are you going?" Jackal caught Penni's waist as she tried to squirm out of his hold.

"If I have to be here, Cruz can watch me until Striker gets here."

"What ant crawled in your panties now?"

"You've done every woman in King's club. Grace said the women who hang out at the Predators' clubhouse joke they should name another day of the week after you. If I say I care, it means something—"

"Really?" Jackal snorted. "I bet Grace couldn't name one of the women who said I fucked them. Can you name one from King's club?"

Thinking back, she couldn't. Mostly, they had stared at him with wishful eyes and veiled assertions of what had taken place with them or other women.

"So, you're saying you haven't slept with them all?"

"I'm saying that I don't keep a fucking roster of how many women I've been with. The women I have been involved with all have a good time, and they don't have to worry about me doing their friends."

"But when you're done, you're done?"

Jackal shook his head. "Not like you're thinking. We both know when it's pretty much over and remain friends. I don't have exes stalking me if that's what you're thinking. Has anyone said I lied or cheated or made promises of a future? No, because I don't make promises I don't intend to keep."

Jackal was tired of beating around the bush. "Why was Train's picture in your bedside table?"

Outraged, Penni straddled his lap and grabbed a handful of his T-shirt. "How do you know what's in my bedroom?"

Gripping her wrists, Jackal used his chest to push her backward until she lay prone on his motorcycle, her legs wrapped around his waist as she struggled to free herself. He circled each of her wrists and his handlebars, effectively trapping her.

"Why are you so embarrassed? Because I saw Train's picture or the dildo?"

"When you let me go, I'm going to kill you!" Penni screeched.

"Did you need the dildo because you're missing him or because you can't have him?"

Jackal watched her reaction to each of his questions. She was furious. When she returned to Queen City, it was a safe bet she would never go out with him. He had nothing to lose and everything to gain.

His aching dick was pressed against her pussy. The seam of her jeans beckoned him, and unable to resist, he rotated his hips, hearing a gasp from her lips.

Jackal lowered his mouth to her throat, breathing in her scent.

"Damn, you smell good."

She snarled up at him. Damn, he liked a woman with some fire in her blood. Penni was like no woman he had ever known, though. Every time he was near her, he was like a blind man gifted with sight, unable to see anyone but her. Only Penni.

"If I kiss you, are you going to bite me again?"

"Try it and find out for yourself!"

Jackal curled his lips up into a smile against the curve of her throat.

"No thanks. I'll try my luck somewhere else." He pressed a kiss to the hollow of her throat, flicking out his tongue to taste her. She tasted as good as she smelled, like peaches on a warm summer day.

She reminded him of when he had been a little boy and stayed with his grandparents for the summers in Georgia. They had an orchard of peaches, and he would help pick them. At that age, he had eaten more than he had picked, loving the velvet texture as he bit into one and the sweet flesh inside.

Sliding his lips upward, he nibbled on her earlobe. "Kiss me back."

"Kiss my ass."

"Don't tempt me." Staring into her eyes, he let her see how much he wanted her.

He was a Predator by name and nature. The brothers would mock him if they saw him appearing vulnerable. Sometimes, however, the predator became the prey.

Risking the chance of receiving another scar, he lowered his mouth to her lips. It would be worth the pain to taste her.

It was a mixture of heaven and hell. While Penni's warm mouth was better than any woman he had kissed before, the knowledge that he might never taste her again was torture.

Step by step, he had led her to discover that he could give her what she needed. He could handle the fire inside her.

Using his tongue to rub against hers, he then twisted hers, leading her into his mouth. Her passion built as she lifted her hips up, pressing against the bulge of his dick behind his jeans.

Jackal was the one who broke off the kiss, pressing his forehead against hers.

"What's wrong?" Penni's raspy voice nearly had him coming in his jeans.

"I have to catch my breath."

"Have you caught it yet?"

He raised up enough to stare down at her. "I have the feeling I'm never going to be able to catch it whenever you kiss me."

She strained at his hold on her wrists. Releasing her, he expected her to smack him, but unexpectedly, she pressed her hands on each side of his face. Her blue eyes stared at him as if she didn't see his scarred cheek.

"You have to remember to breathe through your nose."

"I know how to kiss."

"It was just a suggestion."

Clearly, his kiss hadn't rocked her world. Jackal could understand why her many relationships had failed. Penni's abrasive attitude was a cock blocker. No normal man wanted his ego ripped to shreds. Fortunately, he wasn't normal, and his ego could take it. She might twist his guts into knots, but like the kiss, he would risk it. He wasn't afraid of pain.

He wanted to start his motorcycle and ride until no one could find them. The loud noises from the crowd were a distraction he didn't want. He didn't want anything to take away from this moment…

"You're going to have to save this for later," Hennessy interrupted.

Jackal groaned, lifting his head. Licking his bottom lip, he imprinted her pliant image in his mind then helped her to straighten. She sat mutely, not butting in as Hennessy motioned for the Road Kingz to surround them. *That's a first*, Jackal thought sardonically, not expecting it to last.

The dangerous tension spread among them. Cruz, as Hennessy's enforcer, took his flank. Jackal was impressed as he maneuvered the Road Kingz so bystanders wouldn't be able to see what was taking place from within the enclosed circle.

"If anything goes down, stick to me. Got me?"

"Okay."

He was so proud when Penni didn't show the fear she must be feeling.

Cruz stepped in to allow Striker to enter the circle then closed ranks, preventing prying eyes from watching.

Jackal stood in front of Penni, his hand riding low at his back, under his jacket and on the handle of his Glock. Any move that threatened Penni, he would drop Striker, regardless if Hennessy's life depended on him.

"Where's my money?" Hennessy demanded.

"I don't have it."

"Then there better be smack in that duffle bag." Hennessy raised his T-shirt, showing the Glock tucked into the waist of his jeans.

"How do I know you won't kill me as payback for DJ?"

"You're lucky that you're not already dead." Hennessy's unfeeling voice had Striker's eyes flickering over the men surrounding him.

"I didn't lay a hand on him. I went to take a piss, and when I came out, Ricky had killed him." He leaned sideways so that he could see Penni. "The bitch will tell you that I'm telling the truth."

Hennessy turned so he could keep his eyes on Striker and Penni.

"That true?"

Jackal knew Hennessy was playing with Striker. Penni had already told him Ricky was responsible for DJ's death.

"Tell him!" Striker demanded urgently.

Jackal hid his smile when Penni kept him waiting. Finally, when he rocked nervously back and forth on his feet, as if he were about to piss himself, she spoke.

"Why should I? You didn't care that you were leaving me to get raped and killed."

"He would have killed me, too!" Sighing and turning away from Penni, Striker dropped the duffel bag in front of Hennessy. "It's all there. We good?"

Hennessy used the same tactic that Penni had.

"Shit, Hennessy, let him go before he shits himself," Jackal spoke in the growing silence.

"Apoc, check the bag." Hennessy kept his hand on his weapon.

Apoc bent down, unzipping the bag, checking the contents, and then zipping the bag closed.

"It's good. The same product we sent to sell."

"You and Cruz take it to the car. Tia's waiting by the food truck. I'll see you back at the clubhouse."

"Tia's here?"

"Yes, if you hadn't had your tongue down her throat"—Hennessy nodded at Penni—"she would have said hi."

Tia was Hennessy's cousin. Jackal had met her when she had turned eighteen and her parents had been murdered. He had found her a place to live in Queen City. Then, when Hennessy had left the Predators, she had left with him and DJ.

"We done?" Striker took a step backward.

"We're done."

Jackal kept his eyes on Striker as he walked away. Being an enforcer for the Predators had honed his skills over the years. The uneasy feeling traveling up his spine had him pulling out his Glock before Apoc fell to the dirt, staring up at the night sky.

Hennessy and their men pulled their weapons out as screams filled the night. The red-orange flames from the bonfire glowed across the bloodbath that had begun.

Jackal jumped on his motorcycle, his bike in the direction of the road. They had to get through a half-mile of gunfire to make it to safety.

CHAPTER FIFTEEN

"Get her out of here!" Hennessy yelled, running to the duffel bag Apoc had dropped.

Jackal saw Ice, Max, Stump, and Fade running toward Hennessy and his men as the Unjust Soldiers attacked.

"Hang on," Jackal yelled back to Penni as he started his bike.

The Road Kingz began dropping like flies.

Dirt flew out when his back wheel spun in the loose soil.

Hennessy's large body provided cover as one the Unjust Soldiers pointed his weapon at him. He had to get Penni out of here so Hennessy could focus on keeping himself and his men alive.

Hennessy saw the guns trained on him and tossed the duffle bag to Penni, who managed to catch it. She looped it through her arms, carrying it like a backpack.

"Shit." Hennessy had put a bullseye on them.

Jackal sped through the fleeing bikers all trying to get on their bikes. He slowed his speed to miss a woman who was

117

screaming hysterically. Another biker came out of nowhere, blocking the woman from getting killed. Turning his front wheel, he barely managed to avoid hitting the other bike. If the biker hadn't blocked her, Jackal would have mowed her down and crashed his bike, hurting Penni.

The road was less than a foot away when Jackal spotted a break in the crowd big enough to get his bike through. He rode his bike through the opening in the rows of motorcycles that were at a standstill. The assholes were too fucking busy watching the gun fight to get out of danger.

His bike hit pavement, and he gunned his motor, following the line of red taillights leading toward town.

Penni loosened the tight hold she had on his waist, and Jackal released a sigh of relief that she was safe.

As they neared town, police cars and ambulances sped past them with lights flashing. He hoped Hennessy wasn't one of the bikers who would need a ride to the local hospital.

Jackal parked his bike in front, rushing her into the hotel room then locking the door behind them. Looking out the window, he saw several bikers parking, but none of them seemed interested in them. Jackal bet most of them would just get their things and head out of town before the cops came back.

"Are we okay now?"

Jackal turned from the window at her shaky question.

"Yeah." He pulled out his cell phone, pushing Hennessy's number. When he didn't answer, Jackal called Ice. The phone went to his messages. Shit. He was going to have to wait for one of them to call him.

Frustrated, he ran his fingers through his sweat and smoke-filled hair. "I need a shower."

"Go ahead. If anyone knocks, I'll let you know."

Jackal stopped as he was about to go into the bathroom. Penni had taken a chair, staring at the door. She had handled what had happened better than most recruits would have. She had almost been killed; none of the bikers had given a shit that a woman was in their line of fire. Most recruits had returned to the clubhouse to get drunk or fuck any woman who spread their legs when shit had gone down badly. Hell, his own body was so filled with adrenaline he wanted to bust someone up or fuck. Penni looked as unruffled as if she had just been dealing with the hordes of teenagers she dealt with at concerts.

Shrugging out of his jacket, he was about to lay it down across from Penni when he noticed the bulging pocket. Reaching in, he pulled out her bra and useless cell phone, handing them to her.

"No one will knock." Jackal told her in case she was worried despite her cool-headed appearance. "Hennessy or Ice will call when they can."

Penni bit her bottom lip, bringing blood rushing to the tip of his cock. "Why not call someone else, like Max or Colton?"

Jackal took off his shirt, laying his gun and knife on the small table in front of her. "I don't want to distract them and get them killed. They'll call when they can."

"Okay."

He began walking to the bathroom, unbuckling his belt.

"Jackal?"

He didn't stop, but he did turn his head.

"Can we go home now?"

Jackal gripped the doorknob as he was about to close it. "Yeah, you can go home."

Closing the door before she could see his face, he thought about how Penni had a place to call home, and unfortunately, it wasn't with him. When she returned to Queen City, he would only see her when she passed him in the city or when Grace had one of her parties, giving him the cold shoulder as he passed her.

It was a three-day ride to Queen City. He would drag it to four. He didn't want to let her go. He was dreading it.

CHAPTER SIXTEEN

Groggily, Penni opened her eyes, confused by the terror flood-
ing her body. Reality rushed through her as she awakened in
the dark room. Had she died back at the bonfire and hadn't
known it?

When she opened her mouth to scream, she wasn't able
to make a sound. Mysteriously, the hard arms lifting her from
the bed were gentle. They were restraining her so she couldn't
move, but she didn't feel pain.

As the man carried her across the floor, Penni saw the doorway of the hotel had two shadowy figures. She kicked out, trying to throw herself free, and the hand holding her tightened as
they went through the open door.

Penni looked at the men under the light outside, and relief
poured through her body. Lucky and Rider motioned for her to
be quiet as they moved to a black SUV, which Cash slid out off,
opening the back door.

The man carrying her slackened his hold, sliding her into the backseat.

"Shade, I'm so happy to see you I could cry." Penni wrapped her arms around her brother.

"You okay?"

"Yes, now that you're here."

"Cash and Razer are going to drive you to Treepoint. I'll see you there." Shade stepped back, shutting the door.

"Wait. Where are you going?"

Shade wasn't getting on his bike parked next to the SUV. He had turned back to the hotel room.

"I have some business I need to take care of with Jackal."

Penni easily recognized the cold, ominous gaze turned on her.

"Jackal didn't do anything. He tried to save me. It was the Road Kingz who held me prisoner."

"Penni, I know exactly what happened." Shade didn't try to explain how he knew, and Penni was sure she didn't want to know. Her brother had an uncanny ability to find out information.

"Are they alive?" Penni was startled that she cared. She had begun to like Jackal, despite him being a butthole.

"I'll handle it. Go. Lily's worried."

Penni reluctantly nodded. Shade was done talking.

She leaned back against the leather seats, knowing Shade would do the right thing. He always did.

Penni watched as Cash backed up and slowly drove to the exit, seeing the men standing by their motorcycles. Most of the men she recognized. Viper gave a small wave, and the grim faces of The Last Riders lightened when they saw the movement.

As the SUV passed each of The Last Riders, they hit the roof, letting her know they were glad she was safe.

"They missed you," Cash spoke over his shoulder.

"I've missed them, too."

The last one they passed was the one she had waited for anxiously. His black-blue hair gleamed under the street lamp. When he hit the top of the SUV, Penni held her breath, hoping he would gesture for Cash to stop. He didn't. Train's attention was locked on the hotel where Jackal was.

Why should it be any different this time? He was glad Shade's sister was safe, and that was it. In the years she had known him, Train had never given Penni any indication that he felt anything for her.

She was twenty-four years old; how long was she going to wait before she realized it wasn't going to happen? She was an idiot.

"How's Rachel?" Cash's wife was expecting their first baby.

"Getting used to being a mom."

"She had the baby?" Penny was excited for them.

"A week ago."

"Congratulations. What did you name him or her?"

"She wants to name the baby Mag. I told her over my dead body."

"I don't want him hurt."

"Rachel?" Cash's voice sounded angry. "I wouldn't hurt Rachel because of what she wanted to name our baby—"

"Not Rachel. Jackal. I don't want him hurt."

Razer twisted in his seat to look back at her. "You heard Shade say he would handle it. Jackal should have called the minute you went missing. Jackal and the Predators deserve some questions, and Shade is going to want the answers to be good."

"I'm not their responsibility. The only reason they tried to help me was because of Grace," Penni argued.

Razer shook his head. "King told them to watch out for you. You were under their protection."

"I don't need anyone to watch out for me."

"Obviously, you do." Razer turned to face the front again.

Penni gritted her teeth. Arrogant males were the bane of her existence. Then again, why should she care? Jackal had been a pain in her ass for years. Hell, he had left her stranded at a rest area when he had kidnapped her; not to mention, he had kidnapped her in the first place.

Penni rubbed her hands down the front of her jeans. This time was different, though. She had seen behind the domineering attitude he showed everyone.

He was the exact opposite of Train. Train treated women respectfully. The only time she had seen him lose his temper was when she had been fifteen, and Shade and Train had taken her to a movie while they were on leave.

Penni winced as she remembered staring up at him adoringly, proud of how both the men had walked by her side. A young woman not much older than her had been crying, her hand to her cheek. Three women had been arguing as a man had sheepishly stood next to the woman who had struck the girl.

When his girlfriend had attempted to strike her again, Train had reached out, snatching her hand back. He had been so fast Penni hadn't seen him move.

"Hey!" the woman had screeched, furious at being unable to hit her target.

"Keep your fucking hands to yourself." His quiet voice had drawn the small crowd's gaze from the fight they had been enjoying.

Shade, with his imposing tattoos, had stuck out like a sore thumb in the affluent suburbs where her parents had lived.

The young woman hadn't been used to being challenged. Her expensive summer dress and heels contrasted with the other woman's off the rack clothes.

She had waved her cell phone in Train's face. "I'll call the police."

Train hadn't replied, taking out his own cell phone. Unlike the blustering woman, he had actually seemed to dial a phone number.

"I'd like to report an assault." He hadn't been bluffing.

The woman's mouth had dropped open as Train had given the address of the movie theater. She and her friends had started to move away, but Train had stopped them before they could flee.

"Don't waste your time. I'm sure their camera will show that you all were ganging up on her."

"Do something, Ethan."

The whipping boy couldn't lose face in front of his girl-friend, so he had decided to confront Train. He had been out-matched, though.

Striking out, he had tried to land a punch on his jaw, but Train had grabbed his arm, twisting it behind his back. The worm had wiggled, unable to break his hold. His girlfriend and her friends had begun hitting Train, trying to get him free.

Train had grabbed the hair of the man's girlfriend, turning her around so she couldn't hit him.

Meanwhile, Shade had grabbed each of her friends as they'd kicked and screamed to be let go.

"You need some help?" Penni had unwisely steeped closer to the one Train was holding. The woman had grabbed her, pulling her off balance so that she crashed into her.

"Shit." Train had tried to catch them, but the women had been kicking and hitting as they'd fallen to the ground.

Penni had found herself eating concrete as the woman lashed out at her. She had taken off one her heels and begun beating her with it. The woman might have been from the affluent neighborhoods, but she had fought dirty.

"Shit." Train tried to pull Penni out of the fray yet couldn't separate her from the tangle of legs, arms, and hair swirling around them.

"Fuck. Mom's going to kick my ass if she gets hurt..." Her brother had tried to grab her while Train had attempted to separate the other woman from her. Neither had been successful.

Penni had felt the pain of her blows. Unfazed, she had hit back. Rage had poured out her like never before, but it hadn't frightened her. She had raked her nails down the arms that tried to pin her to the ground. When she'd heard the squeal of pain, Penni had felt a rush of pleasure that she hadn't experienced before. Even when she had felt the teeth clamped onto her own arms, she hadn't cared. She had punched her in the face over and over until she had released her and fallen to the ground.

Penni had hopped up, tossing a leg over her until she had been sitting on her belly, continuing to beat her until blood poured out of the corner of her mouth and covered her chin.

"Stop!" Pleas and hard hands had lifted her, bringing Penni to awareness to what she done.

"Calm down, Penni." Train's low voice had soothed the rage that had nowhere to go. "Go sit on the bench."

She had sat down on the bench as Shade had helped the beaten woman to her feet. Her friends had been too afraid to move when he had ordered them not to.

Penni had buried her face in her hands, horrified at her behavior. She had not hurt so much as an ant before, yet not only had she beaten the woman; she had enjoyed it. What if Shade and Train hadn't been there to stop her?

Penni's stomach had begun to heave, disgusted by the violence she had been capable of.

At that point, the police had arrived, and Penni had started to stand to turn herself over to them.

"Sit still and be quiet," Shade ordered as the two police officers approached.

She had expected to be arrested. Only when the women and man had left an hour later had she realized the police were leaving.

Shade had sat down on the bench next to her, tossing Train the keys to their mother's car they had borrowed. "Get the car."

Train had nodded, laying a hand on her shoulder before leaving.

"You okay?"

"I'm a monster." Penni had stared up at his hooded blue eyes.

"No, you're not." His ironic smile hadn't made her feel better. She'd felt like a disappointment. Their mother had always been so proud of Shade. She had told her friends that he was in the service and told Penni that she should be good or Shade wouldn't come visit her anymore.

"I won't do it again. I promise."

"Don't make promises you can't keep."

"I will." She had reached out to take his hand, but Shade had pulled back. He had never touched her.

When she had been little, she would reach out to him, but he would pull back or briefly hold her then move away. He had never held their mother, and Penni had grown used to seeing the look of pain when Shade visited, assuming it had been because he harbored ill-feelings toward her for breaking up with Shade's father.

As Penni matured, though, she had sensed it was part of Shade's personality. Remaining aloof didn't mean he didn't care. He had visited their mother and her whenever he'd had leave. Each time he had come, he'd brought his friends, which had kept him from spending time alone with her, but she hadn't cared. She had cherished any time she spent with him, but she hadn't cried when he'd left. It was just the way it was.

"You were trying to protect someone you love."

Penni had blushed bright red, embarrassed that he had been voicing her feelings for Train out loud.

"I was just trying to help."

"You succeeded. Maybe next time, she'll think twice about picking on someone defenseless, but I doubt it."

"You're not mad at me?"

"How could I be mad when I've done it too many times to count?"

She had released a shaky breath.

"That doesn't make it right. Train and I were here to watch out for you. If you react that way when you're by yourself, it could be a different story. Don't take on more than you can handle."

"I won't. I'm never going to hit anyone again."

"Yes, you will. You won't be able to stop yourself. You're too much like me."

She had shaken her head. "I wish—"

"You are. I've seen it." When she had kept shaking her head, he had continued, "Mom said you don't have any friends."

"I have a lot of friends," Penni had denied.

Shade had arched a doubtful brow. "Name one."

"Tania, Emily, Katlin, and Val."

"You have sleepovers?"

She had frowned. She'd hated sleepovers. "No."

"Why not?"

She had shrugged. "I don't know. I prefer to sleep in my own bed."

"Then invite them to your house."

"It's hard to when they are so busy. Tania does dance, Emily and Kaitlin do softball, and Val babysits for extra money."

"Do they make time to have sleepovers?"

Penni hadn't wanted to lie to her brother. "Yes."

"Do they invite you?"

"Yes…but I have more homework than they do. My grades are important to me."

"I've seen your grades; they aren't that important. You have a boyfriend or have someone you like?"

"No."

"Don't tell me you don't like boys." Shade already knew the answer.

"I like boys."

"Train won't make a move on you because you're too young and my sister."

Stubbornly, she had looked away. She wouldn't be young forever, and Shade would accept it when they were together.

"Maybe he will one day. You don't know that for sure."

"What do you feel for Train?"

She couldn't believe she was having this talk with her brother. It had been the most words that had ever came out of his mouth. Usually, he'd let everyone talk while he had listened.

"He's handsome, strong, and he doesn't argue when I want to play cards..." Penni had trailed off when she couldn't think of anything else. Then she had finished in a rush. "He's more mature than boys my age."

"Or maybe you're telling yourself that as an excuse for why you're not getting involved with boys your own age. I don't see any tears in your eyes when we leave. As a matter of fact, I never saw you cry at all when you were a baby. Mom used to worry about it...like she did with me."

Penni couldn't tell what point Shade had been trying to make. Of course she'd cried, but it hadn't been often.

"Shit...What do I know? I just wanted you to know that I'm like that, too."

"You have tons of friends, and I've seen pictures of your girlfriends."

"Yes, but I feel differently than they do. I don't love anything or anyone. If any of them walked out of my life, I wouldn't miss them. The difference between us is I don't give a damn about anyone, while you're like the butterfly I used to call you when you were a kid. A butterfly will go from a limb to a flower, attracted by anything that catches their interest. You stay a while, and then, when you're ready, you fly away."

A friend she had known since kindergarten had moved away last year. Though Penni had expected to feel the loss, she hadn't, just found another girl to share lunch with.

What he had been saying couldn't be true, though. She had friends she talked to every day. She had been one of the most popular students in her school.

Penni had searched her mind, not coming up with one close friend she'd shared all her secret with. She would have lunch, movies, and even shopping trips with her friends, but she couldn't recall giving them any clue of the person she was inside.

Out of the corner of her eye, she had seen their mother's car come to a stop. Train hadn't made a move to exit the car, giving them time to talk.

Penni had stood when Shade had, grabbing his hand before he'd moved away.

"So you don't love me?" Penni had asked curiously.

"I feel for you as much as I can feel for Mom and Dad. Mom sent me to psychiatrists when I was in elementary school because I wasn't making friends. She thought it was because we moved around so much and because she had depression, so she couldn't bond with me. I see her watching you the same why she watched me. I thought I'd save you from sitting in a doctor's office once a week."

He hadn't answered her question.

Staring up at her brother, she had understood the words he'd left unspoken. Bravely looking into his beautiful blue eyes, she could see the soul he kept from everyone, including himself.

"Well, we didn't move around when I was a kid, so she can't blame my father like she did yours. We inherited it from her, didn't we?"

"I think so."

Penni had nodded.

He hadn't removed his hand as they'd walked toward the car.

"Shade...Do you think you'll ever love someone?"

"No."

Tightening her hold on Shade's hand, she prevented him from opening the car door.

"I think you're wrong. We can love. I love Mom, Dad, and you. I know you love me..." Penni had rushed to say, not giving him the chance to deny her words. "We are different; I agree with you there. We may not love a lot, but when we do, they're special. You're special, Shade, and one day, you're going to find the woman who proves it to you. Just like I will find the man who proves it to me."

"Like Train?"

Penni had elbowed her brother in his ribs. "It's a secret. He doesn't know it yet."

"Believe me, he knows."

Confidently, she had shot him a calculated smile. "Not yet, but he will."

CHAPTER SEVENTEEN

The slamming of the door had Jackal jerking awake. He was halfway out of the bed, one hand searching behind him for Penni. She was gone, and the room was filled with Last Riders.

Viper was standing at the small table, picking up his gun and tucking it into the back of his jeans.

His gaze then went to Shade, who must have been the one to slam the door since he was standing in front of it.

"Where is she?" Jackal asked.

Shade leaned back against the door, folding his arms across his chest. "Heading to Treepoint."

Jackal picked up the alarm clock on the bedside table, throwing it at the wall across the room. She had left without telling him good-bye.

"Tell me you're not stupid enough to think you could keep her?"

Jackal remained silent, putting on his socks and boots.

Shade shook his head at Viper. "Yes, he was."

"What do you want, Shade?" Jackal huffed. "You have Penni back. I didn't harm a hair on her head. I'm thinking we don't have shit to talk about, so get the fuck out of my room."

Shade lost his indolent air. Striding across the room, he shot out his fist, punching him in the gut. "I think we have a shit-load to discuss."

Jackal doubled over, his hands going to his thighs, wheezing out, "That the best you can do? I'm not going to fight you when you have a dozen of your brothers waiting to take their turns."

"None of them will touch you," Shade promised. "It's one of the perks of being the enforcer for The Last Riders. And it was *my* sister you were snuggled up with in that bed."

"Like I said, I didn't touch her. I was here to protect her. She was kidnapped by—"

"I know what shit went down. The Last Riders will deal with Hennessy and his men when we get back to Treepoint. Viper sent some of the brothers to escort the Road Kingz; we don't want to keep them waiting. Get your things. I don't want to be far behind them."

"I'm not going to Treepoint."

"You don't have a choice," Viper told him. "When Ice didn't call Shade, it became the Predators' problem. King paid the Predators for protection, and what did the club do? Get her the hell out of there? No, you dragged her to a rally to make sure the Road Kingz didn't lose their ass in a drug deal a five-year-old could have pulled off. You nearly got her killed and would have if The Last Riders hadn't bailed you out. When we showed up to get you out of the shootout, the Unjust Soldiers thought The Last Rider's became involved to get a share of the money you stole from them."

Jackal shook his head. "You've lost your fucking mind. I got her out of there myself with no help from you or The Last Riders."

Viper's voice became mocking. "Really? You didn't see our men making two rows for you to ride through? You think Moses showed up to save your ass?" Viper scoffed. "Hell, your ass would have been crows' bait if we hadn't held the crowd back. Rider was the one who kept you from running the bitch down that couldn't move fast enough. Didn't you hear those bullets? I did. I put down four of the bikers who tried to take out Hennessy.

"The Last Riders have their own punishment in store for him and his men who are still alive after that dude double-crossed him.

"When we get to Treepoint, we'll settle the score with The Road Kingz. Then we'll settle with the Predators when Ice gets there. He can help deal with the fallout from the Unjust Soldiers. Until then, you're going."

"Where is Ice?" Jackal reached into his pocket, cussing himself for falling asleep last night and not calling him then. Scrolling, he saw over ten missed calls.

"Grace's mother took a turn for the worse," Viper informed him. "Ice agreed to make reparations after he deals with Oceane."

Jackal snorted. "Like you fucking care."

"We don't take our grievances out on women," Shade said coolly. "Ice knew he fucked up, but we'll take that up with him. You're our collateral until he comes to Treepoint. Since I have a personal stake—being Penni's bother—I thought you would be the best choice."

"Tit for tat?"

"You think this is a fucking joke?" Shade jerked his knee up, crashing it into Jackal's face as he was bent over, tying his boots.

Jackal fell back on the bed. He raised his hand to his face, holding his now bloody nose.

"The Unjust Soldiers saw Hennessy toss you the fucking bag with the drugs," Viper informed him. "You think they aren't going to try to get it? Striker might be dead, but the Unjust Soldiers aren't, and they will be calling. They don't care that Hennessy was doubled-crossed; they lost the drugs and some of their men. Now they are out for vengeance, and The Last Riders are stuck in the fucking middle."

Shade opened the closet door, taking the duffle bag and handing it to Viper. Viper set it on the table, unzipping it and looking inside before he zipped it back up.

"It's a death warrant." Viper kicked the chair back away from the table. "Why didn't Hennessy fucking let the Unjust Soldiers have them?"

Jackal used the blanket from the bed to stop the blood. "He couldn't. Hennessy still owes the money to the cartel he bought them from. Hennessy didn't have the money. Striker stole it from him. The only option he had left was to get the drugs back so that he can sell them to repay the cartel."

"Striker was fucking the Road Kingz and the Unjust Soldiers?" Rider picked up the chair, sitting down on it. "It's a shame the fucker is dead; he would have made a hell of a Last Rider."

Viper's anger showed he didn't agree. Picking up Jackal's wallet, he took out his credit card and threw it at Rider. "Go pay for the room and damages."

"Why are you mad at me? We're all thinking the same thing."

"None of us think like you. Hurry up. I want to get back to Treepoint."

Rider turned serious, losing his joking attitude. They were all concerned about leaving their women alone. And one of those women was Jackal's. Penni might not be there yet, but she would be.

Jackal got up, shoving his dirty clothes from the night before into his saddlebag. Going to the bathroom, he then wet a wash cloth to clean his face.

He gingerly touched his broken nose. If he wasn't ugly before, he was now. His nose was swollen, and his eyes were turning black and blue.

Shade appeared in the mirror behind him. "Let me see."

"Fuck off." Jackal tried to barge past him, but Shade shoved him against the bathroom door, his forearm braced against Jackal's neck.

Jackal simply stood still. He was bigger than Shade, but Jackal didn't want Penni pissed off if he hurt her brother. However, he would make sure she knew Shade was responsible for the marks on his face.

He stood still as Shade straightened his nose then released him. Then Jackal held on to the door knob to keep himself from hitting Shade.

"I did you a favor. It kind of even's out your face."

"Thanks." Jackal slid past him, slamming the door in Shade's face.

He expected Shade to be angry; what he didn't expect was that he would light a fuse that careened them into the bedroom, taking out Viper, Train, and Crash as several others tried to get out of their way.

"What the hell happened?" Viper grunted as he, Train, and Knox held Shade down.

Jackal rose from the floor, using the bottom of his T-shirt to wipe off the blood that had started to pour again. "Shade wanted a pissing contest, and he got one."

CHAPTER EIGHTEEN

"You want me to make you some breakfast?"

"I'm not hungry. We ate at the diner before we came here." Penni sat on the railing of her sister-in-law's front porch.

Lily yawned as she held her son on the swing that Shade had put up for her.

"Want to tell me why you showed up at my door step at seven in the morning?"

Penni didn't know how much Shade would want to tell his wife, so she said, "I can't come for a visit without an excuse?"

"Yes, but it's the seven in the morning that's confusing me. You're not exactly an early riser, and I saw Razer and Cash walking up with you."

Penni remained silent. Shade would answer his wife's questions when he got here. Razer had told her that they would be there before noon.

Lily's house was beautiful. Shade had picked the spot on the land near The Last Riders' clubhouse. The mountains were so high Penni thought she could reach out and touch them.

"Why were you staring out the window so early?" Penni turned to face Lily, seeing the weary circles under her eyes.

"I never sleep well when Shade is away. I thought at first he came back with the ones I saw going into the clubhouse around midnight, but when I texted him, he told me he wouldn't be back in town until this afternoon."

"Who did you see going into the clubhouse last night?"

"I recognize all The Last Riders, but there were a few I hadn't seen before. Some of the men seemed liked they were hurt. That's why I was worried about Shade when he didn't come home last night."

"He's fine. It won't be much longer." Penni turned away to sit down next to Lily on the swing. "He's getting so big." She gently grasped one of John's hands as she leaned her head on Lily's shoulder. Sticking out her foot, she pushed the swing into motion. "I've missed you and John."

"I've missed you, especially when Shade's irritating me by forgetting to pick up his dirty clothes when he showers."

"Missing your old roomie?" Penni missed the years they had shared their small dorm room.

"He's not OCD over cleaning the way you are, which I miss, but I guess I'll keep him, anyway," Lily teased.

"I bet you will." Her sister-in-law glowed in happiness. The shadows in her beautiful eyes that had been a part of her when they had met six+ years ago had disappeared.

"So, you're not going to tell me why my husband had to take off so fast and why he took all The Last Riders with him?"

"Nope."

"You're just like Shade."

She was and wasn't like him. She had learned that as she had grown older. Shade had hit the nail on the head when he had likened her to a butterfly. She had no desire to settle down and get married. She loved her job traveling with the band and making new friends and finding new places to explore. That was why Train would be perfect for her. He would never try to tie her down.

Innumerable friends had been made through her life, but only Shade, her parents, and Lily were the few that she had felt a true attachment to. She had even added Grace to the short list, so she had been glad when Razer had let her borrow his cell phone to call her as they'd driven in to Treepoint.

Penni had felt terrible for Grace when she had told Penni she wouldn't be returning for several weeks. Oceane was dying, and if a heart transplant couldn't be found in time, the chances of her recovering were grim. Penni wanted to fly out to be by her side, but Grace had assured her it wasn't necessary. Besides, Ice was on his way and so was Casey, Max's wife.

She had noticed the two women becoming friends during the months since Casey and Max had married. In a way, they had become sisters in the Predators through marriage, and Penni didn't belong to that club.

Lily handed John to her.

Penni blew raspberries on his cheek. "I've missed you, buddy."

"I wish you lived closer."

"I do, too." She meant it. Penni had thought about moving closer. Her parents were only a state away in Ohio, and she wouldn't miss out on John growing up. Only one thing kept her away: Train. It would hurt that he would be so near yet so far away. Shade had been right; he had never given the slightest hint that he cared about her.

"Is Train seeing someone?"

"No," Lily answered. "Why don't you stay a few weeks? Maybe he'll finally open his eyes and see what he's missing out on."

"I might take you up on that. The band is taking a break. The work I have for booking their next tour, I could do from a computer at your house."

"Shade's got to be happy you're going to stay."

"I don't know about that. He likes it when I keep my visits short and sweet."

"He's only joking," Lily denied.

"Shade never jokes."

"Yes, he does. He's really funny. You'll see. You staying here for a couple weeks will give you time to spend with him."

"You'd better buy a couple of cases of beer and call Tate for an emergency delivery."

"Now you're exaggerating."

They were distracted by the sounds of the motorcycles entering the parking lot.

Lily jumped up from the swing, and both of them moved to stand by the porch rail as the men approached the clubhouse.

"Do you mind?" Lily excitedly stepped toward the steps.

"Go for it." Penni juggled John into a more comfortable position on her hip as Lily took off to meet Shade.

"Get used to it, John. Your mama is crazy over your papa." It never failed to bring a lump to her throat when she saw her brother and sister-in-law together. It was as if they only existed when they were apart, becoming whole when they came together.

John tugged on her necklace, and she gently untangled it from his grip, tucking in the front of her shirt.

Shade had given it to her when she had graduated from high school. The delicate, gold chain was whisper thin with a gold charm in the shape of a compass. The back was engraved with the words: *"Never lose your way."* She never took it off.

Penni gasped when she saw his face. Shade's nose was swollen, and he had two black eyes. Lily was inspecting his injuries, moving aside to let the men walking behind him pass.

As she searched for Train to make sure he wasn't in the same shape, it took a couple of seconds to become aware of the man with a distinctive mark on his cheek. It looked worse than Shade.

She stomped down the steps, swiftly walking toward Jackal.

"Why is he here? I told you not to hurt him!" Penni moved closer to look at Jackal's poor face. "Are you okay?"

Penni ignored her brother's raised brow as she gingerly reached out to touch his bruised cheek.

"Yeah. It looked worse before," Jackal told her.

"It looks pretty damn bad. Do you want me to get you an ice bag?"

"No, most of the swelling has gone down."

"It looked worse before?"

"Yeah."

"You…" Penni was so furious she wanted to pound her big brother.

Jackal had made sure she hadn't gotten hurt when Hennessy had kidnapped her, and how had she returned the favor? By letting her big brother beat him up!

"You do realize my son can hear every word you're saying?"

"What?" She hadn't realized she had been talking out loud.

Shade took his son out her arms. "Is your crazy auntie upsetting you?"

Penni snorted as John shoved his clenched fist in his mouth. Her nephew wasn't in the least upset. The baby only had one thing on his mind, and that was to grab handfuls of his daddy's hair.

"I'll show you crazy if you hurt Jackal again."

"I don't need you to take up for me," Jackal said defensively.

"Isn't this the man you threatened to cut the dick off of for kidnapping you?" Shade quipped.

"I think I'll go inside and make some breakfast." Lily took John from Shade, hurrying inside her house and away from the confrontation.

"He deserved it then, but not this time."

"Jackal's right; he can take care of himself."

If he were the one responsible for Shade's black eyes, Penni had to agree.

"Why is he here, anyway?"

Shade's face became remote. "That's none of your business. Jackal is going to stay here until Ice comes to have a talk with Viper."

From their closed expressions, Penni wouldn't find out until they were ready to tell. She knew whom she was going to have to talk to in order to make sure Jackal or any of the Predators didn't face any repercussions for trying to help her.

"I can't understand why The Last Riders are angry when all they tried to do was help."

"They could have saved their asses if they had just called me when they found out you were missing."

"Because Hennessy used to be a Predator, they probably figured you would kill him. They were being loyal, and I know damn well how much that means to you."

"How about loyalty to King? They promised him they would watch out for you."

"I've told you I can take care of myself. You and King didn't need to ask the Predators to watch over me. Besides, I let you put that tracking device on my phone."

Jackal began laughing, reaching inside his pocket to take out her phone and giving it back to her. "So that's how you found her."

Penni bounced on the balls on her feet, staring at her brother proudly. "I call him every Friday night. I knew, when I missed calling him, he would track my phone."

"I don't leave anything to chance when I care about someone," Shade warned Jackal.

"I thought you didn't love me."

"I don't."

Penni smiled, knowing he was lying. Shade believed admitting to love someone made him weak. However, he had proved he could love when he had fallen in love the first time he had met Lily. As crazy as Penni made him, she knew he loved her, too.

"You're both fucking nuts." Jackal looked back and forth between them at Shade's words.

"It runs in the family." Penni intertwined her arm with Shade's. "Come on; I can't cook worth shit, so I can't help Lily, but I'll make you some toast."

"You'll burn it, and I won't be able to choke it down like I usually do. I think Jackal loosened one of my front teeth."

Penni glared at Jackal over her shoulder.

"Shade, the manager of the hotel called. He said he found your dick in the lost and found."

Penni almost tripped when Shade spun toward Jackal. The two were going at it before she could regain her footing.

"Viper! Train! Knox!" Penni screamed, knowing better than to try to break the two men apart.

The men ran outside the back of the clubhouse, quickly breaking the men apart.

"Motherfucker, who started it this time!"

Knox put Shade in a head lock as Jackal tore away from Train's restraining hold. Before Jackal could strike out, though, Penni took a stance in front of him.

"Don't you dare hit him!"

Jackal, whose eyes were on Shade, turned to Penni, who had moved to protect Train. Varied expressions crossed his face, which she couldn't understand, but thankfully, he stopped fighting, giving The Last Riders time to diffuse the situation.

"Go home," Viper barked his order out to Shade before he grabbed the back of Jackal's T-shirt, tossing him in the direction of the clubhouse. "Go inside."

Left with no choice since Train and Knox were escorting him, he shared steely glances, letting them all know the fight wasn't over.

"Brother, you've got a problem with Jackal; I've got that. But I can't give Jackal back to Ice dead."

"He called me a pussy," Shade managed to speak from between clenched teeth.

Penni hoped Lily's dentist was on speed dial.

"I don't care if he calls you a douchebag; ignore it. Got me?"

Shade reluctantly nodded his head.

Viper took a deep breath, turning toward her. "Winter is dying to see you to make sure you're all right. I'll tell her to come over after Shade eats his breakfast. Maybe that'll put him in a better mood."

"I wouldn't count on it, but Lily will be there, so he'll behave."

Penni followed behind Shade as he walked to his house, deciding to keep quiet so that he could retain his temper before going inside to Lily.

Shade stopped on his front porch.

"He was just being a jackass." Penni couldn't believe she was trying to make amends for Jackal.

"Stay away from him and Hennessy while they're here."

"Hennessy's here, too?" Her mouth dropped open. "But why?"

"Hennessy was hurt at the shootout. Viper brought him here so he could recuperate instead of getting arrested. The Unjust Soldiers would had killed him before he could have made it out of ER."

"That was nice of Viper," Penni said suspiciously.

"Yes, it was. Don't repay him by putting your nose where it doesn't belong. Jackal and Hennessy both have to make amends before they leave. Viper won't tolerate you butting in, even though you're my sister."

"I understand."

"I hope you do, Penni," Shade answered grimly. "Don't expect me to get in a fight between you and The Last Riders. You'll lose."

CHAPTER NINETEEN

The backyard was filled with The Last Riders. Jackal sat on the picnic table, drinking the beer Rider had handed him before sitting down beside him.

"How in the fuck did Shade manage to catch her?" Jackal tipped his beer toward Lily who was sitting at a patio table with Shade, Penni, and Train.

Rider chuckled. "He paid for a personality transplant."

"His doctor should be sued for malpractice."

"You should have known him before he married Lily."

"Bad?"

"More like painful. He had to wait a long time before she noticed him."

"His sister is following in his example." Jackal watched Penni flirt with Train. As they talked, Penni used any reason to reach out and touch Train.

Jackal wanted to walk across the yard, steal her away, carry her to his room, and spank her ass until she couldn't sit for a week.

Two problems stopped him: One, he was forced to share a room with Rider. Two, Rider would enjoy it as much he would.

Rider cast him a sidelong look. "Train thinks of Penni as a little sister."

"You should tell her. She's making a fool of herself."

"If you spent any time with Penni, you'd know telling her anything she doesn't want to hear goes in one ear and out the other."

"You sure he isn't interested?"

Rider tilted his head. "I'm sure. Believe me; Penni isn't the type of woman he goes for."

"What kind of woman does he go for?" Curious, he turned to look at Rider. If he stared at Penni and Train much longer, he would toss him off the hill the clubhouse was built on.

"Look around. Take your pick."

Jackal understood what he meant. The Last Riders didn't lack for female companionship. One or two of the woman had reminded him of how long it had been since he had been laid. When they returned to Queen City, he was going to tell Ice they needed more women, or he was going to become a Last Rider.

A provocative laugh had him changing his mind.

It didn't matter how many women Ice found to fill his bed. None of them would be her, and Jackal was determined to have her.

She had become an obsession. None of the women in that yard had her bottom lip that seemed to beg to suck his dick. He imagined her kneeling in front of him as he thrust his cock in her wet mouth...

Jackal jerked upright, throwing his empty bottle away in the trash can. "I need another beer."

"Help yourself." Rider tugged a sultry woman to him as she passed while Jackal sauntered to the ice chest, taking his time to grab a beer.

"Lily rented the entire series of *My Boyfriend is a Zombie*. Knox and Diamond are going to come over to watch and so are Rider and Crash. Why don't you come, and I'll make a pitcher of Bourbon Sours?"

"Zombie movies give me nightmares." Train smiled indulgently at Penni's disappointed expression.

"You're not afraid of zombie—"

"It's not the zombies that bother me; it's Diamond thinking they're going to take over the world. Knox is a brave man to go home after the nights he works the late shift. He said she's turned the house into Fort Knox."

Jackal wanted to vomit when she laughed at Train's joke. He wondered how fucking funny Penni would find it when he threw him off the hill.

He took a cold beer then leaned against a nearby tree where he was able to listen to their conservation.

He ignored Shade's occasional stare, becoming more and more irritated as the afternoon slowly progressed.

"Viper said the charcoals are ready. Help me carry the meat out?" Lily stood, reaching out to take Shade's hand and giving him no choice but to go with her.

So Lily was trying to play matchmaker?

Her attempt was made in vain, though, as Train stood. "I'll help Viper. I like my steaks rare. If I don't do it myself, he'll burn it to a crisp."

He wanted to shake Penni at her meek reply. "Oh...okay." Since when had she become meek?

Jackal took another beer out of the ice chest then took the seat Shade had vacated, placing the beer on the table in front of her.

"You're never going to get him to notice you by kissing his ass."

"Shut up," she hissed. "You don't know what the hell you're talking about!"

"Really? It's pretty obvious. You licked your lips so often I bet Train couldn't make up his mind if you were thirsty or about to lick him next."

Penni started to stand up. "You don't know me, Train, or women."

He leaned forward in his chair. "You told me a week ago I had all the women in Henry's club."

She paused. "You said that you hadn't."

"I lied." He had never lied to her until now.

"I told Shade you were a jackass. I was wrong; you're a—"

He lowered his voice when he saw Viper and Train look at them. "Be cool. Do you want Train to see you lose your temper?" He could practically see steam pour out of her. "You're smart enough to see he likes passive women."

"That's bullshit. I haven't seen that at all."

"Well, he does; take it from me. I slept in the room next to his."

Penni's expression went pale as she sat back down in her seat. "He's made love to women since I've been here?"

Jackal gripped his beer bottle to keep himself from shaking her. "Baby, what I heard coming from his bedroom wasn't making love, but yes, he has fucked a different one each night I've been here."

He watched as she lifted her beer, drinking it until it was almost empty.

"If you take my advice—"

"Just shut up, please."

"I'm not trying to be mean." Well, he was, but it was for her own good, which wasn't strictly true, either. He had told her for his own good, wanting to further his own chances in getting her in bed. "I can tell you how to have Train eating out of your hand."

Penni arched an eyebrow. "How?"

"Make him jealous. Men like him eat that shit up."

Jackal saw the wheels turning behind her eyes. He knew he had hit pay dirt when she began surveying the men around the yard, trying to decide whom she could use to make Train jealous. He put a stop to that thought before it could get started.

"It can't be another Last Rider."

She glanced back to him. "Why not?"

"The men are used to sharing women in the club. It doesn't cause fights."

Her cheeks were flushed, but she didn't look away.

His dick went hard. Train couldn't handle a woman like Penni.

Once she was in his bed, he would use his body to fulfill any fantasy she could dream up. He had a few of his own that nearly had him scooting his chair forward so no one could see the hard ridge of his cock under his jeans.

He wanted to kick Colton's ass for talking him into getting his dick pierced. He was so hard he felt like spikes had been driven into his dick.

"Who, then? I could pretend I have a boyfriend back in Queen City."

"That's not going to make him jealous. He has to have it under his nose. Use me."

"You?" She burst out laughing.

"What's wrong me?" Jackal asked.

"Well, let's see. To make Train believe it, Shade will have to believe it, too. That's not going to happen. My brother knows I hate you."

"Convince him. Tell him we realized we were attracted to each other when I tried to get you away from Hennessy. It'll work. We spent a week together. Tell him that you wanted to tell him when we got back to Queen City, and I didn't want to wait. That I wanted to face his anger while I was here."

"He'll kill you."

"Not if you convince him not to."

He could tell she was tempted. Her eyes went to Train who was talking to a vivacious woman called Raci. Rider had introduced him when she had pounced on Jackal while he lay sleeping in his bedroom, believing it to be Rider.

"What's in it for you?" Suspiciously, she looked at him over the rim of her beer.

"Other than making your dreams of true love come true?"

"Please...There's no such thing as true love."

"You don't believe in true love?"

"No, I don't."

"Your parents didn't have a good marriage?"

"Their second one. Their first ones ended up in divorce."

"So, if they have a good marriage—"

"You asked me if I believe in true love, and I don't. True love doesn't exist, just like there isn't Superman and no Santa

Claus. True love is a fable made of make believe dreams about someone who doesn't exist. I want a man made of blood and flesh who loves me as much as I love him. The universe only gives us one soul. I don't want to remember what it felt like before him, and I don't ever want to know what it would feel like without him."

"You believe Train is your soul mate?" Jackal saw the uncertainly in her eyes, giving him hope his plan would work. He needed more time to make Penni realize *he* was the man for her.

"I think so..."

"You're not sure? Not that I believe in soul mates, but wouldn't you know?"

"Not necessarily. I'll know when I make love to him."

Over his dead body. Not his own—Train's.

"We going to do this?" Jackal asked as he watched Shade and Lily make their plates. Then he diverted his attention to where Train was carrying two plates before setting them down on the picnic table as Raci brought their drinks.

"You never told me what's in it for you." Penni pointed her empty beer bottle at him.

"I need your help with Viper. If you can convince Viper not to kill Hennessy, we'll call it even."

"Viper won't kill Hennessy."

Jackal rolled his eyes. "Hennessy is lucky he's still alive. You're probably the only one who can change Viper's mind."

"I don't like Hennessy, but I don't want to see any man killed. I'll call Knox and tell him I want to charge him for kidnapping. He'll be safe in prison."

This was not going the way he wanted.

"Do you want Train or not? I think he and Raci make a cute couple, don't you?"

"No. Okay, it's a deal, but no funny stuff."

"Like what?" Jackal laid his hand down on top of hers. Penni started to pull her hand back, but Jackal nodded at Shade and Lily who were getting closer to them.

"Like no touching."

"There has to be some touching, or Shade and Train won't believe it."

"Okay, some touching, but nothing too sexual."

"I thought the idea was to make Train jealous, not turn me into a fucking pussy."

"Okay, we'll play it by ear," Penni conceded as Shade and Lily came to a stop at their table.

Jackal looked up at Shade, confident he hadn't missed their linked hands.

"You going to go fix yourself a plate?" Shade asked as he placed their plates on the table then sat down with Lily at the picnic table.

Jackal had to give Shade credit. He had seen their hands, his frown saying he wasn't happy, but he wouldn't start an argument in front of Lily.

Not about to hide her confusion, Lily asked, "Did I miss something?"

Penni sprung to her feet. "Jackal wants to talk to you. Wow, I'm starved." She disappeared, leaving Jackal to face the couple alone.

Jackal tried to think of a simple way to tell Shade without getting his nose broken again.

"Your sister likes me."

CHAPTER TWENTY

"What are you doing here?"

Penni blocked the doorway after opening the door. She had hoped after finishing her half-eaten dinner that Jackal would return inside the clubhouse. She had only been able to choke down a few bites of her food under Shade and Lily's silent scrutiny.

"Did you forget you invited me to watch the movie with you?" His loud voice had everyone in the living room turning from the television.

Penni stepped onto the porch, shutting the door behind her.

"I did not invite you," Penni hissed.

"I thought this would be a good time to show them we're a couple."

"You already told them; that's all they need."

"Telling them and showing them are two different things. By the way, thanks for the heads up before leaving me alone to tell Shade."

"I was afraid I couldn't keep a straight face." Penni knew she was being a brat, but she had never lied to her brother before, and she still felt angry for letting jealousy over Raci overcome her common sense. "I've changed my mind. I thought it through."

"That's cool." Jackal turned toward the steps. "Train and Rider are playing cards with Jewell and Ember. I'll see if I can join them."

"Wait. Are you sure this will work?"

"Put it this way; what you're doing to catch Train isn't working. The Last Riders have a lot of women. You have to do something to make yourself stand out."

"That's you?"

Jackal lifted his hands up. "By the time I get done with you, Train—hell, all the single men—will be trying to hook up with you."

Her indecision vanished at the picture he had painted. She opened the door, letting him go inside. Then, closing the door, Penni felt Jackal take her hand. She took a deep breath as she led him into the living room.

"He's decided to watch the movie with us." She took a seat on the couch, scooting over so Jackal had enough room to sit down beside her. He circled his arm around her shoulders as Knox pushed the DVR button to restart the movie.

Stiffening, Penni forced herself to lean back against the couch cushion.

Shade, who was sitting on a large recliner, began to rise when he saw him touch her. Pleadingly, she silently begged him not to throw Jackal out.

Thankfully, Lily came to her rescue, pressing a hand to Shade's chest to get him to sit still.

"Would you like something to drink or some popcorn?" Penni offered Jackal.

"No thanks. I'm good."

She chewed on her bottom lip nervously as the horror film became a blood bath that gradually distracted her from the tension in the house.

Diamond and Knox were lying on a large blanket on the floor with a big bowl of popcorn. When the zombie began making moves on his girlfriend, Penni reached down, swiping the popcorn from them.

"Hey, get your own." Diamond took it back, setting it back down on the floor between her and Knox.

"There's enough for ten people," she argued.

"When I get scared, I eat. The movie just started."

"Fine, I'll make mine own."

Penni went into the kitchen, aggravated she was missing the movie.

"You need some help?" Jackal asked, coming in behind her.

"No!" she snapped, listening to the microwave begin to pop the bag of popcorn.

Jackal reached inside the refrigerator for a couple of sodas then set them down on the counter. "I'm beginning to see the problem with Train."

Penni looked away from the microwave. "What do you mean?"

"He's a man to snuggle with a pretty girl, not a bitch."

"I've told you not to call me a bitch." Penni opened the refrigerator door, banging Jackal's shoulder with it as she took out some butter.

"You know what? You need more help to get Train than I can give you. Later."

Jackal went to leave the kitchen, but Penni jerked him back.

"I'm sorry. I don't know why I snapped at you."

"Habit."

She stared at the floor, ashamed of herself, then forced herself to meet his eyes. "I was in high school when I found out Shade belonged to a motorcycle club. I heard terrible things about clubs like his, so even though I didn't get to see him often, I blamed them for how he treated me."

"Shade mistreated you?" Jackal tried to shake her hand off his arm, but she held on more tightly.

"Not like that, no. You don't know him well, so you don't understand how remote he can be. Do you have any brothers or sisters?"

"No."

"At school and at softball games, several of my friends had siblings. They didn't act the way Shade and I do. At first, I blamed my mother and his father's divorce. Then I blamed The Last Riders. Then I realized what was wrong. It was us."

"What do you mean?"

"We don't feel the same way other people do. It never bothered Shade. I still don't think it does. But it bothered me." Penni put her hand on her heart. "I mean, I felt my heart beat, so I knew it was there, but I couldn't *feel* it. I know it sounds stupid, but it's the truth."

Jackal reached out, slipping a hand to the back of her neck then pulling her close to his body. "I believe you think that, but it's not true."

She tried to pull out of his arms. "I know that now, but it took Lily coming into our lives to prove it."

"Lily? How?"

"She's special. She helped Shade find the part of his soul that was missing, and she gave me hope that I could find that, too."

"You think you can find that with Train?"

"Yes."

If he couldn't, who then? She had dated so many men she had lost count. She had believed Train was the one as a young girl, but when he had showed no interest, she had begun to doubt herself, losing interest in the party atmosphere at college. Then, after she had graduated and found the job with Mouth2Mouth, she had accepted any date if she was attracted to the guy. One date with them would prove her wrong, though.

Now she was older, and she had never had a serious relationship. She had become a social butterfly in Queen City, and now she had more friends. Grace was among them, but none of them filled the yearning to fill the hole in her own heart.

She succeeded in pulling away from Jackal. "I think I burned the popcorn."

Penni set the scorched bag in the sink, setting another one in the microwave and turning it back on. Not staring at him, she watched the numbers count down.

"I'm sorry I kidnapped you."

She felt as if a weight had been lifted off her chest. Penni had hated Jackal for kidnapping and holding her hostage four years ago. It had taken him a long time, but this time when he apologized, she sensed it was sincere.

"I forgive you." Before she could burn the popcorn again, she hastily removed the bag, dumping it out in a bowl she took out of a cabinet. "I may even share with you."

Jackal took one kernel, holding it to her lips. She opened her mouth, letting him feed it to her.

"You want me to ask Knox to rewind the movie for you?" she asked when they sat back down on the couch.

"No, I watched it before."

Penni and the others in the room looked at him.

"You've watched this movie?" Diamond asked, taking some off Penni's popcorn and dumping it into her own bowl.

"Yeah, I've seen all three of them. *My Boyfriend Is a Zombie, I Married a Zombie,* and *I'm Having a Baby with a Zombie.*"

"I heard they're making a fourth one." Diamond took the bowl away from Knox. "*I Killed My Zombie Husband.*"

"Figures," Knox mumbled under his breath.

"Why?" Penni opened her soda.

"Men always get killed off in horror movies." Knox kissed Diamond's neck, and his wife giggled, pulling him down for a full blown kiss.

"That isn't true," Penni countered.

"It's mostly true," Diamond countered as if Knox had hung the moon.

Penni rolled her eyes. Of course Diamond would agree with her husband. They were practically necking on the living room floor.

"Why are you taking his side?"

"Because Knox is eating most of my popcorn, and since he's seen it before, he can make some more."

"I can make it—"

"Let him. The house still smells like the one you burnt, and this one is scorched, too."

"I'll do it." Jackal went back to the kitchen.

"You've watched this numerous times; why didn't you make the popcorn yourself?" Penni leaned over to look at Diamond who had pushed Knox back to use him as a big pillow.

"I wanted to ask what's going on with Jackal."

Penni was glad the living room was dark. "I like him." She straightened, not meeting her discerning gaze.

"So you're not serious about him, then?" Shade asked as he shifted Lily on his lap.

Penni thought about her answer. The plan was to make Train jealous, but two of his friends were in the room, so she couldn't admit to that.

"We have a lot in common." There. That was a safe answer. She congratulated herself for her quick thinking.

"Like what?"

"Uh…" Penni's mind drew a blank. "He likes animals." At least, she hoped he did. Most men did, didn't they?

"You don't sound so sure."

Shade wasn't an idiot. She had to own this plan, or it wasn't going to work. If she couldn't convince Shade, Train wouldn't believe it, and she would only end up making a fool of herself.

"I'm sure." This time, she infused more conviction and warmth into her tone. "He helps feed the ducks for me when I'm out of town." It might have been one time, but he had done it. He also hadn't shot her neighbor's dogs when he had jumped the fence at her house. Them not being dead was more than she had expected when he had told her the story.

"That's sweet." Lily patted Shade's cheek at her husband's incredulous look.

"I think it is. He protected me from Hennessy and his men, he's funny, and I think he's cute."

Shade made gagging noises, which had Lily elbowing him in his stomach.

"I think he's cute, too." Lily raised her voice to be heard over the noises Shade was making.

Shade stopped, giving her an irritated glare. "I thought you said I'm the only one you think's cute?"

Penni couldn't help laughing at her brother's jealously. Watching him go from his days of being an emotionless bachelor to being wrapped around his wife's finger was endearing.

Penni tried to imagine Train after she managed to snare him. The weird thing was that she couldn't form the picture.

Jackal came back into the room. "What's so funny?"

"Nothing." She was about to grab another handful of popcorn, but Jackal stopped her, taking the one she had and giving her another bowl.

She took a bite and then another. "Why does this taste so good?" Penni leaned against Jackal's shoulder, going gung-ho to give the impression they were a couple.

"Maybe because I didn't scorch it, and I added some chili pepper."

"It's really good. Thank you."

"No problem."

Toward the end of the second movie, Knox's phone rang. Diamond stopped the movie while Knox talked to one of his deputies. When he ended the call, he stood up, helping Diamond to her feet.

"We'll have to finish this another night. Lyon's wife went into labor; I need to take over his shift."

Lily yawned. "I'm ready for bed, anyway. John will be up early, expecting his breakfast."

Penni gathered the empty popcorn bowls and soda cans as Knox and Diamond left after saying good-bye.

"You and Shade go to bed. I'll take care of the dishes."

"I can do it in the morning."

"Don't be ridiculous. I don't mind. I might not be able to cook, but I can do the dishes."

"All right, then. I'll see you in the morning." Lily stopped on the bottom step leading upstairs, looking at Shade. "Are you coming?"

Shade and Jackal remained sitting, neither man moving.

"Let's go to bed." Lily waited expectantly for her husband.

Sighing, she saw the men were determined to hold their ground. Since it was Shade's home, though, Penni decided to bring an end to the stalemate. Going to the front door, she held it open.

"Good night, Jackal."

Jackal rose and Shade stood, going to Lily's side and following her up the steps.

Penni walked outside with Jackal behind her.

"Your brother is an ass."

Penni gave a low laugh. "He's just being protective."

"You're the same age Lily is."

"Actually, she's older. That doesn't matter to Shade. I don't think he likes you very much. I think he thinks you're an ass, too. It's kind of funny."

"You've got a warped sense of humor." Jackal tugged her down onto the porch swing, his arm resting on the back as he set it in motion.

"I've been told that before." The light breeze felt good as she relaxed.

A light went out in one of the bedrooms of the clubhouse. Penni knew it was the room Train was in.

"I wonder who he's with tonight?" She hadn't meant to ask the question out loud.

Jackal saw the direction she was staring in. He turned to her with the moonlight beaming down on the porch. "Right now, he's watching us."

She started to look up again at Train's room. "How can you tell?"

"I see his shadow behind the window. I bet Shade texted him to make sure I left."

Penni shivered as Jackal curved his hand around her throat, and he lowered his head.

"What are you doing?"

"Giving him something worth seeing. Don't move."

She did what he told her as his mouth brushed her lips, preparing herself for what she saw coming. However, she wasn't expecting the heat that blasted through her core. God, she needed to land Train before she did something stupid.

Her body was screaming at her to pull him closer as he parted her mouth, sliding his tongue inside. Limply, her head fell back on his arm behind her. She slid her arms around his neck and tangled her fingers in the long hair that curled at the nape of his neck.

Jackal slid his hand between her shoulder blades, arching her back so her breasts rubbed against his chest. He parted her lips wider before delving deeper, stroking his tongue against hers.

If he made love the way he kissed, a woman wouldn't be able to take another lover. He didn't kiss like any other men she had kissed before who wanted to build your passion. Jackal thrust you into the fire and wanted you to burn alive.

Moaning, she wanted to curl her toes at the sensations. Pulling him lower so she could explore his mouth, loving the salty, spicy taste that had her wanting more, she rubbed her breasts against his chest, unconsciously digging her nails into his neck.

"That should make it hard for him to fall asleep." Jackal announced as he suddenly stood up, breaking the kiss.

Penni used her foot to stop the swing.

"What...?" She dazedly found herself clutching air. She could barely make out his shadowy outline as the moon slipped behind the clouds.

"Train," he replied. "I better go before Shade comes down with his gun." Jackal went down the steps. "Night, Penni."

"Good night, Jackal." She watched him leave.

Penni heard the loud music coming from inside the club-house as he went in the back door. Then she went back inside, locking and closing the door.

Taking her time, she did the dishes then turned off the lights before she went up the stairs. She took a shower and washed her hair then climbed into bed, turning off the bedroom lamp.

She couldn't fall asleep, tossing and turning, her thoughts jammed in her head. They weren't thoughts of who Train was sleeping with tonight, but Jackal's kiss. She had brushed her teeth before going to bed, so why did she still taste him on her lips?

Turning on her side, she looked out her window, seeing the stars twinkling in the sky above her. It was as if they were laughing down at her.

Giving up, she sneaked back downstairs, settling on to the couch and turning on the television. Penni lowed the volume before starting the movie. The actress of *I'm Having a Baby with a Zombie* gave a blood curling scream.

Who needed men when you could watch a good zombie movie?

CHAPTER TWENTY-ONE

Penni started to sneak past Lily and Shade's bedroom, but the door was cracked open, so she thought they must have woken up when she had gone upstairs to shower and dress. She had fallen asleep on the couch, waking to see the sun shining through the curtains.

Shade and Lily were lying on the bed with John between them. They were asleep. Lily was lying on her side, her head pillowed on Shade's shoulder. John was lying on his front on Shade's chest.

She carefully reached out, closing the bedroom door. The private moment had Penni giving thanks to the universe. In this crazy world where dating had been taken over by apps instead of chemistry, Shade and Lily had both spun the roulette wheel and won.

Downstairs, she began to make a cup of coffee but found only an empty canister. Taking it, she decided to go The Last

Riders' clubhouse. With so many living there, she knew she could find herself a cup and bring some to Shade.

It was a little after eight on a Sunday. Therefore, Penni hadn't expected any of the members to be up yet. The women would be getting ready for church in an hour, so she expected the house to be silent.

At first, Penni thought the music she heard as she opened the door had been left playing from the night before. It wasn't until she was a couple of steps into the room that she discovered the source was coming from the basement. Someone must have left the music on in the gym. That was also where the laundry, hot tub, and a bedroom were located. Willa and Lucky were living there as they built their house.

The kitchen's aroma of brewing coffee and the smell of cinnamon rolls baking didn't distract Penni from going down the basement stairs. Someone had to be awake, or the backdoor wouldn't have been open, and someone had started breakfast.

She had had gone down three steps, bending over to see who was there and alert them to her presence, when it dawned on her that the singing wasn't from the radio. Stunned at the beautiful sound coming from the woman putting clothes in the washing machine, she saw it was Genny.

Penni had met her briefly when she had arrived. Willa had hired the young nineteen-year-old to help cook and clean.

Penni soundlessly sat down on the steps, listening to her sing as she took clothes out of the dryer. It was a common song, but she had given it a sultry, melancholy quality that tugged at her heartstrings.

As she carried the laundry to the bottom steps, Genny gave a small scream, dropping the laundry basket.

"I'm sorry! I didn't mean to startle you."

Penni felt terrible. Hopping up, she went down the steps to help her pick up the clothes.

"It's okay. Did you need something?"

"No, I was just enjoying listening to you sing."

"Genny? Penni? What's wrong?" Lucky rushed from the hallway, wearing a pair of jeans he hadn't taken the time to button. "I heard you—"

"Nothing's wrong. I was just doing the laundry and didn't know I wasn't alone," Genny explained.

"You sure?"

Genny nodded. "I'm fine. I'm sorry I disturbed you."

"I was getting ready to take a shower. You didn't wake me up or anything. I'll see you two at breakfast." Lucky went back through the door that led to his bedroom.

"I'm really sorry. You had folded the clothes in such neat piles. I'll straighten them out as soon as I drink my coffee."

"You don't have to—"

"Please, it'll make me feel better." Penni carried the basket upstairs.

Left with no choice, Genny followed her up.

Penni set the laundry on one of the chairs at the kitchen table before she poured herself a cup of coffee, sniffing appreciatively at the rolls Genny pulled out of the oven.

"Would you like one?"

"Yes, thank you." Penni accepted the plate she was handed and took a seat at the table. "You have a beautiful voice."

"Thank you."

Penni glanced at her surreptitiously as she finished breakfast. Her light brown hair was tied back into a ponytail, she didn't wear any makeup, and her clothes weren't very expensive.

"How long have you lived in Treepoint?"

Genny turned from the stove, her complexion going pale. "A few years."

"So you're not from Treepoint? Where are you originally from?"

"Ouch..." Genny exclaimed, dropping the skillet back onto the burner.

Penni rushed to her side, turning the stove off.

"Put it under the faucet," Penni directed her, turning the water on so the girl could ease her pain.

"I'm fine. It's what I get for not paying attention."

"I shouldn't have distracted you. I knew you were busy. I'm sorry."

Genny removed her wrist from the water, drying it. "It's fine. See? It's barely red."

Penni moved back to the table, sensing the woman wanted to be left alone.

She had finished the last bite when Rider came in from the living room. Genny was standing at the stove as Rider made himself a cup of coffee then took a paper towel to take two of the cinnamon rolls.

Lucky came in as Rider was about to take a seat at the table.

"You ready?" Lucky asked Rider.

Nodding, Rider went to wait at the back door as Lucky readied his own breakfast.

"You're not going to sit?" Penni asked as she started to fold the laundry.

"Can't. My battery is giving me trouble. Rider offered to switch it out with one from one of his bikes."

"I'll see you in church, then."

Lucky was probably the only pastor in Kentucky who rode a motorcycle to church.

Penni finished folding the clothes as they left, deciding to pour herself another cup of coffee.

Penni watched Genny make a large plate of bacon, eggs, and three cinnamon rolls.

"Whoever you're making the tray for will have to hit the gym in the basement after eating all that."

Genny blushed. "Too much?"

"Depends on which of the men you're making it for."

"I don't know. He's staying in the room beside Viper's. I haven't met him yet. From the way he sounds, he's pretty big."

Penni's lips twitched. "He sounds big?"

"His room is over the kitchen. I hear him walking on the floor."

It must be Hennessy she had been hearing. He was certainly large, and Shade had told her that he was next to Viper's room so he could keep an eye on him.

Genny set an empty cup on the tray then turned to fry more eggs.

"His food is getting cold."

"I thought Rider would have been back before now. If he doesn't come back, I'll put it in the oven to keep warm. I'd carry it up myself, but I'm not allowed upstairs."

"I can do it." Penni poured the hot coffee into the empty cup.

"Are you sure? You won't get in any trouble?"

"They haven't told me not to go upstairs." It wasn't an untruth, but it wasn't strictly the truth, either. Usually when she had gone upstairs, it was when Shade or Winter had escorted her, and the men had all been told she was on the floor.

While she and Shade hadn't been raised together, she had traveled with the band members, so she was sure seeing one of The

Last Riders in their underwear wouldn't have her screaming for help. And if she were lucky, she might catch a glimpse of Train.

"Whose laundry was in the basket?" Penni asked, hesitating before sitting on the chair.

"The same man."

"I'll kill two birds with one stone," she joked, setting the tray on top of the folded clothes.

Penni had thought a couple of the T-shirts looked familiar, having seen him wearing them during the rally.

"It may be too heavy..."

Penni lifted the basket easily in her arms. Shade's weight training had come in handy, and she hadn't spilled a drop of the coffee.

"I've got it. Save me four of those cinnamon rolls for Shade and Lily in case Rider gets back before I come back down."

"All right."

Balancing the basket, she went through the living room and up the flight steps. The hallway remained empty as she walked to the door that was beside Viper's. Damn, she had forgotten to ask which room. Viper and Winter's bedroom had two doors next to theirs since it was at the end of the hall.

Left or right? Penni bit her lip in indecision then chose the one on the left, guessing it had a better chance of being directly over the kitchen.

She knocked on the door, hoping she had guessed right. If not, one grumpy biker was going to be pissed.

"Come in."

Hennessy's voice coming from inside the room had Penni opening the door. It was everything she could do not to drop the basket.

Shade had told her Hennessy was hurt, but she hadn't expected how badly he had been incapacitated. Now she could understand why Viper hadn't put a guard in front of his door. His arm was wrapped in a bandage and held in place with a sling. His ribs and upper body were covered with varying shades of blue and purple. It looked as if feet had stomped all over his chest, and his face made Jackal's and Shade's look like they had been done by an amateur. More than one person was responsible for the destruction she saw.

Barely able to hang on to the basket, she set it on the chair beside the bed.

"What are you doing here?" Hennessey tried to lift himself unsuccessfully into a sitting position.

"I thought you might be hungry." She wanted to help him, but she wasn't sure how without hurting him further.

Gingerly, she moved to the other side of the bed, gripping his good arm and helping him to rise to the mound of pillows at his back. When he was settled, Penni laid the tray on his lap.

Hennessy ate hungrily, devouring the cinnamon rolls.

"Did The Last Riders do that to you?" she asked.

"No."

Penni let out a relieved breath. She had hated Hennessy for not letting her go, but what had been done to him made her sick to her stomach.

"Ice and Viper are the reason I'm still breathing."

"Good. I mean, I'm glad you're not—"

"Dead?" Hennessey finished for her.

"Yes."

"It doesn't mean I'll be staying that way."

"If Viper were going to kill you, he would have done it before now. He wouldn't have bandaged you up. He would have let the Unjust Soldiers finish you off."

"He would have done me a favor." Hennessy's grave expression had her wondering how he could eat. Had Viper told him he was going to be killed in retaliation for kidnapping her?

"I told Shade I would stay out of his clubs' business. Jackal wanted me to try, anyway, to smooth things over between you two."

"Don't bother. I wouldn't listen to anything a bitch had to say." Hennessy grimaced in pain, trying to lift his arm into a more comfortable position.

"Fine. I'll tell him you don't want my help."

If he weren't already so hurt, Penni would have pounded him into the mattress.

Penni went out the door and into the hall. She was about to slam his bedroom door closed when she came face to face with Raci as she exited the bedroom across the hall.

She was only wearing a white T-shirt. Her perky breasts had Penni feeling envious until she looked through the opened door and saw Train standing by his bed, about to put on a pair of jeans in his hands. Penni wanted to sink through the floor in embarrassment.

"Excuse me," she mumbled, not knowing how to get out of the awkward position.

"You're not supposed to be up here," Raci said as they stared at each other.

"I was...I..."

The door next to Hennessy's opened.

Was the whole house going to witness her humiliation?

Turning her head, she saw Jackal standing in the doorway.

"I'm sorry. I didn't mean disturb anyone. I took Hennessy his breakfast." Closing the door on Hennessy's curious gaze, Penni tried to pretend it was a natural occurrence to see Train in the nude. "And I wanted to tell Jackal his breakfast is ready."

Since she was in a shitload of trouble, she decided to go for broke. Before he could react, Penni kissed Jackal on his surprised mouth. The kiss lasted much longer than intended, but she blamed him for cupping her butt and pulling her into his hard body.

Leaning into him, Penni stared into his lowered eyes, feeling the world tilt. She imagined she heard the world crashing down around them.

The image of Train in the bedroom faded away as the sensation of Jackal's firm lips on hers brought her mind to a standstill, making her forget they had an audience. Damn, when Jackal kissed, he was like a man on a mission. He didn't try to make them sweet kisses. No, he took no prisoners. You stood transfixed, waiting for each brush of his tongue.

She nipped on his bottom lip when he pulled away.

"Pour me a cup of coffee. I'll be there in a minute."

Dazedly, she took a step past the door he had come out of, seeing the curvy bottom belonging to Jewell facing the open doorway.

Fury had her dodging Jackal's restraining hand when he saw her reaction. First Train and then Jackal; how much rejection was a woman supposed to take? Technically, though, neither man was rejecting her. Train had no idea of her interest, and Jackal was only pretending to be interested.

"I was asleep when Rider decided to have company last night," Jackal explained. "I spent the night in Hennessey room.

I just came out of the shower." Jackal nodded to the bathroom door. "I went to Rider's room to get my boots and a clean shirt."

The thump she had heard wasn't the world stopping, but Jackal dropping his boots.

"So you didn't spend the night with Jewell?" she asked.

"That's her name? How can you tell?" Most of Jewell's body was covered by the blanket. Even a pillow was tossed over her head.

Penni snorted. "I'm a girl, but even I can recognize that ass."

Jewell turned in a huff on the bed. "If you're discussing my ass, shut the fucking the door. I've got an hour before I have to get ready church."

She laughed as Jackal closed the door.

"I'll check on Hennessy. Don't forget my coffee."

"I won't." She started down the hallway, seeing Train standing in his doorway, his jeans now on. "Morning, Train." Damn, now she remembered why she was in love with Train. His body would make any woman stand up and howl.

He didn't speak, only nodded his head.

Jackal's expression became thunderous when he caught her captivated gaze. Penni just shrugged, leaving the three behind as she hurried toward the kitchen.

Genny turned her head at her approach. "Did you have any trouble?"

"No. He said thank you." Or he would have if he had any manners.

Penni barely had time to pour a cup of coffee before Jackal showed up. She had just handed it to him when Train came in. Penni conveniently forgot Train as she hurriedly gave Jackal his coffee then went to the counter for the cinnamon rolls, putting them down in front of him.

"I thought those were for Shade," Genny said as she carefully maneuvered a hot pan she had taken out of the oven.

Penni bit down the inside of her cheek to keep from flushing. "I forgot Shade's on a diet."

"Oh...What about Lily?"

Could the woman give her a break? Penni rolled her eyes behind the men's backs.

"Uh...Okay..." Genny muttered. "I'm getting ready to add icing; you can bring Lily some of those."

Penni took the opportunity Genny had given her to save face.

"They'll be warm," Penni agreed as if that had been the plan along.

Penni took a seat at the table. Neither man noticed. Jackal was too busy eating his food, and Train was watching them. Did he think they would make out at the table?

"Shade awake?" she asked Train.

Train lowered his coffee to the table. "How should I know?"

"I thought you might have texted him since you saw me kissing Jackal...the way you did last night."

"He's your brother. He wants to make sure you don't get hurt." Train didn't deny it.

"I'm twenty-four, not sixteen and never been kissed."

"There's a big difference between Jackal and most of the men you've dated."

"How do you know what kind of men I've dated?"

Train didn't answer the loaded question.

"Shade doesn't even know me, and neither do you. I'm a grown woman. When Shade was a mess because Lily wouldn't give him the time of day, I was the one who kept him from making a mistake. My love life is none of your business, and

I don't need you tattling every five seconds. If Shade wants to know something I'm doing, tell him to ask me his own damn self."

"I will." Train stood, leaving the kitchen.

Penni looked at the swinging door Train had gone through. "I screwed up, didn't I?" Penni asked Jackal, who had torn a cinnamon roll in two pieces, handing the other half to her.

"It could have gone better."

"I better go apologize."

"Sit still. You wanted Train to see you as your own person, not Shade's sister. You've accomplished that. Don't whine about it now."

He was right. It was time Train recognized her as a woman. Whether that determined if they would develop a relationship or not, she had to find out. She couldn't stay in limbo forever. Penni's biggest fear was that life would pass her by in a blink. What if she died in a car accident or any other crazy shit she had a habit of finding herself in before she'd had a chance to make love?

"I finished breakfast," Genny informed them. "I'm going home to get ready for church if none of you need anything."

"No, thank you. I'll see you in church."

Genny didn't seem overjoyed that she would see her there. Penni made a mental note to ask Shade about her.

Genny departed, leaving her alone with Jackal.

"I better go get dressed, too." Penni rose, carrying her cup to the sink.

"What time does church start?"

Penni almost dropped her cup. "You're going?"

"How would it look if I didn't sit in the pew with you?"

"Shade doesn't go to church with Lily."

"I don't mind church. Just don't ask me to give witness or eat dinner with the pastor."

"Too late. You had dinner with him last night." When he looked confused, Penni explained, "Lucky is the pastor."

"And he lives with The Last Riders?"

Penni nodded. "Yes. That's his house they're building next to Razer's."

"And he's a pastor?" Jackal repeated. "He's married to Willa, the woman who makes cakes and cupcakes?"

"Yes."

"The one who makes the peanut butter candy?"

"Yes." Was that a twitch of jealousy that had her clenching her nails against her palms at the rapturous look that came over his face?

"Rider had five pieces of it. Stingy fucker only gave me half of one. That woman knows the way to a man's heart."

"Really? Peanut butter candy and you're for the taking?" Snidely, Penny wondered if her shoe would fit up his ass.

"Hell, nah. The way to my heart is through my dick."

CHAPTER TWENTY-TWO

"Are you going to the diner for lunch?"

Jackal stood in the background as Penni talked to her friends. Strangely, he didn't feel uncomfortable in his jeans and T-shirt. The parishioners were dressed in everything from their Sunday best to jeans and T-shirts.

"No, I'm going to drive to Cash's house and see Rachel and the new baby. I want to introduce her to Jackal." She waved her hand toward him. The pale, blonde woman stared at him curiously as Penni tugged him closer. "Beth, I know you've been busy with the boys having the stomach flu, so this is Jackal, a friend of mine. Jackal, this is Lily's sister."

Jackal shook her outstretched hand. The woman was surprised, and from the looks of the other women gathered around her, she wasn't the only one.

"It's nice to meet you."

Jackal wasn't given the time to say anything else before Penni led him to her rental car.

Viper gave him a glare as he ducked into the front seat, and Jackal pulled down the sun visor to shield Viper's unhappiness that he had left the clubhouse despite his orders.

"If I disappear, make sure you call the cops."

"That wouldn't do you any good. Knox is the sheriff."

"I should get hazard pay for pretending to be your boyfriend."

"It could be worse; you could really be my boyfriend."

"I've seen some of the men you've gone out with. You'd never pick a guy like me if you weren't trying to make Train jealous."

"Why not?" She took her eyes away from the road to shoot him a frowning glance.

"Because I don't kiss your ass."

"Don't be stupid. Do you see Train making any effort to kiss my ass? That's not my priority in a relationship."

"So what about Train does it for you?"

"Train doesn't talk a lot, but when he's with you, you know you're safe. I've known him since I was a kid, and he's never treated me like I was stupid or an inconvenience. When I wanted to shoot a gun, he taught me how. When I wanted to ride on Shade's motorcycle, he sneaked me out of the house and taught me."

"You can ride a motorcycle?"

"No, but he tried. He made up reasons his bike was getting scratched up, and Shade found out. Then he talked Shade into letting him teach me. I gave up after a week."

"So he was like Shade except nicer?"

Penni turned onto a smaller road that was off to the side. The house she pulled in front of was secluded. No one would even know it was there unless they had searched for it. Large trees surrounded the property, and the cabin blended into its surroundings.

"Nice." Jackal got out of the car, walking beside Penni as they reached the front door.

"It's Cash's family home. When Rachel and him got married, they added a couple of bedrooms and the road." Penni knocked on the door.

A gorgeous red head answered the door.

"Hi, Rachel. I heard you decided to have the baby a couple of weeks early."

"Thank God, too. If I kept eating that cornbread Cash was making for our dinner every night, I would be as big as our house."

The two women hugged before moving away from the door and entering the house. Jackal found himself receiving a curious stare as Rachel and Penni sat down on the living room couch.

"This is Jackal."

Rachel gave him a welcoming smile. "So he's your new boy-friend that everyone is talking about?"

"That was quick. The gossips must have texted you before I got in the car."

"It gives them something new to talk about."

"I thought The Last Riders kept the town gossips busy."

Rachel shook her head. "They're too afraid of them to gossip, but your fair game. You're an outsider, and you tend to make a stir when you come for a visit."

"They're exaggerating. When I came to town the last time, nothing happened."

"That's only because you didn't cook, and everyone refused to drink anything you made them. Sex Piston's gang refuses to come to Treepoint if Beth tells them you're in town."

"Sex Piston?" Jackal inquired. He needed to meet the woman. She sounded perfect for Stump.

"You're better off not knowing," Cash said as he came in from a room off the living room, carrying a small baby against his chest. He shook his head when Penni started to explain and said, "She's getting fussy."

Rachel reached up, taking the sleeping infant from his chest. "You couldn't wait for your coffee?"

He bent over, placing a kiss on her cheek. "Want me to get you something?"

"No thanks."

Jackal looked back and forth from the couple. He had researched The Last Riders when he had become interested in Penni. Shade's military record was buried, which had cost King a fortune to find out. Cash's exploits were well documented. The bastard was lethal. He had been a SEAL, and the commendations he had earned in the military had made him a force to be reckoned with as the clubs' lieutenant.

His own father had a brief stint in the military before he had joined a bike gang that consisted of wannabes and drug addicts. It gave them the opportunity to steal money to buy their drugs and little else.

Cash walked across the room, opening a door and leaning in. "You want a cup of coffee, Mag?"

Jackal couldn't see the occupant of the room, but the voice coming from it had him shifting, trying to see inside.

"Lord, why am I still here?"

Rachel smiled, seeing Jackal's concern at that remark. "She's in her nineties. Mag thinks that's long enough."

"You want me to help you into your wheelchair? Penni came for a visit."

"Did she bring any moonshine?" Mag asked.

"No."

"Lord, why am I still here?"

"She brought a friend," Cash added.

"Is he my age?"

"No."

"Is it the pastor?"

"No."

"Lord, why am I—"

"Rachel is going to make some fried chicken for lunch."

"Give me my wheelchair."

A few minutes later, Cash wheeled a feisty grey-haired woman into the living room. She treated him to a narrowed stare then turned toward Rachel.

"You're holding her wrong." Mag stared at Rachel critically. "Hand Ema to me."

Rachel shook her head, handing the baby to her great-grandmother. "Let Penni hold her for a while. I'll go start lunch."

Rachel and Cash left the room, and the stern expression vanished as the old woman held the child.

"Why didn't you bring me some moonshine?"

Penni lifted her hands. "Tate threatened to take away Greer's new truck if he gave me any."

"Since when has that asshole listened to his brother?"

"He loves that truck."

The woman turned her attention on Jackal. "Who are you?"

"I'm a friend of Penni's."

"You her boyfriend?"

"Kinda."

"What kind of answer is that?"

"She's trying to make up her mind."

Mag looked at him from his head to his boots. "You got a college degree?"

"No."

"You been to prison?"

"Yes."

"What for?" She snapped the questions out as if she were a parole officer.

"Drug possession, a couple of times for extortion, and three times for fighting."

"You're not smart enough not to get caught?"

"It was when I was younger."

She nodded. "How'd you get that scar?"

"My father." Jackal surprised Penni by not giving the smartass reply he gave everyone else.

"Son of a bitch dead?"

"No, he's in prison."

"You put him there?"

"No, he's in prison for assault."

"Can I hold Ema?" Penni chimed in.

"You going to bring me moonshine the next time you come?"

"I'll try," Penni answered, carefully taking the child into her arms and sitting back on the couch.

"You got kids?"

"Lunch is ready," Cash interrupted Mag's interrogation.

Jackal stood up, pausing at the sight of the woman gripping the wheels of her wheelchair, despite Cash trying to push her across the floor. Obviously, no one was going anywhere until the old lady got her answer.

"I don't have any children."

The woman leaned in her chair, satisfied he had answered. If the nosy old bat had been his grandmother, he would have put her ass in a nursing home.

Sitting down at the table, Rachel set a beer next to his plate. "Thought you might need that. My grandmother is kind of hard to take, especially when you're sober."

"I thought she was your grandmother," Jackal questioned Cash.

"She doesn't claim me," Cash said sardonically, twisting off the top of his beer.

Penni held the baby as Rachel filled Mag's plate.

Cash reached for his daughter. "I'll take her."

Penni held the baby closer to her chest. "I'll hold her while you and Rachel eat."

"You sure?"

"Absolutely."

Jackal held out his arms. "I'll take her. I had a big breakfast."

Penni gave him a strange look as she handed the little girl over.

Jackal stared down at the baby. She had a thin layer of red hair across the top of her scalp. Her tiny bow mouth scrunched into a cry, and Jackal tilted her upward so she could see her mama. Her gurgling had him smiling down. "Your mama looks better than me, doesn't she?"

"You're damn comfortable holding a baby for a man who claims not to have any," Mag snapped.

"Mag!" Rachel protested.

"It's okay." Jackal flipped the blanket back over the baby's feet when her movements loosened it. "I have a friend who has several children. Sometimes, he has to work late, and I watch them until he gets off. He's married now, but I'll watch them if they want to go to the movies or something."

"That's nice of you." Penni smiled, placing a big chicken breast on the plate in front of him.

"Damn, girl. He just said he babysat them, not gave birth to them." Mag eyed the food on his plate then the chicken leg Rachel had placed on hers.

"Remember your cholesterol," Cash said then mockingly took a big bite from the largest breast on his plate.

"At my age, cholesterol is the last thing I need to be worried about. A good fart could cause a heart attack."

When Rachel was done eating, she took the baby, and Jackal got up to fill his plate, adding a heaping mound of potatoes.

"I thought you weren't hungry?" Penni watched as he put two biscuits onto his plate.

"I've changed my mind." Jackal buttered his biscuits as Mag took Cash's beer away. "Remind me when I get done eating that I need to make a phone call."

"Who do you need to call?"

"I'm going to cancel my gym membership." If Mag was an example of getting old gracefully, he wanted to die young.

CHAPTER TWENTY-THREE

"Are you sure I'm not disturbing you guys?" Penni heard Genny's question as she mopped the kitchen floor.

Penni grabbed a bottle of water out of the refrigerator, avoiding going downstairs to workout, something she had promised she would do after eating the home cooking that was making her jeans skintight.

Train, Hennessy, Cruz, Jackal, and Rider were sitting at the kitchen table, playing cards while Genny had finished serving lunch and was cleaning the kitchen.

Hennessy looked much better since the day they had arrived two weeks ago. Still, it had taken Rider and Jackal to get the large man down the steps.

As she mopped, Genny brushed against Hennessy chair. He moved his chair to the side, and Genny's arm grazed his shoulder. Penni saw her flinch away to mop farther away from him.

"If you need me to move, just say so."

Genny stopped. "I'm finished." She put the mop in the bucket, carrying them down the stairs.

"I guess she doesn't like to be touched by the black man." Hennessy's snide comment had the men at the table stiffening.

Penni's temper exploded, knowing Genny had heard the comment before she had closed the door. "It had nothing to do with your color; it was your size." Penni slammed her water bottle on the table. "You've been in your bedroom since you got here, so let me you tell for a freaking fact that Genny, nor any of The Last Riders, give a damn what color you are. They didn't care when they saved your life, even though you kidnapped me and kept me hostage. Genny didn't care what color you were when she washed your dirty clothes, cooked your food all week, and even made those cinnamon rolls for your breakfast when she heard how much you liked them. I noticed last night when Knox came over to dinner that she's skittish around him, too. You are a jerk…whatever color you are."

Penni snapped her mouth closed, stomping out of the kitchen and going to the basement. She almost said something to Genny, but from her expression, she could tell she didn't want to talk.

She stretched for a couple minutes then turned on the treadmill.

"Hennessy's just irritated from being cooped up," Jackal said as he came up behind her.

"He had no business taking it out on Genny." Penni turned to see Genny dump a handful of clothes in the dryer.

Jackal raised his hands in surrender. "I'm not disagreeing with you; I'm explaining."

"He's a grown man. He doesn't need you to apologize for him, and I'm not the one who deserves an apology."

"It's okay," Genny said softly.

"No, it's not. The next time you fix him a plate of food, bash him upside his head with it."

"I'll keep that in mind." Genny shook her head. "I'll see you two tomorrow."

Penni waved as Genny left. She would be on her way to work for Willa at the bakery for the rest of the day.

She liked Genny. During the past week, she had spent a portion of every morning with her. It allowed her to give Shade and Lily alone time with John. She felt like she distracted Genny from her work, so Penni would take a couple of her jobs to pass the time. Then they would often share a cup of coffee before Genny left.

Genny was a sweet woman with a good head on her shoulders. She worked two jobs: one for Willa baking, the other cooking and cleaning after The Last Riders. She had saved enough money to purchase Willa's home. There weren't many nineteen-year-olds who could accomplish that. Hell, Penni was twenty-four and had shit for money in her checking account. As soon as she could talk Kaden into giving her a raise, she wanted to save enough money to buy her condo.

Something definable reminded her of Lily. Penni couldn't pinpoint what is was, but like Lily, she kept her secrets to herself.

"Want to play some cards? Hennessy and Rider went upstairs, and Train went to work at the factory."

The Last Riders had a factory next door. When Shade had told her that he was working for them and making survivalist equipment, she had been fascinated. Over the years, she had realized how they had helped people facing natural disaster, often donating their time and equipment. The rest of the club members wouldn't be back until their shifts ended that afternoon.

"No thanks. I don't play cards."

"Why not?"

"Because I win, and people—especially men—are lousy losers."

Jackal laughed as he sat down on the home gym, pulling the bar downward.

Penni watched him out of the corner of her eye. His jeans were low enough that she could she could see his abs. He straddled the seat, lifting the weights effortlessly. Penni was tempted to adjust the weights so she could see a sheen of sweat cover his body.

Watching Jackal's T-shirt play peek-a-boo each time he stretched his arms upward raised her lust to a fever pitch.

"Train doesn't talk much, does he?"

His remark had Penni turning back to him. "Not a lot, no."

"Seems to me Rider would be more your type."

"God, no." Penni shuddered. She wouldn't be able to feed him. The only thing he loved more than food was women. "I'd end up having to cut off his dick if he was my boyfriend."

"He's not into monogamy?"

"What do you think? Rider looks at women the way he looks at a smorgasbord. He wants to try it all."

"From what I can tell, Train eats at the same restaurant."

"Are you trying to piss me off?" Penni sped- up the treadmill.

"No, I'm just trying to understand what you see in him." Jackal let go of the pull down bar to take off his T-shirt.

Penni stopped the treadmill. "Why? So you can make fun of me?"

Jackal raised up from the bench, his hands going to the bars of the treadmill. His taut body had her eyes dropping to his tattoos. There was a grim reaper on his chest with a web of strands leading out of his billowing cowl. The scythe led to his shoulder then down the side of his arm. On his other arm was a skull with a red bandana covering the eyes.

"Why would I make fun of you? Because you're wasting your time on a man who doesn't have a problem finding a woman to warm his bed?"

"So?" Rigidly, she stared back at him.

"Believe me, Train isn't shy. If he wanted you, he wouldn't give a fuck who your brother was or whether they were friends or not. If you're not in his bed, it's because he doesn't want you there."

Penni used her shoulder to push him away. "When I want your advice, I'll ask for it! You don't know shit about Train."

"And neither do you. That's not a red flag to you? That if he wanted you, he would have made a move a long time ago?"

"Quit saying that!" Penni lunged at Jackal, pushing him backward, his words lacerating her pride.

He took a step to get his balance, and she vindictively pushed him again, smiling when he toppled onto the couch next to the treadmill.

Penni spun and turned to go upstairs.

"Oh, no, you don't." Penni found herself pulled backward onto Jackal's lap. "You don't get to be mad at me when I'm telling you the fucking truth."

"I can be mad if I want to. Train and I are none of your business!"

"What business?"

Jackal's sarcastic laugh had Penni's temper rising to a boiling point. She had never lost control of her rage to the degree where all she wanted to do was strike out at him.

Instead of trying to break his hold, she leaned back against his chest, turning her head so she could bite his shoulder.

Sickened by what she had just done, she tried to jump up, but Jackal used her movement to bend her over his knee.

"You did that, knowing I wouldn't bite you back."

"I'm sorry." Penni's temper's cooled, ashamed of herself.

"The next time you bite me, bitch, I'm going to give you a bite you'll never forget."

"Don't call me a bitch!" Her demand ended with a yowl of pain as Jackal's hand came down on her bottom. She was wearing a pair of workout shorts and a thin T-shirt, but he didn't care that the material was thin and flimsy or that she could feel the scalding heat of his palm on her butt.

"Calling you a bitch doesn't give it justice. That was for flicking me off."

Penni had known that incident when they had first seen each other had irritated him.

Another smack landed on her bottom. "That was for you telling Ice to tell me to go fuck myself."

She had known that one had stung.

Penni quickly smothered her chuckle when Jackal's hand returned to continue her punishment. He recounted her other offenses, which she lost count of due to the pain that was radiating from her sore butt.

"That was for leaving Casey's lingerie party before I could show up."

"What? Have you lost your mind?" How was she supposed to know he had wanted to give her a ride home? Thank God she had left before he had arrived. She had been drunk off her ass and had eaten too many of her own brownies. To say that he would have been laid that night would have been an understatement.

Penni's thoughts came back to the present with another whack of his hand.

"Then you stood me up and almost killed me with those bees and the dogs…"

The son of a bitch had already spanked her for that one. Clearly, he hadn't gotten over it.

"Okay, okay. I'm a terrible person." She tensed her buttocks, waiting for his spanking to continue. When it didn't, she looked over her shoulder to see Jackal staring down at his hand on her bottom. He was now massaging her buttocks.

"Does it hurt?"

"If I don't answer, are you going to start spanking me again?"

"No."

"No, it doesn't hurt." Penni slipped out of his grasp, sliding to the floor between his thighs. "My butt has hardened to spankings."

"Who in the hell spanked you?"

Unconsciously, she placed her hands on his thighs. "My mama. I stayed in trouble when I was a little girl. She told me it's a miracle she had any hair left. I got out of the house five times before I was four. The last time, I was at a dangerous intersection when she found me. I would climb anything I could. One time, I went so high up a tree she had to call the fire department. I set the house on fire when I was three."

"She should have watched you better."

Penni shook her head. "I was terrible. I admit it. I was a little hyper. That was probably why Shade brought his friends

194

over whenever he came to visit. They could help keep an eye on me. My mother would spend most of the time trying to catch up on her sleep."

"Your father didn't help watch you?"

"Oh, yes, but when I tried to show him I was old enough to dry my own hair, Mama didn't trust him anymore."

"What was wrong with that?"

"I was standing in the bathtub and had grabbed the blow-dryer when he had reached for a towel. I nearly electrocuted my dad and myself, but he managed to jerk it out from the plug."

Jackal leaned back on the couch, laughing.

Desire flooded through her body, and Penni clenched her thighs together as she knelt on the floor.

Penni giggled, and Jackal leaned forward, covering her mouth with his. Her mind was screaming at her to jerk away, run up the steps, but the urge to respond defeated her common sense.

Pressing into him, she felt her breasts tauten under her thin T-shirt.

Reality became just the two of them as Penni felt the passion she had hoped to find in the men she had dated in the past. They had all been different walks of life, but Jackal walked his own road. He didn't cater to her, yet he had made no effort to hide he was attracted to her. Every time he was near, his eyes would appraise her from head to toe, showing he liked what he saw.

She liked what she saw, too. His body would make any woman drool. If he hadn't been such an asshole, she would have found it difficult not to take him on a twirl and find out where their chemistry led. The only thing that had stopped her was, again, he was an asshole, and the gleam in his eyes had warned her he might be too much to handle.

Her parents had told her that she had never felt fear the way other children did, and it was the truth. She still had that. But where Jackal was concerned, her self-preservation had kicked in.

He circled his hand behind her neck, pulling her more securely against him as he leaned back against the couch until she was across him. Penni circled his shoulders, moaning as he fucked her mouth with his tongue. Her pussy ground down on his dick as she felt it harden beneath her.

Jackal raised his hips up, bringing his hands to her hips and pushing her down on him harder. Then, straightening, Jackal moved his mouth down her skin as he tugged her shirt down. The delicate bra she had on was brushed away, leaving her nipple exposed.

"Fuck me."

Penni couldn't tell if it was an expression or a demand. It took her everything not to echo his feelings.

Jackal licked the tip of her breast until she clenched the hair that brushed against her breast. When he touched her, it made her feel invincible, drowning out all the warnings she had never had trouble following before.

"Don't tease me." His tormenting lips were torturing her nipple, grazing the tip without taking it in his mouth.

"I'm trying to make it good for you."

Penni could feel his back shake. He was laughing at her when she was on fire? When she was done with him, laughing would be the last thing on his mind.

She had parts of his body she wanted to explore. The fleeting glimpses had spurred her on.

Penni went to his chest, sucking his nipple into her mouth.

"What did I tell you about biting me?" Jackal's husky growl had her licking the hard nub before moving down to his waist. His abs had been driving Penni to investigate his ridges and dents until she was forced to stop by the top his jeans. "Don't stop."

"I wasn't going to." Penni lifted up only long enough to unsnap his jeans.

Jackal rubbed his thumb over her nipple as she peeled down his jeans and tugged down his underwear. She was gifted with sight of his cock.

Another woman would have hesitated at the amount of piercings on his cock, but Penni had never been afraid of the unknown.

Her lips brushed the head of his cock, feeling the metal hit her teeth.

"If you bite me—"

"A man with that many piercings isn't afraid of a little pain."

After licking the length of his shaft back to the head, she sucked harder on him, determined to savor every minute she had him under her control. Penni wanted to taste him again and again. Each taste brought him deeper into her mouth.

Jackal gripped the arm of the couch as she covered his cock with her mouth again. Each time she lowered and raised her mouth, she tried to take him deeper, using the same rhythm he had used to tongue-fuck her. Penni had always learned by imitation, and her memory didn't fail her now.

She spread Jackal's jeans wider so she could reach the shaft of his cock, massaging his tightening balls.

"Move…I'm going to come."

Penni tightened her lips around the head as he came, his body tautening as he bucked, driving him farther into her mouth.

She lifted her mouth off him when he stopped moving, and then Penni found herself sitting on his lap with Jackal trying to tug her shorts down.

She jumped to her feet, pulling her T-shirt down.

"Get back here."

Penni shook her head, trying to calm her speeding heart. "I need to go. Lily has company coming in."

Practically running to the stairs, she almost tripped over the first step.

"Sit your ass down on my dick. The only company you're going to see is when I shove my dick up your pussy."

Penni wanted to snap at him but couldn't. Shade was standing at the top of the steps, about to come down.

"Sex Piston and her crew showed up early. Lily wanted me to tell you when you didn't answer your text."

Penni couldn't remember where she had left her cell phone.

"Thanks." She bounded up the steps two at a time as Shade moved away from the door.

Avoiding his eyes, she walked by him, pacing her steps, not wanting Shade to think she was running away.

"Coming?" she asked him.

"No, I usually hide out when they show up."

Penni hesitated, worried that Shade and Jackal would have a confrontation. Jackal wouldn't back down from a confrontation with her brother in the angry mood he was in.

"Go on. Lily's waiting."

Penni escaped. Jackal was on his own. She had her own problems, trying to push away the image of when he had climaxed.

She had never intended to go so far with Jackal, yet one touch of his slick flesh had her wanting more. It had become a compulsion, driving her to do something she had never performed on another man.

She wasn't escaping because she had been embarrassed. Shade had been at the door and hadn't seen anything. She had felt uncomfortable facing Jackal after the sexually-charged atmosphere had heightened, reaching a point that, if she had stayed there much longer, there was no doubt she wouldn't have left the basement a virgin.

Train might not be attracted to her, but Jackal was.

Penni consoled herself. It wasn't like she had any feelings for the man other than his body that she couldn't keep from watching or the way he kissed that was like a shot to her needy libido. She was a red-blooded woman and had only hormones to blame.

"Damn." The way he had looked when he had climaxed had aroused her never before she felt kitten instincts that had made her want to purr. The idea of Jackal being a scratching post had her gigging. A girl knew she was in trouble when she began seeing a man as catnip.

CHAPTER TWENTY-FOUR

What the fuck just happened?

Jackal stood, closing his jeans and wanting to smash the work-out machine against the wall. He'd had every intention of fucking Penni. When she had told him that she would know if Train was her soul mate when she made love to him, Jackal had known the only way to get her to care about him was in the bedroom.

That was why none of the men she had dated had lasted. A man could only handle so much of staring at her mouth and tight, little body before it drove him to lose reason.

Jackal wasn't a betting man, but he would bet many of her dates had ended with the men having cold showers or in another woman's pussy.

"Viper wants to talk to you and Hennessy in his bedroom. Hennessy is already there."

When Shade's face remained stoic, Jackal's frustration got the best of him.

"You have something to get off your chest?" Jackal snapped.

"What should I say?"

"I know that camera at the door outside saw Penni and me fooling around." Jackal had scoped out the clubhouse when he had arrived. There were cameras and alarms at every entrance, and the door to the outside of the basement was equipped with an alarm. That was how The Last Riders had kept Hennessy from escaping. Cruz and the other men would have been able to pack Hennessy downstairs, but Shade and Razer would have easily intercepted anyone who happened to make it through the door's alarms. Viper had made sure the members were both protected and prepared.

"If you saw the camera, then you could see Viper turned it down toward the door."

"That's all you're going to say?"

"What do you want me to say? Penni's an adult; she's always kept her head on shoulders when it comes to men."

"Because she's got her sight on Train, and it wouldn't help anything to jeopardize your friendship."

"Is that what you think? You don't know shit about Train. If he wanted Penni, our friendship wouldn't matter. He's flown countless missions, some which he fought on the ground after his helicopter crashed. If Train wanted Penni, I would be honored to accept him into my family."

"Even though one of those crashes was his fault and killed six members in his crew?"

"If the government believed he was responsible for that crash, why would they hire him for a job overseas?"

"Train's going overseas?"

"He leaves in two weeks."

"Does Penni know?"

"No, it's on a need to know basis. I'm sure you'll tell her now."

"You cold-blooded bastard, you should have told her. You know how she feels about him."

"I'd think you would be happy Train is leaving."

He was, and he wasn't. He wanted Penni alone without her constantly looking for Train. He wanted her to choose him because she wanted him.

"So you want me to do your dirty work for you?"

"Other than being worried about Train being safe, why should she care? Why would she be so upset since you are together now?"

Shade was nobody's fool.

"Does someone ever get over their first love?"

"Train wasn't Penni first love." Who in the hell was, then?

Jackal clenched his teeth. The woman better not have let another man touch her. He'd knock the—

"Train was a crush. If she really wanted him, nothing would stop her. If you are in a relationship with Penni, you're the one who needs to be careful. A man who gets Penni is going to be getting more than they bargained for. And don't think I don't know you're hiding your true colors from her. You're a hot-headed son of a bitch. When she loosens her temper, she can be a handful, but make fucking sure, now that you're in a relationship with her, your true colors don't show, or you'll be dealing me."

"I've been dealing with her temper since I met her. Penni's going to be a part of my life whether you like it or not."

Shade shrugged. "I'm just giving you a warning. Whether you take it or not is up to you."

"Since we're all friendly and shit, I'll give you my own warning: she's going to be my property. If you interfere, I'll take that as a sign of aggression against me and the Predators."

"I don't see any of your brothers backing you right now," Shade mocked.

If he weren't Penni's brother, his snide comment would be the last sentence out of his mouth for the two months it took until his jaw healed. But he was, and Jackal had learned that, whenever Penni felt Shade or The Last Riders had been threatened, it took her a while to get over it.

"My brothers are exactly where I need them to be."

"I'm sure King was glad to see some friends from home."

Jackal didn't deny that several of the Predators were watching The Last Riders. Ice might not be in Treepoint, but he wouldn't leave Jackal without someone who could be there within minutes if he called.

"If we're done shooting the shit, I'm going to see what Viper wants. Trying to argue with you is like trying to watch paint dry. It takes all day."

Shade waved his hand toward the stairs, letting him go first. Jackal didn't hesitate. If Shade attacked a man, he would do it facing him, not from his back.

Jackal knocked before entering Viper's bedroom. Cash, Knox, Lucky, and Hennessy were in the room. The man whose presence surprised him was Ice.

Ice held out his hand and the brothers shook before taking the chairs surrounding the couch on the opposite side of the bed.

"Glad to see you," Jackal said, taking a seat on the couch with Ice sitting next to him. "I didn't think I would see you for a few more days."

"Oceane died. Grace wants to stay with her father and brother. I was in the way, so I decided to get this business finished." Ice's expression was somber. Jackal knew how close Grace was to her parents.

"Penni…"

"Grace is calling her now."

Jackal nodded. He wanted to leave the room and make sure she was okay, but from the faces surrounding them, the men had more important things to discuss. As enforcer, he had to stay with Ice, regardless of whether his woman needed him or not.

Viper sat down on one of the chairs with Shade taking the one next to him.

"I'll take the door," Cash said, leaving the room. Jackal knew Viper wouldn't want any of the women coming in to disturb the meeting about to take place.

"Why didn't you call Shade when you found out she had been kidnapped?" Viper started the meeting between the two heads of their clubs.

Ice sat forward on the couch, his hands resting on his thighs. "I was going to call and let you deal with the Road Kingz, but Hennessy used to be a brother, and Jackal convinced me to let him handle it. Hennessy saved Jackal's life when a deal went down the shithole, and Jackal felt he owed him. He didn't want Shade killing him."

"I didn't need his help," Hennessy broke into the conversation.

"Shut up," Ice ordered. "You can answer to Viper for kidnapping Penni. I'm explaining my own actions in this cluster-fuck."

"Penni could have been killed or hurt if I hadn't shown up when I did." Viper's controlled rage had all the men tensing.

"I didn't expect him to piss off another fucking club or that he was balls deep in bed with a cartel." Ice remained unflustered, giving Viper the time he needed to vent.

They had screwed up, and now they were going to man up, whether they wanted to listen to his recriminations or not.

Viper looked at Hennessy. "Now you want me to talk?"

"It would be to your advantage."

Before Hennessy could answer, a knock came to the door, and two men Jackal had never met before entered.

"This is Stud and Cade. Stud is the President of the Blue Horsemen."

"How many biker clubs does this bitch know?" Hennessy asked, running his hand over his bald head.

"Stud and Cade aren't here because of Penni. They're here because of the cartel," Viper explained, his mouth twitching at Hennessy's aggravated expression.

Cade took a step forward. "The cartel is responsible for my wife's father and her sister's death. If they've targeted you, you're not going to get away from them alive."

Jackal looked at the grim faces in the room. All this shit for nothing. Hennessy's club wasn't big enough to deal with the fallout from the cartel and The Last Riders. One was bad enough; two was the end. Hennessy's fixed stare said he knew it, too.

"The Blue Horsemen are willing to help. Fat Louise deserves justice for her family being killed. She risked her life to save her sister from her husband's cartel and bring her back from Mexico."

"We're willing to help, too." Viper nodded.

Hennessy's surprised gaze swung to Viper. "Why would you help?"

"Two reasons: Shade found out the reason you took Penni as hostage was to get drugs back from one of your members who had bought them from the cartel behind your back. Shade said you had no idea that the member had commissioned the drug sale."

"I didn't, but DJ was like flesh and blood to me. I couldn't leave him high and dry."

"Instead, another of the Road Kingz killed him," Shade remarked, going to the small fridge and taking out a bottled water, giving it to Hennessy.

"Yes, I made sure he didn't have any money to buy drugs for himself. I thought he was clean. When I found the drugs in his room and saw he was high, he admitted what he had done. Then I set up the buy with Striker. Since then, it's been one cluster-fuck after another."

"The Silva Cartel is extremely dangerous. Not only do they have a lot of manpower, but they have the Unjust Soldiers to do their dirty work in the States," Lucky commented, leaning against the wall. "If we're going to do this, The Last Riders, Stud's club, and yours will have to take precautions. Not only will they try to attack the clubhouses, but anyone who is connected to them. That means the women or any assets the clubs may have."

"Shit. They're that strong?" Jackal should be worried about the Predators, but it was a blonde his thoughts shifted to.

Lucky looked at Viper who nodded his head. "I dealt with this cartel once before," he admitted. "It was six years ago. I was involved with a task force to stop them from smuggling women out of the United States. We arrested the smugglers but couldn't lay our hands on the cartel. I'd like to even the score for those women and Fat Louise.

"With your help, we could lure them to Treepoint and take them down once and for all. Viper's on top of the security here, but can your clubs handle the fallout?"

Stud, Ice, and Hennessy stared at each other.

"So you're going to use the Road Kingz as bait?" Hennessy asked Viper.

"Yes."

"If my club helps, then you let us leave without any blow-back for Penni?"

"None."

"Then let's fucking get it on, brother."

CHAPTER TWENTY-FIVE

The sound of laughter hit her when she entered Shade's home. Sex Piston's little boy and Beth's twin boys were sitting on the floor, playing with John. The women were in the kitchen and in the dining room, making a picnic, and Fat Louise was sitting on the rocking chair, watching the children.

"You look fabulous," Penni complimented. The woman glowed with happiness. She looked like she was pregnant with a small basketball.

"I look huge." Fat Louise smiled, patting her pregnant belly.

"It's not much longer, is it?"

"Three more months."

"Enjoy. Lily didn't sleep the first four months with John."

"I keep telling myself that."

"I'm going upstairs to change." Penni waved at Sex Piston, Crazy Bitch, Killyama, and Beth as she went up the steps.

She hurried through a shower then slipped on a pair of faded jeans and a flowery top that swung as she moved. Picking up her cell phone, she saw a message she had missed from Lily and a call from Grace.

Sitting down on the side of the bed, she dialed Grace's number.

"What's up, girl? If you're calling me to tell me you can't come back to work yet, I've told you to take—"

"Oceane passed away." Her friend's voice was husky and held a wealth of pain.

"I'm so sorry, Grace. I'm packing my suitcase. I can be there in—"

"No, stay in Treepoint. My dad isn't handling it well. I need to concentrate on him right now."

"What about you? You're important, too."

"I'm fine. Ice stayed and helped me, but we both agreed that Dad and Dax wanted to be alone. I'll stay here for a couple of weeks before I come home. My dad's so angry, Penni." Grace's voice dropped. "I've never seen him like this."

"I wish you would let me come. I could make you some brownies."

"Chocolate won't fix this."

"Not even my special ones?" Penni teased, trying to lighten the conversation.

A small laugh came across the line. "Text me the recipe; I'll make them for my dad."

They continued to talk for several minutes, Penni promising she would call her again tonight.

"Take care."

"I will. Thanks, Penni."

She disconnected the call, thinking of the beautiful woman who was going to be missed so badly by her family.

Penni went downstairs to see the women had moved out to the yard. She stood on the porch, watching the children play, before she walked to the picnic tables where the food had been laid out.

Lily sent her a searching look as she picked up a celery stick to nibble on. "What's wrong?" Lily had been her friend long enough to know when something was wrong.

"Grace's mother passed away."

"I'm sorry." The women sympathized.

"I didn't know her very well. I had only met her a couple of times when she visited at work."

"Are you going to be leaving?" Killyama asked a little to enthusiastically, Penni thought.

"No, she wants time to be alone with her family."

Lily squeezed her hand. "I'm sure she'll reach out if she needs you."

Penni nodded, taking another celery stick before looking dead on at Killyama. "I thought you swore not to come to Treepoint when I was visiting."

"I made the bitches show me everything they put into the food. I didn't trust you not to put something in it that would fuck me up."

"I didn't mean for you to get alcohol poisoning."

"You sure?" Killyama stared at her doubtfully.

"Why would I want to get you sick?"

Killyama reached for the vegetable platter, picking up her own celery stick. "Maybe because Lily told you Train took me for a ride, and I fucked him stupid."

Lily grabbed Penni's arm. "And you haven't been out with him since. You told me you can't stand him."

"I can't."

Penni was unconvinced by her denial. From the way the other women looked, they didn't believe her, either.

"You told her I had a crush on Train?" Penni turned to look at Lily, hurt that her friend had betrayed her trust.

"I did not. I wouldn't do that."

"Then how would they know—"

"Bitch, it doesn't take a rocket scientist to see the way you look at him."

"Oh…" Penni had no intention of getting in a bitch fight with Killyama. Number one, she was smart enough to know she wouldn't win. The woman had been born knowing how to insult others. The second reason was, she might deny she cared about Train, but she did. Killyama was as transparent as she was where Train was concerned.

"You going to fight it out or eat lunch?" Fat Louise stood behind Killyama, trying to reach around for the potato salad.

"No one's going to fight. Besides, there's no need to fight anymore. Penni has a boyfriend."

"Who?" Killyama asked, taking a seat at the picnic table.

"Jackal." Penni thought his name slipped off her tongue too easily.

"You cook for him yet?" Crazy Bitch asked, moving her plate away from Fat Louise when she tried to take the last roll off her plate.

"No."

"Give him my number. When he does, your boyfriend will be looking for another woman. I'm not much of a cook, but at least I won't kill him." Crazy Bitch nearly knocked Fat Louise off her feet when she elbowed her arm, laughing at her own joke.

"The next time I make the candy Willa gave me the recipe for, I won't let any of you have any," Penni bragged, knowing that would take the wind out of their over blown egos.

"She gave you the recipe?" Lily asked enviously.

"Yep, and I'm not sharing. She made me promise." Willa had laughingly told her to make it when she needed to steal a man's heart. Jackal had asked her about it twice since he had been at the clubhouse.

"You gonna put pot in it, too? Hell, you'll take the whole Last Riders' clubhouse down." Killyama's sarcastic comment fell on deaf ears as Lily, Beth, and Sex Piston began talking about planning Fat Louise's baby shower.

Several of the men came out, carrying their lunches from the clubhouse, which Genny had made. Penni volunteered to get more drinks.

"Bring me a beer, and make sure the cap is on it."

Penni wanted to dump her artichoke dip on Killyama's head. Instead, Penni went inside to the refrigerator.

While taking out the pitcher of tea and a beer for Killyama, Penni overheard Genny and Viper talking in the dining room. Jackal, Train, Rider, and Hennessy were also in there, eating their lunches. Penni could tell Genny was very upset from the way she was shaking her head.

"I don't want to move here. I have my own house."

"It's only for a couple of weeks," Train tried to reassure her.

"No."

Viper wasn't going to take no for an answer. "I wasn't giving you a choice. I'll pay you for the inconvenience."

"It's not about the money. If you need me to work longer hours, I'm okay with that, but I want to go home at night."

Genny's face was pale. She was clearly trying to make Viper listen to reason.

Penni was getting ready to interrupt when Lucky walked up behind her.

"Genny, let's go talk in the front room."

Genny turned toward Lucky, instantly calming and going into the other room with him on her heels.

"What was that about?" Penni asked.

Viper took his attention away from the closed door. "We want Genny to move in to the clubhouse until the trouble with Hennessy is taken care off."

"So why not just say that to her?"

"Because, if I told her there was drugs involved, she would quit. The only reason I'm telling you is because you already know the trouble. Rachel, Mag, and Diamond will be moving in, too."

"What about Evie?"

"Some of the Predators will be staying over there."

"Okay." Penni headed back into the kitchen as Lucky came back into the dining room alone.

"She didn't listen, did she?" Penni could see Genny shoving dishes into the dishwasher.

"No," Lucky confirmed with a set face.

"That house means everything to her. She works her ass off to afford it, so she's not giving in just because men tell her to."

"I'll get Willa to talk to her when she gets off work."

"Or could I make a suggestion?"

"What is it?" Viper asked, becoming irritated at having his plans thwarted. At least he was willing to listen.

"You could ask the Porters to watch her at home."

The men stared back and forth between each other.

"That could work. I was going to pay Genny. I'll pay the Porters, instead, and that way, she could stay home and be protected."

"That's bullshit," Hennessy spoke out. "Just tell her no. Tell her she doesn't have a choice. I'd never let a woman tell me no."

Penni clenched her hands. "How well does that work out for you? It's because of you we're all in this mess."

"I'm in this mess because of your crazy-ass, bit—"

Penni strode to the table, placing her palms on the table in front of him. "You're blaming me?" Penni was getting fed up with people blaming her for everything. "If your little dick is as small as how much you know about women, I have someone I want to introduce you to. You're a match made in heaven. Either you will teach her some manners, or you will kill each other. Either way, it's a win-win situation."

Penni was furious at Hennessy for blaming her, and she was mad at Jackal who hadn't met her eyes when she had entered the room, nor had he taken up for her at Hennessy's insinuation.

Penni stormed out of the room, going to the kitchen to take the tea and beer outside.

Killyama took the beer from her when she finally made it out there.

"What took you so long? The beer's hot." She checked the top to make sure it hadn't been tampered with.

Penni tightened her hand on the pitcher of iced tea. *Don't do it. Don't do it*, she kept telling herself.

"Hand me those celery sticks, bitch."

Fuck it.

CHAPTER TWENTY-SIX

"Who's she talking about?" Jackal looked at Viper after Penni had left the room.

"You don't want to know," Viper answered.

"What do you think of Penni's suggestion?"

"I'll get Shade to go talk to the Porters when he gets back from talking to King."

"Genny should be here where no one can get to her." Hennessy shifted his weight, rubbing his hurt leg.

"If the Porters take the job, Genny will be more protected than she would be here. The Porters are fucking nuts."

Hennessy wasn't pacified, but then screams from outside had them running out the back door.

Jackal barely ducked in time to miss a bowl hitting the frame of the door.

"Dammit, when did they get here?" Viper shouted, wading through the women who were blocking them from seeing what was going on.

Jackal moved to the side, trying to see himself. He didn't care about making anyone mad.

Penni was on the ground, fighting a woman who sitting on her.

"Pull her off, Penni," Jackal said as he tried to reach her.

Viper and Train had each taken an arm, dragging the woman back. Penni used the opportunity to kick out, nailing the woman in the gut.

"Stop, Killyama!" Train fell back when the woman jerked back toward Penni.

"Bitch, I'm gonna kill you."

"Quit calling me a bitch!" Penni screeched.

Rider and Razer made Lily and Beth back away as another woman Jackal didn't know tried to bash Penni's head in with the heel of her shoe.

Jackal reached down toward Penni, trying to help her to her feet at the same time Lucky did.

"Watch her teeth," Jackal tried to warn too late as another woman with jacked-up hair jerked back, her hand bleeding.

He reached down, snatching Penni to her feet as she swung her hands in the air at the two women.

"Come on, Sex Piston and Crazy Bitch; you want some more of me? I'll shove that celery up your ass!" Penni snarled.

"Penni, there are kids are here!" Lily had her hands on her hips as she planted herself so the other women couldn't get to her.

Jackal could see reason come to Penni's eyes as she turned to see a pregnant woman ushering the children into Shade's house with Cade holding John and following her inside.

"Please, Sex Piston, calm down. She didn't mean to pour the tea on Killyama," Lily tried to calm her down again.

"The fuck she didn't." Sex Piston straightened her skin-tight shirt down over her leather pants, hopping on one foot until she took off her shoes. One of the high heels had a broken heel.

Stud steadied her, not removing his hand, either to balance her or hold her back from Penni.

"Want me to get you another beer?" Penni taunted the one named Killyama who had apparently set off World War III.

It was only when Shade and Knox arrived in the midst of the brawl that the men were able to get the women back under control. Jackal managed to get Penni to Shade's front porch as the men ordered the women to clean up the mess they had made. He forced her to sit down on the swing, trying to give her time to gather her control. He didn't want to take her inside. He was afraid she would scare the children.

"Want to tell me what happened?"

"No." Penni used her foot to move the swing. "Lily didn't tell me I wasn't the only one who wanted Train." She'd had a crush on Train for so long she didn't know how to handle it now that she had found out another woman might have the same feelings.

"Why not?"

"She said she thought they hated each other."

"I can see that."

Train and Killyama were yelling at one another right this minute.

"Those women should take anger management classes."

Penni sighed. "To be honest, I started it."

"Because you were jealous over Train?"

"Because I wasn't."

Jackal tensed.

"I don't know why I…" Penni looked away.

"Sucked my dick?"

Penni looked up at the porch ceiling. "Yes."

"Anytime you want to do it again, I'm ready, willing, and able."

"I'm not going to do that again."

"Yes, you will." Jackal stuck out his foot to stop the swing. He expected her to argue, but she was watching Train and Killyama disappear into the gazebo.

"He's never going to love me, is he?"

"No." No, he wouldn't. Jackal himself would make damn sure of that. Train had years to make a move had he wanted to. Jackal was just glad he hadn't. "He's being deployed in two weeks."

She turned to look at him. "How long?"

"I don't know."

"Oh." Penni stood up. "I guess there isn't any need for us to pretend any longer." She started to move toward the door, but Jackal reached out, grabbing her arm.

"You weren't pretending when you kissed me, and you weren't pretending when you went down on me."

"Don't be a jerk." She tried to yank away from him.

"How does me telling you the truth make me a jerk? I'm the one being taken advantage of here."

"What?" Penni asked incredulously.

"Did we have an audience in the basement I didn't know about?"

"No."

"I was real with you when I kissed you. You're the one who doesn't want to admit we have something going on."

"Like what?" she snapped.

"I don't know. If you ever get your head out of your ass and quit worrying about Train, we could find out."

"I don't want to know."

"Why not? Am I not rich enough for you?"

"Money doesn't matter to me!"

"It matters a hell of lot to me. I might not be rich, but I work for Henry as head of security and a bouncer, and I've saved up every dime I've earned off the Predators."

"Selling drugs and God knows what else," she scoffed.

"He does know, and I'm cool with that. We don't sell on the streets. As a matter of fact, the ones we do sell to know what they get is clean and won't get them sent to the ER. And we don't finance cartel or gangbangers. What they do with it after we sell to them is on them. None of us takes that shit, and none of us bring it into the club."

"You're honestly telling me you have a clear conscious?" She gaped at him, no longer trying to pull away.

"I didn't say that. I've done things for the club, but I gave my oath as the enforcer, and I won't break it."

"Whatever it takes?"

"Yes."

"Kidnapping wasn't the worst thing you've ever done, was it?"

"No."

"Have you ever killed someone?"

"Yes."

Each question, she became paler.

"Do you sleep with...?"

"Yes."

"Have you ever raped a woman?"

"No." With that answer, he had a clear conscious. "How do you think Shade would answer the same questions you asked me?"

"Shut up. I'm not talking about him; I'm talking about you."

"You can't excuse Shade for the same offenses and then use them to not have a relationship with me. Are you going to walk away from Shade?"

"No," Penni answered.

"Then don't walk away from me."

"I love Shade." Her eyes met his, and the love he saw within them for her brother was unmistakable.

"How do you feel about me?"

"I don't know." The gaze became troubled, showing her confusion.

"Then let's find out." Jackal rose to his feet, taking her into his arms. "It's good, Penni, really good."

He wanted to slide underneath her defenses until there was no getting away from him. If that meant giving Penni time, he could do that.

She bit her lip, staring up at him. "Can you at least try to not be so bad?"

"I can try."

"Will you try to get along with Shade?"

That took effort to answer. "I'll try."

"There's going to be one deal breaker." She pressed her hands flat on his chest.

"What is it?"

"If I ever find out you're messing around on me, whatever this is between us is over."

"I can live with that." He smiled down at her. He tried to place a kiss on her mouth, but she stopped him.

"I'm serious, Jackal. I hate men who cheat."

Thank God Lily had never complained about that to her. She didn't think she could get past that as much as she loved Shade.

Jackal raised two fingers on his hand. "I promise."

Penni melted against him, her face clearing. "We're going to have to get home before we can seal this deal. I can't...you know...do it in Shade's house."

Jackal straightened. "That could be a couple of weeks. There's a hotel in town."

"I'm not going to lose my virginity in a sleazy hotel."

"Babe, I don't think you can still be a virgin with the size of the dildo you had in your nightstand at home."

Penni began hitting him on his shoulders. "I never used it! I was waiting to...use it for a toy when I was involved with someone."

Jackal dodged her blows. "Damn, I wish I had known that."

"Why?"

"Because I cut it up and threw it away."

"You're joking."

"Nope. Babe, all you need is my dick."

"I thought you saw it? Clearly, you didn't see how big it was."

Penni's giggles stopped when Jackal ran a thumb over her bottom lip.

"I'll tell you what; if you can buy a rubber dick as big as mine that feels as good as mine, I'll buy it for you."

* * *

Jackal squashed another bug that came too close. "How the hell can you handle these bugs?"

Mag smashed one on the banister with a bright purple fly swatter. "It's so bad tonight because it's getting dark, and it just rained." She picked up her glass jar, taking a big drink.

It was his turn to watch the front door. He could easily see down the road from where the house had been built. Viper had made it impossible for anyone to attack the front without being seen. He needed to tell Ice he needed to step up his game.

"You don't want to go inside and play cards?"

Since Cash and Rachel had brought her here, Cash's grand-mother had spent most of her time playing cards and sitting on the front porch. Usually, there were two men posted on duty, but one would invariably make an excuse to leave when she was wheeled out.

"You gonna marry that little girl?"

"She's not little."

She made him a sound like he was a dirty old man. "You know what I meant," she snapped. "Well, are you?"

"Couples don't get married; they live together."

"If a man ever told me that when I was younger, I'd have cut off his balls."

"You know, I found out something interesting about women. They all threaten to cut a man's dick off."

"It's because a man will sit up and take notice when their dick is threatened. A woman cares more about how much a man carries in his back pocket than what's behind his zipper." The old woman sniffed. "Believe me; sex isn't all that."

"Then you've never done it with the right person."

"You offering?"

Jackal discreetly backed up a step or two. "God, no."

Mag cackled. "You're lucky I'm not twenty years younger."

"How did your husband die?" Jackal wondered if it had been with the helping hand of Cash's grandmother.

"God took him with a heart attack."

Jackal sat down on the banister, setting down the glass jar beside him. "You sure it wasn't poisoning?"

Mag was still cackling when Penni and Rachel came outside.

"You behaving, Mag?" Rachel asked.

"What do you think? It's not like I can do shit stuck in this wheelchair."

Penni moved closer to Jackal. Slipping his arm around her waist, he pulled her back against him.

Penni wrinkled her nose up at him. "Is that smell what I think is?"

"No." Mag pressed the glass jar between the side of her wheelchair and her thigh.

"You ready to go inside?" Rachel asked, gripping the back of Mag's wheelchair.

"Might as well. The good Lord might come tonight."

Jackal buried his head between Penni's shoulder blades as Rachel and Mag went inside.

"Did you get Mag drunk?"

"Don't blame me. Greer dropped it off when he passed through on his way to Genny's house."

"Well, if God does come, she won't feel it."

"Rider was supposed to take over an hour ago. Want to sneak me into your bedroom? Or do you want to go upstairs to my room? He can have watch duty for the rest of the night."

"I'm not going to lose my virginity when twenty men could hear it."

Jackal picked up his glass, taking a swig. He would make damn sure they wouldn't hear a thing. The shape he was in, it would take him longer to get it out of his jeans than to actually fuck her.

"Are you drinking moonshine?"

"The whole it's burning in my stomach takes my mind off my dick." Jackal teased the back of her neck.

"Ah... You're so romantic. Uh... Jackal?"

"What?" He crossed his arms over her breasts, pulling her back to his chest.

"Do you see the fire coming from town?"

CHAPTER TWENTY-SEVEN

The dark sky was filled with red flames that could be seen over the trees. Penni moved to the edge of the porch, terrified for Genny. The flames were coming from the direction her house was located.

Jackal's cell phone began ringing, but before he could answer it, Viper, Shade, Ice, and Max ran out the front door.

"Genny's house is on fire," Viper announced, halting as the other men ran down the steps toward their motorcycles. "We're going to check it out. No one other than us gets in or out."

Rider came out the door, taking a position next to Jackal. "Is Genny okay?"

"Yes. Greer and Tate took her to the police station to make sure she was safe while the fire station puts out the fire." With that, Viper ran down the steps, not taking any longer to answer their questions.

"Go inside," Jackal told Penni.

She didn't argue, wanting to be with Lily and John. However, Penni did stop and grab his T-shirt, telling him, "Be careful," trying to tell him she was worried without being all girly.

It was hard for her to know how to react. She had considered him the enemy for so long the new feelings he had roused in her made it difficult to respond to him normally.

Jackal didn't have that problem, though. "Go take care of Lily. I'll be fine."

Penni nodded, reaching toward the sky and trying to pull down any good Karma she could, worried about Genny.

Seeing the room full of men tightened the fear in her chest. They were located at every window, two at the door. The women had been ushered upstairs where Cruz, Hennessy, and Crash stood with guns. The large one in Crash's hands had her rushing through the room and into the kitchen.

"Holy Shit." There were almost as many men in the kitchen as in the living room. Lucky and Train were guarding the back door.

"Where are you going?" Train asked as she drew close.

"Shade's house."

"They're down in the basement with Beth."

Penni nodded before going downstairs.

She steadied her nerves, not wanting Lily to see she was worried.

Bliss, Diamond, Willa, and Winter sat stoically on the couch, Lily held a sleeping John, and Beth paced back and forth, watching their children play. Cash, Razer, Drake, and Stump stood by the door that led to the outside. There were more men upstairs than there were down here to protect the children.

Cash saw her staring at the door with a worried expression and assured her, "The door is steel, and the window is bulletproof. If I hit the button, the door at the top of the steps closes, and no one can get in or out."

"Is it steel, too?" Penni asked, reaching down to pick up the pretty, little girl who had wrapped her arms around her legs.

"Yes." Cash's stony countenance wasn't what she was used.

Penni was surprised that he had been willing to be left behind at the house, but now she knew. He would die to protect every woman and child in the room. All of the men would.

Bliss rose to take the beautiful child in her arms. "Sorry. When Darcy gets tired, she wants to be held."

"I didn't mind."

Penni had met Bliss several times when she had visited Shade, but she had never become friends with her.

The love she held for the little girl she and Drake had adopted as she sat back down, singing softly to her, showed how content Bliss was in her new life.

"Does anyone know what's going on?" Willa murmured, not wanting to wake Darcy who was beginning to fall asleep. "Lucky just told me to stay down here and then went upstairs."

The men hadn't told any of them what was going on, but they had come down here, anyway. It was a testament to the love these women felt toward their husbands—respecting and trusting that it was for their own good.

Unfortunately for them, Penni thought they deserved to know.

"There's a fire at Genny's home." When Willa seemed about to jump off the couch, Penni reassured her, "She's at the sheriff's office; she's fine."

"Thank God." Willa and the women didn't want to alarm the children, so they talked softly.

Willa and Beth carried the children to Lucky's bedroom, settling them so they could sleep as they waited.

"Chance and Noah think it's a sleepover." Beth had given up her pacing to sit down next to Lily, running her head over John's hair. "He gets more beautiful every day. Women aren't going to stand a chance from falling in love with him."

"If he takes after his mama, it will be love at first sight."

"That's not exactly how I remember it." Penni snorted. "You were afraid of your own shadow then. I had to drag you out of the dorm room to go to a party, and you hugged the wall the whole time."

Lily laughed. "I may have been exaggerating a little bit."

"A little?" Penni and the rest of the women laughed with her.

Diamond turned the television on, starting the third movie in the series, *I'm Having a Baby with a Zombie.*

"Uh…Diamond, do you think it's a good idea to watch this now?" Penni really didn't want to watch a zombie movie when the clubhouse was under attack. She personally didn't think that a blood and guts movie would take their mind off their fears.

"If I die, when will I get to watch it again?" she retorted.

Cash, Razer, Drake, and Stump didn't look like they appreciated her humor.

"You're not going to die, but it will take our mind off being worried about Genny." Penni settled down on the other side of Lily. She wanted to call Jackal to see what was going on, but she didn't want to interrupt him.

Once the movie ended, they were about to start another one when Cash stopped them.

"They're back."

Penni followed the women upstairs, anxious to find out what had happened.

The living room was crowded, so Penni stood in the open doorway. She could barely see Genny shivering beneath a blanket.

"I'll make some coffee," Penni said to no one in particular, turning toward the kitchen and filling the empty pot.

Viper led Genny to the kitchen table, telling everyone, "Go to bed. The fire is out. Train, Rider, and Max will keep an eye on the house."

The crowd began to dissipate.

Willa sat down next to Genny, taking her hands in her own. "What happened?"

"Greer took Genny to the grocery store. When he came back, he saw someone had been in the house. He got her out as the house exploded. Knox said the fire department thinks it was a gas leak." Viper put an arm around Winter's shoulder.

Penni stared at Genny in horror. She knew how much the woman had loved her new home.

"Was it intentional?"

"Yes," Viper revealed the answer everyone had been waiting for.

Genny buried her face in her hands, which were shaking.

Hennessy, who was standing by the kitchen door, slammed his fist into the door, making it swing madly. The wood splintered as the door parted from the doorjamb then leaned drunkenly to one side.

"I take it that one wasn't made out of steel," Penni muttered to Cash as she passed him to gather coffee cups.

"I must have missed that one."

Penni passed out coffee to the ones left in the kitchen. Ice and Jackal stood by themselves, shaking their heads when she offered them some.

"How did you get so dirty?" she asked Jackal. His face was covered in grime, his T-shirt was ripped, and his jeans were torn almost completely off.

"Genny had a new kitten that became scared when she tried to catch it. It climbed a tree, and I tried to get it down."

"Where is it?" Penni looked at Genny who was still crying helplessly in Willa's arms.

"When I tried to get it, it jumped down and ran into the road."

Penni wanted to tell her how sorry she was, but she didn't want to bother her and Willa. Plus, she was gradually getting herself under control.

When she managed to quit crying, Penni went to her, patting her shoulder. "Let's go get you cleaned up. You can share my room at Shade's home. There are twin beds. I promise not to snore."

"Go ahead," Willa urged. "You'll feel better when you get the smell of smoke off you."

Genny nodded, letting Penni lead her away.

At Shade's, she gave Genny a nightgown to wear and showed her the bathroom before leaving her alone.

Penni rubbed her aching brow. Genny seemed so fragile. She had told Penni that she had been in foster care before finding jobs in town after she turned eighteen. Penni hadn't pried to see why she had been in foster care. After all, Genny was private and didn't like talking about herself.

Penni knew she and Willa had a close relationship, but even when they had hung out together in the kitchen, Genny had seemed solitary. It hadn't taken long to realize who Genny reminded her of.

It was Lily. Her best friend had never shared secrets with her, and Penni didn't see it happening with Genny, either.

Genny took the spare bed when she came back into the room, burrowing beneath the covers.

"I'm sorry about your kitten."

Her only answer was a lone tear steaking down Genny's cheek.

"Can I get you something to drink?"

"No, I'm just going to go to sleep. I have to be up at six for work."

"You're not going to work tomorrow—"

"Yes. It will take mind off Smokey." A sob caught in her throat. "I jinxed him by calling him that."

"No, you didn't," Penni soothed her, turning the light off. "I'm going to watch some television downstairs. I'll make sure not to bother you when I come back." She wanted to give Genny some privacy to take in what had happened tonight.

"Thank you."

Penni softly closed door, turning to see Shade carrying John to his room with Lily following as she went to their bedroom.

"How is she?" Lily asked quietly.

"Not good. I wanted to leave her alone for a while. I'm not sleepy, anyway. I'll see you in the morning."

"Good night." Lily went into the bedroom where Shade was leaning over John's crib, watching him sleep.

"How bad was the fire?" Penni asked when Shade came out.

They moved to the edge of the stairs so the women couldn't hear them.

"It's gutted."

"Her insurance will—"

"Genny bought the house a few months ago. Willa practically gave it to her. Even with the insurance, Genny can't afford to buy another one."

"Surely, you and the rest of The Last Riders can help? I can, too."

"We already have. She refused our offer. She knows we're the reason the house was destroyed."

"It just happened. Give it a couple of days, and hopefully, she'll change her mind."

"I hope so. I'm going to bed."

When he turned away, she blurted, "Shade, when is this going to be over? I can't stay indefinitely. I need to get back to work."

"It won't be much longer. The fire showed they're getting frustrated because they can't get close to us. They'll make a mistake, and we'll have them. Until then, you're staying."

"Yes, sir." Penni snapped a salute before she sauntered down the steps.

Shade leaned over the stair railing. "You're not too old to get spanked."

"That's what Jackal said." Penni started to provoke Shade for his overbearing attitude then thought better of it. "Never mind."

"Thanks. That was a TMI."

"Sorry, I'll be more careful next time." She was smart enough not to poke a tired tiger when he was getting ready to go to bed.

Penni was about to sit on the couch when she heard a knock on the door. Raising the curtain, she saw Jackal standing outside.

Penni opened the door and went outside, afraid that their voices would keep Shade from going to sleep.

"I wanted to kiss you good night."

Before she could respond, Jackal placed a scorching kiss on her lips.

"Damn, how's that supposed to help me sleep?" she mumbled around his lips.

"Too much?" Jackal eased the pressure on her lips to place a tender kiss on the corner of her mouth.

"Not enough." Penni jerked his face back to hers, not waiting for an invitation.

She tugged at his bottom lip, making room to explore his mouth, while pressing her hands on his chest.

Every time they kissed, she discovered something new about Jackal. His body would tense as if he were holding himself back. It was exciting to have a man who wanted you so badly he found it hard to control himself. Penni felt the same way toward Jackal. Invariably, she was the one who was unable to control herself.

"Let's go to the hotel," Penni panted out when she broke the kiss.

Jackal groaned. "Now you want to give in? Ice is waiting for me to talk."

"It can't wait until tomorrow?" She raised her hips up to notch her pussy against the bulge she could feel straining against her.

Jackal pressed his forehead against hers. "It could, but I don't want Ice interrupting when I'm fucking you."

"I can wait until you're done." Penni couldn't understand the sense of urgency that was filling her with dread.

"I've waited years to get you in my bed, so I can wait one more night to make it good for you."

Penni laid her head on his chest. "I can't change your mind?"

"You can, but Ice will change it back if I keep him waiting much longer."

Penni sighed, giving him a parting kiss.

"You going to dream about me?"

"I don't have dreams," she confessed.

"Everyone has dreams. You must not remember when you wake up."

"I don't." Penni shrugged.

It was when she had heard children describe their dreams or nightmares in school that she had realized how unusual it was not to have them.

"You won't have that problem after tomorrow night. I'm going to make your first time so memorable you'll dream about it every night."

Penni burst out laughing. Slapping her hand over her mouth, she turned toward the house to make sure she hadn't woken the others up. When she turned back toward Jackal, she could make out his scar in the darkness. She thought his powerful silhouette seemed more sinister than what most women would consider dream-worthy.

"Maybe you'll be the one dreaming of me."

"Babe, that's nothing new. I dream of you every night."

CHAPTER TWENTY-EIGHT

Ice was waiting for him at the picnic tables. The front door was being guarded by two of Viper's men, while Ice had offered to watch the back.

"What do you think?" Ice asked at his approach.

Jackal knew something was wrong when Ice had told him he wanted to talk where no one could hear them.

"I think it's a little convenient that they managed to rig the gas when no one was watching. Viper installed security cameras when Genny was at work after she refused to move into the clubhouse."

"Viper said he checked the security camera. Whoever it was came in through a window. They managed to avoid the security camera and knew to set the fire when Greer and Genny left the house."

"Someone's feeding them information."

"Yeah." Ice sat down on top of the picnic table.

"Any idea who?"

"No, and neither does Viper. This place is as tight a drum. Viper said his club in Ohio is, too."

The men remained silent, staring into the dark night. Jackal speculated on who would have the opportunity to know exactly when Genny was going to the store.

"I'll talk to her in the morning. She cooks breakfast for the men," Jackal informed.

"Viper's checking everyone's cell phone, but it's going to take a couple days to get the information."

"We don't have two days." The person who had leaked the information of Genny going to the grocery store was a time bomb. The details provided could prove to be fatal to another member, either in Treepoint, Ohio, or Queen City. Jackal didn't want to take that chance.

"No. The cartel wants Hennessy dead. To them, he stole their drugs without any intention of paying. Then, when they used the Unjust Soldiers to get them back, The Last Riders succeeded in taking out more of their men than they expected. It was the final nail in his coffin."

Jackal sighed. "I told Hennessy to walk away from DJ."

"He didn't listen to your advice any more than when I told you the same thing about Hennessy."

"Hennessy's a good enough leader that he can turn the Road Kingz into a club to be reckoned with. I didn't want him holding the grudge against the Predators for throwing him out. I still don't."

"If we don't stop the cartel, you're not going to have to worry about Hennessy much longer."

Jackal raked his hair back.

Ice rested a booted foot on one of the picnic benches. "It has to be one of the women."

"Why?" Jackal asked.

"Genny doesn't talk to any of the men except Lucky, and I trust him."

"I do, too."

"Which means one of the women sold The Last Riders out."

"Maybe no money was involved," Jackal suggested.

Ice gave a whistle. "Cade said they use any means necessary to get what they want."

"I'll ask Shade to get information on them, but I already know he won't tell me. He'll recheck them himself. I can use my connections, but again, that takes time."

"When you want information from a woman, there's more than one way to skin a cat."

Jackal nodded, his mind going back to last night when Penni had told him that being with another woman was a deal breaker.

"Rider told me the women can't be with a man who doesn't belong to The Last Riders. The one I can talk into breaking their oath will be the one betraying the club."

"Bingo."

"Fuck me," Jackal cursed.

Ice stood up, smacking him on the back. "Sorry, but the sooner, the better. Whichever bitch is doing it could get us all killed."

"When Penni finds out, I'll wish I were dead."

"Not many men would complain about putting their dick on the line for their club."

"Stump could do it."

"You want to put your faith in Stump? He's more likely to get us killed before the cartel has a chance."

Stump loved to fuck, and women smelled it on him. He could talk a woman out of her panties with her husband within earshot. The man had caused more fights than any other man in the club. There were always numerous boyfriends or husbands who had come searching for revenge, and because he loved to fight as much as he loved to fuck, he usually ended up behind bars for a couple months out of the year. The only reason he hadn't been on the wrong end of a bullet was his connection to the Predators.

"Think about it. It's not like you have to make a decision tonight; all the women are settled for the night. Talk to Genny in the morning." Ice shrugged. "You might have to do it, but then again, you might catch a break and figure out who fed the information to the cartel."

"Since when have I ever caught a fucking break?"

"When you became a Predator."

"You don't know Penni. Any chance I have with her will be gone. She's like no other I've met before. How did you feel when you lost Grace?"

Ice had cheated on Grace to prove to the men that he wasn't fucked in the head after what had happened to him in prison. And Jackal had been one of the men who had expected him to prove himself.

"Brother, I could order you to fuck the bitches, but I know you're going to do what's best for the club. Just as I did." He nodded with an evil grin. "Payback is a bitch."

In other words, the choice Ice was offering him was no choice at all.

* * *

Jackal shook off his sleep as he entered the kitchen where Genny was already at work, and it was only ten to six.

"Any coffee?"

"It just finished." Genny nodded at the coffee pot.

Jackal liked the girl. She would cook for the men, but she wouldn't let them take advantage of her.

"I have a favor to ask," Jackal told her, standing at the counter as he blew on his coffee.

"What do you need?"

"Can you remember who you told you were going to the store yesterday?"

"Viper already asked that question, and he still has my cell phone."

"Humor me. Maybe you forgot someone."

Genny shook her head, shoving a baking sheet of hash browns into the oven. "No, because I didn't tell anyone."

"So it was a random trip to the store?"

Genny frowned. "No, Willa had gotten a large order for her chocolate cookies, and we were out of chocolate chips, so she asked me to pick them up and bring them when I came in today."

"Did anyone hear her asking you?"

"Everyone; it was right after lunch."

Fuck, he was right. He wasn't going to catch a break.

"Can you at least make me a note of the women who were there?"

"That, I can do."

Jackal sat down at the kitchen table, watching her work on the note as she cooked. Ten minutes later, she handed him the list.

He glanced at the names as he refilled his cup. He had already memorized the names of the women.

"Can I borrow your pencil?"

Genny shrugged. "Help yourself."

Jackal crossed out the names of the women who were married, figuring if any of them were the one who had betrayed them, then they were already fucked. That whittled down the list.

"You sure this is all of them? You didn't leave anyone out?"

Genny nodded. "I'm sure."

That left him with Ember, Raci, and Jewell. It could be worse. As many women as they had, the number could have been much higher.

Jackal pulled out his cell phone, pulling up the text Viper had sent him last night of the employee's work schedules, thinking how the women all hung around the club room when they got off work.

He stared down at the paper again. Ember had been sleeping with Train more often since he had gotten there, Raci was the friendliest, and Jewell would be the hardest nut to crack. He circled Raci's name, thinking she was least likely, but maybe he could use her to find out about the other two.

Jackal shoved the list in his back pocket as Viper and Ice entered the kitchen, Winter following behind more slowly as she went to the refrigerator.

After taking out a lunch box, she kissed Viper on the cheek. "I'll see you when I get home. Rider's waiting for me in the parking lot. I already texted him and told him I'm on my way."

"I could have taken you."

Winter shook her head, avoiding his gaze. "Stay. I know you have business to discuss." She then left without another word.

Maybe it *was* one of the married women. Jackal had been witnessing the escalated tension in the couple since he had arrived there. Maybe she was sick of playing second fiddle to a group of bikers. Razer and Shade had their own homes, so it could be that Winter was sick of sharing her husband with the men and women twenty-four hours a day.

Jackal knew Winter was one woman he wouldn't be able to trick into revealing anything if she were the one betraying the club. To be honest, he wasn't man enough for that job. Stump wasn't, either. The fear of Viper was enough to shrivel any man's dick.

Jackal waited until Viper and Ice had fixed their plates and went to the main dining room to talk without being overhead.

"Anything new?"

"Shade took Genny's phone after I gave it to him. No one texted her yesterday. Genny didn't have any texts for the last month other than Willa, and those were all work related."

"Damn, I knew it wouldn't be that easy." Jackal stared down at the empty coffee cup in his hands. "I talked to Genny. She said Willa asked her to go to the store yesterday. She made a list for me, and I've managed to narrow it down to Ember, Raci, and Jewel." He had debated over telling Viper, knowing Viper had asked her the same question.

"I'll text Shade and tell him," Ice said. "He's already pulled everyone's messages and phone calls. It will save some time."

"All three women followed the club from Ohio," Viper told them. "I'll call Moon. The clubhouse there is on alert, as well. I'll ask if any had any contact. If Shade and I question the three women, though, it will make them suspicious." Viper pushed his plate away, staring at them.

Jackal didn't respect many men, but Viper was putting the club's safety ahead of his pride, and that was worth his respect.

Ice and Jackal hadn't intended to tell him about their plan. He still didn't, and now he wouldn't have to. Viper already knew.

The three men didn't need to discuss the strategy to catch the traitor; they all knew time wasn't on their side.

"One thing for fucking sure: today is going to be an interesting day." Viper's eyes focused on him.

"Yes, it is."

CHAPTER TWENTY-NINE

Penni brushed the tickle attacking her noise away as she woke up. Blinking, she stared up at the baby blues of her nephew. Lily's giggle had her turning her sleepy gaze toward Lily as she picked up John.

"I'm sorry. He was playing on his blanket when I went to make his breakfast."

Penni raised up on the couch she had fallen asleep on last night after Jackal had left. "That's okay. I didn't mean sleep so late. I'll never get back on schedule when I get back to work."

"Maybe Kaden will fire you, and you'll move to Kentucky. I'm going to miss seeing you every day."

"You have plenty friends to keep you occupied."

Lily's face fell as she sat down on the couch beside her. "Are you mad at me because of Killyama?"

"Kind of." She and Lily had been friends long enough that she felt Lily could have given her a heads up.

"I'm sorry, Penni. I should have told you, especially when I egged you on to try to make Train interested in you. As far as I know, it was the one time, and the two fight all the time. Killyama insults him more than flirts with him. But that's no excuse. I guess I've been missing you so much I lost my judgement. That and I'm not allowed to talk about anything that involves the men."

"The bro code?"

"Yes." Lily laid her head on her shoulder. "Can you forgive me?"

John sat on Lily's lap, tugging at the dangling tie of her blouse.

"That depends on whether you make me French toast for breakfast."

"With strawberries?"

"I forgive you." Penni hugged Lily then lifted John onto her lap. "Your mama knows I can't resist a good meal. Is that how you get Shade to stop being mad at you?"

"Yeah, sure." Lily blushed, getting off the couch.

"Jackal said the way to his heart is through his dick." Penni fell back on the couch cushions, laughing when Lily's face turned even redder.

Lily picked up one of the pillows, hitting her with it, making sure she didn't hit John.

Penni only shook her head at Lily as she left to make breakfast.

* * *

A knock came to door as they were finishing breakfast. Penni smiled when Lily opened the door to find Jackal filling the doorway.

He came in, sitting down at the table with them.

"You want some breakfast?" Lily offered.

"No thanks. I'm not hungry."

Penni knew Jackal wasn't a man who smiled a lot, but his flinty expression had her wondering what troubled him so early in the day.

"Willa is going to take Genny clothes shopping in Lexington."

"That's a good idea. I told her to help herself to my clothes, but nothing is like having your own."

Was his distant behavior just because of the fire last night?

Penni reached out, covering his hand with hers and giving it a tight squeeze.

He pulled his away. "Genny asked if you want to go."

If she went, they wouldn't be able to sneak out to the hotel tonight. It would take at least three hours to drive there, so by the time they shopped and drove back, it would be late.

"Willa wants to make a day out of it, staying for dinner and then staying in a hotel and driving back tomorrow. She thinks giving Genny a day away from Treepoint will help instead of having to drive back and forth to work and seeing the shell of her house."

"Is it safe? I thought Viper wanted us to stay near the club." Penni asked. She wanted to help by spending time with Genny, but dammit, she had waited a long time to lose her virginity, and since making her mind up that Jackal would be the one, she was anxious to be with him.

"Viper will send Cash and Shade with you."

Yep, they would be safe.

"Then of course I'll go." Penni's disappointment burned a hole in her chest.

"Since Shade is coming, do you think you could go?" Penni asked Lily just as Lily got a text message from Shade.

"Looks like John and I are going, too. We're going to have so much fun!"

"Yippee," Penni said, trying to cheer herself up.

"I'll go and get John and myself ready." Lily picked John up from his highchair.

"Go ahead. I'll be up in a minute." Penni rose from the table when Jackal stood up, heading toward the door. Penni caught his hand as he was about leave. "Is something wrong?"

Jackal didn't smile. "No. You go and spend time with Genny."

"I was looking forward to tonight."

"I was, too. We can do it another night when this mess is over."

Penni's face fell. "Are you trying to tell me that you want to wait to make love to me until after we get back to Queen City?"

"I think that's for the best." He didn't meet her eyes, which wasn't like him.

"I don't understand. If you're changing your mind about us, then just tell me so." Penni felt a sharp pain she had never experienced before. Maybe she should cancel going with Genny and go to a doctor.

Before she could analyze where the sharp pain was coming from, Penni found herself pinned against the wall next to the front door.

"I haven't changed shit about how I feel about you. You're mine. You have been since I made you get on my bike and duct taped your hands around my waist. I can't feel bad about it, even if I know it made you hate me, but I did what I had to for the club. I will always do what I have to do for the club.

"I never had a home before the Predators. I had been living on the fucking streets since I was fourteen years old. The only time I had a roof over my head was when I was in juvie. My father made sure that he scared potential foster parents from taking me in."

"I'm so sorry, Jackal."

Penni had her parents, Shade, and even Shade's father had been kind to her, making sure she had felt like a part of their family. Meanwhile, Jackal had no one. His father was the one he should have been protected from.

"Don't be. I'm not the first runaway who found themselves on the streets, and I won't be the last. We live in a fucked world, and it just becomes more fucked every day."

"That's not true... There are good people everywhere."

"That may be true, but they didn't do shit to help me. I survived by doing anything and everything I had to in order to put food in my stomach and sleep in a bed. I'm not going to lie; I've done things that would make you sick. It makes me sick.

"Ice took one look at me, Hennessy, and DJ and fed us, gave us our rooms, and gave us a family. DJ was willing to give it up for the drugs, Hennessy for DJ, but me? Hell no. I'll stand behind the Predators until I'm dead and gone."

Penni felt the tears slip out of the corners of her eyes. Jackal brushed them away with his callused thumbs.

"I understand."

"You don't, but you will. There are going to be a lot of fights between you and me over the club. There's going to be times you hate me and walk away, but I'm not going to let you go."

"You're not?"

"Hell no."

Penni let her head drop down on Jackal's chest. "Is that a promise?"

"It's an oath." Jackal's arms tightened around her, nearly cutting off her breath before he loosened his hold and stepped back.

She watched him go, wanting to pull back and barricade the door against the world. Lily would complain, but she would get over it.

Penni shook her head. It was a sad when she was thinking about taking her sister-law and nephew hostage just so she could have sex.

"Dammit, am I ever going to get laid?" she asked the closed door.

"Uh…Are you talking to me?" Lily said, coming down the steps.

Penni turned around to face her friend. "Do you know how many men have tried to get me to sleep with them?"

"Uh…No, and I probably don't want to know."

"Hundreds." Penni's anger had her exaggerating. "I damn near shot one's dick off."

"Okay…"

Penni released a loud sigh.

Lily juggled John on her hip. "Feel better?"

"Not yet, but I will by the time I get dressed and ready to go."

Penni stomped upstairs to her room, going to the window to slide it open. Raising her hand, she threw her negative emotions out, and there were a lot. When she was done, she slammed the window back down before they could return to her. If that didn't help her to get laid, nothing would.

She rubbed her hands together, as if she were shaking them off. Bolstered by a fresh aura, Penni dressed, and by the time she had come downstairs where Shade was now waiting with Lily, she was in a better mood.

"Ready?"

"Yes."

"The others are waiting in the parking lot," Shade said as he carried John and Lily packed the diaper bag.

Penni raised her eyebrows when she saw Winter sitting in one of the backseats with Genny. Beth and Razer were sitting in a car with their two children, parked alongside Lily's van.

Penni climbed into one of the backseats as Shade buckled John's car seat.

"I didn't know Beth was coming." Lily waved at Beth as she got in the front seat.

Shade slid behind the steering wheel, and Cash got in the back seat. Then Shade drove out of the parking lot with Razer following behind.

"We thought you women deserved a break," Shade commented.

Penni saw Winter's frozen expression.

Lily and Shade talked as the car traveled out of town.

"What about Willa?" Penni asked as they passed the church.

"Willa and Lucky are ahead of us," Cash answered from the seat behind hers.

Penni and Lily talked during the drive while Genny and Winter remained silent. When she tried to talk either of the women, their replies were monosyllabic. It was a relief when they reached the shopping mall.

"I hope you're ready for me to spend all your money?" Penni teased her brother.

"Viper is financing this shopping trip, so buy whatever you want," Winter chimed in before Shade could answer.

"Which store should we hit first?" Penni asked Genny.

"You pick."

"Let's start at the end and work our way back down to where the cars are parked," Winter voiced her opinion.

"That sounds good." Genny showed her first smile since they had left Treepoint when Willa and Lucky rose from a bench.

The large group walked through the streaming crowds, coming to a stop in front of a department store.

"Why don't you men go take the kids to the food court while we shop here?" Winter asked Shade who was closest to her.

"We stay together." Shade started past Winter who remained standing still.

"This store has security at both entrances. It'll be easier for us to shop without the kids."

"That's a good idea." Beth nodded, agreeing with Winter. "I can text you when we're ready to go to another store."

Shade looked down at the twin stroller that Chance was already trying to climb out of. "Text me when you're in the checkout line," Shade gave in, taking the stroller from Lily as Razer wheeled the twins to the food court.

Lucky and Cash looked relieved to get away from the store.

"I know he wasn't looking forward to waiting for us to shop." Willa smiled at the women as they walked into the store.

They found the women's department, each going their own way to look at the multitude of clothes. Penni and Winter took the same rack, sliding the clothes as they looked.

"You don't find it strange that the men were so ready for us to go shopping on a Friday night?"

Penni looked up from the clothes to see Winter staring at her. "Why does it matter that it's Friday?"

Penni saw the women move from their rack to the one she was at, giving Winter strange looks.

"Well?" Penni asked, seeing the women's eyes warring with each other.

Winter jerked her gaze away from the other women. "Friday night is party night."

"Every night is a party with The Last Riders," Penni scoffed, pulling out a red flaring skirt she was thinking about trying on.

"Not like Friday. Look around us, Penni? Do you see Viper here, even though he asked me to get off early? It was when I was in the van that I found out he wasn't coming." Winter's eyes stared fixedly on the clothes.

"So you think he is going to use the opportunity of you being gone to cheat?" Willa whispered.

Winter lifted her gaze. "Yes or...Jackal."

"Jackal was as disappointed as I that we couldn't be together to night. We had plans...until Genny asked me to come."

Genny shook her head. "I didn't ask you. Willa called and asked me this morning. I'm glad you're here, but I didn't ask."

The women looked at Willa.

"Lucky suggested I ask Genny today. He said we could make a day out of it."

"That's what Razer told me when Lily asked me if I wanted to come."

Penni thought about how Jackal had looked so sincere when he had told her about his childhood...

"I'm sure it was just a misunderstanding."

"Want to find out?" Winter dropped any pretenses that she was looking at clothes.

"How?" all of the women answered, their suspicions making her nervous.

Winter looked Penni straight on. "We can leave and go back to Treepoint while they're busy with the kids. They won't even know we're missing until the store closes."

"You can take my car." Willa reached into her purse for her keys.

"We're going to look crazy when we walk in, and they ask why we left." Penni's trust in Jackal was beginning to slip. It didn't help that all of the women were convinced the men were up to no good.

"What if they just wanted us gone to handle the situation with Hennessy?" Penni grasped at a final straw.

"Do you really think Viper would let his best men leave if he were expecting trouble?"

Winter had her there. They would keep them back to protect the clubhouse.

Penni took the keys out of Winter's hand. "I'll drive."

CHAPTER THIRTY

"You want me to take the bullet for you?" Stump took a beer out the cooler behind the bar.

"If I thought you could keep your mouth shut, I would." Jackal stifled the urge to knock Stump's teeth out.

"I never could keep a secret."

"Maybe you're the one we need to watch." He surveyed the clubroom, searching for the woman who was the first target.

"If you want to fuck me, all you have to do is ask."

Jackal choked on his beer, managing to get away from the bar before he dunked Stump's head into the cooler.

He used the opportunity to head over to Cruz who was close to Raci. She and Jewel were talking to another woman, sitting on the middle steps. Jackal and Cruz's backs were turned to the them, but they would be able to hear as they talked.

"You ready to go back on Sunday?"

Viper had decided that was the bait they would drop to make them expose the traitor and draw the cartel out.

"Hell yes. If I listen to that old bitch bang on the wall next to my head much longer, I'm going to strangle her," Cruz complained. "How did Viper keep her from coming down tonight?"

"I gave her the last of what Greer brought. She won't want to leave that room."

Jackal didn't feel guilty. The old woman had more color in her fleshy face since she had been in the clubhouse. Cash had called Evie to stay the night with Mag until Rachel came back the next day. Rachel had taken Cash's daughter to spend the night with her brothers at their house as suggested.

It was like a wall of dominoes that he felt was about to crash around him. Jackal hoped the women wouldn't let it slip to Penni if he touched a woman. Otherwise, she was going to hate him more than before.

"You want go play a video game in the basement?" Jackal threw out the bait. If neither came down, he could cross two off his list.

"No thanks," Cruz declined. "I think I'll go get another beer."

The men parted, going through the room. Jackal went through the kitchen and down the basement steps. The room was empty.

Sitting down, he turned on the Xbox. It was hard to wait to see if one of the women would show.

After ten minutes had passed, Jackal was about to stop playing the game when he heard someone coming down the steps.

He watched her feet appear then saw Raci's grin as she practically bounced across the basement. She was wearing a black miniskirt that came to the tops of her thighs with a blue off-the-shoulder top that showed her tits.

"Can I play?" She sat down next to him, watching him play.

"Go for it." Jackal motioned for the controller next to the Xbox then restarted the game to see if she really wanted to play or if her intent was to get information out of him.

When her breasts brushed against his arm, he had his answer.

"How long have you been a Predator?"

"Twelve years," Jackal answered noncommittally, wanting her to think he wasn't aware that she really wanted to find out.

"That's a long time," she practically cooed.

"Yeah."

"Do you like being in their club? I like being in The Last Riders, but it's boring sometimes."

"It's okay." Jackal shrugged, keeping his eyes on the TV screen.

"I bet you're really good at being a Predator. What position do you hold?" She pressed her tits harder against his arm.

"I'm their enforcer."

"Wow. Train is our enforcer."

He almost snorted at her lie.

Raci dropped her hand to his thigh, and Jackal dropped the controller, turning toward her.

"Is this one of the times you're bored?"

Raci nodded, settling on the couch cushion. "It gets boring fucking the same men all the time. I could talk to Viper about him getting you in if you want."

Jackal almost flinched when her hand slipped higher against the bulge of his jeans.

"Jeez, you're really packing, aren't you?" Raci rubbed his dick as she unsnapped his jeans with her other hand.

Jackal peeled her hands away from his limp dick. Either he made her talk, or his dick was about to show her how uninterested he really was.

Jerking down her top, he took her nipple in his mouth.

"I can make you feel so...good." Raci brought her hand once again to his dick.

He yanked her hands back, holding them behind her back. "Did I tell you that you could touch my dick?"

Raci leaned forward, running her tongue up the side of his neck before stopping at his earlobe and sucking it into her mouth.

"You want my dick? Ask for it."

"Can I suck your dick?"

She moaned when he yanked her skirt up, baring her to her waist. He brought his hand between her thighs, and Raci spread her legs as he slid a finger inside her pussy. Raci twisted on his fingers, sprawling her legs wider.

"How long have you been with the Last Rider's?"

Raci moaned louder. "Several years."

"That's a long time."

Raci frantically nodded as Jackal began to pump his finger into her drenched pussy.

"I bet they took one look at a beautiful girl like you and thought they hit the jackpot."

Surprisingly, she shook her head. "My cousin had to talk Viper's brother into letting me join. It's not easy to become a Last Rider."

"Where is he? I want to thank him."

Raci tried to open Jackal's jeans again, and Jackal saw the flicker of fear enter her eyes.

"She doesn't live in Treepoint."

"Where is she? Call her. I'm tired of the Predators. We could meet up. We can start our own club," Jackal said as he rubbed her tit with his free hand.

"Crystal has an old man."

"Introduce me to her. I can take care of him."

Raci shoved her hand down his jeans, taking out his cock. "I haven't seen a pierced dick since Diamond married Knox," she whimpered. "Fuck me."

Jackal pulled his hand out of her pussy. The fact that she hadn't noticed his dick wasn't hard showed she wasn't into fucking him.

Clenching his hand on her thigh, he smeared her juices on the inside of her leg. "I think we need to get Viper down here to enjoy this party."

"Viper's busy."

Jackal jerked back at Penni's choked voice. He didn't spare a glance at the woman who was trying to tug her skirt back down as he shoved his dick back into his jeans.

Penni turned and ran up the steps, and Jackal ran across the room, his hand reaching out to try to catch her. Penni dodged his hand, turning to face him.

"Don't you dare touch me when you still smell like her!"

Jackal jerked his hand back. "Listen to me—"

Penni clenched her hands into fists. "I'm going to walk up these steps and go to Shade's house, and you're not going to fucking touch me. Do you understand?"

The fury blasting from her told Jackal she wasn't ready to listen to anything he had to say. It would end a fight and give her something else to hate him for. Therefore, he would wait until morning to talk to her.

"Yes." He nodded once.

Raci tried to slide past them.

"We're not done." Jackal pulled her to his side. Then he wanted to kick himself at his choice of words as he saw Penni blanch then run up the steps.

"I hate you!" she yelled. With each step she took, more expressions of animosity came out. "God, I hate you!" Her voice became shriller.

Jackal barely had time to move away from the bottom of the steps as a chair came tumbling down.

"Get away from me!" Jackal heard her furious scream from the kitchen, but he wasn't stupid enough to attempt the steps. It was lucky he hadn't. Plates came flying down, crashing onto the floor.

"She's gone crazy. Maybe you should go talk to her?" Raci whispered when a large cookie jar joined the pile.

Jackal looked at Raci as if she had lost her mind. "If you're so brave, you go up there."

"Never mind."

"Shit." She was pissed off.

"Fuck that asshole!" Penni screamed down the stairs.

A laptop splattered in parts, the screen cracked.

"Come on, Penni. I'll walk you home." Winter's calm voice tried to reason with her over the men telling her to calm down.

"He was fucking her!"

Jackal heard her moving away from the door to the basement and yelled back, "I was not!"

"What the hell did he say!"

He peered up the steps, hearing a struggle. Concerned, he started up the steps.

"FUCK!" Jackal ran back down the steps, taking Raci with him into the hallway, and then he heard shots ring down, sending plaster raining from the wall across the steps.

"Fuck that!"

"She's pretty mad," Raci panted, crouching down.

"No shit." Jackal had his gun to protect himself, but he really didn't want to shoot the crazy bitch.

Jackal had learned his lesson. This time, he was smart to stay quiet until he saw Train and Viper come down the steps.

"You okay?"

Train's amusement had Jackal shoving Raci toward Viper. He wanted to spank Penni's ass red.

"I've been better."

"Did a bullet hit you?" Viper went to the laundry, taking out a roll of paper towels and tearing some off before he handed them to him.

"No, that was glass from the cookie jar."

The men stared at the disaster that Penni was responsible for.

Jackal stepped on a cookie, smashing it with his boot.

"No one is going to want to clean this mess," Train said as he took a chair from in front of the couch.

"Penni made it; she can clean it up," Viper said as he pushed Raci onto the couch, standing over her.

"You going to be the one to tell her?" Train arched his eye at his leader.

"Never mind. Raci can do it."

"Me? I'm not going to clean up her mess!"

"Why? You have something better to do than fucking Jackal?"

"I didn't fuck him!" Raci denied. "Who are you going to believe, me or Jackal?"

"Penni was the one who was screaming it."

"We were just messing around. That's not against the rules. It's not fair, anyway. The men don't have any problems fucking anyone they want, so why can't the women?" Raci began crying. "Besides, I didn't want to." Her eyes pleaded with Viper.

"Then why did you? You have plenty of Last Riders to keep your pussy warm."

Raci's shoulders began to shake. "I didn't have a choice. They threatened to kill Crystal."

Train reached out, taking Raci's wrist and tugging her onto his lap. "Then we have to stop them, don't we?"

Train's gentle words had Raci's tears drying. "Yes, we do."

Ice, Hennessy, Max, Stump, Cade, and Rider came downstairs.

"Where's Winter?" Viper asked Rider.

"Upstairs in your bedroom. She left a blanket and pillow in front of your door."

Viper's expression hardened. "Talk!" he snapped at Raci.

"I got a text from Crystal for me to call Deron. When I did, another man answered. At first, I thought I had dialed the wrong number." Raci shuddered.

"It wasn't?" Jackal prompted when he saw Viper was getting irritated. He wanted to be with his woman as much Jackal wanted to be with Penni.

"No, but I didn't know who it was. He told me that he had Crystal and Deron, and if I didn't do what they wanted, they would kill her. You know how close Crystal and I are. What was I supposed to do?"

"You could have told me or Shade."

"He said he would kill her if I did. He said someone else in the club was watching me."

Viper folded his arms across his chest. "He was bluffing."

"I didn't know what to do. I was scared. He made me tell him who was in the clubhouse and when they left the house." Raci gave Viper a terrified glance at that. "I told them Genny was the only one who left the house. I made sure they wouldn't hurt Willa."

Jackal looked away. The bitch was excusing herself because she had been willing to get Genny killed instead one of the members' wives.

Raci had known that, if one of the men had found out, they would have killed her. She had been right.

"How did you talk to them? Shade checked cell phones."

"They mailed me a disposable phone. Since I offered to check the mail, no one noticed me taking it."

"Jewell is going to be furious you did it." Rider's low whistle had Raci crying again.

"Do we have to tell her?"

"Yes. Where's the cell phone now?" Jackal's sharp voice cut through her tears.

"I hid it upstairs in my bathroom, under my sink. It's at the bottom of a box of tampons."

Viper motioned for Rider to retrieve it.

"Sorry, Viper. I didn't think to look there."

"I wouldn't have, either." Viper nodded to Rider to go. "What else did you tell them?"

"I told them that I heard Jackal and Cruz talking about leaving, but I wanted to find out more before I called them back. The last time I didn't have anything, they made Crystal scream." Raci buried her face in Train's shoulder.

Rider came back with the phone, talking into another phone.

"Shade just found out Winter and Penni are missing. He wants to know if you want them to come back or stay in Lexington?"

"Tell them to stay. The kids have to be tired. They can come back in the morning."

"Why did it take them that long to notice they were missing?" Jackal's loud voice must have been heard on the phone because Rider winced.

After a few minutes, he hung up the phone. "Shade said that Lily and Willa kept telling them they were in the dressing rooms."

"It took a long time to say all of that," Jackal said suspiciously.

"He told me to shove my phone up your ass." Rider shrugged. "Any other time, I would help him out, but it's a new phone."

"What's our next move?" Ice's cold gaze went to Viper.

"Raci's going to make another call. She's going to tell them the Predators, the Road Kingz, and The Last Riders are going to attack the Unjust Soldiers' compound. They'll think our women will be guarded by a small amount of men. When they show up, they'll have a surprise waiting."

"You going to bring them to The Last Riders' clubhouse? Isn't that risky?" Jackal didn't want Penni near the cutthroats when they attacked.

"They won't expect all of us to be here, plus the other clubs."

"They'll kill Crystal and Deron!" Raci sobbed.

Jackal and all the men stared down at Raci.

Cade laid a hand on Raci's shoulder. "They're already dead. The cartel doesn't keep hostages. I'll check with the police to see if any unidentified bodies have shown up, but I doubt it. They hide them to keep their relatives under their control."

Raci shook her head. "I heard her scream..."

"It was probably one of their women. My sister-in-law was dead before her father could pull money out of the bank."

Jackal couldn't bring himself to sympathize with a faceless woman when his was still hurting.

"If you don't need me, I want to go talk to Penni."

"Stay away. She's sitting on Shade's porch with a gun," Rider warned him as he helped Raci straighten her top.

"Where did she get the gun?" Jackal growled.

"Sorry, brother." Stump grinned. "She snatched it out of the back of my jeans."

"She's Shade's sister; I would give her a wide berth for a couple days," Viper advised.

Jackal acknowledged that Viper might be right.

"I'll talk to her tomorrow," he said, going back to his original plan.

"Like I said, take a couple of days. I've taken enough beatings from Shade to know what I'm talking about."

Jackal ignored Viper's advice. Shade would take the gun away when he came home. Once she was rational, she would see reason. Penni might be hot-headed, but when she calmed down, she would be more level-headed. That was a woman's role when they were involved with bikers, so she might as well learn that lesson now.

She's mine. She's mine, he kept repeating to himself. He had sworn an oath, and he intended to keep the one to the Predators and the one he had made to her. He would keep it tomorrow and every day until the day he died...if she didn't kill him first.

CHAPTER THIRTY-ONE

Penni sat there, staring into the dark night. Her cell phone kept pinging, but she didn't want to talk to Shade, Lily, or Winter. Jackal, at least, did not call. *Then why are you checking to see if he did?*

The drive back to Treepoint had been tense, both she and Winter imagining what they would find when they arrived at the clubhouse.

"Want me to stop and get you something to drink?" Penni had looked at Winter who had been staring out the window. When she had turned her head, Penni could see her cheeks were wet.

"No, we don't have time. We'll be lucky if we make it before they know we're missing."

Penni licked her dry lips. "Winter, Viper wouldn't do anything to jeopardize your marriage."

"Viper's not the one who's ruining our marriage. I am."

"I didn't realize you were having problems. You just seem so happy together." Had she been so involved chasing Train and immersed in Jackal that she had missed that the marriage was crumbling?

"Viper and I both want to keep our problems to ourselves. We didn't want any of The Last Riders to give their opinions."

"Why would they give their opinions? Your marriage is just between you and Viper. It's none of their business."

"I want a child, Penni. I want one so badly I can barely breathe."

"Then have one," Penni said matter-of-factly. "I can see why it could be a problem. Raising one in a clubhouse would be hard, but Razer and Shade make it work."

"I can't have children...Well, I can, but I can't." Winter took a breath before explaining her confusing answer. "When I was attacked and left for dead, my spine and hips were injured. My doctors say there's a chance I wouldn't survive."

"Holy shit! I can see why Viper doesn't want you to do it. Have you thought about adoption?"

"Yes, but the baby wouldn't be mine and Viper's. We filled out the paperwork to start the adoption process, but we were denied."

"Assholes. You would make the perfect parents."

"I know. That's what I think, too, but they did a background check and found out he's the president of The Last Riders. They don't think we'll make suitable parents. We even tried to take in foster kids, and they turned us down for that, too."

"Winter, if there is anything, I would—Hey, I could be your surrogate."

Winter shook her head. Smiling, she pulled out a Kleenex to wipe her face. "I would take you up on your offer, but Viper would kill you if you didn't hand over the baby after it was born. You wouldn't give up a child after carrying it that long. You have a hard time being away from your ducks. You drove Jackal crazy every day by making sure Colton was feeding them."

Penni thought about it, but she didn't agree. Penni knew she could admit her own flaws, and she wasn't possessive. When men stopped calling her, she didn't get offended, chalking it off as another failed attempt to get Train off her mind. The child would be Winter and Viper's, not hers. She was sure she could do it, but she would give Winter time to think over her offer.

"If you change your mind, let me know."

"I will. We'll work it out...if he's not doing something he shouldn't be doing."

"He won't be." Penni waved her hand in the air, releasing her own worries and any she might have caught from Winter. Then she put her hand back on the steering wheel. She was determined to make Winter lighten up. "You think Kaden would give me maternity leave, though, since technically I wouldn't be keeping the baby?"

Winter leaned her head against the window. "You're a nut." When she managed to stop laughing, she put her tissues back in her purse. "Will you do me favor?"

"Of course."

"Don't tell anyone. I let my emotions get the best of me. I really want to keep this between me and Viper."

"No problem."

The Last Riders had become a family. None of them would want Winter to jeopardize her health.

"I wish I could have seen Shade's expression when he discovered we were missing."

Winter brought her hand to her mouth. "I wish I could have seen Cash's. He was guarding the backdoor. If the clerk hadn't shown us the employee exit, we wouldn't have managed to get away."

For the rest of the drive, they talked about how the boys at the school where she was principal always believed they could pull the wool over her eyes. Winter told Penni several of the more humorous anecdotes, not stopping until she parked in The Last Riders' parking lot.

Because they were driving Willa's car, the two men on the front porch went back to leaning against the door.

"We're here," Winter said unnecessarily.

"Are you sure we should do this?" she whispered. Whether Winter went or not, Penni had every intention of seeing what Jackal was doing.

"Yes."

"Remember, let's be cool. Whatever we see, we don't want to give them the satisfaction of knowing they've hurt us."

"I'll be calm. I promise. We'll go in the front door. If they're not in the living room, they'll either be in the kitchen or the basement. The men won't take the women upstairs to mess with; they'll be too afraid of Mag barging in."

"You remember she's in a wheelchair?" she said as they quietly made their way up the large flight of steps.

"Tell that to Rider. I don't know how she managed to get in her wheelchair, but she opened Rider's door and caught him with Jewell."

"I think she has a crush on him."

When they reached the door, Penni saw it was Train and Crash on guard duty.

"What are you two doing here? You're supposed to be in Lexington. Where are Shade and the rest—"

"We decided we didn't want to stay the night. Excuse us." Penni attempted to get to the door, but Train and Crash both blocked it.

Their guilty expressions made her sick. Winter had been right; the men had wanted them gone.

"Move, Train...*now*."

Train and Crash stepped to the side, letting them open the door.

Penni looked over the crowded room. The members were having such a good time. Music was blaring, and several of the women were dancing. Several of the men were at the bar, watching a boxing match on the big screen.

"I see Viper." Penni pointed at Viper, who was sitting on a stool with Ice and Cade on each side of him. "I told you that you didn't have anything to worry about. Do you see Jackal?" Penni asked Winter, but her attention was on Viper who had turned to stare at them, his phone in his hand.

"I guess the secret's out. Go. I'll try to distract him from calling Jackal until you can find him."

Penni had seen Jackal wasn't in the living room, and the kitchen was practically empty. The few members back there were watching the boxing match in the room off the kitchen. They didn't pay attention to her as she went down the steps.

The couple hadn't heard her come in. Raci's hand was on Jackal's dick, and her breasts and pussy were bare. He was finger-fucking her. Then he slid his hand out, wiping it on her thigh.

After that, she didn't remember much of anything. It was as if she were staring down at herself.

The rage that blindsided her didn't leave until she was sitting on Shade's porch swing and Winter left. Shade had warned her about the killing rage he was capable of, but she hadn't expected it to be so intense to actually shoot at some-one. Technically, she hadn't shot him, but she hadn't been aiming...Okay, she had been aiming at his dick, but she had missed it.

Son of a bitch! Penni breathed in through her nose and out her mouth, calming herself again.

The son of a freaking bastard-bitch-snake-in-the-fucking-grass deserved more than the three bullets she had sprayed down the steps.

When she couldn't think of any other names to call the ass-wipe, Penni decided to go to bed. She couldn't leave before Lily returned from Lexington, but when she did, Penni decided it would be time to head out.

She knew Shade would try to talk it her out of it, but she didn't care. If the cartel was stupid enough to try to intimidate her, it would be the last thing they ever did. With the mood she was in, she could take on the whole freaking cartel. Maybe she could give them Jackal...

* * *

The next morning, Penni was up early. She showered and got dressed in a pair of grey leggings and a black and grey T-shirt that had crisscross straps on the back. The outfit was deceptively simple, the shirt falling past her hips. The leggings were tight and showed off her bottom, and the expanse of her back was left bare.

Penni turned her back to the full-length mirror, turning her head to see the full effect. She smacked her ass. The five pounds she had gained looked good on her.

She had finished packing her bags when Penni heard Shade and Lily come in. She zipped her suitcase, leaving it on the bed.

She would ask Shade to pack it into the car when she was ready to leave.

Penni took her time coming down the steps, seeing Lily holding John as Shade set down the shopping bags on the couch. Shade and Lily watched her as she came to a stop.

"Did you know?"

"Lily, take John upstairs and put him down for a nap. Wait for me in the bedroom."

Her friend sent her a sympathetic glance, but followed Shade's order.

Penni went toward the living room. "Don't tell me you're angry at Lily."

"My wife lied to me when I repeatedly asked her where you and Winter were. She has a habit of keeping information from me when it involves the women. Her loyalty belongs to me, not to every harebrained idea the women come up with."

"You trying to rationalize the men deliberately wanting us out of the house so they could cheat?"

Penni shivered at the blue eyes that drilled into hers.

"Viper didn't want Winter out of the house so he could cheat, and I didn't know which man had been picked to try to get information out of the woman they believed was betraying the club."

"What?" Penni's voice rose.

Shade waved his hand to silence her. "I had my suspicions it was Jackal, but that was left to Viper and Ice. If they had asked me my opinion, I would have chosen Jackal, too. Only someone from the club would have known Genny was going to the store. We needed to know who it was before someone was seriously hurt."

"They chose Jackal?"

"Yes."

Penni stared down at the floor. "Did they give him a choice?"

"I'm assuming yes."

There was a whole clubhouse of men; Jackal could have said no. It had come down to a choice between the Predators and her, and he had chosen the Predators.

"Did he find out who the traitor was?"

"Viper told us it was Raci this morning. He's going to call a meeting to vote whether she stays in the club or goes. They won't vote her out, though. Raci has been a good member for years. Her cousin and cousin's husband were taken by the cartel. Raci was trying to save their lives."

Shade had never discussed club business with her, but he knew Penni would see Raci every time she came for a visit. Poor Genny. She would be the one who would have to look at Raci every day and know she was responsible for almost getting her killed and the destruction of her home.

"Thank you for telling me."

Shade held out his hand. "Where's the gun?"

Penni went to the kitchen, taking it off the top of the refrigerator and giving it to Shade.

"Did you leave any bullets?" Shade defrosted slightly when she handed it to him.

"A couple. If he hadn't run like a sissy, I would have emptied the chamber."

"Don't be too hard on him. I would have run when I saw a gun in your hand, too."

Penni punched her brother in his shoulder.

"Ouch, that hurt." Shade actually smiled at her.

Damn, Lily was good for him.

"I'm leaving after lunch."

Shade's smile dropped at her words.

"Listen. Please listen. When I'm done, if you still say to stay, I will. Okay?"

Shade nodded. "Tell me the plan."

* * *

Penni made her way to the clubhouse where she found Genny busy cleaning up the kitchen after breakfast.

"I thought I would give you a break by fixing lunch if you don't mind?"

Genny kept mopping, answering, "I don't mind at all."

Penni didn't have to broach the topic on whether or not Viper had already told Genny who had been responsible for her house being destroyed. It was on her face.

She went toward the basement door, knowing there had to be a mess left over from last night.

"Raci already cleaned it. She was doing it when I was talking to Viper," Genny said, stopping her from going down.

"Genny, I wish there were something I could do to make you feel better. I know how much that house meant to you."

"Really?"

Penni nodded. "I've been lucky. My parents had a wonderful marriage, and they gave me a home I'll always cherish and can tell my children about one day. One day, I'll have enough to buy my own home."

Genny began crying, placing her head on the handle of the mop. "I worked so hard for that house."

Penni moved toward Genny, patting her on the back. "Whoever blew up your home didn't only destroy your home, but your dream. But you can buy another one. Viper probably feels bad enough that he'll buy you a bigger one."

Genny lifted her head, laughing. "He already did. He offered to buy me the house next to Mrs. Langley's home, and it's bigger than hers. I told him I wouldn't want to clean it on the weekends."

"If it were me, I'd get Viper to make Raci clean it every Saturday." They laughingly came up with other chores to make Raci do. Then Penni went to the counter, beginning lunch. She was going to make The Last Riders a meal they would never forget.

She worked as Genny cleaned the rest of the kitchen then left to work on the rest of her chores.

It was lunchtime when Winter came in to the kitchen.

"Something smells delicious."

Penni tossed the broccoli she had been cutting into a bowl. "Thanks. Lunch will be ready in a few minutes."

Winter poured herself a cup of coffee. "Have you seen Viper this morning?"

"No, and I haven't seen Jackal, either." She picked up several cloves of garlic, mashing them with her sharp knife.

"They left to go to town to see Knox," Genny said, having come back in, as she took the plates out of the kitchen cabinets. "Viper told me this morning before you got here."

"Oh, thanks." Winter moved away from the smell of the garlic. She stared at the food spread out on the counter. "Uh... Penni, what's in the crockpots?"

"Meatball stew and barbeque hotdogs."

Winter opened the crockpots then closed them. "Did you mean for the food to look this way?"

"What's wrong with it?" Penni scraped the garlic from the cutting board into a bowl of vegetables. She set another five cloves on the cutting board then mashed them one at a time.

"Never mind. Isn't that a lot of garlic?"

"Yes…it…is." Penni scraped the garlic into the salad then poured on the dressing. Using tongs, she tossed the salad before setting it on the buffet. Then Penni went to the pantry and fridge before coming back to the counter.

"What are you making now?"

Penni opened the bread. "Making you a sandwich."

"I was going to eat in my room, but I wouldn't miss this, even if the house caught on fire." Winter winced at her word choice. "Sorry, Genny."

"None taken. I'm supposed at be at work in an hour for Willa at the church. When I saw the way Penni was cutting the hot dogs into small pieces, I figured I could risk being late. Did you see the way she cut the broccoli? She cut off the heads."

Penni garnished the cheese ball with a small slice of red pepper then stabbed a small knife into the center for the men members to use.

Winter took her sandwich and went to sit at the kitchen table. "I need a front seat to enjoy this."

Penni saw Viper, Jackal, Ice, Cade, and Hennessy come into the kitchen. They hesitated before coming forward to take their plates and get in line.

"Hello. Are you having a good day?"

Penni shot Viper a spearing glance, not answering his question.

Viper hurried through the line.

Raci, Jewell, and Evie came into the kitchen next, followed by King, as Shade came in from the back door.

Jackal was next in line. "I want to talk to you after—"

Penni picked up the sharp knife she had used to cut the vegetables. She began cutting the large carrots into slivers.

Jackal blanched, moving away.

The line moved along, none of the members brave enough to talk.

Evie took a bowl next to the crockpot, asking, "What is it?"

"Meatball stew."

"You go, girl!" Evie grinned, closing the crockpot and putting the bowl back.

The members continued to pass her one at a time. Raci looked like she wanted to bolt from the line.

Raci raised her eyes after she had put salad on her plate. "Penni...I—"

"No worries. Here, have some more." Penni put another mound of salad on her plate. "Enjoy."

"Thanks." Raci moved away in relief.

I wish I had put another ten cloves of garlic on the salad, Penni fumed internally.

"Do you want me to turn down the crockpot? It looks done." Genny's hand went to the power switch.

"No. I will after lunch."

"Okay."

Penni waited until all of the men were settled before she went to stand at the table where Viper was sitting with Shade, Jackal, and Ice.

"I want to talk to you."

"Can it wait until after lunch?"

"No."

Viper sighed, starting to get up. "Fine, we can go in the living room."

"Don't bother. I just wanted to tell you I'm leaving."

"You can't leave yet…" Viper and Jackal spoke at the same time.

Penni put her hand in front of Jackal's face. "Don't talk to me. The only reason I'm talking to Viper is as a sign of respect for Winter."

Viper's face grew cold.

"I hired Alec to protect me, so there's no reason for me to stay. I'm going to meet up with the band in Reno. With Alec and their force, I'll be well protected. If anyone tries to stop me, Alec has my permission to call the State Police. He's waiting for me in the parking lot now."

"Shade?" Viper's voice was hoarse with anger.

"She'll be fine. Alec hired extra men, and he understands how dangerous the men he could be dealing with are."

"I guess I have no choice other than to let you leave, then. I wish you would wait, but I won't stop you."

Penni nodded, turning toward the kitchen.

"This is horseshit. You're not leaving!" Jackal tried to take her arm, but Penni jerked away.

"I told you last night not to touch me." Penni strode by angrily as Shade and Viper stood up to make sure Jackal stayed seated.

Penni went to the kitchen counter, making a bowl of stew, then carried it to the table where Jackal was sitting.

"I made you a bowl of meatball stew."

"I don't want any fucking stew. I want you to listen to reason. There were reasons—"

Penni dumped the contents of the bowl on his lap.

Shade and Viper sprang away from him while Ice simply leaned away from the droplets of stew that were flung his way.

"You crazy bitch!" Jackal jumped to his feet, trying to tug the hot material away from his skin.

Penni picked his still full plate up then slammed it down on side of his head.

Jackal fell like a brick wall.

"I warned him not call me a bitch."

CHAPTER THIRTY-TWO

"Is he breathing?"

Jackal blinked up at the ceiling, seeing Stump bent over him, filling his vision.

"Of course. She just rattled his brain." Viper tried to lift him.

"Give me a minute." Jackal was going to lose the small amount of food he had forced himself to eat.

"Whoa, brother, you need a breath mint." Stump's face disappeared from his sight.

"Ready?" Shade's face took his place.

"Yeah." Jackal let Shade and Viper lift him. Swaying a bit, he took a minute to feel steady on his feet. Then Jackal nodded his head for them to let him go.

A series of explosions went off in his head.

"Give him a chair."

Viper moved so Shade could slide a chair under him.

"What did she hit me with?" Jackal held his hand to his aching head.

"Your plate."

Shade's muffled voice had Jackal wanting to look up, but he knew he would vomit if he moved.

"That bitch took him out!" Stump chortled. "If she weren't your woman, I'd marry her."

"Where did she go?" Jackal asked as the men sat back down at the table. He couldn't make up his mind whether he wanted to know to protect himself or kill her.

"She went to say good-bye to Lily and Beth."

Shade's amusement had Jackal wanting to hit him with another plate on the table.

"I'm going with her," Genny announced, standing in the doorframe of the dining room.

"Genny, don't go." Winter placed an arm around her shoulder.

"Penni offered me a job as a caterer for the band the night my house exploded. I've thought it over, and I think it's the best for me."

"Where will you live?"

Winter's tearful voice had Genny's face crumpling.

"I'll be living on the bus with their other workers. Right now, I don't want to live in another house or apartment. When I'm ready, I'll find another place to live. I have no ties, so I can live wherever I want to."

"You have ties. Willa and I will miss you."

"I can Facetime you and Willa, and I can see you when Penni comes in to visit. I can ride in with her." Genny sounded positive, but the pain in her eyes showed it was a lie. When Genny left, she wouldn't be coming back. "I need to go and tell Penni I'm going to take her up on her offer and pack my bags."

"I'll come help," Winter told her.

The two women exited the room, leaving them all staring after them.

"Does this mean that we'll have to start doing chores again?" Ember broke the silence.

Raci ran out of the room, crying.

"Do you want me to stop her?"

Viper shook his head at Shade. "No. Tell Alec to watch her. I'll add her to the payroll."

Jackal took a drink of his water. His head began to feel like it was attached to his shoulders again.

"I have to go get showered and changed. Don't let Penni leave before I can talk to her."

"No, you're going to stay away and let her leave. I need your head on straight until we can get the cartel taken care of. Then you can chase after Penni," Ice ordered.

Jackal managed to stand up despite his swimming head. He glared at Hennessy. "I should have killed DJ myself. I knew he was a fuckup; you knew he was a fuckup—hell, DJ knew he was a fuckup. The only reason we're all in this position is because I didn't kill him when Ice told me to."

Hennessy started to lunge toward Ice, but Jackal pushed him back down.

"I knew DJ was going to drag you down. I lost my brother"—Ice smacked a hand on his chest—"when you turned your back on the Predators."

Hennessy relaxed back in his chair. "I couldn't leave him."

"And we couldn't let him stay. You have your own club now. You've learned a hard lesson, one Viper and I already learned. A weak link will destroy your club. You can't break the chain if it's made of steel."

"I can't handle this deep shit. I'm gonna go change my jeans." Jackal walked through the dining room.

"Lunch ready?" Max asked as he swerved out of Jackal's way when they passed on the landing. "You smell and look like a vampire pissed on you."

"Penni cooked lunch."

Max gave him a pitying look. "She try to kill you again? Brother, when you gonna understand that bitch wants you dead?"

"When she marries me, you can be my best man," Jackal said half-jokingly.

Max took out his wallet, taking out a card and handing it to him. "Call her."

"Who is she?"

"My life insurance agent. Take out enough for me to bury you. If not, then fuck her. At least she won't kill you."

"I like to live dangerously."

"How do you think being dead will feel?"

"She wouldn't seriously try to hurt me."

Max looked at him incredulously. "How'd you get that blood on your forehead?"

"Penni hit me with a plate."

"You sure you don't want me to ride her out in the mountains and leave her?"

"She's a bad Penni; they always show up," Jackal wisecracked.

Max slapped him on the back, knocking him into the wall. "Keep your sense of humor. You're going to need it."

"Which jackass is making all that fucking noise?" Mag bellowed from inside the room.

Max went pale, running down the steps like a bear was chasing after him.

"Lord, what have I done to deserve you sending me to live with this pack of heathens?" Mag lamented. "Heavenly Father, call me home."

"Lord, either you answer her prayer, or I will."

* * *

Jackal was jerked awake when the alarms blared throughout the hallways. He jumped out of bed, already dressed, reaching for his gun. He then ran from the room.

Jackal almost fell down the flight of steps when he saw Mag on the landing.

"Why in the hell aren't you in your room?"

"You worry about your own sorry ass, and I'll worry about mine!" the old bitch mouthed off to him.

He was ready to throw her over his shoulder and carry her back to her room when Cash came running up the steps, tossing Mag a rifle.

"First man who comes out the door I don't recognize, I'm gonna blow their heads off! I ain't afraid of no damn cartel. I was raised to shoot at revenuers when they came snooping around."

Cash took his place on the landing next to her, telling Jackal, "Go on downstairs. I've got the upstairs covered."

Jackal saw the three Porter brothers running up the steps. He expected them to line up beside Cash, but they didn't.

Dustin stopped on the last step, the step down was Greer, and the next step down was Tate. Dustin and Greer braced their shotguns on their shoulders. All three were aiming at the door. Rider stood by the door with a pistol in his hands.

Jackal ran into the living room. He was going to take the spot behind the pool table, but Train and Razer were both there with AKs. Therefore, he hastily took a spot behind the bar where Drake, Hennessy, and Cruz were.

Viper came out of the swinging door from the kitchen. "As soon as we open the door, Knox and Stud's men will block them in the parking lot so they can't escape. Both basement doors are locked down. The Predators have the kitchen." He took a quick glance around the room. "Rider, open the door and let the sons of bitches in."

Jackal aimed his Glock at the door, watching Rider open the door. The men running into the room didn't know what hit them. They made it past the entryway before they started being gunned down, the sound of gunfire deafening.

A few turned back toward the door, but men coming in blocked their path. Others tried to run into the dining room, and the sounds coming from there showed they had met the same end.

Viper kicked the bodies to the side, opening the way to let men inside. Blood blossomed on Viper's leg then, showing he had been hit.

Holding his position, Jackal shot the man as he was lifting his gun to shoot Viper again.

Jackal then moved from behind the bar, kicking more bodies out of the way, positioning himself next to Viper. "Get behind the bar."

Viper didn't move, shooting at more coming in through the door. Then Jackal and Viper moved backward as the bodies fell.

One man came in, terrified, and tried to grab Rider. As they struggled, Tate put a bullet in his skull.

When those outside stopped trying to get inside, the Porters, Rider, and Viper moved toward the door, going to them.

Jackal waited inside with the rest of The Last Riders, checking to make sure those littering the floor were dead. Those who were still living had their guns removed and were lined against the wall, moaning in pain.

Viper came back inside, limping. "That's the last of them. The DEA is here. Train, call Shade; tell him it's over. We won't let the women up until we have the mess cleared." Viper had moved the women into the basement last night. "Anyone who doesn't want to have their guns checked for ballistics, give them to Drake. He'll stash them until the DEA leaves."

Jackal handed Drake his weapon, and several others gave theirs. Then Drake went to the kitchen, coming back with an armful of guns before going up the steps.

"Show me where you're putting them. You have your hands full." Tate took his brothers' shotguns, following Drake.

"You need to go to the hospital to get that leg checked out." Jackal gave Viper a bar towel to stem the blood soaking his leg.

"Train will patch me up. I'm not leaving."

"Suit yourself." Jackal shrugged, raising his hands in the air as the DEA agents came in with raised guns.

It took four hours before Viper let the women come upstairs.

Jackal went behind the bar, taking a bottle of whiskey out of the cabinet under the bar. He was surprised it wasn't broken with the amount of bullets that had hit the bar from the front.

Train went to the kitchen, coming out with paper cups. Jackal poured all the men a drink.

"Fuck, the television has a crack on it," Rider complained.

"None of the liquor was broken, but your TV is fucked." Jackal took a drink of his whiskey before pouring one for Ice.

"That's because Viper had a sheet of steel running through it." Rider took several bottles of beer out of the cooler behind the bar, placing them on the bar for the men to reach.

Jackal and Ice stared at the men, taking the whisky bottle and passing it around, instead.

"I told you that you had to step up your game. That's a five-hundred-dollar bottle of whiskey," Jackal chided Ice.

"How many bottles does Viper have under there?"

Jackal poured himself a cupful. "I saw three or four."

"Slip them out here and put them in my saddlebags. As soon as the shit clears, we're out of here."

"If you're going to steal from a man, at least wait until I can't hear what you'll be taking."

Ice took the whiskey back, pouring some in Viper's cup. "Call it a parting gift. I was going to take the TV."

CHAPTER THIRTY-THREE

"You sure you don't want me to stay?" Alec asked, coming back into the room after he had checked out her upstairs.

Penni placed her makeup case on the small, round table in the area off the living room. "No thanks. I'm just going to bed and sleeping for a week."

Penni locked the door after Alec left before going to the pantry and pulling out a bag of duck feed, shoving three scoops into a large baggie.

Going outside, she walked through the small neighborhood. It was only a short walk to the lake that faced the back of her condo. She could have easily climbed over the wall, but she had no desire to get stung if there were any stray bees that had been missed by the college when they had come to remove the hive. She would wait to check out her backyard when she wasn't so tired.

She would feed the ducks first. Then she promised herself the sleeping marathon she had told Alec about.

There were several people around the mini-lake. It was barely ten in the morning, and the lake was secluded, but many in the community liked to sit there and eat their lunch.

The peace stole over her as she fed the ducks. Penni then sat on one of the benches under a large, shady tree when the bag was empty.

Leaning her head back, she closed her eyes, letting the shadows hit her eyelids. She stretched her hands, reaching out and letting the peace and tranquility invade her soul.

"I've never seen you sit still."

"Go away." Penni didn't raise her eyelids. She had no intention of seeing Jackal's face again.

She felt him sitting down next her on the bench.

"I'm not going away. I've been take caring of your ducks for weeks now; the least you could do is look at me."

Penni snapped her head up. "Colton's been taking care of them."

"Colton did it until I got back in town. I've been doing it for the last three weeks."

"I'm back now, so you won't have to do it anymore." Penni tried to sound grateful yet failed miserably. She waved him off with a shoo gesture.

Jackal shoved his hands into his pockets. "How's Genny doing?"

With a disgruntled sigh, she answered, "Good. She moved in with one of the backup singers who needed a roommate."

"I'm surprised you didn't offer for her to move in with you."

"I did. I think she wants a fresh start without being reminded of Treepoint every day. Shade said that Hennessy is back in Colt, Arkansas."

"Yeah, he left the same day we did. The DEA and the Mexican police arrested those who orchestrated the attack on The Last Riders' clubhouse. Viper said the Mexican authorities were relieved to bring the cartel up on charges and arrest them." Jackal's skeptical tone had her finally looking at him.

"You don't believe them?"

"The cartel had too much power to have gone unnoticed for as long they did. They have to have someone in their pocket, shielding them."

"At least they're too busy now to give Hennessy anymore trouble." Penni gazed at the lake, unable to look at him any longer.

"Lucky, Shade, and Cade are going to make sure there won't be any chance of them escaping justice this time. They're trying to get them extradited to the United States."

"What about the Unjust Soldiers?"

"There aren't any left."

"I'm glad. I don't like Hennessy, but he was trying to help out a friend. That, I can understand."

"You're going to give Hennessy a break and not me?"

"I'm not going to talk about what happened." Penni tightened her lips, forcing back the volatile words she wanted to spew at him.

"You're not ready to talk about it yet?"

"No." Penni jerked her gaze back to the lake.

"Okay."

A duck waddled to the edge of the water with her seven ducklings following her, popping into the water one after another.

"Why did you stick so many forks and spoons in the ground?" Jackal pointed at one of the utensils buried in the dirt.

"How did you know they were there?" Penni asked sharply.

"Busted my front tire on one."

"That's why," she chided. "Motorcyclists and bicyclist ride on the grass. Two months ago, someone ran over and killed one of the baby ducks."

"Oh. Why not just post 'no riding on the grass' signs?"

"Like that one?" Penni pointed at a sign on the wooden pole a few inches from them.

"I didn't see it."

His contrite expression had her thawing her frosty behavior toward him.

"Most people don't. I tried to get them to post larger signs, but the HOA that established the lake doesn't want to spoil the natural beauty of it. They only recently started putting cameras on the light poles and posted signs so people would know they were being watched. So having to make a bigger sign telling them to stay off the grass has them dragging their feet."

"Why the cameras? Are people stealing the ducks to take them home?" Jackal joked.

"No. Someone is killing them. The last one was right before I left. They killed a swan. It was horrible. Swans mate for life. Its mate kept swimming around, calling for it." Penni swallowed the painful lump in her throat at the memory of it.

"Damn. Which one?" Jackal asked, staring at the lake.

"Why? Are you going to tell him you're sorry?" Penni barely held back her laughter.

"Don't give me that crap. I know you know which one it is."

Penni nodded toward a spot where a beautiful swan was gracefully gliding along the water not far from where they were sitting.

"See? I know you."

Jackal's complacency had her looking away, her smile dying.

"You don't know me at all. You don't know that I felt like an outsider in my own age group, that I couldn't measure up to my mother's expectations on how I should act. The only time I felt alive was when I was doing something that could have gotten me hurt.

"When Shade came to visit, he could make the emptiness go away. Then he would leave again, and it would start over. He used to take me to a park a couple of miles away from our home, and we would stare out at the lake.

"He taught me how to breathe, Jackal. How to breathe in and out until I could feel my heartbeat in my chest. I finally understood the difference between being alive and just existing.

"Shade felt empty inside, unable to connect to others. I did, too, but to a different extent. I felt too much. It was as if I were living my life running a marathon, and I could only do so much to accomplish everything I wanted.

"One day, I talked a little girl who lived next to me to walk to the lake with me. It was near a freeway. My mother noticed us missing from the backyard and found us near the onramp. My mother couldn't understand why I'd done it. Shade did.

"When he moved to Treepoint, I saw a light I had never seen in Shade before. One night after Lily had become my roommate, I saw him sitting outside our window, so I went outside to talk him to him." Penni took a deep breath before continuing her story. "I saw in him pain, a pain I never believed he could even feel. He couldn't stand being separated from Lily, and they weren't even a couple yet.

"I missed their wedding, but saw a video of it. His face... God, his face. It was like nothing I had seen before. He was happy. Shade was happy. Love and joy shined in his eyes. It was if he had found all the answers in life I had been searching for.

"Then, when Lily was almost killed by a stalker of Shade's, she couldn't bear that she was responsible for someone's death. She was in a coma, and the doctors thought she would be too traumatized to pull out of it. Shade stayed by her side; he wouldn't leave her. They said he kept calling for her over and over. He called for her until she came back. Like the swan, Shade would call for her. Lily is Shade's soul mate."

Penni took another breath before looking at Jackal. "I won't take any less for myself. I have to find my soul mate so I can finally stop running. I thought I could make Train love me, but I couldn't, and finally, after all these years, I know now I never loved him. If I had, I would have stopped running long before now."

"Penni, you never stood a chance of being with Train."

"Wow. That hurts. I know I'm not as attractive as most of the women he's been with at the club, but I'm not exactly puppy chow, either."

"The way you look isn't the issue. Babe, you were mine when I saw you flip me off as you came out of the hotel."

"You kidna—"

Jackal covered her mouth with his hand, cutting off her words.

"I'm never going to live that down, am I?" Jackal removed his hand when she tried to bite him.

"No."

"I can live with that…just like I'm going have to live with you seeing me with Raci."

"Yes, you are!" Penni snapped. The fury that had subsided over the last three weeks flared again. She stood up to stare down at him. "You want to know something funny? I forgave you for kidnapping me. I forgave you for leaving me at the rest area. I even freakin' forgave you for the duct tape you put on my mouth when I called you a spineless needle dick for kidnapping me. I forgave for you for all of that, but what I can't or won't forgive is you being with Raci."

Penni began walking away from him.

"You can keep walking away from me," Jackal raised his voice when she didn't look back, "but you're still going to hear me call after you. I love you, Penni. No matter how many times you don't want to hear me say it, I love you."

Penni began running as fast as she could. She had heard the aching pain in his voice. With every beat of her stuttering heart, she heard him calling to her.

She opened her front door, slamming it behind her before sinking down onto the carpet.

A whisper filled the silent house. "Jackal."

CHAPTER THIRTY-FOUR

"You still moping? Brother, you're taking the life out of the party."

"I haven't seen anything cramping your style. How was the bitch with the Mohawk?" Jackal's sarcastic question sailed over Stump's head.

"She was confused, but she isn't anymore," Stump gloated, throwing himself down on the old chair next to his.

"I bet she never wants to fuck another man."

"Why should she? She just fucked the best one," Stump boasted.

"Brother, you make it hard to be a man."

"I know."

Jackal ground his teeth together, hoping the girlfriend of the bitch who had sneaked into Stump's bedroom shoved Stump's dick down his throat. The bastard would probably enjoy it, though.

"Where is Max tonight? He was supposed to go on a beer run when he got off."

"He's working tonight. He wanted to finish the bench for Lily. There's a delivery truck going near Kentucky, and Shade's meeting it to pick it up."

"If it takes much longer, we'll make him get his ass home instead of bringing the beer." Stump started to get out of the chair. "I might as well go get it myself."

"Max just came in the door." Jackal saw Max was empty-handed.

Stump looked around the room before narrowing his eyes on him.

"What's up?" Jackal said, already beginning to get up as Max came toward him. By the look on Max's face, something was wrong.

"I passed by the area where Penni lives, and I saw cop cars. I couldn't see what was..."

Jackal didn't wait to listen to the rest, already running out of the clubhouse with Stump and Max a step behind him.

Jackal gunned his motor, driving toward Penni's house. It was ten minutes away, and each minute, he told himself Max didn't know if the cops were at her house or at someone else's home in her neighborhood. He made it to the street before hers, the one that led to the community lake.

Dammit, to reach her condo, he had to go that way, and it was blocked off at the lake.

Jackal parked his bike, taking off toward her house. Jackal was intending to satisfy his curiosity then go back to the clubhouse when he saw the cops weren't at Penni's. They were down by the lake, and as he reached it, he saw detectives taking reports.

Two women were standing near a rope, blocking anyone from coming closer.

"What happened?"

An older woman turned to look at him sadly. "Someone killed several of the ducks, swans, and their babies."

Jackal's stomach recoiled at the thought that someone could do such a senseless act. He had to get to Penni and tell her before she found out. He didn't see her with the rest of the bystanders.

He was walking away when he saw her crouched down by the shore of the lake, her brown top blending in with the tree she was under.

He raised the caution tape so he could slide under, and a cop tried to stop him.

"I'm with her." Jackal pointed at Penni, and the cop let him pass.

Jackal broke into a run as he drew near. She was sobbing, trying to soothe the large bird lying limply in front of her.

"Let's go." He tried to pull her to her feet.

"Who would do this?" she cried out, shrugging away from his touch.

"I don't know, but I promise I'll find out."

"Is the vet here yet?"

Jackal bent over the bird, seeing it was the one she had showed him the other day that had lost its mate.

"Is that him over there?" There was a man the cops were escorting under the tape.

Penni turned to look, nodding and waving the man to hurry.

He did hurry his pace when he saw her.

She moved out of the way as he examined the swan.

"Can you go to my car and bring me a cage?"

Jackal followed the vet's directions to his van, deciding to bring two of the cages in case there were more birds that could be saved. He hurried, and it wasn't long before he was placing the cages next to the dying bird.

He reached down and lifted Penni to her feet. This time, she didn't resist him, burying her head in his shoulder.

The vet placed the swan in the cage. "I want to check the other birds to see if I can help. The police want me to bring the rest to my office so I can tell them how they died. Could you drive this one to my office? My partner should be there."

"Yes," Jackal answered. "Penni, stay here, and I'll get your car. Where are your car keys?"

"In my house, by my front door. But my house is locked from the front. When I heard the police cars, I jumped over the back wall.

"It doesn't matter. I have a key to your house." Jackal took off, coming back in a matter of minutes.

Penni got in the front seat as he loaded up the cage. He didn't think the bird would live, but he wanted to try for Penni.

As he was getting in the car, he saw the vet coming toward him with the other cage.

"I found three ducklings that need to go, too." He shoved the other cage in the back seat.

Penni gave him the directions to the vet's office then said, "Thank you."

"You're welcome." Jackal did a U-turn, driving toward the office on the other side of town.

"He's not going to make it, is he?"

"I don't think so, sweetheart."

The waiting vet came out of the office as soon as they pulled into the parking lot.

Jackal tried to talk Penni into leaving, but she refused, sitting down stubbornly on one of the waiting room chairs. Therefore, Jackal sat down next to her, taking her hand in his.

Twenty minutes later, the vet came out and told them the swan had died, but the ducklings hadn't been harmed.

"If I hadn't been watching television, I would have heard who did it," Penni said later as Jackal drove them back to her house.

"Babe, whoever did that was fucked up. You could have been the one hurt for trying to confront someone with that kind of anger. Whoever did that was in a killing rage, using the ducks to make them feel better."

"That's sick."

"Yeah."

"The police are taking the video tapes. I hope they catch whoever did it."

"Me, too."

Jackal parked her car in the driveway then walked her to her door. He opened the door to her condo, expecting her to tell him to leave, but she didn't. Instead, she went into her kitchen to make coffee.

Jackal leaned against the refrigerator. "If you drink that, you'll be awake all night."

She turned off the coffee, staring down at the coffee pot. "Let me have my key back."

Jackal turned and opened the refrigerator, taking out two waters. "No."

"I don't want to argue with you tonight." Her voice broke.

"Tonight was the first time I've seen you cry. The last thing I want is to make your night worse, but I'm not giving the key back. I need it."

She slammed her hands into his chest, pushing him back against the refrigerator. "You didn't care that you fucked Raci instead of me, so why do you care about a stupid key?"

"I didn't fuck her—"

"You touched her. I saw you. Your dick was hanging out. I might have interrupted her, but you were a second away from screwing her."

"No, I wasn't. If you saw my dick, you'd know I wasn't."

She stared him in confusion, her hands dropping from his chest.

"I couldn't have fucked anyone with that limp dick. The only reason Raci didn't notice was because she was trying to get information out of me."

Penni backed up until the counter stopped her. "You touched her..." He saw the pain in her eyes.

"Yes, I touched her, knowing you would probably find out and hate me. I hated myself, but I gave an oath as a Predator, and I kept it, even though it was going to fuck up things between us. An oath isn't easy to keep. Men have died for generations to keep them. Should I have let Ice or Max been the one to do it? Grace is dealing with her mother's death, and Max has only been married less than a year."

Her aghast expression answered his question.

"Using one of The Last Riders wasn't an option," he continued. "It was a setup to find out who was betraying the club. Should I have let Stump do it? He would have fucked her and told her what we had planned. Hennessy would have been suspicious. Cruz would have beaten it out of her. Cade could have, but Fat Louise is pregnant. Stud could have, but if that bitch of a wife of his found out, she would've—"

"Jeez." Penni shook her head, stopping him. "So you're the go-to guy when the Predators need a dirty job done?"

"Yes."

Penni raised her hands in the air. "What do you want me to do? Accept that you're going to fuck a woman if Ice orders you to?"

"No. I told him I won't do it again." Jackal gave her a twisted smile, hiding how painful it had hurt him to make that ultimatum. "I told him no, that even if it meant I'd have to walk away from the Predators, I would."

Penni gave him a trembling smile. "You said that?"

"Yes."

"You said that even though you didn't know if I would take you back?"

"Babe, there was never any doubt that you were going to take me back."

Penni started walking around the kitchen huffily, and Jackal braced his hands on the counter.

"You're my soul mate," he told her.

"You think you can convince me that you believe in something I know damn well you don't?"

"What makes you think I don't? Who else do you think would put up with your crazy ass? You almost shot me! When haven't I been there when you needed me? Who else were you ready to jump into bed with? Who else would I walk away from the Predators for? Not...one...woman...but you. Only you."

Penni walked back over to him and laid her head on his chest. "I don't know what to do."

Jackal placed his hand on the nape of her neck, tilting her face up to his. "That's a start. I can deal with that. What I can't deal with is not being a part of your life." He kissed her as he had never kissed her before. "I couldn't fuck another woman when the only one I want to fuck is you."

He stroked her tongue with his, pressing his flush against hers. His dick was so hard he shuddered when he ground his cock into her pussy. If she were wearing anything other than her tight jeans, Jackal didn't think he would have been able to stop from releasing his dick to fuck her right there.

Penni began kissing him back, burrowing her hands under his T-shirt to run them across his waist then reach around to the small of his back.

Jackal lifted her onto the counter before pulling down her blouse, baring the lacy, pale blue bra. He pulled her breasts out of the cups, sinking his mouth onto one taut nipple.

"I want to fuck you so badly!" he groaned, blowing his heated breath over her wet nipple.

"I didn't mean I was going to make up my mind tonight." Penni circled her thighs around his hips.

"I'm not going to fuck you tonight after what happened, and I have to work for Henry tomorrow night. That gives you two days to make your mind up."

"If I don't, what then?"

"I'll make it up for you." Jackal tugged her legs down, unsnapping her jeans. He took the jeans and wispy panties off, dropping them to the floor.

She curled her hands over the countertop, licking her bottom lip. "What are you doing? You just said I had two days—"

"Helping you make up your mind." He buried his face in her belly, tracing her belly button with his tongue. "Your body is so hot. It makes me want to do everything nasty I can think of to you." Jackal caressed her flesh until he reached her pussy, spreading her legs wider.

"Like what?" she croaked.

"Like this." He used his thumbs to part the lips of her pussy, sucking her clitoris into his mouth.

"Oh, God..." Penni moaned. "What else?"

He lowered himself to his knees then blew on her shiny bud. "I'm going to make your pussy cry for me."

He licked the length of her cunt then drove his tongue into her pussy. Penni reached to the cabinets above her head.

"You taste like peach rum."

Her moist pussy was almost pushing him to his breaking point, but he wanted this time to be all about her.

He searched for the spot she was the most sensitive. When he found it, she started whimpering.

"That's not as good as my dick is going to feel."

"It's pretty good now," she panted.

"Only pretty good?"

"You like to talk too much," she complained, bringing her hands to his hair to push him back down.

"I thought girls like that shit." He placed his hands on her hips so she didn't fall off the counter.

"I'm not most girls."

"No, you're not."

Jackal used his tongue to torment Penni's pussy, sliding in and out of her then lashing her clitoris before sliding back inside. Her wetness spread, making it easier for him to slip deeper inside her pulsing muscles, driving him on, becoming drunk on her taste.

"Say my name," Penni moaned. "Say my name," she repeated.

"Penni..."

"Jackal...if you ever fuck around on me again, I'll kill you," she moaned.

He took her warning seriously. The woman didn't do anything in half measures. She was all in...or she was away. Jackal wasn't going to let that happen.

Her throbbing pussy was the only one he needed, the only one he couldn't live without tasting. And right now, it was convulsing, nearly making him come as she shattered on his tongue.

When she sat on the counter like a limp doll, he pressed kisses on her belly then each of her breasts then on her waiting mouth. Then he helped her off the countertop and back into her jeans.

He shoved her panties into his back pocket.

"Give those back."

"No. I'm going to put them in my nightstand."

She blushed, reminded of what she had kept in her nightstand before he had destroyed it.

"Are you going to cut them up, too?" Her mouth was still wet from his kiss.

"Fuck no," Jackal teased. "You probably don't want to know what I'm going to do to them when I get home." He plucked at the front of his jeans, trying to ease the material from strangling his cock.

"That's definitely TMI."

"You can have them back in two days." He walked to her door. If he stayed much longer, he would be using her pussy to ease his aching cock instead of her panties.

"You can have them."

Jackal pulled her in for one more kiss. "Lock the door after me."

"Why? The only pervert I need to keep out is you, and you have a key."

Jackal smacked her bottom as he went out the door, barely making it out before she slammed it behind him.

"God, I'm going to marry that woman."

CHAPTER THIRTY-FIVE

Penni looked up from her computer screen when she heard the office door open.

"What are you doing here?"

Grace came into the room, wearing a gorgeous dress that had her self-consciously straightening her casual top over her black pants.

"I decided to come back early." Grace smiled at her, putting her purse on the desk catty-corner from hers.

"I told you to take the rest of the month off."

"Dad told me to come home, that he needed to be alone." Her smile slipped then firmed. "He's going on a road trip. I think it will be good for him. He's bought a motorcycle and will ride throughout the country until he decides which movie he's going to direct next."

Penni and Grace talked every night. The father and daughter were close, but she could understand him wanting to mourn in private without his son and daughter as witnesses.

"Since you didn't take my offer for more time off..." Penni picked up a sheath of papers, handing them to Grace. "This is the contract for the Atlantic venue. Make sure Kaden has his own dressing room. He can't be a diva if he doesn't have fresh fruit, coffee, and an air purifier."

"Ax doesn't want a personal chef?"

"I already hired one to go on tour with us."

"Thank God. It was a pain in the ass when the venues' hired cooks who didn't make what he wanted."

"I don't think Genny knows how to make Sushi, but she'll learn," she stated confidently.

The women spent the day getting caught up on their work. Then Grace went out to get take-out for lunch. Shoving her paperwork out of the way, they sat at Penni's desk to eat.

Grace brushed a crumb away from her expensive dress. "So, Ice said you and Jackal are a couple."

Penni lowered a chip that she had been about to eat, taking her time before answering the question and finally giving the only she could.

"I'm thinking about it."

"Is it ten percent or fifty percent odds?"

Penni thought hard. "Uh...I don't know. More like seventy percent sure."

Grace frowned. "More than fifty percent? I thought you would be, like, less than ten percent."

"That was before last night."

"What happened last night?"

Penni didn't answer, shoving a chip in her mouth.

"Did you have sex with him? You swore you'd never want anything to do with him."

"No, I didn't have sex with him, but I'm thinking about it. He's kind of sexy."

"Do you think he's ten perfect—"

"What's going on? When did you become a freaking mathematician?"

Grace looked down at her food. "If you tell, I'll get in trouble, but Max started a bet over whether Jackal could...get you in bed," she answered delicately.

Penni could just imagine the words Ice had used.

"Max said Jackal couldn't get you in bed even if he had Stump's dick."

Wow, that must have hurt Jackal's pride. Then another thought struck her. Had Jackal been trying to win a bet?

Penni stiffened in her chair. "Does Jackal know?" She would cut off his dick and shove it up his ass!

"No...No, he didn't. He didn't until this morning when Ice told him. Ice wanted to figure out whom to place his bet on. Our hot tub is on the fritz...We enjoy our hot tub," Grace admitted, embarrassed.

"What did Jackal say?"

"He told Ice it was fifty percent."

Penni relaxed back in her chair. She could live with that answer.

"Well?" Penni raised her brows at her.

"Who did Ice bet on?"

Penni nodded.

"He placed on you, but he wanted me to make sure he shouldn't change his bet."

Now Penni could understand Grace's impromptu return to work.

"You might want to tell Ice to go ahead and change his bet."

"Really? Um...I'm happy...if you're happy." Grace carefully cleaned away the remains of her lunch. "But I wanted to make sure before he risks our money on a stupid bet so we don't lose."

"What do you mean?"

"Nothing's going to change your mind, right? Even if one of the men tell you something that will upset you?"

Penni folded her hands together on the desk. "Spill."

"It's just that Ice is worried one of the men will tell you something about Jackal that would keep him from winning the bet."

"Like what? If it's about Raci, we talked, and that's why I'm still making up mind about him. Before that, he had a solid ninety percent chance of getting me in bed."

"See, that's what has Ice worried."

Penni noticed that Grace had downplayed her own worry.

"What kind of things do you think they would tell me?"

"I don't know. If I knew, I would tell you. You're my friend, and I wouldn't keep anything from you that I thought you deserved to know."

"That's good to—"

"Except…" Grace became flustered. "You are aware he's one of the bouncers at the Purple Pussycat?"

"I'm the one who took you there to show you where the Predators hang out. I also know he's…slept with most of the women."

"Cool. I was worried I would have to tell you. I admire you," she said in a truly awed tone. "I don't think I could take Ice watching the women working with their clients."

Penni's chair fell back as she quickly rose. "What'd you say?"

Grace paled. "I thought you said you knew?"

"That he was lying to me about not sleeping with the strippers. I knew he threw drunks out or men who got too touchy-feely with the dancers, not watching them fuck!" Penni picked up her chair. "Never mind. Tell Ice his bet is safe." She sat back down, pushing her chair forward to her desk. "Let's go back to work."

Grace stood uncertainly. "I feel terrible. It's not like they're in the same room. He stays in a separate room behind a two-way mirror so the women stay safe. Usually, it's high profile men who want a place to have sex without being seen. The men pay for the room and the women with neither of them knowing each other."

"How do you know about it?"

Grace threw their trash away, going back to her desk. "Ice and I went there a couple times," she muttered. "You know, to spice things up."

Penni couldn't help giggling. "Did it work?"

"God, yes. We usually don't have a problem, but damn, it was...fantastic. Vida and Colton have, too. And I think that Max wants to, too, so bad. The room is expensive." Grace waved her hand in front of her face. "If I didn't want the hot tub fixed, I'd get Ice to splurge on another night."

Penni went to the temperature control, turning the air conditioner down.

"Do any of the bouncers watch when any of you—"

"Hell, no. Only the customers get watched because Henry doesn't want any of the women or men to get hurt. Some of their clients have a lot of money and think them giving a beating is included in the price. Ice said one of the men tried to break one of the women's arms a couple of weeks ago, and Jackal jacked him up." Grace rolled her eyes at Ice's choice of words.

"Some of the male workers earn money that way?"

Grace nodded. "A couple of them do. Some of the bartenders are very good-looking, not that I noticed."

"I have." Penni picked up her cell phone. She noticed Grace watching her as she asked the voice on the other end of the line to speak to Henry. Penni almost started giggling again as Grace listened to her requests.

When she hung up the call, she turned to her computer.

"Did you just rent Henry's room tonight?"

"Yes." Penni read a new email that came in during lunch.

"But…It's Monday. Jackal's working there tonight."

"I know."

* * *

"You sure you're not here to start trouble?" Henry's skeptical gaze took in her appearance in her brand new red dress that was so tight and short she had to resist the urge to tug it down.

"I promise."

Henry held out his hand.

"What?" Penni asked in confusion.

"Your card was denied."

Damn. She reached into her purse, taking out the card she used for emergencies. She would pay Shade back. *It's kind of an emergency*, she consoled herself as Henry went into his office, coming back a minute later and handing the card back.

"It's the room on the right, off the bar." Henry's big body blocked her view as he keyed in a series of numbers for the gold door at the stairs of the strip club. "Enjoy."

She almost snapped back at the amusement he made no effort to hide.

"You didn't tell, did you?" Penni asked.

"No. I keep my promises." Henry gave her another warning look.

Geez, what does he think I'm going to do?

Penni almost tripped over the plush carpet as she scoped out the room. Damn, she had been missing out. The bar room downstairs looked like a dive compared to the expensive furniture in this part of the club. The black booths were padded, and a small candle gave their occupants privacy. She was going to hit Kaden up for a higher salary if this was one of the things money could buy.

Penni saw the door off the bar, going to it and keying in the numbers Henry had given her.

She turned the knob, entering the dim room. Then she walked toward the bed, dropping her purse onto it before turning to face the mirror that she knew was a two-way looking glass.

She cleared her voice. She could almost sense him from the other room.

"Please don't come out. I need to say something to you." She took a deep breath, trying to begin the speech she had rehearsed in her head on the way to the bar.

"I told you I would know my soul mate after I slept with him, but I don't have to know that now. I'm not scared of seeing the real you. You think I don't remember that you've been an ass in the past? Did you seriously believe that, when you suddenly turned over a new leaf and became normal, I wouldn't notice?" Penni shook her head. "Really?" she scoffed. "Some of the women even know what day of the week you'll take them to the Predators' clubhouse to fuck.

"Despite what you told me last night, I don't believe you're capable of walking away from the Predators. You're a dangerous, lethal, hot-tempered, risky asshole who will never change, but that doesn't frighten me, either. I think, after you get tired of me, I will become just another day of the week to you. However, if I can jump off a limb, nearly set my house on fire, and almost electrocute myself, I think I can handle you."

Penni walked across the room, placing her hand on the mirror where she imagined his face was. "I wish so badly that I felt the same way about you that I did before Hennessy kidnapped me, but I don't. I love you, Jackal. I'm dropping out of the race. I'm going to stop and smell the roses and find out what it feels like to be loved by you." Her hand dropped to the top button of her dress. She slowly unfastened it.

"I'm not going to spend the rest of my life missing you, so before you open that door, make sure that you want me, too, because I'm not going to give you your soul back. I'm going to keep it, even if you try to take it back." She undid the last of the buttons, laying the dress on the chair next to the bed and giving him a view of her ass with the thong riding up it. Facing the mirror again, she slipped her arms behind her back to unhook the red lacy bra then placed that on the chair.

When Jackal hadn't come through the door after several minutes, her heart broke. He had made his choice.

She had started toward her clothes when she heard her cell phone ringing in her purse. Dammit, it was not the time to answer the freaking phone. But feeling embarrassed that Jackal had decided not to take her up on her invitation, she searched for her phone.

Seeing it was Jackal calling, she put it to her ear, turning toward the mirror.

"Can I come in now?" His hoarse voice put her fears to rest.

"Yes." She was still laughing when Jackal came through the door, already taking his T-shirt off and throwing it to the ground.

"The observation room is soundproof to avoid anyone knowing they're being watched." Jackal toed off his boots, unsnapping his jeans and kicking them away as he stepped out of them.

"Oh..." Penni backed toward the side of the bed. "Are you sure?" She began retreating, only to have Jackal push her on the bed.

"I'm sure."

Her body reacted to the dominance that was stamped across his face.

"You took a piece of my soul the first time I saw you. It's only fair I take a piece of yours."

She melted into the coverlet on the bed. "I know this is insane to ask this now, but is this clean?"

Jackal laughed. "Yeah. Henry gets a discount from a factory then gives them to the homeless shelter after they're washed."

"No wonder he charged so much for the room."

"If you had told me what you were planning, I would have talked Henry into giving you a discount."

"I don't think he would've. I don't think he likes me."

"I'll give you back the money for the room," Jackal offered, covering her with his body.

"Don't worry about it. I'll get it back when Max pays Ice for the bet I got him to place for me."

"Damn, I'm going to marry a smart woman."

Penni would have jumped from the bed, but Jackal kept her pinned under him.

"I didn't mean tonight. I can't believe you weren't afraid of me, the Predators, or Hennessy and his men, but I mention marriage, and you're ready to run screaming from the room."

"Marriage scares me," Penni confessed. "I've had this weird fear since I was younger that I would end up being one of those women who have multiple marriages. I have an uncle who has been married five times and an aunt who's been married six."

"How many times have your parents been married?"

"My mother was married to Shade's father and then my dad."

"Have you met Shade's father?"

"Yes, and I like him a lot. My mother was just tired of being alone. He served overseas and wasn't ready to retire. He spent a couple of vacations with Shade when he remarried and retired."

Talking had her relaxing back on the bed, becoming aware that he was stroking the pulse on her throat with his thumb.

"You're only going to get married once...to me. But I can wait until you're ready."

"As long as you understand that it is going to be a looong time before I'm ready." She looked down her body to stare at Jackal. "What are you doing?"

"Trying to make love to you."

"Oh...That feels good." Her head fell back to the pillow.

The muscles in her pussy were already in need, wanting him to fill the ache that had begun when she had seen the full view of his naked body.

Jackal circled her nipple with his tongue, making it pebble in arousal. He put his hand between her legs, playing with her pussy as if they had all the time in the world.

"Mmm, that feels really good, but I only bought the room for an hour." She circled her hips, raising them and trying to hurry him along.

"I'll pay him for the rest of the night."

"That'll be expensive!"

"It's my treat," Jackal grunted, moving toward her other nipple.

Penni's eyes started to roll back in her head, but her eyes were held by the image above her. A mirror above gave a view of Jackal. His ass was magnificent, his skin tan, and his muscles coiled as he moved. She could climax from looking at his body.

He moved to the side, rubbing his cock between the folds of her pussy. Penni couldn't see the balls of the piercings she had seen when she had given him a blowjob, but she could feel them against her skin, giving her friction that had her ready to jump into the unknown pit of desire where she was afraid she wouldn't find an opening to reach air ever again.

"Jackal..." She bit her lip when she felt him enter her.

"Babe, it's going to be all right."

"Maybe you should take a couple of those balls off."

"Babe, trust me; you're going to beg me to get more."

Where would he put them? They already traveled the length of his dick.

Penni's curiosity disappeared when he tried to put his cock in her pussy.

"It's not going to fit." Penni began to panic, slapping his back when he began to laugh.

"You had a rubber dick in your nightstand, and you're worried about how big my dick is?"

"I told you I never used it."

Penni trembled as he worked his dick into her. Sweat dripped down the side of his face. He looked like he was in more pain than she was.

"Woman, you're tight..." Jackal raised himself, bracing a hand beside her head. "Sweet Jesus...You feel good."

Penni circled her hips, trying to make him move faster. His slow movements were sending shockwaves throughout her until it was everything she could do not to scream.

Their playing around fell away as the intensity built between them. Instinctively, she rocked her pussy as he thrust inside of her. Pleasure enveloped her as she sank to the bottom of the pit of fire.

Penni shut her eyes, afraid Jackal would see the emotions rolling through her body.

"Open your eyes." Relentless, he moved harder and faster inside of her. He then tugged her hair until she opened her eyes. "Watch."

Penni gripped his shoulders, unconsciously digging her nails into his flesh. Trying to hold on to him was the only way out of pit that was consuming her.

She screamed and heard Jackal murmur something, but she couldn't make out his words. Her climax was so close she could only writhe with each of his strokes.

"Penni…" He was calling her name, each syllable leaving a mark on her heart. "Penni!" he shouted, grinding his cock so high into her that she shattered into a million pieces.

She wasn't aware she was crying until Jackal shifted to his side, brushing her tears away.

"Babe, did I hurt you?"

Penni shook her head. "You're not going to give it back, are you?"

The ruthless man that Ice had made his enforcer knew what she meant. "No, I'm not giving it back. It's mine."

CHAPTER THIRTY-SIX

"Think I can make it?" Penni leaned over the pool table, lining up her shot. Her tight jeans had more than one of the Predators sauntering over to watch the game taking place.

Jackal leaned on his pool cue, appreciating the sight of her ass bent over the table.

"Take your time," Stump said appreciatively, sitting on a bar stool that he had pulled over to watch.

Jackal gave him a warning glare as she made her shot.

Penni gave a loud whoop, casting him a gloating smile. "You owe me a beer."

After setting his pool cue on the table, he put an arm around her shoulders before leading her to the bar.

The brothers were gathered, making it hard for them to find a spot.

"You've eaten enough of those brownies she made. Move." Jackal let Penni have the last stool at the end of the bar. He reached for the platter, seeing Buzzard maneuvering it toward him.

"That wasn't nice," Penni reprimanded him for making Buzzard move, giving her sweet smile to the meanest brother in the club. "You should be more polite, like Buzzard. See? He saved the brownies so you can have one."

"Buzzard? Polite? Shit, how do you think he got his nickname?"

Penni reached out and took one of the brownies, breaking it in half. She gave him the other half. "Why?"

"Because he would eat the beak or the feet of a chicken if he was drunk enough."

Buzzard nodded proudly, as if he were honored.

Penni's eyes narrowed on Buzzard in interest. "I've wondered how they taste. I've seen them prepared on cooking shows, but I've never been brave enough to eat them myself."

"They taste like fucking chicken."

Jackal shoved himself in the spot between the two.

Penni gave him a baleful look. "You have no sense of humor." She reached past him to take another brownie, giving the whole thing to him this time.

"Are you trying to get me high?"

"Will it put you in a better mood?"

"Babe, if you want to put me in a better mood, let's go to my room." Jackal gazed at the cleavage exposed by her blouse.

Penni lowered her lashes. "You don't want a rematch?"

Jackal popped the brownie in his mouth. "Rave, give me that bottle of rum." Taking the bottle in his hand, he spun Penni off the stool, steering her through the throng of brothers and bitches hanging around.

"Why do you want to go to your room so early? It's only ten."

"I'm not spending my whole night off with the brothers when I can spend it fucking you."

Penni took a step backward after he closed the door.

He didn't bother with the lamp; he could see her well enough from the light left on in his bathroom.

She loosened the ties at her throat, showing the lacy peach bra that had teased him throughout the night.

"Haven't you had enough of me yet?" she teased him, taking off her top and letting it slip through her fingers.

In the two months they had been together, Jackal had discovered Penni wasn't shy. She enjoyed sex as much he did. She could play shy, but then she turned into a vixen without blinking an eye. She could flirt one day then be standoffish the next day, making him work to get her in bed. She had crumbled any preconceived beliefs he'd had about women. When Penni had made her mind up that she wanted him, there had been no half-measures; she had given herself fully and expected the same from him. But his favorite act was what she was doing now: baiting him, showing the sexy attitude that could bring him to his knees.

She took her time wiggling out of her jeans before bending over to show her breasts that were almost spilling out of her bra.

"Not yet." He huskily groaned when she walked to the new bed he had bought last month.

She had refused to sleep over until he had bought it, joking that his old one had cooties. Jackal hadn't wanted her to be reminded of the other women he had been with when he was fucking her. Therefore, he had paid for the bed, but Penni had picked it out. It was fancy for his taste, but she had insisted, so he had given in.

Ice had laughingly said Penni had him by the balls, and he'd admitted she did, especially when she gave a performance the way she was now, gripping the metal post at the corner of the bed.

"Are you hard?"

"You want me to show you?"

"God, yes." She licked her bottom lip.

Jackal set down the bottle of rum on his nightstand before turning on the lamp. Then, removing his clothes, he stepped over them, reaching for her.

The tsk-tsking sound had him clenching his hands to keep from jerking her to him. Penni crouched down by the bed, giving Jackal a view of the peach panties covering her pussy.

"Who gave you that move?" he asked.

"Sherri. You like it?"

"Yeah. She give you any other pointers?" Jackal's hand went to his dick, rubbing his thumb over the head.

Penni pranced forward before dropping down in front of him. Brushing his hand out of the way, she circled the head of his cock with her mouth. As she twirled her tongue over him, unbelievable pleasure tore at his restraint.

She flicked her tongue down the length of his cock, gently taking each of the nine balls along his dick into her mouth before releasing it.

"Careful."

"Don't you trust me?" She laid the side of her face on his pelvis, her hand sliding up and down him.

Jackal jutted out his hips, silently demanding for her to take him into her mouth. "If I didn't trust you, you wouldn't be so close to my dick."

She chuckled, her golden curls dancing in the light from the lamp. Jackal used the opportunity to twine his fingers through her hair, holding her steady.

"Babe, you're driving me crazy."

"It's supposed to be sexy."

"Who told you that?"

"I read it in a magazine."

"Can I borrow it when you leave on Monday?" Jackal was already resenting the two weeks she would be gone when Mouth2Mouth left for Canada.

"I'm going to bring you a big stack of magazines. They'll keep you busy while I'm gone. Besides, you might learn a thing or two."

"Like what?"

"Like, there are hundreds of ways we can have sex besides the two you like."

"Babe, I like what I like."

Penni fell to the floor, laughing. "I love when you joke around with me."

Jackal sat down on the floor, leaning back against his bed. He grabbed one of her feet, slowly dragging her closer to him. She stared at him, startled.

"If you want something different, I can do different." He took her other foot in his hand, pulling the lower half of her body up to his.

After dropping her feet, he gripped the lace of her panties, ripping them apart. Then he lifted Penni by her hips and placed her over his jutting dick, positioning her pussy where he wanted it.

Penni stared into his eyes as she sank down on him, her head falling back and her tits turning as peach as her bra when all of his cock was buried in her.

Giving her a minute, he caressed her back until she began sliding up then down on him. He let her fuck him at her own speed. She was so tight he couldn't believe she could move at all.

He put his hand on her pussy, rolling his thumb over the bud of her clitoris, and Penni squirmed on him, her wetness surrounding him and making it easier for her to move on him.

Braced between his hands, he held her, urging her to move faster while taking a nipple in his mouth. He almost bit her when her muscles clenched on his dick.

"Woman, you need to quit reading so much." Jackal raised his hips as he thrust higher into her.

Penni's pleasure-filled expression showed she was affected as he was. She arched her back, moving faster, and Jackal's balls tightened.

Spreading his legs, he shifted, lowering her to the floor, and then he was over her, relentlessly pumping his aching cock into her pussy.

When she began screaming, she flung her hand out, grabbing his T-shirt and biting it to muffle her screams.

Jackal wiped the sweat out of his eyes, waiting for her spasms to stop before he flipped her onto her stomach and started fucking her again. She began clawing the carpet, grabbing the T-shirt she had slipped off of him to bite it, stifling the moans she couldn't hold back.

"Any more positions you want to try?" Jackal goaded, trying to hold back his loud groans.

She shook her head, unable to answer.

He paced his thrusts, using the head of his dick to hit different spots along the walls of her slick channel. When he found the spot he wanted, he butted against it rhythmically until even his T-shirt couldn't muffle her screams.

Jackal stiffened over her, unable to hold back the release he knew would send her over the edge with him.

"I guess we need to turn on the music next time," Jackal muttered, dropping down beside her on the carpet.

"I'm not leaving this room until everyone is gone." The only part of her body she could move was her head, and she only turned that so she could glare at him.

He slid his hand down to cup the prettiest ass he had ever seen. "Believe me, your screams are nothing to be embarrassed about. I can do what Stump does and turn on a porno. He said it gives him inspiration." Jackal rolled his front toward the ceiling. "It's a good way to slip a bitch in your bedroom that you don't want the brothers to know you're fucking."

Jackal knew he had said the wrong thing when she raised up to sit on the floor. He laid his head on the curled up shirt.

"Like you do when you slip in Henry's girls?" Her face turned serious, calling him out on the lies he had told her.

"Yes."

"Are you—"

"I haven't fucked any of them since Hennessy kidnapped you. I don't plan to as long as you keep me happy."

Air was pushed out of his lungs when she sprang up to sit on his waist.

"I don't think that's funny!"

Jackal raised a hand to the nape of her neck, pulling her down to his mouth. "Who can't take a joke now?"

"I can't stand the thought of you with another woman."

He teased the corner of her mouth. "Me, neither. You've turned me against wanting other women."

"Quit teasing me. It's not funny anymore."

Jackal tangled his fingers in her hair. "Babe, I'm deadly serious. Why would I want second place when I can have the best?"

"Aw, you may have dug yourself out of the dog house."

Jackal gave her a hungry kiss, as if he hadn't just fucked her. "You ready to get a shower?"

Penni pinned his shoulders down. "Keep going. You're not finished digging."

* * *

Jackal leaned through the rolled down window to kiss Penni's pouting mouth.

"You sure you don't want to take me out to breakfast?"

"I can't," he told her. "I'm meeting someone in thirty minutes."

"Okay, we can do it tomorrow."

Jackal watched her drive away before going to his bike where Max and Fade were waiting, already sitting on their bikes.

"Let's get this show over with." Max started his motor. "I have an hour."

"Why are you working on a Saturday, anyway?" Jackal straddled his bike, starting his own motor.

"Brother, you know how many kids I have, and they all need new shoes." He grinned, backing up.

Jackal turned around, maneuvering his bike to take the lead with Max and Fade riding behind. It was ten minutes to the house that sat on the corner of a street where the residents were afraid to go out after dark.

Fade cut his motor. "Son of a bitch has bars on his window."

Jackal parked his bike next to theirs. "He's expecting me. I don't know how many of his friends are going to be in there. You cool going in?"

"Hell, brother, I woke up to give an ass whooping; the more, the merrier." Max kept his voice low as they walked up the driveway.

Once Jackal knocked on the door, it took several minutes for it to open. A pimply punk answered.

"Jackal?"

"Reefer?"

The dumbass straightened his shoulders when Jackal addressed him. Then the wannabe stepped back, letting Max, Fade, and Jackal inside.

Jackal surveyed the living room, seeing a coffee table covered in dirty dishes, and the couch was so filthy Penni would recoil in horror.

A muscled dipshit stood up, crossing his arms over his chest, trying to give the impression he could deal with the trouble that threatened his friend.

Jackal pointed at the door to the side of the room. Max nodded, going to the doorway, but the dipshit tried to block his path.

"If you want to buy my shit," Max said, "I'm going to make sure there aren't some friends waiting to shake me down. If he doesn't move, I'm out of here."

"It's cool. Move, Keg," Reefer said.

Max walked into the other room. The men stayed silent as Max went through the other rooms before coming back to stand by the kitchen door.

"No one else is here besides them."

"Can we speed this up? My mom's coming by to clean my house."

Jackal stared at the room in disdain. "Call her and tell her not to come for a couple of hours."

"Why?" Reefer lost his punk-ass air, trying to take a step toward his backup.

Both froze when Fade pulled out his gun. The two pussies then tried to run, but Max blocked them, his arm knocking the bigger guy in the gut.

Keg fell to his knees, vomiting.

"Damn." Max laughed. "He pissed himself."

"Here, you can take my money!" Reefer tried to dig into his pockets, but Fade stopped him, twisting his hands behind his back.

"I don't want your fucking money. I'm giving you another chance to call your mommy. If you screw it up, I'm gonna take you somewhere else, and your mommy will be burying your body instead of being here to drive you to the hospital. Give him his cell phone, Fade."

Reefer almost dropped the cell phone. He was barely able to press the buttons as Fade watched him with the barrel of his gun held against Reefer's temple.

They listened as Reefer followed his orders then gave the phone back to Fade, who crushed it under his boot.

"I've got to get to work," Max reminded him.

"Just take my money and go. I don't want trouble." Reefer had gone from a punk-ass to a whiny bitch.

"Did it feel good when you killed those ducks?"

"Huh?" Reefer's mouth dropped open. "I didn't..."

Jackal punched him in his lying mouth. "Lie to me, and I'll cut out your tongue."

Fade pulled a long, vicious knife out of his boot. "You didn't have a problem bragging about it during the pot parties you've been giving."

"You're going to hurt me over fucking ducks?" Reefer's wide-eyed appearance showed disbelief, unable to comprehend that Jackal was threatening him over something as inconsequential as ducks.

"I like ducks, especially the ones my woman loves."

"Hey, man, I didn't know your bitch was—"

"Now you do." Jackal punched him in his stomach.

Reefer took a punch better than his friend—at least he didn't vomit.

Keg tried to get up to help his friend, but Max grabbed his shoulder.

"A smart man would stay down and let the punk-bitch take the beating that's coming to him."

Keg took Max's advice, staying down.

Jackal kicked him in the ribs, and when he fell down, he planted his foot on Reefer's chest. "How does it feel to have someone kick the shit out of you?"

"Please, stop…"

"That was only for the first one you killed. You killed five. I'm just getting started."

* * *

Max waved to them as he turned his bike toward the street where he worked. Jackal and Fade were pulling into the parking lot as Ice got off his bike.

"How'd it go?" Ice asked as they went into the club together.

"He was crying for his mommy when we left him." Fade snickered.

"He's lucky I left enough of him for her to take to the hospital." Jackal went inside to his bedroom then came back to the bar to pour himself a drink. "He's learned a hard lesson about keeping his fucking mouth shut."

Ice lifted a brow at his choice of drink. "Since when do you drink rum?"

"I've developed a taste for it." Jackal was taking another sip when Ice's cell phone rang. The expression that came over his face had Jackal ready to get the men out of their beds.

He was the first one heading toward the hallway when he heard Ice's yell.

"Get out! Get out of the clubhouse!"

Jackal opened Stump's door, seeing him in bed with Rave. They were already moving.

Jackal then ran down the hallway, slamming open doors and making sure the men and women were getting out. In the last room, Isla was trying to heave Buzzard out of bed.

"Get out! I'll get him." Jackal went to the bed, lifting Buzzard to his feet. "Brother, you picked the wrong time to get drunk off your ass."

"It was the brownies. I ate most of the them."

Ice ran to help them. They were going out the door when the explosion hit the club.

"Son of a bitch, *run!*" Ice roared.

The explosion sent a ball of fire chasing them, knocking them to the concrete. Jackal grabbed Buzzard's arm, lifting him and half-dragging him across the pavement to the end of the parking lot.

Fade and Griffen were trying to pull the bikes back, but they gave up when another explosion shook the clubhouse. Consequently, the brothers simply stood back, watching their clubhouse disintegrate until the police and the two firetrucks' sirens had them moving farther away.

Ice stonily stared at the fire that was destroying the clubhouse. "If Lucky hadn't called, we would all be dead."

Jackal hated himself at that moment. He had failed as an enforcer. If Lucky hadn't given them the warning, each of them would be dead, burnt to the point that even their families wouldn't have been able to identify them.

"Who did it?" Jackal already knew, but he wanted it confirmed before he set his wrath on the one deserving his vengeance.

"Raul, Fat's Louise's ex-brother-in-law. He escaped from the Mexican prison. They didn't even know he was missing until this morning. Lucky was with the team that was extraditing Raul to the United States. He didn't have time to warn Hennessy before the bomb he planted killed three of his men. If Lucky hadn't called us, we would have been hit, too."

Jackal wondered which of the hanger-on's in the club last night had planted the bomb. Raul would be long gone, hiding out with someone who could protect him.

"I'm going to kill the bastard," Jackal vowed.

Cars were lined up on the street to watch the fire. One car braked, and then Grace was running toward Ice, throwing herself into his arms.

"Oh, God! Are you okay?"

Ice pulled her close. "I'm fine. I told you I was okay when I called."

Grace burst into tears. "I've never been so afraid in my whole life. I couldn't bear to lose you and my mother—"

"I'm here, Grace. The bastard didn't come close to taking us out," Ice lied to keep Grace from knowing how close she had been to losing her husband.

Jackal recognized the car double-parking beside Grace's. Penni's terrified face had his stomach churning, but he braced himself for what he had to do.

When she threw herself into his arms, Jackal kept them to his sides, stepping back.

Her startled face stared back at him. "Are you okay? What happened? Why didn't you call me? Grace called—"

"Go home."

"I'm not leaving...Are you hurt?"

"No, I don't have a mark on me." Jackal ignored the burning pain on his back where the fire had scorched his T-shirt. The injury he felt from when he had dragged Buzzard across the pavement was hidden where she couldn't see.

"Thank God you aren't hurt."

"It wasn't God who saved us; it was Lucky."

"Lucky? How did he save you? Is he here?" Penni looked at the faces in the crowd.

"No, he called Ice, warning us to get out. If hadn't, we would be dead. I failed the club." Self-loathing filled him, hurting him more than the blisters on his back.

"You blame yourself for this?"

"Who else is here to blame but me? I should have known the cartel wasn't going to allow their men to be killed without repercussions."

"Jackal—"

"Go, Penni." Jackal reached into his pocket, taking out his keychain and sliding off the key for Penni's condo, trying to give it to her.

She shook her head, tears brimming her eyes. "I don't understand—"

"You were right; I'm never going to walk away from the Predators. If I hadn't had my mind on fucking you, this wouldn't have happened."

"You're blaming me?" Penni whispered.

"Aren't you listening to me!" Jackal yelled. "I'm blaming myself. I didn't do my job, and because of me, these men almost died!"

Penni took a step back at the anger he didn't try to hide.

"Get out of here! I don't want to see your face again." Jackal shoved her key in her hand. "Go."

Jackal would never forget how she looked when she turned to flee from his harsh words.

Grace caught her, going with her while giving him dirty looks as she helped Penni into her car.

"Brother, this is not your fault. Go after her before it's too late," Ice said, breaking through the agonizing pain of having his soul ripped out of him.

"It's already too late."

CHAPTER THIRTY-SEVEN

The green room was larger than most with several rooms where the performers could rest before going on stage. This one had several couches and plush chairs that would fit all the members of the band with a table placed against the wall for all of Genny's cooking.

"How does it look?" Genny asked apprehensively.

"It looks fantastic. You did a great job." Penni pushed several of the bottled waters into the ice bowl.

"I'm getting better."

That's an understatement, Penni thought. The young woman had successfully made sushi that would give the finest restaurant a run for their money.

"Take a break. You and your crew can break it down when the band gets back on the bus after the show."

"Thanks. Where are we heading this time?"

"New Jersey." It was a stop that was halfway through their tour. It would be another two weeks before they made it back to Queen City.

"I've never been to New Jersey. I'm excited."

"Me, too." Penni remembered when she had first toured with Mouth2Mouth. Each new city had held something new to discover. Now, they just ran together.

Genny yawned. "If you need anything, just call."

"I will."

Penni sat down on one of the chairs when Genny left, listening to the music coming from the stage. She closed her eyes, seeing Jackal's face, and her hand went to her heart.

The ache had grown each day since he had told her he never wanted to see her again. She was dying inside, and it wasn't anything a doctor could fix. She knew it because she had tried that. The doctor's answer had been to prescribe anxiety medication, which she hadn't filled.

She hadn't believed a broken heart could affect her so badly. She knew better now. She had known it would be heartbreaking if Jackal had grown tired her. The reality, though, was killing her.

"What's up, butterfly?"

The voice from the doorway had her lifting her head.

"Shade?" Penni used her hand to raise herself from the chair.

Her brother's penetrating gaze bore into her. He didn't say anything, just held out his arms for her.

Penni took faltering steps until she found her enclosed in his arms, laying her head on his chest.

"What...are...you doing here?" she managed to get out.

"You didn't sound like yourself when you called me."

Penni gave him a slight smile. "I'm just tired from being on the road."

"Is that all? It doesn't have anything to do with Jackal?"

She dropped her arms, turning toward the food table. "Are you hungry?"

"No, I'm not hungry. You should eat some food yourself, though. You look like you've lost weight."

"Not really. I just took off the weight I gained from Lily's cooking."

"If you keep losing weight, I'm going to tell her, and she'll come and put it back on."

Penni shrugged. "That might not be necessary. I'm thinking about coming for a visit when the tour ends. I'm missing you, Lily, and John."

"Really? That would be good. It would be better than what you have planned for when you get back to Queen City."

"How do you know what I have planned?"

"Grace said you're planning on tasering Jackal's ass to make him listen to you."

"I might have been exaggerating," Penni lied, glad she had left her purse on the bus. "I said that because, when I tried to call him, he wouldn't answer my calls. I've texted him, but he won't even answer those, and I've sent over a hundred. I begged Grace to ask him to call me. I even took a flight back to Queen City to talk to him, hoping that giving him a week alone after the bombing would make him ready to talk to me again. Casey told me he was living in a hotel room, but they wouldn't give me the room number. The hotel manager called the police on me." Penni shook her head wearily. "I almost called you to come down and help me knock some sense into him," she admitted ruefully.

"Why didn't you?" Shade's unemotional voice didn't hint how he would have responded to her request.

"I didn't want you to think I was chasing after Jackal the way I did Train."

"Penni, I can see the difference between the way you feel about them. You love Jackal. You never loved Train."

"I know." She choked back a sob. "Has Ice told you how Jackal is doing? He won't say anything to Grace because he knows she'll tell me."

"Sit down, Penni."

She wanted to remain standing, but she walked across the room, sitting on the couch.

Shade waited until she was seated before he sat down next to her, taking her hand and holding it tightly.

"I've seen Jackal. Physically, he's fine. He's actually why I'm here." Shade's face became closed off. "He wants you to stop calling and texting him." When Penni tried to jerk her hand away, Shade held it more tightly. "I know this isn't easy, but what you're doing is distracting him, and he can't deal with that right now.

"Jackal has been with me and Cade, searching for Raul. The son of a bitch almost cost twenty men their lives, and Jackal would have been one of them if I hadn't called in time. He had to leave you behind to do a job he feels needs to be done, or none of us are going to be safe. Not Lily, John, the Last Riders, or the Predators and their families.

"Hennessy lost three men, and Jackal wants that to be the last three people who are killed because of that cartel. Cade and I are flying home, though. I can't leave Lily and John any longer, and Cade's baby is due anytime. Jackal, Fade, and Hennessy are trying find him on their own with the DEA's help."

"All he had to do was tell me. I can understand wanting to keep his friends safe. I can handle Jackal being in danger. It scares me to death, but I can deal with that. It's losing him I can't—"

"You're missing Jackal's point of sending me here. It's not so you will feel better and think you can wait for him until this situation is finished. He wants you to understand the relationship is over. He wants the texts and calls to stop. He wants you to move on with your life."

"How am I supposed to do that? I hear his voice in my heart. My mind tells me it's over, but my heart won't give up. I can't give up. I love Jackal. I always will."

The silence between them was broken when they heard Kaden tell the audience "Good night," and the band began to play their final song of the night.

My love for you consumes me, drowns me.
Baby, why can't you see you're mine for eternity.
Like a bird in a cage with nowhere to go,
These tainted hands hold your soul.

I will make you love me, crave me.
Baby, just you wait and see. I will become your disease.
Like a bird in a cage with nowhere to go,
These tainted hands hold your soul.

You flew away.
You didn't stay.
Baby, why didn't I see you could be stolen from me.
I'm like a bird in a cage with nowhere to go,
These tainted hands need your soul.

You came back.
My heart was black.
Baby, look and see. You have finally rescued me.

Like a bird in a cage with nowhere to go,
These tainted hands won your soul.

The song had never been so poignantly beautiful to Penni.

"I need to go. The band will be coming in."

Shade looked down at her. Taking her hands, he helped her to her feet. "I have a flight to catch. Take care, butterfly." Shade hugged her tightly.

"You haven't called me a butterfly since I was a little girl." Penni laid a hand on Shade's beating heart.

"I remember you always wanted to jump on the bed when I tried to make you go to sleep, telling me to catch you."

Penni felt a lone tear slip down her cheek. "I felt invincible then. I'm all grown up now, and I know I'm not. Jackal wants me to forget about him. He gave back the key to my apartment, even sent you here to make sure I get his message, but he didn't send me back the most important thing I need. Tell Jackal, until I get that back...I'll be waiting."

Shade brushed her tears away. "I'll tell him."

Watching Shade walk away was the hardest thing she had done in her life. She wanted Shade to take her to Jackal. However, she gathered every ounce of control she was capable of and watched him walk out the door, taking the only link of talking to Jackal with him.

She was still Jackal's woman, even though he didn't want to accept it. When he had made her his woman, she had become a Predator. What a Predator takes, they don't give back, and she wasn't giving Jackal back.

He's mine.

CHAPTER THIRTY-EIGHT

Jackal turned the motorcycle Rider had let him borrow six months ago. Wearily, he stared at the new Predators' clubhouse that Ice had built while he had been gone.

He was tired, and every bone in his body hurt. He had ridden the last leg of the journey home alone, leaving Hennessy in Colt, Arkansas. And Fade, he was gone.

Jackal went to the door, expecting the room to be half-empty, but all the brothers were waiting for him. Their cheers and yells were a hollow comfort due to the brother he had left behind.

Ice slapped him on his shoulder, shaking his hand. Max gathered him in his bear hug, lifting him off his feet. Stump handed him a bottle of beer. One after another, the brothers greeted him while the women all tearfully kissed him.

Jackal went to the bar, speaking to each of them as he passed until he reached the women lining the bar, the ones who hadn't been waiting to kiss him hello.

"Hey, Grace, Vida, Casey."

"Jackal, we're glad you're home." Grace hugged him.

Casey and Vida each waited their turn. He expected recriminations for his treatment of Penni. Instead, they went to their husbands.

"We'll see you guys later. We're meeting Sawyer and going shopping." Grace kissed her husband good-bye.

Casey held her hand out to Max, who grumbled, getting out his wallet to hand her a couple of twenties. When she didn't move away, he gave her the rest of his cash, showing her it was now empty.

Vida laughed at Colton, who just handed her his credit card.

"You make us look bad for making our husbands give us shopping money," Casey complained.

"I made Ice fork over some, too. I asked for his credit card this morning before he left. He's in a better mood before I get him out of bed," Grace confided.

"I'll have to try that. Max holds onto his wallet like it will save him from drowning."

"Grace, wait," Jackal cut in.

Grace and the other two women turned back to Jackal.

"Where is Penni? I rode by her condo, but she wasn't there. I called Shade, but he thought she was at her condo. He even checked her cell phone, and it showed she was at home. When I broke into her apartment, though, it was empty. Ice said he didn't know where she was, either. So, where is she?"

Jackal ran a hand through his long hair. He hadn't wanted to call, too afraid she would hang up on him. His plan to show up at her door and beg his way back into her life had failed.

"Penni made us promised not to tell you," Grace told him. "She said, if you want to see her, you know where to find her."

Frustrated, Jackal stared at her. "If I knew where she was, I wouldn't have driven to her condo or to her office. I even checked to make sure she wasn't feeding the ducks before I came here. So, where is she?"

"We can't tell you," Vida said, giving him a sympathetic glance.

"Is she with a man? Is that why you won't tell—"

"Penni said you would know how to find her," Grace cut him off. "Get some rest. Ice told us you haven't had time to sleep since you killed Raul. When you get some sleep and are thinking more clearly, you'll know how to find her."

Jackal wanted to throw a bar stool at the wall. Ice must have known he was at his breaking point, because he blocked the women from his view.

They left, laughing as they walked away.

Jackal pressed his fingers against his tired eyes. "They think I deserve to suffer."

"Brother, go to bed. I saved the end of the hall for you. It has a brand new bed. It'll feel good after sleeping in all those hotel rooms."

Jackal had to admit to himself he was too tired to ride anywhere until he got some sleep.

"I'll get a couple hours sleep, but if I can't figure out where Penni is, your wife will be my next stop, and I won't be taking no for an answer the next time."

Ice nodded. "I'll warn her. Go to sleep."

Jackal nodded, passing Ice who stopped him, holding out his hand.

"I'm glad you're back, brother. It hasn't been the same without you."

"Thanks, Ice. I won't let you down ever again."

"You've never let me down, Jackal, not once."

The two men leaned into each other, slapping each other on their backs before stepping back.

Jackal finally made his way down the hallway, seeing Ice had added more rooms to the new clubhouse. He was too tired to appreciate the changes, though. Right now, all he had on his mind was getting enough sleep to figure out where Penni was.

He had googled her tour schedule. Mouth2Mouth's next concert was a month away. If he couldn't find her by then, he would drive there, even if it took him all night.

Jackal went into the room Ice had told him was his. Turning on the light switch, he closed the door behind him. There was a large bed taking up half the room.

Jackal sat down on the end of the bed. It reminded him of the one Penni had picked out before the clubhouse had been destroyed.

Jackal ran his hand over the metal frame then dropped his hands into his lap. Penni's face swam in front of him.

Jackal buried his face in his hands. "Where are you?" he groaned out.

Suddenly, he lifted his head. Jerking himself to his feet, he strode down the hall, coming to a stop in the clubroom. The men turned to stare at him.

"I know where she is," Jackal said huskily.

Ice stood up from the new, blue La-Z-Boy rocker. "I knew you were a smart man and would figure it out. Grace left her car here. I'll drive you because no way in hell are you driving yourself."

"Where is she?" Max yelled out before they could get out the door.

"Fuck you, Max. You figure it out."

* * *

Ice found a parking space, and Jackal opened the car door, beginning to get out.

"I'll wait ten minutes to make sure she's there. I was supposed to call Grace and tell her if you left the clubhouse so Penni would be there until you showed up."

"Thanks, Ice."

"No problem."

Jackal went into the Purple Pussycat. He strode through the room and up the stairs to the large door where he keyed in the code for the bouncers that gave them access to each room of the club.

Jackal's heart beat hard as he neared the door where Penni and he had stayed when they had made love the first time.

Henry was talking to one of the bartenders, but he turned to watch him cross the room.

Jackal keyed in his number, but the door didn't turn. Henry had overridden the door's commands.

"What are the numbers?"

Henry raised a brow at Jackal's menacing tone.

"I don't know what you're talking about it." Sherri's, Henry's girlfriend, gloating face showed she didn't know she was risking her own life by thwarting his attempts to enter the room that Jackal was even more sure Penni was in. There was an easier way to find out without killing the woman, though.

Jackal went to the middle door where the bouncers could look into both rooms while the clients used their services. Jackal keyed in his number again, and this time, it worked.

Jackal gave Henry a killing look before going inside.

The mirror showed that the room on the left was empty. Jackal stepped to the right mirror, and his breath caught. Penni was sitting on the bed, facing the two-way mirror and staring down at the phone in her hand.

Jackal hadn't cried since he was kid when his mother hadn't come home, and his father had made fun of him for it. But he cried now, knowing no one could see him.

It had been six months since he had last seen her. Shade had offered to send pictures of her, but Jackal had told him no. Jackal had known that, if he had seen her, he would have broken and gone to her. However, he'd had an oath to keep, and he had been determined to keep it. Too many lives depended on him succeeding, and one of those lives was hers.

His blood still ran cold at the thought of her being there when the explosives had been detonated. If he hadn't scheduled the meeting with Reefer to sell him a dime bag, they would have been in his bed at the clubhouse that Saturday morning. The only reason Ice had been up was because Ice had made it a rule that, when someone was out on a job, someone had to keep watch, and he had known the rest of the brothers wouldn't want to get up so early.

He saw that Penni had lost weight. She had been a tiny thing before, but now she looked so fragile a gust of wind could blow her away.

He walked closer to the mirror, wanting to run from the room and into the one she was waiting in. Knowing Henry wouldn't give him the number until she told him to was the only thing stopping him. He couldn't even fucking call her since her cell phone was at her condo, and he didn't know the number to the one she was holding.

Jackal was about to take his cell phone out of his pocket to call Ice and tell him to call Grace and beg her to call Penni to let her know he was here when Penni suddenly lifted her head, staring at the mirror. Then she dropped the cell phone onto the bed.

She rose unsteadily to her feet. The peach teddy she wore wasn't seductive or playful like she usually liked to wear. It enticed. Tiny straps led to her satin covered breasts, and then her skin was exposed all the way to the small patch of satin that covered her pussy. It was an all-out assault on a man's dick.

"I know you're there." Her soft voice filled the small room he was in. "I can feel you." She placed her hand on the mirror, and Jackal lifted his to place it in the same spot.

"I've missed you so badly."

"I've missed you, too." Jackal replied, despite knowing she couldn't hear him through the soundproof glass.

"Before I tell you the combination to the room, I want you to listen to what I have to say."

Penni raised her other hand to the mirror, and Jackal mirrored her movements.

"I love you. I love you so much I don't even care what you've done since you've been gone. I don't care if you've fucked a hundred women. I don't care who you killed. I don't even care if you love me. *I just want you.*

"I don't want to hear any excuses for why you wouldn't see me, and I certainly don't want to know who the women you fucked are. I don't want any more oaths or promises, even if you plan to keep them. I just want you. I will always want...*you.*" She gave a shuddering breath, stepping away from the mirror.

Jackal waited for her to tell him the combination or to keep talking. When she did neither, he began to laugh. She had forgotten to give him the combination.

It took him a minute to get Ice to quit laughing before promising to call Grace, He waited breathlessly for her phone to ring.

When she went to answer her phone on the bed, he was already debating smashing through the mirror. However, her soft laughter had him calming long enough to hear her tell him the combination.

Jackal practically tore the door off its hinges as he left the viewing room, going to the locked door. He had to key in the numbers twice because of his bumbling fingers. Then he rushed inside, slamming the door by kicking it closed.

Penni was laughing so hard she fell back on the bed. "Do you know how long I rehearsed that speech?"

Jackal stood, staring down at her. "I take it you forgot to rehearse the number part of it."

"Yes." Her poignant eyes stared up at him. Penni raised herself back up, reaching her hand out to cup his cheek. "I've never seen you cry before."

"I love you. And there haven't been any women to tell you about. I didn't want another woman. I'll never want another woman but you."

"I told you I don't want to talk—"

"Too damn bad. You deserve to know that."

Penni took his T-shirt, raising it to his chest so she could press a kiss on his abdomen. "Go ahead, then, but I'm not listening." She snapped open his jeans, parting them then pulling his dick out.

"Uh...I guess we can talk later."

"You took off the metal balls?" Penni angrily glared up at him.

"I was riding so long my dick was killing me." Any other woman would cuss him out for leaving her, but the only thing Penni was pissed about was piercings?

"Can't you put them back in?"

Jackal gaped down at her. "Right now?"

"Uh...yeah." Penni laughed, rolling on the bed as he laid down beside her.

"Woman, I can't put them in right now. Do you not remember how many I had? And I only had that many because I was drunk off my ass when Colton did it. We'll have to go back to the clubhouse to put but them back in. I'll have to be drunk to even put the Apadravya back in, and the nine balls in my dick, so no, I can't do it right now."

"All right, there's no need to be grouchy about it. I'll make you a pan of my brownies. It'll work better than alcohol."

"I'll stick with my rum. I'm afraid, if I eat your brownies, I'll end up with more of them."

Penni propped herself over his chest. "Is it going to hurt?"

"Babe, it's gonna hurt like a son of a bitch, but for you, I'll do it."

"That's the sweetest thing you've ever said to me."

"I have told you numerous times how much you mean to me—"

"But none that involve pain."

"Babe, believe me; it involved a lot of pain to stay away from you. Sending Shade was hard on both of us, but neither of us wanted you to mourn me if Raul killed me." He didn't try to hide his anguished expression. The months he had been away from her wouldn't be easily forgotten.

"When you have the piercings back in, we'll call it even."
Penni flicked his nipple.

Jackal slid the teddy straps off her shoulders. "You've lost
weight."

"I'll gain it back. Lily is coming for a visit. She's a good
cook."

He hoisted her farther up the bed so he could get a better
view in the mirror on the ceiling.

"Shade coming?"

Jackal groaned when she trailed her mouth down his abs
to his dick that was so hard it was reaching toward his belly
button.

"Mmm-hmm. So are my parents and most of The Last
Riders."

"What's the occasion?" Jackal raised himself onto his
elbows to look down at her sucking the head of his cock into
her mouth.

She lifted her mouth off him to raise her head, staring into
his eyes. "I thought we could get married."

"You're asking me to marry you while you're giving me a
blowjob?"

She gave him a trembling smile. "I thought it would be
harder to say no."

"God, I love you."

She gave a shaky laugh. "Is that a yes?"

"It's a big fucking hell yes."

Penni straddled his legs then reached under her crotch to
unsnap her teddy.

"I always wondered how bitches did that."

Fascinated, he watched as Penni tugged it over her head,
tossing it over her shoulder. Then he lost what mind he had

left when she slipped her palm up his cock, taking it into her mouth.

"Every night I went to sleep, I imagined your mouth on me." Unconsciously, Jackal's hand went to his side, clenching the coverlet in his grip.

She took him to the back of her throat as she fondled his balls.

He wanted to jerk her down to the bed and thrust into her balls deep, but he sensed she wanted him in her control. She'd had no control when he had left her, so she needed to regain her power in their relationship, and Jackal let her have it. She deserved more for what he had put her through.

Her little nipples grew taut, flushing as her excitement grew. When she moaned, Jackal couldn't take another second.

He rolled her back to the bed, sliding his legs between hers. Plastering his mouth to hers, he figured, if he was going to drown, she was going down with him.

He slid his cock into her weeping pussy an inch at a time. It was like taking one piece of her at a time.

At first, her pussy was tight, but then it loosened as he moved, relaxing as excitement built, as he touched each of her contracting muscles. She trusted him to give her what she needed, to take the ascent they were both trying to reach.

Thrusting deeper, he put his mouth to her ear. "If I never have another moment on this earth, I want to spend the last with you like this: with my dick in you, giving my soul to you. You're the only reason my heart is still beating.

"I rode across most of the United States and Mexico, just so I could come home and breathe again. Fade was killed, and Raul turned his gun on me. I wasn't even afraid of dying, because I knew we would be together again. It might have taken years and years, but you would be with me again in eternity. I knew you would find me when it was your time to pass. You would hear me calling to you until you could find me."

He thruster harder until he was pounding her into the bed, grasping the mattress so they wouldn't fall to the floor.

"Penni...Penni...You're my own Penni from Heaven." His raw emotions lit a passionate fire in her that had Penni curling her legs around his, slamming her pussy up to take what she needed from him.

Jackal...He heard her calling his name over and over without a sounding passing her lips. Their souls were claiming each other back, erasing the pain of the last six months and replacing it with a joy that would last through the lifetime that lay ahead of them.

When he could breathe again, he was able to focus on her face as they lay curled into each other, stroking the each other, unable to believe they were together again.

Jackal curled an arm over her shoulder, enjoying the serenity of the climax she had gave him and holding her close again.

He lifted one tired eyelid to see hers scrunched in worry. He hastily closed his eye, not wanting to know what was going through her mind.

Damn, he was tired...and Penni was obviously not.

When Jackal couldn't ignore her jostling his shoulder anymore, he raised both of his eyelids to look at her.

"What?" he grumbled.

"We have to leave. Henry charges double on Friday nights."

"I'll pay for it. Go to sleep." Jackal closed his eyes tightly, hoping she would take the hint.

"Uh...You promise you won't be mad?"

Jackal opened his eyes.

"I had Ice place another bet for me, and I placed one for you, too. I thought it was a done deal. How could we lose?" She bit her bottom lip.

Any other time, he would give her something else besides her lip to nibble on. Right now, though, she had his undivided attention.

"I really thought it would take you longer to figure out where I was. Max won."

"How much did you bet?"

"I only bet a hundred for myself," she hastily told him.

"How much did you bet for me?"

"I knew you needed a new motorcycle, so I bet five hundred for you."

Jackal sprang out of bed, shoving his head through the opening of his T-shirt. When he picked up his jeans, he quickly tossed Penni her clothes. "Get dressed."

She climbed out of bed, clumsily getting dressed. "I'm so sorry. I mean, how could we lose?"

"You said that," Jackal snapped, putting on his boots then helping Penni button her blouse.

"You're mad," she stated the obvious.

"It's okay." Jackal remembered the phone that had fallen to the floor, handing it to Penni. "You can make it up to me. I bet Max we would have more kids than him."

Penni hurried across the room as Jackal opened the door. "Does the one I offered to be a surrogate for with Winter count?"

Jackal crashed into the doorjamb at her words. "No, it didn't include..." He lowered his voice, seeing everyone in the room watching them. "We can talk about this later."

"Okay, we'll wait until you're in a better mood."

No matter how good of head she planned to give him, she was not going to convince him to let her have Viper's baby.

"Jackal, I need to talk to you before you leave." Henry said as he left the booth he and Sherri were sitting at.

"Can it wait?"

"You need to pay for the room. If I let you get away with it, then the other employees will expect it, too."

"I already paid!" Penni exclaimed.

"Your card was declined."

"I have another card." She began to open her purse.

"The credit card company told me to cut it up. They said the cardholder had closed your account."

Penny pouted. "Shade closed my account?"

Jackal ground his teeth. After reaching for his wallet and taking out a card, he gave it to Henry who walked away happily with it in his greedy hand.

"You've been using it every time we rent Henry's rooms?" Jackal spoke out of the corner of his mouth to keep from yelling at her.

"He said it had to be an emergency when I used it."

"Remind me why I want to marry you." Jackal commented as they walked out of the club after he had put his card back in his wallet, the sunlight hitting his bloodshot eyes.

"That hurts." Penni put her hand dramatically across her heart. She looked at the row of cars parked in front of the strip club. "Where's Grace's car?"

"Your car's not here?"

"No, Grace dropped me off. My car's in the shop."

Jackal mumbled something under his breath.

"What did you say?" Penni tilted her head toward him.

"Nothing."

Jackal called Ice, moving them into the shade so he could see.

"It won't take him long to get here," she soothed, patting his arm.

"You're going to make this up to me...a lot."

"Yes, Jackal," she answered submissively. "You don't happen to have a spare key to my condo, do you? I forgot to take it off my key ring when I dropped the key off this morning."

Jackal was afraid to answer her question, seeing spots dancing in his vision.

The door to the Purple Pussycat opened, and a man his age came out, seeing Penni standing by his side.

"Didn't I see you come out of there?" The drunk winked at her.

"Mind your own damn business," she snapped.

"Bitch, I have a stick bigger than he has—"

The man's head hit the brick wall.

"Do not call me a bitch!"

Jackal grabbed her around the waist.

"I'm calling the police." The man whined, trying to find his cell phone.

"Here, take mine." Jackal handed him his cell phone, listening as he called the police.

"Why did you do that? They'll arrest me." Penni looked around, trying to find a place to hide.

"Don't worry about it. I'll tell them I did it. He's so drunk they'll believe anything I tell them. Call Henry and tell him to destroy the video of the front door."

"I'm not going to let you go to jail for me," Penni protested, but she did call Henry to destroy the tape. "Why are you doing this? We still have time to get away; Ice just pulled up."

Jackal refused to budge, waving down the police car as it approached.

"Ice can bail me out in the morning after I get a good night's sleep."

"What happened?" Ice asked, getting out of the car. "You want me to handle...?"

When the cops got out of their cruiser, they pinned Jackal against the wall with Penni screeching at them to let him go.

"I'll get his paperwork started while you find out what happened," The officer that arrested him shouted as they led Jackal toward his cruiser.

Feeling grateful, he sank back into the leather seat, exhausted. He watched Ice try to pull Penni toward his car, but she refused to budge from where she was listening to the drunk tell his story to the other police officer.

Jackal was worried she was going to get herself arrested if she didn't back off the drunk. When the officer trying to take his statement gave Penni a warning, she finally relented, going to Ice's car. Then he saw Penni slip the drunk's wallet into her purse before flicking the drunk off as she climbed inside.

Jackal began laughing so hard the cop in the front seat turned to stare at him over his shoulder.

"You better not vomit in my car!"

Jackal wiped his tears of laughter on the arms of his T-shirt. "I'm going to marry that woman."

EPILOGUE

"Ready?" Jackal asked as he waited impatiently by the open door.

"No, I've changed my mind. I can't do this." Stubbornly, Penni shook her head.

Jackal sighed, shutting the door then striding across the floor. He crouched down in front of the chair she was sitting on. "Babe, it's too late to change your mind."

"Quit saying that." Penni heard the edge of hysteria in her own voice, but the fear that was pushing her down wouldn't let her get to her feet.

"We've been through it before. It's...too...late."

Penni started crying. Did he have to say that?

"Okay, okay. Quit crying. It tears my soul apart when you cry."

"Give me a couple days, and then I'll be able to do it," Penni pleaded.

"Everyone is already waiting: your parents, Shade, Lily—hell, even all the Predators are there except Max."

Penni's head fell back on the chair. She stared up at the ceiling, counting the seconds between contractions. When she could she lifted her head again, she said, "Tell him about losing his bet. I'm never having another baby."

"Yes, you will. It's just nerves—"

"That's easy for you to say!" she snapped. "These contractions are fucking painful!"

"Then let's go. If my baby is born here instead of at the hospital, I'm going to be pissed."

"This is all your fault!"

"You're the one who kept forgetting to take the pills. I kept telling you I would use a condom until you were ready to have a baby."

"If you joke one more time that I'll misplace the baby, so help me God, I'm going to cut off your dick."

"I was teasing you. You're going to make a wonderful mother." Jackal brushed her tears away.

"See? The contractions have stopped. It was only a false alarm."

Jackal stared at her doubtfully. "I think we should go to the hospital just to make sure."

"All right. Just so you'll feel better."

"Thank you." Jackal helped her to her feet, and Penni waddled to the front door with him on her heels.

Jesus, did he think she would run upstairs and lock herself in their bedroom? That was tempting, but the fact that Jackal could outrun her was disheartening.

His helping her as she lowered herself into the front seat of the car lifted a tiny bit of the fear that had been escalating since she had found out she was pregnant. Jackal then started the car before backing out to the street. As he made a left, he drove past the lake, coming to a stop at the stop sign. The ducks and swans glided across the water, impervious to what was going on inside the car.

When Jackal would have made the turn that led them to the hospital, Penni reached out to stop him.

"Look," she said softly. Two swans swam next to each other, their necks arching together, coming together to look like a heart. "It's a sign."

"Sure it is, babe. Can I go now?"

"Yes." Penni felt the last of her fear slide away. "Everything is going to be okay. I can feel it."

Jackal smiled. "I've been saying that for the nine months."

Yes, he had been telling her, but she hadn't believed it until now.

The contractions began again, but she didn't tell him, not wanting to distract him from driving.

It was a relief to pull up to the emergency entrance. She wasn't able to wiggle out of the car before he was back with a wheelchair. Thankfully Jackal hadn't listened to her, and her doctor was standing by, waiting for her.

Another contraction hit as she was wheeled away. Jackal was by her side as she was rushed to the birthing room. The sight of the bed would have had her in hysterics if she hadn't seen the sign the swans had gifted to her.

"Get her hooked up to the monitors, STAT," her doctor ordered.

Penni was in too much pain to realize the room was filling up with nurses and technicians.

When she caught a glimpse of Jackal's face, she tried to ease his worry. "I'm fine."

He only nodded, moving out of the way so the doctor could work.

Penni held out her hand to him, feeling him take it in his.

"We can do this." Penni gave him a trembling smile.

"No more. One is enough."

"We'll see." Penni tried to arch up as the pain radiated through her body. "My chest is hurting." She began gasping for air as the shrill scream of the monitors filled the room.

Penni saw the fear on Jackal's face as she began to lose consciousness.

"No...Don't you fucking dare take your eyes off of me! Penni...Penni!"

* * *

Was he ever going to shut up? She was sleepy; why wouldn't he stop?

She tried to search for the warm, soothing abyss where she could hide from the pain, but he wouldn't let her. If he knew how badly it hurt, he would leave her alone.

She tried to tell him to let her sleep, but he wouldn't listen. Over and over, he called her name, and Penni couldn't make him stop. Then, when she heard the sound of his voice again, she didn't want to. She quit struggling to return to the warm abyss, trying to find his voice, instead. She couldn't stand hearing him in so much agony. She would gladly wake if that was what it took to end his suffering.

When he didn't respond, she realized he couldn't hear her. Then she could barely hear him, and the warm abyss was gone. Taking its place was total darkness, and she couldn't find her way out.

She wanted to give up. Multiple layers kept her from reaching Jackal, forcing her back under. His voice, which had been close, was becoming farther away. She was losing her battle to stay with him, with their child.

She wanted to cry but couldn't, no longer even able to her own voice. She was about to give in, the pain too relentless. She felt her heart faltering one beat at a time, becoming fainter with each beat.

She stopped struggling to reach Jackal. It was useless...

His voice called her name again. That was when she remembered something Shade had taught her.

She listened to her heart, making herself take one breath at a time, forcing her heart to beat faster with each breath she took, not letting the lifeline float away. Little by little, she felt her faint heartbeat become stronger and stronger.

At first, she couldn't see anything. Then she saw her husband's face staring down at her.

"Don't you dare leave me again." His voice was so hoarse she could barely understand him.

She tried to talk but couldn't.

"You can't talk. There's a tube in your throat. Stay, babe, stay with me."

Penni gripped his hand, trying to tell him without words that she wasn't going anywhere, but then she fell away again.

* * *

Each day, she grew more coherent until the third day when she became alert to what was going on in the room.

Shade and Jackal were standing by the window, talking. She tried to tell them she was awake, but her throat was too sore.

"It was the doctor who saved her life. If she hadn't recognized the symptoms of amniotic fluid embolism, Penni would have died. She said sixty-eighty percent of women who have that happen don't live." Jackal pressed his hand against his eyes. "If you hadn't talked me into making Penni give up on using a midwife, she wouldn't have made it."

Jackal rubbed his face with both hands. "God, since the first time I met Penni, it's like I've been chasing a rainbow before it disappears, trying to catch her with a butterfly net, because I was afraid she wouldn't stay."

"Do you know why I kept giving you hell when I found you didn't call me about Hennessy?" Shade said, not waiting for his answer before continuing. "Whenever Penni was in town, she fussed about something you had done to piss her off: that you were doing the strippers, even how you look in your favorite dark navy shirt.

"You didn't have to catch her with a net. I just wanted to make sure you deserved her. You took my shit and held your own. I couldn't ask for any better for her, and I know Penni felt the same. The doctor may have saved her life, but you're why she wanted to stay."

Jackal gave a half-hearted chuckle. "Penni told me once she wanted to stay and smell the roses. She had already planned to stop touring with the band and stay home with the baby."

"I know Penni. What can go wrong, usually does." Shade turned toward the bed. "She's awake."

They moved to tower over her bed.

"I heard that." She winced as the words came out.

Jackal raised her head, giving her a drink of water. "Better?"

Penni nodded, not ready to chance the pain returning by talking again.

Shade moved closer to the head of the bed, leaning down to brush a kiss across her forehead. His expression softened.

"You did good, butterfly." Raising up, Shade put his mask firmly back into place before striding across the room to the door. "I'll leave you alone for a minute. Then Mom and your dad want to see you."

Her hand brushed her abdomen when she tried to sit up straight.

"The baby?" Memories struck her, and she tried to sit up, but Jackal placed a hand on her shoulder.

"Stay still. I'll raise you up." Jackal raised her bed slowly.

Penni's eyes bulged at the pain in her chest and abdomen.

Shade gave her a shuttered look before leaving the room. "I'll give you a few minutes before I let them come in."

Was there a reason her brother had left so quickly? Penni wanted to scream at him to go get her baby, but as she opened her mouth, she saw Jackal go around her bed, bending over. Then he turned back to her again with a blanket against his chest.

Jackal held the baby to her, and Penni tenderly stared down at the tiny being who was sound asleep.

"He's beautiful," she whispered.

"*She's* beautiful," Jackal corrected.

"A girl...The sonogram said it was a boy."

"Babe, when have you ever done what you're supposed to?" Jackal chuckled.

"Are you sure she's ours?" Penni ignored the pain in her throat and the rest of her body. She couldn't believe the beautiful child was hers.

When she ran a caressing finger down her soft cheek, the baby lifted her curious eyes up to her. They were cerulean blue like hers. Then her little rosebud mouth curled into a twisted smile like Jackal's.

"I'm sure."

Also by Jamie Begley

The Last Riders Series:

Razer's Ride
Viper's Run
Knox's Stand
Shade's Fall
Cash's Fight
Shade
Lucky's Choice

Biker Bitches Series:

Sex Piston
Fat Louise
Merry Blissmas

The VIP Room Series:

Teased
Tainted
King

redators MC Series:

Riot
Stand Off

Porter Brothers Trilogy:

Keeping What's His

The Dark Souls Series:

Soul Of A Man
Soul Of A Woman

Made in the USA
Coppell, TX
09 April 2024

31115681R00218